SATOR THE SOWER
AREPO THE PLOUGH
TENET THE HOLDER OF MAGICAL VOW
OPERA OPENS THE MYSTIC GATE
ROTAS TURNS THE WHEEL OF FATE
LET PATERNOSTER FROM THE STONE EXTEND
MAY ALPHA START FOR OMEGA MUST END

*"See, I am coming soon; my reward is with me, to
repay according to everyone's work.
I am the Alpha and the Omega, the first and the last,
the beginning and the end."
Revelation 22: 12 - 13*

THE SATOR SQUARE

A MICRO DISK
with images intended to plunge the monarchy into crisis

A SECURITY CHIEF
intent on damage limitation at whatever the cost

A YOUNG JIHADIST
on a path to suicide - terrorist or unwitting puppet?

A DETECTIVE
faced with a series of unexplained deaths

A MIDDLEMAN
ruthless and unscrupulous - is his only interest the money?

PAPAPICMAN
The elusive pope of the paparazzi and harbinger of death

ALL BROUGHT TOGETHER BY THE ENIGMATIC CODE OF THE MYSTIC SATOR SQUARE

Geoff Cook

THE SATOR SQUARE

PART ONE – SATOR – THE SOWER

PART TWO – AREPO – THE PLOUGH

PART THREE – TENET – THE HOLDER OF MAGICAL VOW

PART FOUR – OPERA – OPENS THE MYSTIC GATE

PART FIVE – ROTAS – TURNS THE WHEELS OF FATE

Published by New Generation Publishing in 2017

First Edition

ISBN 978-1-78719-279-9 (paperback)
ISBN 978-1-78719-280-5 (hardback)

www.newgeneration-publishing.com

New Generation Publishing

In Loving Memory
Rita and Vic
My Inspiration

In Living Memory
Stephen, Simon and Daniel
My Expectation

BOOK ONE – SATOR – THE SOWER

One - @GerbenRosenberg

"Gerben?"

He detected both surprise and curiosity in the way she had framed his name. Surprisingly, there was no trace of hostility. He put a mental tick in the positive box. Even so, her ample frame blocked the doorway, defiantly barring access to the apartment. Still fences to mend.

On impulse, he took her hand and planted a delicate kiss, his lips hardly brushing the back of her fingers. As her gaze followed this gesture of outmoded chivalry, he ran his right hand up from the waistband of her loose fitting cream silk dressing gown, avoiding her breast and gently squeezing her shoulder. She shuddered, a brief, but unequivocal response, yet there was no defiance. Another tick in the box.

"Why?" she asked, standing erect, pulling the dressing gown straight and tight around her, re-knotting the belt and folding her arms – actions that all said don't do it again, but she hadn't slammed the door in his face.

"I wanted to see if you had forgiven me, Chantelle. It's over two years now." Should he ask to come in? Better not force the pace.

"And you feel this is the right approach? Touching me up like fruit at a market stall? Come on, Gerben. Get real!" A trace of a smile creased her cracked lips.

She wasn't conventionally beautiful. Yet her heavy features and unkempt appearance somehow enhanced the earthiness. He'd never asked her age. Early thirties, he guessed. She'd look like shit when she was sixty. Chauvinist maybe, but true.

"Words when dealing with emotion are so often misunderstood," he answered. "They tend to over or understate your intentions. Actions provoke an immediate and singular response. They can tell you much more and a lot quicker." He smiled. "Besides, I couldn't resist the temptation."

"You never could, as I recall, Gerben. A bet, wasn't it?

The memory seemed to bring a flash of anger to her eyes. Her hand smudged yesterday's mascara across her eyelid.

Going back over that incident was dangerous. He decided to fast forward, buy some reconciliation time. "I came to your office nine months ago to apologise, but you wouldn't see me." The recollection jarred. "You sent down some snotty little hag of a secretary to tell me to bugger off in front of everybody in reception. It must have made the little cow's day." How could he still be so angry? Wounded pride? If he could just have put his hands around that bitch's throat.

"You didn't come to apologise, Gerben." Her voice cracked. "You came to sell me some smutty little photos, like all the other times. You must have thought I'd got over our little encounter. What was the bet? Five hundred Euros if you managed to shag a lesi? Well, let me tell you, Gerben. Your little bet cost me a long term relationship and a great deal of heartbreak." She sounded annoyed, but he felt somehow that it was staged for his benefit.

"You got over it." He sounded unrepentant.

Once again, she retightened the belt of her dressing gown. "The bitch had been having an affair for over a year. I never guessed. I was well shot of her."

Gerben went to speak, but she jumped in first. "If you're going to say 'Well, lucky I helped you out or some such other banality that lets you off the hook, forget it. You fucked me for a bet and that's about as low as it gets."

"I wasn't." He shook his head. "I was about to say, it was a pity you didn't buy the images of that footballer on the boat with his lover. They made a fortune for Paris Match. I heard you got grief from the owner for missing out on that deal. Mustn't let our personal lives interfere with business, must we?" he goaded.

She looked through him.

Got you, he thought. You're still standing here talking to me for one reason. You're afraid; afraid that if you send me away, you could be missing something your boss will make you feel sorry for. So you stay with it, but you're dying to shut the door in my face.

"Well, lovely talking to you, Gerben, but I can't believe that a good Yiddish boy who thinks he's a woman's dream in the bedroom would come half way across Paris on the Jewish Sabbath to apologise for his behaviour a year ago." She looked hard into his eyes. "So what do you really want, Gerben?"

"Can I come in?"

"I've got company."

He gave a twisted smile. On that one night they had spent together, she had told him that it reminded her of a fifties film set. He recalled her words. "How did you put it?" he said. "I think that I detect the aura around you. It's a mix of the stench of sexual abandonment, body fluids, perspiration and stale cigarette smoke; obnoxious, but, somehow, strangely compelling and so appealing to our basic animal instincts."

She shook her head disdainfully, waves of peroxide blond hair falling around her ears. The quiff above her forehead was almost yellow, much blonder than the rest of her hair. It was as if the perpetual trail of nicotine in the smoke from her cigarettes had, over time, somehow dyed it.

"Can't you get rid of her? We have to talk. It's really important."

"I promised myself a weekend away from the office. Can we make it some other time? Say Monday?" It was more a plea than a statement of intent. Time to press home the advantage.

"Look Chantelle." He took a step closer to her. "Last time you missed a scoop by sending me away. Today, you can multiply the word 'scoop' a hundred fold and still fall way short. I have something that will make your career, believe me!"

She looked hard into his eyes, turned and went back inside the apartment. He took it as his cue to follow her as far as the lounge. He exhaled with relief as she closed the bedroom door.

4

From what he could remember, little in the apartment had changed. He slumped into the recliner that faced the TV. For someone on a mega salary, the place was small, pokey almost and sparsely furnished. It wasn't a home, just somewhere to pass through as the days changed.

The floor was littered with copies of weekly magazines in various languages. The competition. He flicked through a Danish glossy. So much syndicated shit. It wasn't a patch on *Bien a Vous*. Chantelle Dubois was a highly talented, professional editor with a gift for putting together the right journalistic mix needed to produce a successful weekly 'kiss and tell' ratings winner. *Bien a Vous* or *BV* as it was known in the trade was owned and backed by an Indian banking magnate who treated the magazine and, by default, Chantelle, as his toys. Expense was no object and he was prepared to lavish millions, as long as the deal was an exclusive and would keep *BV* at the top of the pile. That was the precise reason why Gerben Rosenberg was sitting where he was on the Jewish Sabbath and not in the synagogue in Montreuil where his parents, sister and two brothers with their families would have already noticed and frowned upon his absence. He was the black sheep. It would have to be a convincing excuse.

The raised voice from the bedroom sounded vaguely familiar. It was not Chantelle's. Strident, high pitched and angry, it was full of venom, past reason, past Chantelle's vain attempt to seek a compromise. Gerben was beginning to enjoy himself. Nothing like being a bystander at a catfight. How long would Chantelle keep her cool? Should he get involved if they started getting physical?

The shouting and pleading stopped as suddenly as it had started. The bedroom door swung open, the handle crashing heavily into the partition wall. He looked down at the floor. The footsteps accelerated across the room and stopped abruptly alongside him. There was no option but to look up. It was the hair that confused him initially. The last time he had seen this human version of a stick insect with bumps, she had dark hair tied up in a bun. Now, it was short, red and shaped around her ears. But there was no mistaking the raw anger in those eyes, framed by the thick rimmed glasses. He had seen it once before.

"Bastard!" she spat at him and then turned and stomped out of the apartment.

As the front door ricocheted on its hinges, Gerben's thin lips extended into a self-satisfied smile. Getting your own back was a gratifying experience, even something as petty as this. That forlorn creature was the secretary who had once taken so much pleasure in evicting him from *BV's* offices. What a result!

"Well?" Chantelle was walking from the bedroom door to the armchair opposite him. She had changed into slacks and a loose fitting open weave jumper. She was wearing no bra, the silhouette of her breasts far more sensual to him than had she appeared bare-chested.

He forced himself to look into her eyes. "I seem to be making a habit of accidentally screwing up your relationships. I'm sorry."

She seemed nonplussed, but he could tell she was putting on an act.

"Then make it worth my while. What have you got?" She edged forward on the armchair, her legs closed, hands clasped around her knees.

For the first time since she had opened the door, Gerben felt on home territory. He swung into sales mode with the involuntary gestures of gently stroking the tip of his classic hook nose and then moving his hand to wipe the moisture from his balding head. Somebody had once suggested that he should either shave all the hair off or pay for a transplant. The wispy strands that stretched from the middle to the back of his cranium were neither one thing nor another. But Gerben had resisted. He was prone to perspire heavily and the remaining hairs helped to keep his skullcap in place whenever religious etiquette demanded.

He lurched forward on the recliner, nearly losing his balance as he tried to sit upright. His centre of gravity was continuing to move south. Now into his forties, he had to work harder in the gym to stall the traces of a spare tyre around his waistline, product of too many business deals over dinner. He struggled briefly for breath. "As you know, Chantelle, I represent the interests of a number of experienced photographic journalists, artistically and technically talented individuals who rely on me to get the best commercial leverage for their output."

She mimicked a soccer referee, blowing a make-believe whistle and showing an imaginary card. "Cut the crap, Gerben, please. I don't need nor have time for the sales pitch. You're a tenacious, lowlife, grubby agent for a bunch of equally lowlife paparazzi who daren't show their heads above the parapet for the risk of having a dozen and one writs shoved in their unshaven faces." She waited for a response, but there was no reaction. "Now, what have you got and how much is it? Two simple questions."

Her technique was easy to recognise. She was trying to gain the initiative from him, muscle the negotiation so that she called the shots. No chance of it working in his case.

"Before we discuss the sordid details, let me just say one thing." He stopped for effect. She had raised one eyebrow way above the other in an inverted V. How the hell did she do that, he wondered.

"A dozen other publishers would murder for what I'm going to show you, Chantelle, but I had to give you first refusal. I felt really bad about what happened that night and I'd like us to put our relationship on a new footing. You get my drift?"

He leaned forward and placed his hand on her knee, which she casually brushed off. "Listen, Gerben, let's get this horseshit out of the way once and for all." Her voice was calm, emotionless. "You're one of the few men I've screwed in my life and, I have to say, I guessed there was some ulterior motive right from the start. As it happens, it was a very pleasing and rewarding night's work which is in the past and which I have no intention of repeating. Whatever you despicable motive, you were a very subtle and considerate lover. I have to say that in the intervening months the experience seems to have aged you quite considerably. Your limited physical attributes appear to have turned to fat."

He didn't feel like laughing, but he did. "That's a hell of a backhanded compliment!"

"As to your selfless gesture of coming to see me first," she went on. "Forgive me if I don't buy that either. *BV* is about the only magazine that could raise big money in short order. All the others you'd have to go through the senior editor; the management committee; the finance director; probably the proprietors; not forgetting the legal eagles." She waited for a reaction. "I'm right, aren't I?"

He wasn't about to admit that she was spot on.

"With me, it's a quick phone call to Benny in Dubai and the money's as good as in your account. So, let's forget the foreplay and go straight to the climax!"

He leaned back in the recliner, resting his feet on the raised stool. "Two million Euros, paid today into a nominated bank account in the Caymans. If you're quick off the mark, you'll easily treble that. All global syndication rights pass to you. As soon as Benny says yes, you call the shots."

She looked into his eyes, but he avoided her gaze. "You're either mad or you've..." She hesitated. "No. Two million? You must be joking."

"I've never been more serious," he replied.

"Show me," she demanded.

Gerben took an inexpensive camera from his floppy briefcase. "Don't worry," he said. "They weren't taken with this. Probably something a metre long with six different lenses. You know how these lads work." He handed it over to her. "For God's sake, don't press the delete button by mistake. There are no copies. Guaranteed."

She studied the camera. "It's on a memory card?"

"Yes. Protected. You have to use an SD adapter with that camera. It's getting on."

"How about I put the card into my mobile and check

what you've got?"

"No way. Don't even think about it. I know what these smartphones are like. You blink and some app syncs everything to some album or a cloud in the stratosphere and the next thing you know is that the whole bloody lot is featuring on U Tube or your Facebook page. No way. This little beauty stays right where it is, the original with no clones."

"You're absolutely certain?"

"Stake my life on it. I paid a small fortune for this little lot."

She looked surprised. "You're the principal? You're not commissioned on this one?" The first image appeared in the viewfinder screen.

"I've pledged my life savings, Chantelle. It's all mine to sell."

She wasn't paying attention. She clicked onto the first image and studied it closely. "Is this who I think it is?" she asked. "It doesn't look like him."

With a sigh, she clicked onto the next frame. Gerben had just started to relax when the camera landed back in his lap. She was shaking her head. "This is what's supposed to make my career? You spoil my weekend for this? I think you've lost the plot, Gerben. I wouldn't give you twenty grand for that lot, let alone two million." Her frustration was beginning to show.

"No?"

"For months now, the rumour has been doing the rounds that he was gay. So what? Sexual preference is not mutually exclusive to any one section of society. All you've got is a nice set of photos of various guys in the throes of getting it together. Sweet. Marketable? Barely. Confirms something most people suspected. Half the world say "Aah" and the other homophobic half say something offensive. Big deal!"

"How much did you say?"

"Maybe twenty grand and that's pushing the boat out."

He released the micro card, taking another from the

small case into which he clipped the first and then handed the camera back to her.

"OK," he nodded. "So, it's twenty grand for that set and one million, nine hundred and eighty thousand for this one."

"Is this some sort of a game?"

"No game."

With a look of resignation she brought the first image into the viewfinder. Although her expression remained impassive, Gerben noticed her fingers begin to tremble as she moved through the frames. She could have studied no more than six images before the camera slipped from her grasp. "We'll never get away with it." She looked up at Gerben. "This is dynamite. You could destroy a monarchy."

Gerben was on his feet. Before she could react, he had taken the camera back from her and switched it off. "They don't get any better," he said. "Sixty images in total. My guess is you could probably publish about half. The rest you could try and sell back to the victim."

"Blackmail?"

He laughed. "Don't be silly. That's criminal. The danger is that if you've got these images in the public domain, they are bound to end up on the internet. Best if they were out of circulation. Don't you agree?"

Her mind was elsewhere. "These are kosher photos, right? No funny business?"

"Of course not. You'll get your guy to verify anyway. But I'll guarantee legitimacy. Taken over the course of this past Wednesday and Thursday. I completed the purchase last night and you're my very first port of call."

"Who took them?"

"You know I can't tell you that, Chantelle." His tone was conspiratorial. "Best you stay out of the loop, anyway. I'll just say it was one of my clients."

"Knowing your clients, there's a dozen copies stored in cyberspace. By tomorrow, they will be all over the internet, whether you like it or not. You can't stop the momentum."

"Don't take me for an amateur, Chantelle. My source is impeccable; knows the value of sole exclusivity. A single leak and the merchandise is worthless. We all lose. The seller doesn't get his hands on the cash I've deposited with the lawyers and my two million evaporates into thin air.

"They'll be on to me like a pack of hounds cornering a fox. Once this breaks, every lawyer in Paris will be instructed to go after my blood. They're bound to get an injunction to hand over the material."

She was beginning to backtrack, but he had planned for a cold feet reaction. "As you can imagine, I've given this a lot of thought overnight. This is your timetable. We do a deal this afternoon and you schedule an eight page supplement plus new title page for the print run on Sunday night. Nobody in *BV* must know anything about it." He could feel the adrenalin begin to take hold. His mouth was dry. "Any chance of a drink of water?"

She leaned across to the fridge, took out a bottle and, after taking a large swig herself, passed it to him. It was fizzy, but it did the trick. "Go on," she said impatiently.

"We spend tonight and tomorrow working on the supplement. You get your best graphics designer to come around in the morning to work on the cover story. It must be done here. Complete secrecy is essential."

"We?" she queried.

"Figure of speech. Who's your main man?"

"That will be Bernhard," she said.

"Tomorrow night, you email one of the photos to an address I get for you. You offer him thirty similar originals and you name your price. Then,. . . "

She stopped him in mid sentence. "You've thought all this through. How much do you suggest?"

"Ask for six million and settle for three."

"You're out of your tiny mind." She looked incredulously at him.

"Believe me, they will bite your hand off."

"And?"

"Monday morning, you prime all the likely sources to which you can syndicate the publishable images to look out for the midday release of this week's *BV*. Name your price, do deals and supply the product before the day is out. Job done."

She stood up and walked over to him, stretching, off balance, to reach for the water bottle. He kept a tight grip on the neck, forcing her to fall against him. Alert to the tactic, she prized the bottle out of his hand and forced the base hard into his crotch. He gasped with pain.

"I told you, Gerben. No funny business. I'm not interested." She released the bottle and stood up.

"Don't blame me. It's such a waste of . ." She snatched the bottle out of his hand and threw it at him, narrowly missing his head.

"I know, Gerben, I've heard it all before. Why such a woman as me should be lost to the pleasures of mankind. You men really think you've got what it takes to satisfy every woman's physical and emotional needs. It's a load of crap. Men are from Mars and they should have stayed there. Now, get real! When we publish, all hell will break loose. How do you suggest I handle it?"

He squirmed in his chair. The bottle had hurt him. Silly bitch! "It will be Tuesday afternoon or Wednesday before they can mobilize, probably Friday before they get a magistrate to listen and next Monday before there's a hearing. That will probably give you another week's publication with some more money-making revelations."

"They'll go for invasion of privacy, demand the product and force me to name the source. It's a big gamble."

"Well. I'm no lawyer, but there is a defence of disclosure in the public interest which could be used to counter the privacy allegation. After all, there's so much outing in the press at the moment. Your legal team will be better placed to comment than I am. But I ask you, would you want someone like him to put his arm around your young nephew?"

12

She nodded her acknowledgement. "And your position?"

"If you're forced to, you name me. It's obvious. I'll look after myself. It's built into the price."

"I was coming to that. Benny's going to have to take a lot on trust. He can't put it through the lawyers first. I might be able to convince him to go to one, but two is a big gamble. How about it?"

Gerben gave her that 'don't give me all that crap' look. "Good try, Chantelle, but two million Euros is the starting and finishing point." He put the camera back into his briefcase. "Take it or leave it." He walked toward the door. Time was passing. He had to close the deal. "I'm out of here."

"Do me a favour, Gerben. Give me a couple of hours. Go to your synagogue and pray. This isn't going to be easy."

As he opened the front door, he glanced back. She was reaching for her mobile. Benny wouldn't let this scoop go to somebody else. Gerben Rosenberg was home and dry.

Two - @Chas.Broadhurst.kp

Questions! Why so many damn questions?

God knows, there's something to be said for military discipline. He would not accept that a soldier was any less curious than a civilian, but he could not conceive that any of the officers who had served under the SAS command of Captain Chas. Broadhurst would have dared to challenge an order with "What's all this about?"

Not so the glorified arse lickers of the Royal press corps, whom he was supposed to handle with a kid glove. God forbid that he should offend their fragile sensibilities!

Never mind. Just two more to go and that was everyone dealt with.

He guessed it must be around three in the morning and

his piles itched, a sure sign that he was feeling the stress. Wriggling in the armchair in a futile attempt to alleviate the irritation, his mobile slipped to the floor. Touching the switch, a soft glow from the table lamp pricked the darkness, casting shadows around the lounge of his grace and favour apartment. The motor in the security camera whirred as it registered the activity, then silenced as he located the mobile and extinguished the light once more.

Broadhurst preferred it that way. His most successful deployments in the Falklands and then, in the Balkans just prior to his discharge, had been night special ops. His senior platoon leader, Lambert, was now his second in command in the Kensington Palace security hierarchy. It had been a right royal battle to secure Lambert's appointment against the concerted opposition of those pen-pushers from human resources. What did those grey men know about real life? Alright, maybe Lambert was a ladies' man, but Broadhurst would not have survived Bosnia had his sergeant not taken out that sniper who had him in his sights. The shot that would have shattered his skull into pieces had ricocheted into the back of Broadhurst's knee. Months of surgery and rehabilitation had left him with a limp and, from time to time, a nagging ache whenever he overdid the exercise. In the world of personal security, the competence and loyalty which Lambert had displayed were both essential and invaluable.

A woman's voice, brusque and husky from sleep, answered the phone. Broadhurst was about to speak when the phone had obviously been taken from her.

"Yes, Sir?" Lambert's voice. Broadhurst's explanation for the call was received in silence and acknowledged with a second, "Yes, Sir."

He pushed the speed dial a second time. "Sarah? It's Broadhurst."

Another female with a gruff, disoriented voice. "What time is it?"

"Just after four."

"Who is this?"

14

"Are you alright, Sarah? This is Chas Broadhurst."

No reply. The only sound was some heavy snoring in the background.

Finally. "Sorry. You woke me from a weird dream. For a moment, I couldn't work out if this was real or not."

His apology for waking her was cursory. Sarah Hansom was the media relations reporter at the press corps with a fairly predictable routine. Today was different.

"Is there a problem?" he asked.

"Must have been last night's takeaway," she explained. "Lamb Jalfrezi. Terry insisted on extra spicy. Tasted like a puncture repair kit and now I feel like throwing up."

As keen as he was to get to the reason for his call, her comment reminded him that his own takeaway meal for one dietary plan had recently been missing a good Indian component.

"Something bad happened?" she asked.

He was getting good at ignoring questions. "The eight o'clock meeting is cancelled."

"Thank God," she replied. "I could do with an extra couple of hours in bed."

"Sorry to disappoint. You need to be at the Palace by six. A car will pick you up."

The significance of his last remark would not be lost on her. It must be serious. Taxis were never used whenever there was a panic. Palace officials working outside of their normal timeframes would prompt the more savvy taxi drivers into passing the information on to their contacts in the tabloid press. Unusual behaviour provoked curiosity and speculation, a staple diet for the suspicious journalist.

"OK," she acknowledged. "Anything I need to know?"

"We won't be in the green room. Go straight to the cellar."

This had confirmed her worst fears. The cellar was rarely used. The room was in a nuclear blast proof underground complex in the east wing of Kensington Palace, surveillance swept every thirty minutes and policed by a group from Special Forces

"Do you want me to contact Rashid or the others?" she asked.

"It's done," he replied. "Just get yourself there on time and it's code one. No pillow talk."

The snoring in the background had become even more energetic.

"No fear of that," she said.

Three - @GerbenRosenberg

Gerben extended his legs over the arm of the sofa. The small of his back ached. Two nights huddled up like a foetus, his neck crooked at an unnatural angle, exhaustion was beginning to overtake the adrenalin buzz that had kept him so pumped up. That and those funny little pink pills she kept in a pin box in the sewing drawer. He couldn't imagine Chantelle being into crochet or knitting a jumper. For the first time in the crazy thirty six hours they had just lived through, from late Saturday afternoon when Benny had finally sealed the deal and transferred the down payment to just four hours ago when the magazine had finally been put to bed and released to the printers, he realized just how shattered he was. Six hours sleep over two nights, coffee after coffee. And the result? A work of art, even if he did say so himself!

Following all that archive research, photo setting, discussion, rejection and acceptance a new level of respect had been established with Chantelle. Their joint effort had been immense. The interchange of ideas; the arguments; the conclusions; the battles had been fought with consummate professionalism. As much as he still fancied her physically, he had come to admire her clinical approach to the challenge. He could only hope that she saw something more in him than just a rather shallow and solitary middle-aged gigolo.

On the downside, the one negative had been Benny's

insistence that Gerben stay with the deal once terms had been agreed. For his part, Gerben had pressed for a simple arrangement where he received the two million, handed over the goods, a polite thank you and exit stage left. No way. Unless he stayed on side, there was no deal. Benny or, the correct spelling as Gerben had learned, Beni Ram was a Hindu, originally from Mangalore, who had ended up as an influential middleman in Dubai, working for wealthy clients around the Middle East and, as a consequence, had become very rich himself.

As arranged, Gerben had returned to Chantelle's apartment that Saturday afternoon, to find himself in a video conference call with Benny and his lawyer. They wouldn't argue about the price, only the way it was paid. A ten percent down payment today and the balance following Monday's publication of *BV*, at which time Gerben would meet up with a partner from the lawyer's Paris office to iron out the legals and get his hands on the balance. Gerben respected the tactic. By Monday evening, Chantelle would have sold the rights around Europe and Benny would have already covered his outlay.

With two exceptions, there was also agreement on the marketing strategy that Gerben had proposed. The first of Benny's demands was that Gerben join Chantelle in preparing the supplement for the magazine. She was obviously not happy and plainly confused at Benny's insistence that Gerben be allowed to meddle in editorial issues, but Benny didn't seem like somebody you argued with too much. The second was that Chantelle could not be involved in any proposal to sell the more compromising photos to the Prince's representatives. That would be best done by a middleman.

"Do you know anything about Hinduism, Mr Rosenberg?" Benny had asked. There was a time delay on the line. He was dressed in traditional flowing Arab robes, sitting on a large cane chair with elephant's ears. Gerben guessed that they were of an age. The one striking feature about Benny's shiny coffee coloured face was a cleft in his chin so prominent that it could have clasped a coin.

"I spend enough time trying to please my parents by keeping up with the traditions of Judaism, let alone other faiths," he replied.

"The dharma we Hindus follow is one that treats men and women as equals, but insists that we revere and protect our women from the evil in this world. I could not allow Chantelle to front such a proposal."

"You talk about a middleman, Benny. You mean you want me to front it?"

"I was coming to that, if you let me finish. You are bound to be implicated anyway. Our lawyers will have to eventually disclose the source of this revolting material. You might as well take centre stage from day one."

"If I'm going to do that, I might as well make my own deal for six million. Why do I need you?" Gerben countered.

There was a pause, and then Benny laughed. "Two reasons. One; you have to sell the photos as one package and not in two hits. Nobody in their right mind would buy half a camel. Two; you know as well as I do that once the legal wrangling starts, your two million will evaporate into legal fees like steam out of a kettle. You need *BV's* legal backing to defend your butt from the red hot poker they will try and stick up it."

He had been spot on and Gerben's vain attempts to wriggle out from under Benny's foot were just that - vain attempts. Five minutes later, the deal was sealed.

Chantelle had seemingly appeared from nowhere and was standing in front of him. "I couldn't sleep either," she said. She was back inside the cream silk dressing gown again. "Too much going on. What do you think they'll say to your mail?"

"Nothing. We know the mail was opened, but they won't reply. I suspect their main thrust will be to do everything possible to stop publication of *BV*. There are probably fifty lawyers in France working on that right now."

He pushed the blanket aside, standing to reveal a pair of striped, baggy boxer shorts. "I'll just go and freshen up. This could be a long day. The next contact will probably come from one of these lawyers, threatening you with God knows what if you don't stop the magazine going on sale and me with charges of criminal intent if I don't cooperate and deliver up the goods for zilch. Hold tight. This is going to be a bumpy ride."

The bathroom door slammed shut behind him, but opened again quickly. "I suggest you give your young graphics artist a call," Gerben said, referring to the man who had spent a day in the apartment working on the front cover of the magazine. "Make sure he stays indoors, away from the workplace and talks to no one."

"You already covered all that with Bernhard when he was here," she replied. "He's reliable."

"Maybe so, but we can't take any chances."

A flash of anger crossed her face.

"You don't mind do you?" he added as a sop, retreating back into the bathroom.

Chantelle reached for the handset and knelt across the sofa to pull back the curtains, revealing a murky dawn, the sky full of dark, threatening clouds. Spots of rain began to splatter on the window pane. The streetlights on the road below were still on, casting shadows on the confusion of parked cars that occupied every conceivable space available. She noticed the Renault Espace simply because it stood higher off the ground than the vehicles around it and it was the only one she could see that was occupied. She made out the silhouette of two figures, one in the driver's seat, the other, diagonally behind him. Curious. She waited, but the car did not move.

There was no reply from Bernhard. Putain! The day hadn't even begun and she was getting bloody paranoiac! Pull yourself together woman! She leaned back across the sofa, her hand seeking leverage under the cushions. There was something hard to the touch. She pulled out a striped zipped toilet bag that Gerben must have put there. Strange he hadn't taken it into the bathroom with him. Curiosity got the better of her. The little hard covered black book that sat on top was bound shut with an elastic band. Her instinctive reaction was to push it down between the cushions. A face towel was folded to cover the bulky object that lay below. She pulled out an ancient looking handgun by the barrel. A dozen or so little bullets clinked together in the bottom of the bag. What did he think was going to happen? A western style shootout in her apartment? This was all getting out of hand. She replaced the zipped bag under the cushions and looked out of the window again. The Renault was still there. "Gerben!" she called anxiously.

He heard the telephone ring. "Just give me a few more minutes, will you? I need to take a shower. Every bone in my body aches." As an afterthought, "Is everything OK?"

There was no response. She must be dealing with the phone call.

"Gerben?" It was a whisper. She was pressed up against the bathroom door. "Gerben? That was the printers, phoning from Nancy. They told me one of the four colour machines they need to use for the supplement has gone wrong. They don't have a replacement. A technician has been called, but it could be hours before the repair is completed."

He had wrapped a towel around his waist and, as he opened the door, she nearly fell into his arms. "I told you so," he proclaimed. "The wheels have started turning. They're just faster out of the blocks than I thought they'd be." He held her by the arms. "You look as though you've seen a ghost."

"I have. Two of them." She told him about the car. There was a moment's hesitation, as if there was something else she needed to say, but she turned and walked into the kitchen.

"Tea?" she shouted.

"No, thanks." He checked to ensure that the toilet bag remained hidden.

"I'll finish showering, then, we'll talk it all through."
He walked back to the bathroom.

"You knew they'd get to the printers, didn't you?"

"I thought it was a possible, Chantelle. Just as well we split the job and gave part of the print run to your standby contractors in Prague and Talin. What time do the flights arrive?"

"In four hours," she replied. "We'll have the magazine on the newsstands just as the crowds start building for lunch."

He put the shower on pulse mode. The stream of water made small red welts on his pallid skin. "You'll have to do better than that lads to get one over on Gerben Rosenberg." His voice was lost in the sound and the steam of the water from the shower.

Four - @Chas.Broadhurst.kp

Broadhurst checked his watch. The briefing had been going on for a little over two hours when he stood to make a few prepared closing remarks. A rousing call to incentivise a squad of battle hardened soldiers was in his comfort zone. Extolling false optimism to a band of spoon-fed, marshmallow journalists, trained like Pavlov's dogs to following royals around as they patted babies on the head, was definitely not. As those around him rose from their chairs, the expressions on their faces said it all. Not one of them was yet mentally prepared to face a series of meetings with a bunch of hard-nosed red top and broadsheet editors to do what it took, plead, threaten or cajole, into cooperation with the Palace. He just prayed that as the reality sank in, they could steel themselves to the task.

The cellar had been in darkness when he had arrived at just after five. The room was huge with a circular table large enough to accommodate the war cabinet and senior military advisors in a time of national crisis. The longer wall was filled with a series of large white screens, faced by an array of IT style desks complete with monitors and keyboards. Broadhurst had positioned himself facing a large one way mirror, behind which was an observation room and a door leading beyond to a private area, which he had never seen.

Under normal circumstances, the Monday video conference briefing would have been chaired by Duncan White, the senior press officer, with Broadhurst in attendance in an advisory capacity. Today, although he had briefed White about the one item on the agenda, Broadhurst would take control.

As the small group seated themselves next to each other around one small segment of the table, an elderly man limped from the observation room to a chair facing the group. The stick he had used to support him was now placed between his legs, both hands clasped around the round chrome ball at the top. His most striking features were a head of long, white grey hair, tied back in a ponytail and those piercing violet blue eyes that had so mesmerised Broadhurst when they had met earlier.

They all turned toward him, waiting for Broadhurst to make the introduction which did not come.

"I'll not mince my words," Broadhurst had begun. "You tell me every week how difficult your work is becoming, how out of touch is the attitude of the monarchy with public . sentiment. Recession and austerity have produced a groundswell of federalism. Only last weekend, thousands protested in Trafalgar Square demanding change, a popular theme echoed by large sections of the media. None of you would contest the viewpoint that the Royal Family faces a serious threat to its very being."

He could only imagine the reaction his words were having on the Royal party listening behind the one-way glass partition.

"Well, let me tell you," He went on. "The problem has just got a whole lot worse. Last week, we dealt with the final arrangements for a private visit by Prince Arthur to an event sponsored by the Anglican Cultural Exchange. I'll use the synonym ACE. The meeting was at a Buddhist retreat in southern Portugal on Wednesday and Thursday past." He stopped for a drink of water. "As we understand it from the Bishop, ACE is a respected body that handles seminars for deacons training for ordination as priests so that they can appreciate and work with different faiths. Hence the visit. Are we all on the same page?"

Heads nodded around the table. Prince Arthur was the youngest of the King's four sons, twenty three and a bachelor. Sarah had written a piece on him for release to some high society magazine a few months earlier. He was almost two and a half years into his clerical training, had already been ordained as a deacon and, when compared to his other three brothers, he was a paragon of virtue, uncontroversial and rarely in the public eye.

Broadhurst explained that the Prince had travelled on a scheduled flight to Lisbon using the name Deacon Baxter, an alias which he had previously used when renting a private apartment in Belgravia a year earlier so that, according to the official version, he could study in peace and quiet. Two personal security guards had travelled on the same flight, but their presence was low key and they had stayed in a visitors' guest lodge on the perimeter of the retreat away from the main building. "I've debriefed the two men thoroughly. There was no hint of any problem or suspicious elements in the vicinity."

Sarah looked over questioningly at Ata Rashid. Where was all this leading? Rashid was the overseas, foreign press liaison officer and her ally in the press corps. He looked as bemused as she was.

"The visit went as planned and the Prince returned safely on Thursday evening." Broadhurst was sombre."Yesterday, late afternoon, the Prince's private secretary received an email from a sender in Paris. The identity of the person concerned is classified."

Duncan White looked askance. Without some

clarification, this bland statement excluded his team from information that would be needed when checks were made. There was already enough treading on toes and internecine warfare between the Palace press corps and security forces as it was. This issue was too big for internal wrangles.

"It's a temporary measure," White interrupted. "We need to deal with this person's affiliations, political and international, before we can brief you. It won't be a long delay."

"Anyway," Broadhurst went on, "be it as it may. . ."

"Gender?" This time it was Gerald Crichton interrupting. Gerald was number two in the press corps. Unlike his boss who had been recruited from Fleet Street, Gerald was old school tie. Eton and Oxford, a contemporary, two years older than Prince Arthur, he was closely associated with the Royal family and had, apparently, been a regular guest at shooting parties hosted by the King.

"Sorry?" Broadhurst queried.

"Can we at least know the gender of the sender?"

"Irrelevant." The security chief almost spat the word out. "Now, for God's sake, let's get on." Once again, he looked across at the observation room. "This person's email had an encrypted photograph of the Prince attached. To say the least, it is highly compromising."

"Can we see it?" Sarah asked.

"No." Again there was no explanation. "Late yesterday afternoon, we transferred the Prince from London to a secret location where he will remain indefinitely. The official line is that he has gone to a private retreat where he can further his ecumenical studies without interruption."

"Why?" Crichton asked.

"To take him out of circulation. Now if you can stop interrupting and let me finish."

As irritable as he had become, he could sympathise with the sense of foreboding that everyone in the room was experiencing. It was the stuff you read in novels. This never happened in real life.

Yesterday evening, the Prince had been subjected to extensive interrogation. That was where the strange old man with the ponytail had become involved. Broadhurst had eventually introduced him to the meeting as Professor Speir, a consultant hired to assist the Royal family. Again, there was no clarification, or any sought.

The Prince had been both contrite and forthcoming. Within the organisation of ACE, there was a splinter group, known as Synergy, a private and restricted number of clerics with the official objective of encouraging clergy from other faiths to sympathise with and support the objectives of the Anglican movement. Prince Arthur was a member, known under his alias of Deacon Baxter. Every three months or so, invitations were sent out to selected members to attend "bonding" seminars at various locations around the world. Certain key words in the invitations would tell the participants what to expect.

"Synergy is run by a lay preacher named Hemmings. He's travelling, but I have arranged a meeting with him via his wife for later today." Broadhurst hesitated, conscious that he needed to choose his words carefully. "To put it bluntly, it appears that the real purpose of these gatherings is to put practicing gays within the Anglican clergy into a private and relaxed environment where they can enjoy and feel at ease in physical relationships with each other and with other participants. The Prince describes it as a release valve."

There was a collective intake of breath around the table. Crichton stood up, his hands supporting him as he leaned forward to make his point. "I sincerely hope you're not going to say what I think you are. Arthur has no such leanings, I'm certain."

Broadhurst recognized the outburst for what it was, a calculated, cynical attempt to curry favour with the observers behind the one way mirror. "I'm not making this up," he said, gesturing for Crichton to sit down. "This is the Prince's account. In today's permissive society, we can probably survive with the disclosure of a sexual liaison between consenting males, even if prostitutes are involved. There has been rumour and speculation about his preferences on the internet for some time. It's unlikely to come as a real shock. Unfortunately, the photograph in our possession suggests that his activities could be deemed criminal. I emphasise 'suggest'. One photo proves nothing."

"What about the Buddhists?" Sarah asked. "Were they a party to this?"

"There were no Buddhists," Broadhurst answered. "They have rented out the retreat over the next month, while they all go back to Nepal."

"Didn't your lads check this out when we knew where the Prince intended to go?" Duncan White had recognized that security issues were at stake and Broadhurst's slow, measured shake of the head told him that somebody in the embassy in Lisbon was going to get a bollocking.

"Let me finish, please," Broadhurst continued. "Somebody knew, a; exactly what was going to happen and, b; that the Prince would be present. A photographer was hidden in the grounds. We don't know who. He took around sixty stills and, as far as we understand, if you accept the emailer's categorisation, around thirty are of consenting males in various stages of intercourse and the other thirty, sexually deviate to hard porn to, regrettably, criminally improper. They all feature the Prince in one form or another."

"My God." Crichton slumped back in his chair. "How do we deal with this?"

Broadhurst turned to say something to Lambert who had, so far, remained stone faced and emotionless throughout the entire proceedings. He whispered a response to his boss, got up and left the room. Broadhurst indicated that he was now prepared to let White take the floor.

Duncan White had a far more inclusive style of

delivery, plainly designed to make his staff feel more at ease. "There are two aspects for us to deal with immediately," he explained. "The first is to stifle the baby at birth. Let me explain. The Mirror Group told us last night that their Danish associate publication has received an approach from *Bien a Vous*, the French magazine offering syndicated images of a member of the British Royal Family which are designed to both shock and enlighten. The associate was asked to refer to today's issue of *BV*. Unfortunately, the Mirror only owns a small minority stake and has no editorial control. They believe their Danish associate has agreed a conditional deal."

"If that's the case," Rashid said, "it'll spread all over Europe, maybe the world, like the plague. We're assuming then that *BV* has purchased the pictures?"

White nodded. "Yes. At least, some of them, shall we say the selection that outs the Prince as a practicing gay."

He stopped to wipe the perspiration from his forehead before going on to explain how they were trying to get *BV* to pull the print run. Lawyers in France had been instructed to obtain an injunction, but the process was lengthy and could take days. The King's equerry was trying to contact Benny Ram, the magazine's proprietor to enable the King to make a personal appeal. So far, no success. Mr Ram was on a confidential business trip, he was told. As soon as he was back in contact with his office, rest assured, he would be immediately informed.

"Incredible. Unbelievable in this day and age of instant communication. What about the editor?" Crichton asked

"Chantelle Dubois? We know very little about her." He turned to Sarah. "That's what I want you to work on later. Find out everything you can."

She nodded.

"There is no private telephone number listed for her and no answer from her office," White continued. "In any event, as she wouldn't have pressed the go button without Ram's say so, I doubt she could do anything even when we do get access to her."

Lambert had come back into the room. He took his cue from Broadhurst. "We have an address for her. Two of our men from the Paris embassy are on stakeout waiting for instructions." He spoke with a Northern Irish accent.

"The second objective is straightforward damage limitation," White emphasised. "There is a small window of opportunity. One firm of lawyers acting for us also represents the graphics company which prints *BV*. They have managed to stall the production run for a few hours, but it will happen later today unless there is legal intervention." He hesitated. "We must assume that, at best, by late afternoon, these pictures will be in circulation and, doubtless uploaded onto the net. Under no circumstances, do we want any UK or Irish publication to follow suit. That's your first priority."

As detailed instructions were issued to each member of the press corps regarding the appointments, strategy and backup to be provided for each of the publishers they would visit, Broadhurst and his aide broke off into a huddle with Professor Speir out of earshot of the rest of the meeting. After a series of whispered exchanges, they returned to their seats.

Broadhurst tapped the table. "Look. There's work to be done and this meeting needs to end. Can you please deal with the rest of the specifics afterwards?" It was more of an instruction than a question and the 'please', more a threat than a courtesy.

"Shall we cover the arrangements for the batch of photos that are not to be published?" White queried.

"I was coming to that," Broadhurst replied. "In short, the person who sent the mail is offering to sell us the collection for six million Euros. The preamble is couched in all sorts of conciliatory language about not wanting to damage the Royal family's image; the huge cost borne by this person in acquiring the photos; all that sort of garbage to avoid letting it seem like the blackmail it is. Anyway, at this stage it's a security issue and we'll be dealing with it today.

"Is that it then?" White queried. "I'm keen to get my people on the job."

Broadhurst put up his hand. "Not so fast," he said. "There's one more thing. Apart from the two security personnel assigned to accompany Prince Arthur, nobody outside this room knew anything about the visit to Portugal. The Prince is adamant that nobody in Synergy knew in advance of Deacon Baxter's attendance, that is, apart from Hemmings. We'll soon see if that stacks up when I have had the opportunity to interview this Hemmings character."

"What are you driving at, Chas?" White was suspicious. None of this had been covered at the pre-meeting briefing.

"By the end of the day, each of you will have had a chat with Professor Speir. That's an order from on high."

"Do we have time for this?" White asked.

Broadhurst displayed the trace of a smile. "There's a credible case for investigating the suspicion that someone around this table leaked details of the Prince's visit to a contact in the paparazzi. If they did, I intend to find out. Whoever, it was, they had better start shaking in their boots because their days are numbered."

Lambert stood looking out of the window in Broadhurst's office as the rain swept across the courtyard below. He watched as Sarah Hansom pulled up the raincoat over her head and scurried toward the open door of the staff car. "She's a very sensuous young woman, don't you think, Chas?"

"Who?" Broadhurst sat down at his desk and started to thumb through the pile of notes and telephone messages.

"Sarah," Lambert replied. "She has a sort of catch me if you can eye play. Bet she's good in bed."

"You recent divorcees have only one thing on your mind," Broadhurst replied. "Until six months ago, Alice was the only woman for you. Then, Soraya came along and now she's the passion in your life, the only woman who has ever understood you." He laughed at the other man's obvious discomfort. "What's happened now? You blowing hot and cold?"

"No. No. Nothing like that," Lambert replied hastily. "She's just moodier than Alice. Difficult to know what she's thinking."

That's an essential ingredient of the female psyche." Broadhurst watched as Sarah's car pulled away from the main gates. "I just hope and pray that the editors she's on her way to meet find her argument as compelling as you do her body."

Professor Speir tapped politely on the open door. "You asked to see me before I start?" he queried.

"Yes. Thank you, Professor." Broadhurst indicated for him to sit down. "The two security men who accompanied the Prince are waiting for you downstairs. Use the interrogation room. It will have more impact. What are your initial reactions? Have you detected the mole in our midst?"

The Professor stared intently at his clasped hands. "If you mean do I consider that anybody at the table knew what was going on with this Synergy group beforehand, my opinion would be no. If you mean do I think there were speech, gestures and body language signals which pointed to someone as the possible informer, I could not yet exclude anybody." He looked up at Broadhurst. "Not very helpful so far, am I?"

As Lambert ushered the old man out of the room a few minutes later, Broadhurst indicated to shut and lock the door. "What was all that about?" Lambert asked contemptuously.

"It's the King's idea," Broadhurst replied. "He's into this behavioural bullshit. He says it's foolproof. Well, let me tell you, whoever the grass is, he's no fool. The only way we're going to get to the bottom of this is good old police work, not looking for someone with sweaty palms! Now let's get down to business"

Two of the palace security staff had flown to Paris on a plane from the King's flight at six that morning. Maxwell had been chosen because he was a fluent French speaker, Lewis because he was a clinical and ruthless thug. They were now waiting for instructions.

"Tell them to take over the surveillance of this editor woman's apartment from the embassy boys," Broadhurst ordered. "If we have to break in. we don't want any witnesses around."

"We wait until she leaves?" Lambert asked.

The intercom buzzed. Broadhurst picked up the handset and made a series of notes as he listened. "Good work" was all he said as he hung up. "Research has come up with a recent copy of *Bien a Vous*. The publisher's credits include the name of the graphics design editor." He consulted his notes and turned back to Lambert. "It's a Sebastien Bernhard. He has to have been involved in processing the images over the weekend for today's issue. He's listed in the Paris phonebook. Here's the address. Apparently, it's an arrondissement where the Paris arty set hangs out."

"Maxwell and Lewis?"

"Yes. Tell them to go there first before taking over at the editor's place." Broadhurst paused. "Do they have credentials?"

"Forged Police Judiciaire warrant cards. What used to be the Sûreté in our day." Lambert replied. "It's a high risk strategy."

"I'll pretend I didn't hear all that." Broadhurst sounded deadly serious. "We need to know what this graphics man has in his possession. More importantly, what medium is carrying the originals? Are there any copies and who has them? We have to strike before this business snowballs."

"Which means?"

"As a last resort, Lewis can use his strong arm tactics, but, for God's sake, tell him to act with discretion. He and Maxwell have to remember they're operating on somebody else's patch."

"Understood," Lambert replied. "I'm going to my office. I'll call in a few favours. We need to find out where this Rosenberg character is hiding. I should have a profile and personal details by now. I'll mail them across to you."

Broadhurst nodded reflectively. "You know, Lambert. I thought that when we got son number three out of the shit with the poker and drinks fiasco, that that was that. No more hassle. We've always known that number four was gay, but to discover he's a paedophile." He left the sentence hanging in the air. "He's fourth in line to the throne for God's sake. It could tip the monarchy over the edge."

Lambert unlocked the door. "He's fourth in line at the moment, but that won't last. Remember, one and two are married now. It won't be long before they're breeding like rabbits. By the time he reaches middle age, he'll be lucky if he's twentieth." He closed the door behind him, turning to face the opulence of the grand staircase leading down to the entrance hall. "Mind you, hc'll be first in line on the sex offenders' register."

Five - @Bizzybuzzybee

Benny Ram detested the desert. The sand got into everything; the infernal dust storms; the countless miles and miles of barren landscape. No wonder the people were so boring. It wasn't that he had a general dislike for Arabs with their fundamentalist attitudes and customs steeped in tradition. It was more a case that he understood where they were coming from, but he was confused by the fervour now sweeping the Middle East to subscribe to an ideology so out of touch with the modern world in which he thrived.

The fact that fate had locked him into the Babel of Dubai to make his fortune may have been the reason why he had been obliged to compromise his youthful ardour to become a social reformer at the university in Mangalore, but he did not discount the past. His mother's passion for fairness amongst the castes was engrained in his being and he begrudged nobody the right to succeed, with the one proviso that they did not get in his way.

He used his thumb and forefinger to part the Omar Sharif style moustache, forcing the grains of sand lodged in it to fall onto his bulbous cheeks to be brushed away. If there was one thing he hated more than sand, it was sitting in the back of a military style jeep that jarred every bone in his body as it careered along a dirt road. The two Kurdish militiamen had said nothing to him since they had crossed into Syria. Their concentration was on the horizon and the possibility of a chance encounter with an enemy group. The town of Ayn Issa to which they were headed was no more than fifty kilometres from the Turkish border, but it had only recently been recaptured from the rebel forces and bands of armed stragglers still terrorised outlying hamlets.

The out of focus image of the minaret came into view. Distorted by the heat and clouded by the sandstorm, the tall, thin tower from which the muezzin would call the inhabitants of Ayn Issa to prayer appeared as if it were built of three disjointed sections. Nevertheless, after the tension of the journey, it was a welcome sight.

Not so, as they entered the main thoroughfares. The poorly constructed buildings that straddled the narrow roads had been decimated by small arms and mortar fire. Balconies, collapsed or barely suspended by metal construction bars revealed jagged tears in the buildings that forced his gaze to intrude on the remnants of the lives of those who had once lived there. Pictures on charred walls, a broken vase resting on a ledge, a singed child's teddy bear wedged into the balcony railings; the scene reminded him on a smaller scale of the firestorm in Dresden after the bombing in 1945.

Another Kurdish fighter, a slim, older man with a pronounced limp, led him in silence to a small storeroom in an alleyway leading from the vandalised mosque. The building in which it was housed was relatively undamaged and, as far as he could see, the sacks of flour and rice stacked on pallets had all been slashed open. The sound of rats scurrying for cover was the only noise he heard. From the corner of the passageway, a doorway led to an open area where communal bathing must have once been the order of the day. Now, little more than fifteen centimetres of liquid sludge covered the mosaic flooring of the pool, littered with snack packaging and the decaying bodies of rodents tossed to their death. To one side of the room was a set of swing doors into the toilet and changing areas.

Mullah Hashen stepped forward, a smile of relief on his face, as he embraced the newcomer. The Kurdish soldier nodded and retreated back along the passageway.

"Is this our man?" Benny asked, as the Mullah stepped aside.

The body lying on the floor was chained by both wrists to the iron pedestal of a wash hand basin. His black tunic and trousers were ripped and torn, revealing the scars of torture and beatings all over his body. Benny prodded with his shoe at the boy's chest. The eyes opened immediately, alert, taking stock of the situation. He was slim, above average height with a head of curly black hair, now caked with dirt and streaks of blood. His nose was squat, with a bump halfway up, as though it must have been broken at some time, but his eyes were the most outstanding feature. They were deeply inset into his skull, but so striking was the turquoise with just a pinprick of a pupil, that they radiated from within like the stare of a bird of prey as it assesses its target.

Benny retched. Alongside the toilet bowl were mounds of faeces and puddles of urine. The chains did not stretch to allow the captive to sit on the toilet, so he had got as close as possible. The stench was unbearable. Benny had expected no less. Armed conflict and personal hygiene were no bedfellows. Both the boy and Mullah Hashen had a puzzled expression on their faces as he took the half orange from the plastic bag in his pocket and thrust it under his nose. He took several deep breaths.

As the eldest son of a family of wealthy and influential

silk traders, Benny had followed the classic affluent Indian first son route to relatives in England and an education at Winchester and Oxford where he had majored in economics. His position in Mangalore's society had been assured.

By way of an explanation, he said, "In Tudor Britain, royalty and the aristocracy would only take to the streets of London holding a scented handkerchief or an orange under their noses to combat the stench of the unwashed masses and the filth around them. I find the stench of war particularly distasteful."

The boy studied him. "Have you come to kill me?" he asked with a perfect English accent.

"Your name and age?" Benny demanded.

"Darek. Twenty one."

Benny was surprised. He barely looked old enough to shave.

Mullah Hashen smiled as he experimented with the orange. "Darek was captured by the Peshmerga when they retook the town. He was being trained by the Jihadists as a suicide bomber. I thought he might suit your purpose. I convinced them to stop the punishment and wait for you." He tossed the squeezed orange toward Darek who ate it hungrily.

"So you want to be a martyr, do you, Darek?" Benny asked.

The boy was studying him in an offhanded way, his mind obviously in another place. Eventually, he spoke. "The Mullah said you are a powerful friend, a man who must be treated with respect, whose counsel I must follow. I praise Allah that I may rid this world of infidels before I reach his eternal paradise."

"Your command of English is very good," Benny said.

Darek looked up at the ceiling. "My father was English, from London. He came to teach at the Elementary School in Damascus. I adored him. He met my mother and, for her sake, he converted to Islam and became passionate about the teachings of Mohammed. He considered he had an obligation to speak out against the government. It was pointless." He stopped to count on his fingers. "I was twelve," he continued. "The Mukhabarat came to take him away from us. They said afterwards that he saw the error of his ways and confessed before he took his own life. You know that suicide is a sin in Islam which condemns a man's soul to hell and damnation.

"And what about your mother?" Benny asked.

"You will not know that my mother was the sister of a very powerful man in our government."

"Really?"

"She was forced to testify at my father's trial, to denounce him. My mother was so full of shame that she pleaded with the mullahs to take me into their care so that she could return to her birthplace in the mountains."

"Is that where she is now?"

"I have no idea," he said without any trace of emotion. "I haven't seen or spoken with her since the day she left."

Benny stared at the man in silence. Almost ten years of continuous daily indoctrination, learning to hate a way of life which he had never experienced nor embraced, to kill indiscriminately and take his own life in the process. In that split second before he pressed the button, would this man, Darek, question an ideology that said his father's supposed act was a cardinal sin, whilst his would lead to an eternal paradise?

"You understand that the Mullah may have a mission for you to fulfil?" Benny asked.

"I look forward to the opportunity to prove myself worthy to Allah,"

"It will not be easy," Benny continued. "You will have little time and a lot to learn about the shameful behaviour of the western infidels, a religious doctrine which is not yours and which you will find difficult to accept."

"Whatever is necessary, I will succeed." Benny detected a real determination in the man's reply. "An honourable death for me means that my father will be released from his torment, for us to enjoy eternal happiness and fulfilment."

Mullah Hashen led the way back out of the building toward the Peshmerga command centre. The two men who had accompanied Benny from the Turkish border were waiting, smoking and laughing as he approached. His tailored suit and Egyptian cotton shirt were obviously the butt of their humour. He would change into something less conspicuous for the next stage of his journey.

"Will he do?" the mullah asked.

"I guess so. My only concern is his immaturity. He has no experience of the outside world, no sexual experiences unless he was fucked by some of his comrades in arms. You must impress upon him that he is likely to experience acts which he may find distasteful, but he has to treat it all as part of the plan."

"Where do you want me to take him?"

"I'll let you know tomorrow. I'm meeting his controller this afternoon. He'll organise a schedule of intensive training and then send him on. Tidy him up, Hashen. Get him out of those chains and into a shower. Just a minute." Benny had reached the door of the senior Peshmerga commander's office.

He knocked and entered without waiting. The woman who had been sitting on the man's lap, turned and smiled. Unhurried, she pulled the brassiere back over her ample breasts.

"What the . . ? The Kurd stopped in midsentence as he recognised Benny. One hand shooed the woman out of the room; the other pulled roughly at the zipper on his trousers. The man was unshaven, without headdress his hair hanging limp and greasy down to his neck. He looked to Benny like an immigrant worker on a Dubai construction site, but here, this desert outpost was his empire and this unruly bunch of brigands, his slaves.

"So?" The man asked.

Benny reached inside his jacket. "Ten thousand dollars, as agreed. Hashen will move him out tomorrow. Here's another hundred for his taxi ride to Turkey. We'll give you the address."

Wondering where it had just been, Benny resolutely took the outstretched callous hand, returning the forceful grip.

"Nice doing business with you, Mr Ram." He laughed. "Let me know in good time if you need any more of the bastards. Otherwise, we make their journey to paradise as painful as possible."

Benny left his two Kurdish escorts at the border with a handsome tip. Life had taught him that you never knew when a contact would come in handy in the future and money always made these casual friendships more memorable.

The border town of Akcakale was heaving with Syrian refugees, a human tidal wave, confused and disturbed, anxious as the Turkish authorities attempted to register them. His car and driver were waiting at the only fleapit of a hotel he had been able to find.

With some relief, he changed out of his suit into a traditional dishdasha. The long flowing blue gown was cool and he could now circulate without attracting attention. There were several missed calls on his mobile. He could guess who was after him. They would have to wait. All hell must be breaking loose in Paris, but Chantelle could handle it. At least, for the time being. He selected another of his private mobiles and made the call.

"Sator," he said and waited.

"How long?" came the reply.

"Soon. We need to meet."

"It will have to be this afternoon. I must leave this evening."

"When and where?" Benny asked.

"Sator. . . . That's really good. Really good." He followed up with a GPS reference and a time.

They would meet in the Courtyard Restaurant of the Manici Hotel in Sanliurfa. Benny calculated it was no more than sixty kilometres away. With any luck, he would be there by two in the afternoon. Time for a late lunch.

The traditional hotel was a good choice. He booked a suite for the night. Tomorrow, he would re-surface to deal with the flack from his magazine's exclusive story.

The restaurant was left with just a sprinkling of diners by the time Benny was escorted to a table with a view over the city renowned as the birth place of the prophet Abraham that had now become the temporary home to a half a million Syrian refugees.

Now dressed in a casual silk shirt, sleeves open around the cuffs and with two buttons undone to reveal broad, muscular shoulders and the suggestion of a mat of hair on his broad chest, the virile image was only distorted by the lower two buttons which strained against a pot belly, under which a leather belt supported his linen trousers. Benny would claim that his waist measurement had remained unchanged since his university days, but in a more expansive mood, he would also agree that, in compensation, it would appear that his legs were getting shorter.

He had decided against the Urfan speciality dish of the day and opted for a grilled fillet steak with fries, preceded by a pickled vegetable starter which he had almost finished by the time his fellow diner arrived.

"Good to see you again, Mr Ram," the tall man said, offering his hand.

Benny lowered the fork, carefully wiped the olive oil from his mouth with a starched white serviette and stood up. He avoided the hand and held his arms forward to embrace the man, kissing his cheeks in a symbolic greeting.

"This is the way we welcome friends in my homeland, Terence. Please, no more Mr Ram. From now on, it's Benny."

Obviously taken aback by this physical approach, Terence Hemmings moved quickly to his chair, much to Benny's amusement.

"Drink?" he asked, as he recalibrated his memory of their first meeting. Hemmings had an undeniable military bearing and attitude. Although in his late forties, Benny guessed that he must keep himself extremely fit. His face had aquiline features, spoiled by some boy like freckles that suggested innocence and ginger hair which, naturally curly, had been swept back severely and bedded with hair cream. Looks were often deceptive; the crooked smile none more so than in this man's case.

"They have alcohol here?" he asked with surprise in his voice.

"I'm pleased to say they do," Benny replied, holding up a Bloody Mary as proof.

Hemming settled for a bottle of beer and followed Benny's choice of a steak, but with a green salad.

"Sorry I'm late," Hemming apologised. "I had to pack and leave the seminar in Van earlier than I anticipated. I'm off to the airport as soon as we are through. Back to London. Somebody with Palace security needs to speak with me."

"You're from Devon or Somerset, are you?"

Hemmings smiled to reveal two chipped teeth on one side of his mouth. "You recognise my accent?"

"My university roommate was from Chard. No offence intended, but I have to say it's always been an accent I associate with people who are thick. Maybe, because of my roommate."

"That's me, Benny, the harmless country farm boy with a straw between his teeth and a haystack for a brain."

"I very much doubt that, Terence. You have a more sinister air about you."

"That's why we're in business together."

"Talking about that, we did agree on a price, did we not?"

"Twenty five million dollars."

Benny grimaced. "The sum is correct, but I think you have the currency confused."

Hemmings ignored the remark. "Is everything in place?"

"I told you the die is cast. Your urgent meeting in

40

London is already evidence that this is so. Some of the photographs are now in circulation and the boy will be with you tomorrow."

"I need him sent up to Van as quickly as possible. We still have to instil the mission into him, make the video and organise the travel arrangements. In as little time as is necessary, he must be ready to leave."

"Hashen will bring him as far as the Syrian border by nine tomorrow morning. You take it from there."

"I'll get Mullah Omar to meet up with them. Do you trust Hashen?"

Benny smiled, more to himself than at Hemmings. "As much as you trust Omar. They are religious capitalists who enjoy their well paid extra-curricula activities. Yet, their secular reputations are unblemished. What more could we hope for?"

"And the potential threat from the Israelis. Do you have someone in mind?"

Benny nodded. "I do. He fell into my lap, so to speak. I've had the man in my sights for some time. He sold me the images."

Hemmings had finished his meal and was preparing to leave, but Benny could tell there was something else on the man's mind.

"Can we finalise the financial details?" Benny ventured.

Hemmings sat back down. "You are a very rich man. Twenty five million dollars is not such a sum that would entice you to put your livelihood, probably your life, at risk. Is there, perhaps, another motive which prompts you to pursue this venture?"

Benny smiled. "We all have our weaknesses. I believe in the monarchy, politics and religion, but not all practiced together. History has taught us that it is a lethal combination."

"Forgive me if I do not recognise you as a man with such high altruistic objectives."

"Appearances can be deceptive. By the way, if you

recall, it was good old British pounds rather than dollars that we agreed upon."

Benny matched the stare. It wasn't the money, he guessed. Hemmings was weighing up the risk of moving forward into a position of no return whilst still unsure of Benny's commitment. He was asking himself whether Benny could be trusted or if there was some bigger game he was playing?

Hemmings shrugged. "As you suggest, I am a simple foot soldier. I understand the temptations and can react rationally. Many of my colleagues are more influential than I and, alas, more impetuous. I cannot guarantee your safety should the assurances you offer prove to, how can I say, contain elements of deception."

"Then I shall have nothing to fear," Benny replied. "The fee is agreed?"

Hemmings nodded. "Paid how and when?"

"No later than tomorrow, into escrow with a firm of lawyers in Zurich." He gave the name which Hemmings noted. "Twenty four hours after the event occurs, the money is released to my order."

"You seriously propose to place the detail of our transaction with a third party, albeit a discreet Swiss lawyer?"

"Terence, you underestimate me. The trigger necessary to release the money will simply be the proof of deaths of a young suicide bomber, name Darek, and his accomplice, a man by the name of Gerben Rosenberg."

Six - @banderboyseb

Sebastien Bernhard had a studio apartment on the fourth floor of a tenement terraced house in the 18th arrondissement. The Goutte d'Or district was mainly inhabited by working class families and young aspirant artists, actors and writers whose limited incomes kept them outside, but within touching distance of Montmartre, the artistic heartbeat of Paris.

Not for long, Sebastien thought. When his masterpiece was complete, he would escape from this dump to a world of inspiration where the industry leaders in computer graphics and animation pursued their art. Sebastien saw himself as a true artist, not some Photoshop hack churning out pages of sensationalist trash for the masses. *Bien a Vous* paid the bills, but had about as much artistic merit as an exhibit in a Turner prize gallery.

The missed calls while he had been asleep were all from Chantelle. She could wait. He walked out onto the small railed balcony, stretching his small, wiry body, his arms raised outward. It felt as if he were to try hard, he could almost reach across the gap to touch the balcony across the narrow, cobbled street. At the very least, if somebody was on the other side, they could touch each other's hands. In the films, it would be an abandoned sex-starved beauty who craved his body. In reality, it was an elderly man, crippled by deformity and with a hacking cough that kept Sebastien awake at night. Never mind. Any day now, it would all be just a bad dream.

That reminded him. The Wi-Fi connection in the apartment had been on the blink for over a week. The provider had said it was a router problem, but nobody had showed up to fix it. He needed to back up his project on the cloud server. If he lost the last two month's work stored on the hard drive, he would never forgive himself. He was not going to work today; Chantelle's orders; so there was no excuse. He would buy a mobile broadband dongle this afternoon, without fail. After he had uploaded the files, he would get into the editing. Jacques & Gillian was an adult animation, real life images cartoonized and converted into a no holds barred, sexual fantasy with some clever graphic techniques. His film even made Prince Arthur's antics look tame by comparison. He laughed at the thought. The horny content had been officially approved a couple of nights ago by Sebastien and two friends who had jerked each other off as they watched it. Now, it was just a question of contacting the right people and the money would start to roll in. The market was enormous, beyond belief.

He walked back into the studio just as the lock on the front door shattered and the two men forced their way into the room. Sebastien instinctively backed away, pinning himself against the IT table. "Who the fuck?" he shouted out of bravado.

"Police Judiciaire!" Maxwell waved his phony credentials in Bernhard's face. Lewis followed suit.

"We need to know if you have or know where we can locate the original source of the images you've been working on these past days." The concierge had already confirmed that Bernhard had moaned to him that he had to traipse half way across Paris to work over the weekend.

"Get a court order!" Sebastien replied, slightly less nervous now he knew he was dealing with the police.

Maxwell nodded, the prompt for Lewis to send a fist with the knuckle on the third finger extended, into the man's right shoulder blade. Sebastien fell onto one knee, his left hand clutching the top of his arm. "What was that for?" he screamed in pain. "Who are you?"

Maxwell bent down, his face inches away from the frightened man. "Listen. We don't have time to piss about." He glanced at the computer screen. The activity around the IT table had jarred the machine out of sleep mode. The *BV* cover page came into view. "Where are the prints you used for this?" he indicated.

Sebastien glanced at the screen and then back at the man. He reached into his shirt pocket and retrieved a USB stick. "They're on this." He said, nervously.

"All of them?"

Sebastien shook his head. "I think there's about half. They were already copied onto the stick for me when I arrived."

"From what?"

"I don't know. They didn't tell me." He was almost

crying. Maxwell had moved back to let Lewis take his place. "Please, please don't hit me again," the man pleaded. "I honestly don't know."

Lewis reacted to the tap on his shoulder by stepping back and unzipping his green bomber jacket. "Who is 'they'?" Maxwell was in his face again.

"Chantelle and Rosenberg."

"Rosenberg?"

"I assume he's the man who sold her the photographs."

"This Rosenberg was at your editor's apartment? Is he there now?" Maxwell's voice showed a trace of excitement.

"He was, up until a few hours ago." Sebastien followed Lewis' movement as he walked behind the table. He watched the man as he closed the lid of the laptop. "Don't touch that. It's got my film on it." He tried to get up, but Maxwell restrained him. "I haven't got a copy. Oh, please, no."

"I want you to tell me everything. From the moment this Chantelle called you to the time you stepped back inside this front door." He looked around at the remnants of the door, swinging slowly on one hinge. "Well, what was the front door," he said. "Don't leave anything out and don't waste time if you want your computer to stay in one piece. Understand?"

Sebastien nodded, managing to get back onto both feet. "Please, please, don't lose all my work. It's got nothing to do with what you're interested in," he pleaded.

Nervously, he stuttered through a timeline of his weekend. Maxwell seemed satisfied.

"No!" he screamed. Lewis had the machine above his head. Sebastien launched himself at him, tearing at the man's face and drawing blood in welts down his cheek. Lewis swore, thrust the laptop to the ground where it shattered into four pieces, and moved towards his assailant.

Sebastien backed off.

At that moment, the French windows of the apartment

45

opposite opened and the old man staggered into view. "What is going on?" he shouted at the figure of Sebastien who had turned around to look at him. Maxwell and Lewis retreated into the shadow of the room.

This was his one chance. Running onto the balcony, Sebastien climbed onto the railing and launched himself into the air toward the balcony opposite. "Get help!" he shouted at the old man. His body bounced against the outside of the iron struts as his hands gripped the handrail. For a matter of seconds, he hung in the air above the street below before he started to climb upwards. The old man was powerless to help, his face aghast as Sebastien searched for a foothold.

Maxwell looked on. It must have been Lewis' punch that frustrated Bernhard's climb. His right arm appeared to lock, dislocating his shoulder and forcing his hand to lose its grip. There was a look of disbelief on his face as his left hand, unable to sustain his weight, slipped from the handrail. The piercing scream ended as his body hit the ground below and lay lifeless, a single trail of blood seeping over the cobbles.

Maxwell thrust the USB stick into his pocket and shoved Lewis in the back, through the doorway. "The fire escape!" he shouted as they ran to the rear of the building.

On the floor of the apartment, the remnants of the laptop, screen, keyboard and motherboard lay on top of the hard drive. On the sofa, the smartphone began to ring.

Seven - @GerbenRosenberg

Chantelle threw the handset onto the sofa. "Why doesn't he answer the damn phone. I've left six messages already," she said. "I told him to stay indoors, not to go to the office. I didn't tell him to become bloody incommunicado!" She looked over to where Gerben stood, to one side of the window. "Are they still there?" she asked.

"They are," he replied, "but there's some activity. I can't tell exactly what's going on."

She walked over, pushing past him and looked directly out of the window. "They know that I live here," she emphasised, making it obvious she was watching them. "It appears they are getting ready to leave. One of them is outside the car, cleaning tree debris off the windscreen, the other is wrestling to get his coat on. Thank God!" She retrieved the phone. "Let me try him again."

"Can I make a suggestion?" he asked, without waiting for an answer. "Let Bernhard be. He's probably just sleeping. Remember, you kept him up half the night. Do this! Change that! More colour here! Put the image up a bit! He's probably sick of the sound of your voice."

"I'm his employer, damn it! He's got no right to be sick of the sound of my voice." She laughed. "Damn you too, Gerben! Why have you got me into this business? I'm beginning to sound and feel like a nervous wreck."

The phone in her hand vibrated. "It must be him," she said. But it wasn't. She listened intently, finished the call with a simple 'thank you', checked her watch and then looked hard at Gerben. "*BV* has made it to the newsstands. The clock is ticking. I need to get to the office."

"Remember what we agreed. Act totally normally," he urged.

"I'm later than usual. About an hour," she said. "I take the metro to the Isle d'Italie, walk the few hundred metres to the office. What more?"

"Watch your handbag," Gerben replied. "There will be muggers with a special interest in its contents.

Wrapping a bottle green raincoat around her shoulders, she reached for her mobile and stashed it. "Liberated females don't need handbags," she said, walking to the door, hands in her pockets. "If one of them starts to follow me, send a text. I need to know." She looked quizzically at him. "I don't understand why Benny insisted you hang onto the memory cards."

"Because he trusts me. We have a gentlemen's

agreement and that's good enough."

Bullshit. If only you knew the truth, Gerben, she thought. Benny was no gentleman and trust wasn't in his vocabulary. A calculated distraction on the Sunday had given her the opportunity to follow his secret instructions. Gerben was none the wiser. The original cards were now in a secure place. He now had two identical virgin cards which she had arranged for Bernhard to purchase on his way over to her apartment.

He was back at the window. "It's what I thought, a change of shift. They've driven off, but a black Merc has taken its place."

"What are you going to do?" she asked.

"I'll give it five minutes to make sure that no one comes sniffing around the apartment and then I'll get back to Montrieul. I need to follow up on our approach to the Prince."

Two minutes later, he watched as one of the new men on surveillance, a tall, thick set guy, wearing a green bomber jacket, got out of the car and started walking toward the metro.

Gerben dutifully sent off a text message. He was curious. Chantelle intrigued him. She may be into women, but that doesn't mean it had always been to the exclusion of men. Her bedroom was as basic as the living room, a simple double bed, matching side tables and a pine wardrobe. No pictures or photographs on the walls; nothing more than a place to sleep.

He wasn't sure exactly what he was looking for, until he found a well-worn Gucci suitcase, cabin size, under the bed, filled with non seasonal clothing and a small photo album. There were just eight photographs, neatly mounted, one per page. The first two must have been taken recently, within a couple of years, if he had to guess. They were, obviously, the sort of time delayed exposures you took by balancing the camera on a wall and, then, rushing around to pose before the shutter opened. She was embracing a man, smiling at the camera. In the first, his head was only half-turned toward her; in the next, he was looking adoringly into her eyes. The remaining six photographs were much older, unmistakeably her as a young girl, ten or eleven. They looked to have been taken all on the same day, at the same place, somewhere near a lake, eucalyptus trees dotted around. Five showed her happily playing with a younger boy. In the last, she was standing on the porch of a country house, this time holding hands with an older man. They were smiling at each other.

He flicked back to the first two photographs. So, there had been a relationship, he thought. She must have been so badly let down that she had categorised all men as bastards. It was a self-serving explanation which allowed Gerben to let his fantasies run wild.

The sound of a key in the front door lock sent a cold shard of fear through his body. His first reaction was to turn toward her bathroom and the fire escape visible through the window. That was no good. He'd never make it before the intruder was on to him. His next reaction was to find the cushion under which he'd hidden the gun.

There was the sound of someone turning a key, trying to find a purchase in the lock, then a man's voice cursing in English. The thought crossed Gerben's mind that he wouldn't be making so much noise if he expected to find someone else in the apartment. At least, that would give him the element of surprise. To do what? He was no trained fighter. The pistol, a relic from the Algerian conflict, had been bought clandestinely on a whim a few months earlier following a set-to with an angry journalist who had threatened him, but he had no idea how to use it or even how to load it with the ammunition. A trained professional would realise that in an instant. He put it back under the cushion.

He heard retreating footsteps and chanced a glance through the peephole. The intruder's key had not worked. The concierge would have a spare. Gerben had to get out while he could. He looked around for the camera, checking that the memory card was in place.

Gingerly, he opened the front door. He could hear the overweight concierge complaining as he made his way up the staircase from the floor below. The only way out was up. He shut the front door behind him and ran for the stairs, around two corners and on to the landing above. His impetus nearly carried him headlong into the old lady who was trying to manoeuvre a wheelchair out of her front door.

"Call yourself social services!" she complained angrily. "Merde! You're never here on time and the lift is broken again. Why doesn't the condominium fix it once and for all? They charge enough! If my husband was alive to see it!" She broke off. "You're not Anton! Where's Anton?"

He helped her into the chair, covering her legs with the blanket. "Anton is ill. He couldn't come today."

"Don't tell me! Liver problem. Am I right?" She wasn't waiting for an answer. "Can't keep off the Beaujolais. I've told him. If he carries on, he'll end up in one of these things before his time." They were approaching the staircase. "Your name?" she demanded.

"Oliver," he replied.

He guided the chair slowly down, one step at a time. "Careful!" she urged. "I want to get to the Centre in one piece. The way you're going, I'll arrive as a collection of bones!"

The camera in his pocket was chafing against his hip. Gerben took it out and laid it in her lap under the blanket. "Keep hold of this for me," he said. He placed her hands firmly together on top of the blanket over the camera. Her skin was flaking, ice cold to the touch.

She looked up at him. "Bit old to be a carer, aren't you, Oliver?" They were nearing the bottom of the stairs. "My first husband was named Oliver. Useless bastard he was! No good in the sack either! Are you married Oliver?"

Gerben glanced up. The concierge and the stranger were busy with the pass key; a casual glance at Gerben and then back to the task at hand. After ten seconds, another more penetrating look, as if he recognised the face. Gerben began to panic. The wheelchair was almost level with Chantelle's front door.

"I asked you . . ." She broke off, recognising the presence of the concierge. "What are you doing, Henri?" she asked.

"Nothing, Madame de Lafayette," the portly concierge replied self-consciously.

"It doesn't look like nothing, Henri," she replied imperiously. "Anyway, she's not in. I saw her leave the building about twenty minutes ago. Had a man in there all weekend. From time to time, I could hear his raised voice. Not dissimilar. ."

She broke off as Gerben jerked the wheelchair to one side. "What was that for Oliver?" She raised her hands in alarm. The camera slipped out from under the blanket and bounced off the step of the wheelchair onto the carpet, coming to rest at the stranger's feet. He smiled at her, bent to retrieve it and place it back in her lap.

"Where's Anton today?" the concierge asked. "Haven't seen you before."

Gerben had already begun to push the wheelchair toward the next step of stairs. "We're late," Gerben offered as an excuse.

She was looking at the camera. "What is this thing?" she enquired.

Gerben felt the eyes staring into his back. Someone was whistling a tune at the bottom of the stairwell. "Sounds just like Anton," she said. "It's one of his favourites."

Both the stranger and Gerben understood the implication of her comment at the same time. The man began to run toward Gerben, who, grabbing the camera, span the wheelchair around and propelled it forward to collide with him. Gerben made a dash for the stairs, turning the corner to career headlong into a heavily built young man with a surprised expression on his face.

"Sorry," Gerben said. "There's a man up there, trying to mug Madame de Lafayette. See if you can stop him!" He gasped for breath. "I'm going for the police."

The young man took off. Gerben raced for the next set of stairs and the corridor leading out of the building. As he reached the front door, there was the sound of a single gunshot. He didn't stop running until he reached a street full of shoppers where he could get lost in the crowd.

Sitting in a café with a large latté in front of him, he began to regain his composure and take stock of the situation. That had been a call to close for comfort. Whoever was after him was prepared to use force, guns and, whatever it took to get the pictures. He took the camera from his pocket. It was probably best to ditch it and keep the card somewhere safe. He checked the spring loaded slot for the micro card. It wasn't there anymore.

Eight - @renemarchal

Someone had put a copy of *Bien a Vous* on his desk. Very thoughtful, I'm sure, but nobody at 36 made such gestures without an ulterior motive. Capitaine René Marchal picked up the magazine and began to flick casually through the pages. He sighed out loud. The British Royal family careered from one crisis to another. How long would it be before Britain did away with the monarchy and established a French style republic? With scandals like this, it couldn't be too far away. The images he merely glanced at. Would the young man actually be grateful that he had been forced out of the closet? He closed the magazine and studied the cover. The aspect that really intrigued him was how a second rate publication like *BV* could summons the financial clout to get hold of such an exclusive. There must be some big bucks behind it.

Marchal had been at 36 for twenty eight years, man and boy. In three weeks, they would be throwing a surprise party for his retirement, just like they did for all the old farts who were being put out to graze. He couldn't wait.

36 was the number by which the Police Judiciaire was

commonly known. The address, 36 Quai des Orfèvres, was wrongly believed by most Parisians to be the home of the PJ, the French equivalent of the CID. In fact, few people realised that the PJ is headquartered in the main Ministry of the Interior Building and most of the 2200 policemen are spread across Paris in various buildings. For the last ten years, Marchal had worked in the first division of La Crim, the Brigade Criminelle, from the third floor of a very unimposing building in the Avenue de Marigny, not far from the Champs-Elysee.

"Who left this for me?" he asked, as Lieutenant Peltier hurried into the office, looking stressed as always, a sheaf of papers clasped untidily in his hand.

"The Commandant. He asked for you to make yourself available after lunch for a meeting." Peltier had discarded the papers in a pile on his desk, his attention on the cover of the magazine which he was trying to read upside down. "Fancy Prince Arthur, a pédé. They've blurred the picture, but it looks like he's about to give that bloke a blow job. Don't you think so?"

"Surprised you find it so titillating, Peltier." Marchal looked half amused.

The young man looked away quickly. This slur on his heterosexuality was, obviously, a sensitive issue, his voice never having properly broken.

"Did the Commandant say what it was about?" Marchal went on.

"No. Your mobile's ringing. Can't you hear it?"

He didn't want to admit he was going deaf, but it was one of the reasons for which he grateful to be leaving the force. "The ring's progressive. It gets louder," he explained, excusing the lapse.

The call was brief and found Marchal in a taxi on his way to a fashionable restaurant on the Left Bank.

"I've borrowed the manager's office," Commandant Arnault indicated. "He's a good friend. Do you use the restaurant?" He made it sound like a public convenience.

Marchal shook his head.

53

"The scented beef haché is out of this world. You should try it." Both men sat either side of the desk.

A Big Mac from McDonalds and a vinegar sachet was the nearest Marchal got to the recommended dish, but he said nothing. "We have a problem?" he asked.

"I want you to have a look at an incident for me. The SP is investigating an apparent accidental death, a fall from a building in Goutte d'or." Arnault just managed to get the words out before he belched.

"Why us? If there are no suspicious circumstances, uniformed are supposed to handle it. And even if there were, the 18th arrondissement is 2nd Division's patch. I don't want to go treading on toes."

"You won't. Believe me, 2nd don't want to know. They're too busy." He looked down at a new message that had just activated his mobile.

"Sorry?"

"I'll brief you when I've got some more details." He pocketed the phone. "Listen. The caretaker from the apartment block where the death occurred said that two PJ officers were in the building looking for the victim. They showed her warrant cards. She indicated which one was the man's studio."

"Studio?"

"Yes. The place is full of bohemian types, apparently." He sounded disparaging. "The problem is that uniformed has contacted all the divisions to trace the officers involved, only to find that nobody was officially assigned to this address."

"So, we've either got two phony cops or a couple of rogue elements."

"Exactly," the Commandant said. "The Commissary has asked me to get it dealt with right away, to use somebody who was beyond reproach. I thought of you."

Liar, Marchal thought. I'm the only field officer you can spare. He was being phased out. New cases were being assigned to younger men. "Very kind of you, Sir," he replied. "And this?" He held up the rolled copy of the

54

magazine.

"Disgusting, isn't it?" Arnault reached out to take it back. "The magazine has its offices on our patch. Presumably, there's going to be a lot of legal flack flying soon. I want us to be on top of the situation in case of any criminal allegations. But it can wait. This is more important."

"Shall I hang onto that?" Marchal asked, indicating the magazine.

"No. The wife hasn't seen it yet. She asked me to pick up a copy."

Marchal had an aversion to driving around Paris, so he took taxis whenever he could. Admin wouldn't be too hard on him over his last expense account.

The narrow cobbled street was about a hundred metres long and had been sealed off at both ends. Crowds pressed against the makeshift barriers to get a glimpse of the police activity. The body laid where it had fallen, partially covered by a sheet. A pathology intern was standing over it, obviously anxious to leave the scene along with the three uniformed officers who had been instructed to wait for Marchal's arrival.

He asked to see the body. It was a straightforward case. She indicated the balcony on the fourth floor from which he had fallen. Suicide or accidental death. His back was broken and God knows what his insides were like. There was a single head wound from which some blood had seeped. Tomorrow, the autopsy would disclose if there were any substances in his body.

Marchal pulled back the open shirt to inspect the torso and looked upwards. There were no balconies on the first three floors, just simple ledges on which window boxes had been placed. All were intact.

"There was nothing to break his fall. He landed on his back. Correct?"

The intern nodded.

"How do you reckon he got this nasty bruise on his front shoulder blade? It's not consistent with the fall?"

She studied the wound. "I'd assumed he'd struck something on the way down. It's a single, heavy blow,"

Marchal turned to speak with the gendarmes. The victim's studio apartment had been sealed off, nothing touched. None of the neighbours had seen anything.

"Where's the caretaker who spoke with these two officers?" he asked.

The caretaker turned out to be a woman in her fifties, a cigarette, trailing ash, lodged in the corner of her mouth. She hadn't paid much attention to the two men. They were tall and broad, just like policemen always are. They flashed identity cards as one of them, black wavy hair with a cold, threatening stare, asked in which apartment Bernhard lived.

"Did the identity card look like this?" He opened his wallet.

She nodded. They made their way upstairs to the fourth floor. Marchal ignored the taped doorway and walked to the rear of the building. "Do you always leave open the window to the fire escape?" he asked.

She didn't and, no, she hadn't seen the two officers leave, but there was such pandemonium going on in the street. She had tried to find them, but somebody had already phoned for the police and when the uniformed officers arrived, she hadn't thought any more about the two men.

"How long after they went up was it that the man fell?"

"Twenty minutes. Maybe less. I was busy, I didn't look at the clock."

Other than a collapsed front door and the remnants of what had once been a laptop computer, nothing else appeared to have been disturbed. They made their way toward the balcony, treading carefully between the debris. An officer was bagging the hard drive. Who did this Bernhard work for?

A magazine. She wasn't sure which one. He spent a lot of time at home. No special girlfriend. People came and went. Mainly men friends. No, he wasn't like that.

The bookcase was next to the French windows. He ran his fingers across the various books and files kept randomly on the shelves. The thin file with payslips written on the spine told him what he wanted to know. Coincidence or something more sinister? Sebastien Bernhard was the senior graphic designer with *Publications Bien à Vous S.A.*

His eyes were involuntarily drawn to a movement of the curtains in the apartment just across the street. Standing on the balcony, it looked a lot further to fall than it did from the ground. "Hello! Can I speak with you, please?" He addressed his request to the balcony opposite. There was no reaction.

One of the policemen had followed Marchal into the apartment. "An old man lives there alone. His name's Forlan, but he wasn't in when we called around." He pointed toward the ground. "The medic wants to get off. Can they move the body now?"

Five minutes later, there was no trace of a fatality in the street, the area was no longer a potential crime scene and people were again milling to and fro. Callous, Marchal thought as he climbed the staircase in the adjacent building. The pressures of life were so great that something as profound as death evaporated into the business of the day as seamlessly as if it had never happened.

Banging on the door, coupled with a shouted rant had absolutely no effect. Fortunately, the spare key was under the doormat. The figure in the armchair with its back to the door was watching the television. The old man started as Marchal put one hand on his shoulder, extending his warrant card with the other. Saliva was dripping from the side of the old man's mouth. He sucked it back in, then swallowed it.

"Sorry to alarm you, Monsieur Forlan, but we were afraid you might be ill."

The old man fiddled with something in his old jacket pocket, retrieving a white plastic disc which he placed in his ear, the wax squelching as he did so. A little white box in his hand was emitting a high pitched sound which oscillated as he turned the control. The noise suddenly stopped. "It's wireless," he said, as if he knew what he was talking about. "I'm deaf without it. Say it again! You scared the life out of me.

Marchal repeated what he had said.

"I didn't see anything," he said, straining to get up from the chair.

"Didn't see anything of what?"

"Whatever you've come round here to talk about."

"I think you did, Mr Forlan," Marchal said softly. "Let me say something. A young man fell from this balcony today, a young man whose life had barely started. You must have said 'hello', waved to him from time to time. I bet you did." He could see from the old man's eyes that he was right. "I don't want his life to be wasted and I'm sure you don't either. We owe it to him to discover exactly what happened and I think you can help the police find out who was responsible. So, why don't you tell me?"

The old man shuffled nervously around the room. "They might come for me."

"They won't. They'll never know you told us." He put both hands on the man's shoulders. "I'll never say."

"There were two of them, big guys, looked like flics. They couldn't recognise me. Sun was in their eyes."

"What did you see?"

"Nothing until they were close to the window, just shadowy figures in the background." He gulped fresh air. "The boy was kneeling on the floor, holding his shoulder. He looked real scared. The bigger of the two guys, the one who didn't say anything, took something out of a computer and gave it to the one who was doing the talking. Couldn't hear what he was saying. Didn't have this on." He gestured at the hearing aid. "Not allowed to wear it near the balcony. Lost the last one. It dropped while I was trying to look down. Lovely woman. Big ..." He gestured with his hands cupped in front of his chest. Social services said that was it. If I lost this one, I could just stay deaf. Cow, that Madame Tamarinde!"

"Can we stick to what happened, Monsieur Forlan?"

"Big guy smashed the computer; it was one of those ones you carry around; into little pieces. It was then that the boy made a dash for the balcony. He looked petrified. I struggled out onto my balcony and shouted. He had already climbed onto the railings. The men didn't follow him. They backed off, but they were still talking to him"

"You didn't hear what was said?"

"Like I said," Forlan complained, "I can't take this outside. I took it off."

"So the man jumped to his death?"

"No, of course not." He sounded irritable. "He was trying to reach my balcony, but he didn't quite make it. I couldn't help him. I'm so old. No good to anyone. Twenty years ago, I could have saved him."

"Don't blame yourself. It's not your fault."

"When you get to my age, nothing ever is." He looked up at Marchal. "He was holding onto the outside of the railings. I thought for a moment he was going to make it. Then his arm gave way. He shouted for help, but he knew I couldn't. As he let go and started to fall, he said "he's not French." Then he disappeared. Such a weird thing to say."

"But you couldn't hear him?"

"That old cow at social services kept me waiting years. In the meantime, I learned how to lip read."

Marchal nodded. "It's not so odd. People falling to their death are often heard saying the strangest things. It's as if their conscious mind won't let them accept what's happening. Maybe, they think it's going to be like the movies, a soft landing in a garbage container or on top of a truck full of mattresses. What did you think he meant?"

The old man fell back into the chair, the exertion apparent. "Not for me to say, but I guess he wanted to point the finger at the men who were responsible for his death."

The mobile vibrated in Marchal's pocket and then

59

began to ring. It was Commandant Arnault's office, but only a secretary relaying a message. He left the old man cursing as he fiddled with his hearing aid.

The taxi took him to an address on the west side of the city. Parked vehicles on either side of the tree lined street had forced the squad car to double park outside the apartment block. Two uniformed officers in front of the front door were watching a young woman walk her dog. A muscular young man and a sullen faced concierge sat in the lobby.

"Whose apartment were you trying to gain access to?" Marchal asked the concierge.

"Madame Dubois's. She's the editor of *Bien á Vous*. The police have tried to contact her, but she's too busy at her office to deal with them."

I bet, Marchal thought. From the stuttering and disjointed narrative of the two men, the policeman began to piece together the story. On reflection, the concierge had recognized the man who had pretended to be Madame Lafayette's carer and who had run off. He had been visiting with Madame Dubois over the weekend. No, he had no idea what his name was. Without a second thought, Anton had rushed into the hallway and launched himself at the man who had told the concierge he was a policeman. The description fitted one of the men who had visited Bernhard's apartment earlier that day. As Anton had bundled him to the floor, the man had wrestled a handgun from his pocket and fired a shot into the air. In such a confined space, the noise had been shattering. Shards of plaster had fallen from the ceiling. Poor Madame Lafayette. She had had a seizure. The *flic* had run off, leaving Anton to call for an ambulance.

Someone had already spoken with the hospital. The old lady was in a drug induced coma. It was fifty, fifty. If she came through, tomorrow would be the earliest she could be resuscitated. Forensics had already been asked to check the crime scene and remove the bullet for examination.

Marchal returned to 36 to be greeted by the sight of his

assistant, head obscured from view, attempting to blindly negotiate a pile of lever arch files out through the doorway. "What are you doing, Peltier?" he asked.

The unexpected sound of the Marchal's voice caused the young man to lurch forward, sending files and loose papers all over the floor. His face was bright red with embarrassment. "Sorry, Capitaine." He stuttered. "I've been ordered to clear my desk."

"What for?"

If it was humanly possible for him to sound even more embarrassed, Peltier succeeded. "As from tomorrow morning, I've been transferred to immigration," he said. "They need more manpower. Slave trafficking, I'm told."

Marchal felt the bile rise in his throat. "On whose orders?" he asked.

"Commandant Arnault." Peltier was recovering his composure. "He told me I'm not an intern anymore. I've been recommended for promotion as a full lieutenant." The young man must have recognised the flash of anger on Marchal's face. "The Commandant came looking for you, but you weren't around, Sir."

Marchal bit his tongue. It wasn't anger, more the frustration of no longer being treated as part of the chain of command. Peltier had bent down to pick up the paperwork.

"Leave that!" Marchal ordered. "As of this afternoon, you're still working for me and I need you to do something."

Peltier needed no prompting. He stood to attention.

"You told me once that you had a relative in the London office of *Le Monde*, if my memory serves me right?" Marchal asked.

"A sister in law. She's a journalist, married to my elder brother."

"I need a favour from her. I can't go through official channels. I'm pretty certain that the two incidents we're investigating involving these phony policemen are linked to *BV* and this exposé of Prince Arthur. My guess is that these men are trying to get to the source and our victims were in the wrong place at the wrong time."

"What do you want her to do?" Peltier asked.

"There must be a security force that is responsible for protecting the Royal Family. I need names and bios of the men concerned. Do you think she can help?"

"It's a tall order, Capitaine. I can only ask."

"Tell her there's a story in this and as soon as I get to the bottom of it, I'll give her the inside track. That should be enough incentive for any journalist."

There was a gasp of exasperation from outside the doorway. The Commandant had come across Peltier's impromptu filing system. "What the. . . !"

The young man wheeled around, a look of horror on his face.

"My fault, I'm afraid Sir," Marchal interjected. "We bumped into each other as I came into my office." The look of relief on Peltier's face did not go unnoticed.

Commandant Arnault motioned the Lieutenant to gather the papers and leave the room. He closed the door behind him. "Are you sorry to be leaving us, René? It must be a wrench for you?"

The use of his forename; the caring question; the slow build-up; Marchal resigned himself to a sucker punch. "I must say, I have mixed feelings," he replied. "I've promised myself to spend more time with my grandchildren."

Arnault was about to say something, ask a question, but he simply nodded as if the other man's remark was nothing more than commonplace. "Peltier has told you that he's been reassigned?" Marchal nodded. "Orders from above, I'm afraid. You won't miss him, will you?"

"It depends very much how this investigation develops." Marchal replied by following up with a brief summary of his progress to date and the initial conclusions he had drawn.

"That's one of the matters I wanted to discuss with you. It sort of dovetails in with a conversation I had this afternoon with a senior civil servant at the Élysée Palace."

"The Élysée?"

"Yes," Arnault replied, "someone high up in the Interior Ministry. This business has some very political overtones. They want us to tread softly and not make any waves that could upset the British."

"What does that mean?"

"Look, René. You've got a couple of weeks left to do before you retire. Give yourself some personal space and time to get things in order. Concentrate on the handover to your replacement."

That was the first Marchal had heard about a substitute, prompting his curiosity to ask questions. He decided against it. He did not want to get sidetracked. "You've lost me, Commandant." He was irritated. "We've got one lad who was probably coerced into jumping to his death and a gun fired in the common area of an apartment block that has caused an old lady to have a seizure. Hardly incidents which want to make me rush for my fishing rod and sit by a lake all day, in the comforting knowledge that somebody will start worrying about it in two week's time."

"No crimes have been committed, to the best of our knowledge, other than those relating to the possession and discharging of a firearm. That's right, isn't it?"

Marchal looked quizzically at his superior. "You mean other than impersonating police officers, threatening behaviour, possible assault, damage to property, attempted breaking and entering? No. There's no problem. Everything's totally kosher!"

"I don't appreciate your facetious remarks, René." Arnault retorted. "These issues are never black and white. Politics are at play and we have to respect and deal with the evidence accordingly. We're operating in a wider context than just a couple of local incidents." He stopped to draw breath and assess the other man's reaction. "Look. The British are totally embarrassed by this Prince Arthur business and rightly so. They need our help and we need theirs to counter some proposed German amendments to the Europol convention we don't like. The Brits are on their back with their legs open, begging for cooperation. Let's give them what they want. Get my drift?"

Marchal shrugged. "You're in charge. I just want to get to the bottom of it. You and your superiors take it from there." He was keen to end the conversation. "Is that all?"

"Just one more thing." Arnault's tone was conciliatory. "Now Peltier has gone, there's a spare desk in your office. I thought it would be a good idea if we could assign a slot to the detective who'll be taking your place. Get them into the swing of things." He stopped to gauge a reaction, but there was none. "Colbert will be joining you tomorrow."

"I don't know him," Marchal said.

"From Lyon, I understand." Arnault hesitated. "Look, I know this is trivial, but try and arrange the office so it doesn't look as you've got the biggest desk and Colbert is somehow made to feel inferior. We don't want to get off on the wrong foot, do we?"

They'll have me outside on the sidewalk before my time's up, Marchal thought. He could have hidden the sarcasm, but damn it, what would Arnault do; fire him?

"I tell you what, Sir," he said. "Why don't I go through the motions of transferring everything in my desk into Peltier's and then Colbert can sit at what was my desk and feel superior. Good idea?"

"Great. I knew you'd see it my way, René."

Nine - @ChasBroadhurst.kp

Broadhurst pushed the copy of *BV* into the centre of the table around which they had all met earlier that day. It felt like an eternity ago. He rubbed his eyes hard. It seemed like there were pieces of sand in them that he just couldn't get rid of. He looked up to see Lambert follow Duncan White into the room.

Looking as exhausted as he felt, they sat down, waiting patiently for him to speak. "It's been a long day so far, gents and there's still a way to go. So let's make this meeting as brief as possible. I have to report to His Highness. He's resting at the moment. Duncan? Press black out?"

"Complete, but with conditions," White replied. "The team has done a good job. Press, radio, TV, we have secured a twenty four hour stay of execution. With the enquiry into the conduct of the media still looming fresh in everybody's mind, nobody wants to step out of line."

Lambert interrupted. "What you mean is, everybody wanted to step out of line, but nobody dared for fear of being blacklisted."

"Correct." White continued. "Broadcast news coverage of the revelations is, of course, the lead story in all the bulletins, but there will be no visuals. We've issued the agreed statement that the Palace does not comment on the private lives of members of the Royal Family. All the broadcasters have asked for interviews on the evening news bulletins. At this stage, all have been politely declined"

"That's your view?" Broadhurst asked.

"My initial reaction was a blanket refusal, but I think, on reflection, that would suggest weakness and indecision on our part. My proposal is that we go with the BBC on Newsnight. It carries more weight than any of the other news programmes."

"What's your reasoning?"

White gripped the edge of the table with both hands. "Everyone we have talked to today insisted that the Prince's homosexual behaviour is a matter of public interest and that the facts should be aired. This twenty four hour stay of execution is a sop. If we're not granted an injunction in France stopping *BV* by this time tomorrow, the images will be everywhere. We have to bang on hardball about the privacy aspect. There will be some public sympathy for the Prince and we need all we can get."

"Who are you proposing does the interview?" Lambert

asked. "The Newsnight presenters are a tough, persistent bunch."

"I know," White replied. "I've given it a lot of thought. Gerald Crichton's my suggestion."

Broadhurst gave a hoarse laugh. "Holding yourself as a hostage to fortune, Duncan, aren't you? Crichton's an upper class, public school boy with a plum in his throat. Hardly going to endear himself to Joe Public, is he?"

"Precisely my point," White replied. "The only way we can present this issue to the world is as an extension of some public school larking about behaviour. Boys will be boys, especially in the dark. People see the aristocracy as a class apart, not integrated by breeding into the real world. It's the only avenue open to us."

Broadhurst nodded. "I take your point, but he'll have to be well briefed. In my view, he's got all the makings of a loose cannon. And he pricks too easily. Once those presenters get under your skin, well. ." He left the sentence unfinished.

"Leave him to me," White said. "I'll make sure he stays in line. Just give me the OK and I'll get him sorted."

Broadhurst drew a line on the page. "Alright, when we're done, I'll take it upstairs. You'll know in thirty minutes." He turned to Lambert. "What have you got for us?"

The report was succinct. Maxwell and Lewis had made good progress, but, in the process, had attracted unwanted attention from the French authorities.

"I understand the King has spoken to the PM on that score," Broadhurst interrupted. "She's dumbfounded about the whole damn business, but has agreed to speak to someone with authority in the Interior Ministry at the Élysée. I presume that's happened. You were saying? Go on."

"Maxwell is convinced that the source material is on one of these micro cards you buy to add storage capacity and it's in the possession of this Rosenberg character. In fact, he thinks he has seen the camera in which the card is lodged."

Lambert went on to outline the details of the incident at Dubois's apartment door. "When Maxwell realised that the social security carer was an impersonator," he went on, "he put two and two together that the man must have been in the apartment when he went to gain entry, heard the noise and made his escape whilst Maxwell was downstairs getting the concierge."

"Unlucky," Broadhurst said. "How have you left it with them?"

Lambert had instructed his men to maintain a low profile until he managed to get a photograph of Rosenberg to them. They had to be sure that the police weren't actively pursuing them. For the time being, they would continue to maintain surveillance on the Dubois apartment.

"I thought there was to be a meeting between this Rosenberg character and our lawyers today?" White inquired.

"That was the intention," Broadhurst replied. "They've been ringing the mobile number he posted in his email, but no reply."

"Can't he be contacted through the magazine? Maybe, he's found someone else to pay more."

"Possibly. If so, very little we can do about it until the next person makes contact." Broadhurst replied. "We must assume the Dubois woman is not really in on the deal. The King's equerry has been on and off the phone all day trying to contact Benny Ram. Apparently, he's due back in Dubai about now. The lawyers are on stand-by, all night, if necessary."

"At a thousand pounds an hour at two in the morning, it's probably the most expensive night-time profession out there!"

Broadhurst reacted with a tired smile. He had defined two objectives. The first had been partially successful; to minimise the fall-out from the publication of the intimate photographs already in the public domain. At worst, some were offensive, but with an explanation coupled with an expression of regret and the passage of time, the situation could be controlled and, eventually, resolved. However, paedophilia was a word that instilled disgust and hatred throughout society. And quite rightly so, Broadhurst thought to himself. The monarchy was unlikely to survive such a scandal and that was precisely the issue they faced with the remaining images. It was imperative that they never saw the light of day.

"For all we know, there could already be a hundred copies in existence," Lambert said.

"Possible, of course," Broadhurst replied. "That's the unknown, but I somehow doubt it. The existence of just one copy would destroy Rosenberg's negotiating position. He must realise that nobody is going to hand over six million or whatever sum he'll settle for in exchange for a piece of plastic without ensuring proper safeguards are in place."

"I don't know how you can possibly engineer a deal like that." White checked his watch.

"I'll leave it to the lawyers," Broadhurst replied, "but I guess it'll have to be some form of pension fund arrangement; money put in escrow for x number of years, payable if none of the images find their way into the public domain in the meantime. . . ."

"Listen, Chas," White interrupted, "I've got an appointment now with your professor fellow and I want to be free when you've cleared Crichton for the TV appearance. So, if we can break for a while?"

"He's also asked to see me," Lambert chipped in. "Surely, I don't have to go through with this charade?"

"They are not my orders. You know that." Broadhurst opened a folded sheet of paper he had taken from his pocket. "My instructions are that everybody at the original meeting has to undergo this behavioural evaluation and that includes me. Based on this timetable, all Duncan's people have already been interviewed. It's just us three to go."

Lambert was persistent. "I thought the most likely

candidate for tipping off the paparazzi about Arthur's presence in Portugal would be this Hemmings fellow. Aren't you supposed to be seeing him today, Chas?"

Broadhurst nodded. "He's been out of the country. According to his wife, he should be landing at Heathrow around about now. He's been primed to come straight here."

White stood up to leave. "It's difficult to imagine it could be anyone else," he said.

Broadhurst leaned back in his chair so that his feet could rest on the table. The sensation in his eyes was both painful and infuriating. He had to get some drops.

"You never know do you, Duncan?" he said whimsically.

"I'd better go too," Lambert said. "I need to contact Maxwell."

"Just hold up for a minute, will you," Broadhurst ordered, looking around to ensure nobody else was in earshot. "Switch the monitoring system off, please."

Lambert followed the instruction. "What's up?" he asked.

"I've been giving some thought to our Mr Rosenberg and his sleazy pics." Broadhurst studied his colleague's expressionless face. "There are two other courses of action."

"Go on."

He swung his feet off of the table and leaned forward. "Since this business at Dubois's apartment, he's bound to be running scared, probably hidden this micro card or whatever it's called in some place nobody will ever find it. If we can organise a safe house, we get Maxwell and Lewis to pick him up and interrogate him."

Lambert laughed. "Interrogate being a euphemism for put pressure on him until he tells us where it is?" he queried.

"That sounds like another euphemism, but, unequivocally, yes."

"And the alternative course of action?"

"If that's not on, we gamble that the card will never come to light and arrange for Mr Rosenberg to have a very permanent accident!"

Ten - *@GerbenRosenberg*

She flung open the door to the apartment, kicking her shoes off across the room in theatrical style and launching herself onto the sofa. What a day! From the moment Chantelle had walked into her office, a maelstrom had hit her full on. The telephone had not stopped ringing. The fax, email file, everything had gone berserk. Her secretary was inundated with messages and with over a hundred tweets and dozens of new followers on *BV's* Twitter account, coupled with an avalanche of activity on its Facebook page, the international profile of the magazine had reached new heights.

Over thirty draft contracts had been issued by her lawyers to publications around the world. By the close of business, twenty deals had been completed; funds transferred and encrypted files made available to the purchasers. Conditional contracts had been signed with eight UK publishers. As soon as the twenty four hour voluntary blanket news blackout had been rescinded, these transactions would also be completed.

Contact had also been made with the firm of specialist international lawyers Benny had instructed over the weekend to delay any attempt by Prince Arthur's advisers to obtain a summary injunction. As Benny had calculated, an application to the Tribunal de Grande Instance in a Paris suburb to move for an injunction had been made and successfully deferred until later in the week. Celebrity sexual misconduct didn't appear to warrant the urgent attention in France which might be the case in certain other countries.

All in all, it had been a very rewarding day, so why

didn't she feel elated?

Her biggest regret had been Nana. Since her lover's summary departure from the apartment on Saturday, there had been no contact between the two women. Late in the afternoon, their eyes had met briefly across the general office. Nana had looked away, her expression a mixture of hurt and anger that said come after me and make me feel better, but Chantelle had been too busy. She was full of regret and contrition and desperately needed a comforting embrace that said everything was alright. She couldn't make up her mind whether she should make the first move by a telephone call or to just turn up at Nana's condo. As soon as she had cleared up a few loose ends, she would decide what the best course of action was.

The other little niggle was the arrival, just as she was leaving the office, of that pompous little policeman, what was his name, Arnold or something like that. Yes, he was on a fishing expedition. Who was it who had sold her the pictures of the Prince? How many photos were there? Who had taken them? She had fielded all the probing with non committal answers or don't knows that had started to annoy him. Then came the veiled threats. People in high places were concerned; international relations could be prejudiced; did she realise that she was playing with fire? Her personal safety could be at risk. Certain elements might be very upset by her behaviour. Instantaneous bravado had prompted her to tell him to fuck off, but, as time had passed, his words had begun to disturb her. She kept remembering that sideways look as he turned to leave and that final comment. "I'll be watching developments very closely, Mademoiselle Dubois," he had said. "Take this to heart. Don't make an enemy of me. I can be a very dangerous adversary. It would be pointless to put everything you have achieved at risk for the sake of some smutty exposé."

The all too familiar ring of her mobile brought her back to the moment. Benny's Dubai number flashed on the screen. "Hello, Princess. How you been getting on?" He reacted in his normal cheerful fashion as she recounted the events of the day.

"So, we're already showing a profit on day one?" He was buoyant. "Thanks to you. Keep it up. There's a long way to go. Carry on selling. You're dealing in packs of five images, as we agreed?"

"Yes," she replied. It's the same five images this week to everybody and then another set as soon as you give me the green light."

"Good. Just to keep you in the picture, if you excuse the pun, I've just finished a call with the King's personal assistant. It was a rather strange concoction of fire and brimstone mixed with a grovelling appeal for cooperation."

"And your response?" She was wary.

"I gave him the normal claptrap about not being involved in the magazine's content and not interfering with editorial decisions etcetera."

Chantelle laughed. "That'll be the day!" she exclaimed.

He ignored the rebuttal. "I told him I'd do what I could. Anyway, the long and short of it is, they'll be pressing for an injunction and damages this week. The lawyers will go for public interest overriding the privacy aspect and we may have a chance. If not, you'll get a fine and have to hand over the photos."

"All of them?" she queried.

"No." The lawyers tell me that any decision against us will relate to the five photos you've published and will only be binding in France. They'll have to go charging around the rest of the world like the little Dutch boy trying to plug the dyke."

"Sorry. Don't get you."

"Never mind," he replied. "It's just an old fable I learned at school. Legally, Rosenberg still owns the remaining images and will release them to you as and when I say." He drew breath. "That's why I'm ringing, in fact. I've been expecting his call all day. He's supposed to be going to see Mahesh Kamal, my private attorney, to arrange for the transfer of his money tonight. Not a word. I warned him against any funny business. You've got his mobile number, haven't you?"

Chantelle reached for her handbag to find the relevant piece of paper. The first note she drew out was the one the night porter had given her as she had come in. It was an urgent request for her to contact the concierge and gave his home number. Her brow creased. "Just a second, Benny," she said. "It was the wrong piece of paper. I haven't heard from Gerben since I left him in the apartment around midday." She rummaged around in her bag until she found the scrawled number. "It's been a very popular request today," she continued. "Gerben's telephone number, that is." She told Benny about her conversation with the policeman.

"Don't pay any attention to him," he said. "It's all bluster. You've not committed any crime. If he comes back at you, refer him to me. Understood?"

Her next call would have been to satisfy her curiosity and contact the concierge, but in looking for Gerben's number, she had also come across the little black book she had found that morning in the toilet bag along with the gun. Gerben might return to claim his property at any moment.

She was doing the right thing, wasn't she? Richard needed her help. They had made a commitment. They. . ., no he, had to have closure. There had been a time when she had felt as determined as he was, but, now, was the death of their natural father so black and white? Could blame be so easily attributed? Could revenge be so total? He thought so. She flicked through the book and found the entries in his tiny handwriting that he would need, and then dialled the number.

A man's cautious voice answered.

"Listen, I haven't got long," she said. "How are you? I miss you. Will you come to see me before you go back?"

"Yes, yes, yes," was the impatient reply. "Have you got something for me?"

"When we spoke on Sunday, I said I was working with the middleman, the agent for the photographer. Remember?"

"Of course. For goodness sake, I'm fed up with hanging about! The funeral was days ago."

"Well, I've got some information you might find useful. Got a pen?"

"Go on." She recited a series of names, email details and numbers.

"That's the break through we've been waiting for," he said. "It's bound to be one of them."

"Are you in Paris? I must talk to you. It's dangerous."

"No. I'll go where I have to. I'll be alright."

"When do you have to be back?"

"They gave me a week. I said I had to sort out the old bastard's affairs!"

As she went to comment, there was a noise. Somebody was shifting around on the carpet in the hallway outside her front door. Her voice was reduced to a whisper. "Got to go. Call you back."

A mobile rang close by. The noise outside the apartment stopped. The phone kept on ringing. It was coming from inside the apartment. She jumped to her feet. The flashing light from the screen reflected on the floor under the sofa. "Hello," she answered after fishing for the mobile with her hand.

"What are you doing answering Rosenberg's phone, Chantelle?" Benny asked.

"He must have forgotten to take it when he left the apartment. I found it on the floor."

"When he turns up, tell him to contact me immediately!" There was frustration in Benny's voice.

The noise had returned. She looked through the spy hole in the front door. Nobody to be seen, but the noise hadn't gone away. She carefully put the security chain on the door and gingerly opened it to reveal Gerben, on his knees; his head bent forward, fingers pressed into the carpet pile. He looked up sheepishly at her.

She released the security chain and opened the door. "What is this, Gerben?" she said, hands on hips, "some sort of Jewish prayer position?"

"After a fashion," he replied. "I felt something fall out of my pocket as I fiddled for the key you left me." It was the first thing he could think of. "Probably a coin."

There was no trace of the micro card. Either he wasn't looking in the right place or somebody had come across it. The only crumb of comfort was that, if it had been found, it wasn't the bad guys. They were still parked in the adjoining road and although not close enough to get a view of the front door of the building, they still had a long distance view of Chantelle's lounge window. He had spotted the Renault before they could have seen him and had used the cover of the dozens of residents' parked cars to reach her apartment block. If the man had found the SD card, they'd surely be long gone by now.

"Well, forget about it," she said. "If you can get your act together, you'll be a very rich man by the time the evening's out. Benny wants to speak to you urgently."

"I can imagine," he responded, glancing around the lounge. He asked her to pull the curtains closed. "Act normally," he said. "Just leave a small gap in the middle."

"They're still out there?" There was fear in her voice.

He nodded and then went on to tell her about the drama that had followed her departure earlier that day. "I can't tell you how it all ended, only that there was a gunshot that scared the life out of me. I've been keeping a low profile all afternoon." He looked around again. "I must have. . ."

"You're looking for this?" she interrupted, holding up his mobile. "You seemed to have left half your belongings here. Your toilet bag is on the table." His black book and the gun were back in their rightful place.

He made no move to take the bag with him. "Look after this for me, will you. Put it in a drawer somewhere until I can take it with me."

She was looking at the note taken from her handbag, seemingly ignoring his request. "This business in the hallway must be what the concierge wants to talk to me about. I'll speak to him. Why don't you give Benny a call while I'm finding out what happened?" It was more of an order than a request.

It was a one-sided conversation. Gerben listened obediently while he was chided for being out of contact all day and, again, as Benny gave him specific instructions on where and how he would spend the remainder of the evening. His lawyer, Kamal had been briefed to arrange for a solicitor from an associate practice to represent Gerben at a meeting with the Prince's representatives. Benny was convinced that they would be anxious to conclude a deal as quickly as possible. "For a man who is about to receive a large amount of my money, you seem a little downbeat, Gerben. I assume everything is exactly as we agreed?" Benny's tone was hollow, almost threatening.

"Of course," Gerben lied. "I just don't like being shot at." He went onto describe the events that were still so vivid in his memory, leaving out the fact that the micro card had gone missing.

"This memory chip thing is safe?" It was as though Benny was reading his mind.

"Yes," Gerben lied again.

"It could have been worse," Benny suggested. "You're not dealing with a group of honourable, upper crust Brits who take adversity on the chin. They're a hundred times more cynical and ruthless than you could imagine. They'll do anything to protect the integrity of the Royal Family and that means taking whatever action is necessary. So, go and get this deal done and you'll stop being a moving target."

As instructed, just before ten that evening, Gerben sat in a poorly lit waiting room in a grey stone building just off the Rue Saint-Florentin, within a stone's throw of the Place de La Concorde. The list of partners engraved into a hardwood plaque on the wall showed that Mahesh Kamal was quite a long way down the pecking order in the firm of Cabinet Martin, although Gerben doubted that his take home pay reflected this mediocre status.

During the twenty minutes he had been left on his own to admire the water cooler, the coffee machine, today's FT and a range of outdated magazines that would have shamed even his dentist's reception, Gerben had become more and more depressed. The chances of recovering the micro card were remote, a needle in a haystack. It could easily be stuck to the sole of a shoe, inside the dust bag of a vacuum cleaner or, worst of all, picked up by a passerby who just happened to spot it. His retirement fund had disappeared with it. On top of that, his entire life savings had gone up in smoke and, to round it off, Chantelle had learned from the concierge that the gunshot into the air had caused the old lady to have a seizure; a revelation that, for some reason foreign to his nature, troubled him. And if the men who were after him, eventually ensnared their prey, how much pain would he have to suffer before they finally accepted that he really had lost the card. The future was bleak.

"Mr Rosenberg?" A small, slightly built Indian with angular features and a receding hairline greeted him without the trace of a smile. "Follow me!" he said. "Your identity card, please."

As they walked, Gerben fished in his jacket pocket and handed it over to a secretary who seemed to appear from nowhere. "Sit down!" They were in a meeting room with computer monitors spread around a large oval table.

"My instructions are to transfer one million eight hundred thousand Euros. ."

"Pounds sterling," Gerben interrupted.

"Pounds sterling," Kamal corrected himself, "into a Cayman Islands account that Mr Benny Ram has set-up for you. Is that correct?"

"Yes."

"In exchange for a mobile data storage card which contains some sixty original images and which I am to inspect and verify, plus a declaration from you that it is the original and that no other copies exist of these images." He looked up at Gerben, the stare of an unbeliever. "If such a declaration is found to be untrue, you will refund all monies received. Correct?"

"Correct."

Kamal hesitated. "Well, hand it over then," he demanded.

Gerben tried to sound as incredulous as he could conceivably be. "I obviously don't have the card with me. It's in a safe place. People are after it. People with guns. I'll retrieve it by tomorrow."

"Did Mr Ram not explain the nature of the transaction to you? I can't proceed without the card."

Gerben tried to sound distraught. "I assumed that as he has already had access to half the photos, the funds would be transferred on trust. I can't walk around Paris and take a risk that the card might be stolen."

Kamal laughed out loud. His smile revealed a selection of gold fillings that decorated his mouth. "How wonderfully naive you are, Mr Rosenberg," he said, but there was no humour in his eyes. "Either that or you're a fool. Take it on trust? This is a law firm, none of this my word is my bond on a handshake crap here. Bring the card and I'll wire the funds. It's as simple as that." He slammed his blotter shut.

Gerben rose to leave, but an angry hand motioned him to stay put. Kamal stood up. "I don't like having my time wasted. It's offensive," he added," but Mr Ram has asked me to brief you on the posture you are to take at the meeting you are going onto with the Prince's lawyers."

Gerben nodded. He was beginning to feel like a naughty schoolboy. He should have refused at the outset to act as Benny's middleman. Greed had clouded his judgement. It was a big mistake, but with the card gone, there was no turning back at this stage.

"Before I do," Kamal went on, "let me give you some advice. I sense that something is not as it should be. My client is a formidable opponent in the business sense with contacts and allies around the globe. You go against him at your peril. Do you understand what I'm saying?"

"Yes." More than you can conceive, Gerben thought.

Ten minutes later, Kamal stood up. There was no handshake.

"Don't forget this!" Kamal held the other man's identity card in his outstretched hand.

Kamal walked toward the window, where he waited until he saw Rosenberg emerge from the building into the Paris nightlife. "What a pitiful bastard," he said to himself as he turned back to his desk and punched a number into the telephone.

"Mr Ram. It's Kamal." He explained why the funds had not been transferred. "I sensed there was something on his mind," he said in answer to Ram's question. "I wouldn't like to suggest a double cross, but we'll have to be wary."

"Did you get the copy of his identity card I asked for?" Ram asked.

"Yes. It's been digitalised," he replied. High resolution. I've mailed it on to your safe storage box along with a head and shoulders of him I took with the webcam. Both files are encrypted, as requested."

"Good. Let's trust that this card business is just a reaction to his nervous state of mind." There was a moments silence on the line. "He's on the hook and I don't propose to give him a minute's peace."

Eleven - #Memory Card

The afternoon shift on the intensive care ladies ward at Cochin Hospital was coming to an end and the young nurse was anxious to leave. The clock said ten twenty, which meant that her replacement was already five minutes late. She looked back at the old lady, lying in an induced coma, her face a picture of peace. How different it had been earlier that afternoon. It was sixty/forty she wouldn't make it to the end of the day, but she was a tough old bird. Her vital signs were now near enough normal and she had been taken off of the respirator a couple of hours ago. She had an aristocratic face the young nurse thought.

Absentmindedly, she reached for the blanket that was draped over the chair next to the bed. It had covered the old lady's legs when they had brought her in. As she went to fold it, a gold coloured speck was momentarily caught by the light. She fed the blanket through her hands until she could see what it was. Carefully, she detached a small black memory card with four gold coloured contacts, placed it on the chair and painstakingly folded the blanket.

"Sorry I'm late," her replacement said. "Traffic, as always."

The young nurse nodded. She held out the micro card along with the blanket. "Put these with Madame Lafayette's personal belongings in the nurses' staff room, will you? She's in bed number seven. I'd do it, but my new date's waiting for me. Don't want to make a bad impression, not just yet, anyway!" She skipped out of the room, a smile splitting her attractive face.

Twelve - #PruneInTheMouth

Gerald Crichton hated the foundation make-up they put on your face before a television appearance. He'd only had it done once before, but the experience hadn't made it any easier this time round. It seemed to stop you sweating until your skin began to feel uncomfortably warmer and it seemed as if your face would explode. That recollection nagged at him and they were barely into the filmed introduction to the news segment in which he would participate.

It had been a long, tough day. Following the early morning meeting, he had had two bruising engagements with the publishing houses responsible for the UK's leading daily broadsheets. White had joined him for the second meeting, and they had finally won through, if only for twenty four hours. He had sensed that both publishers were anxious to go to print, but were concerned about stepping out of line with the rest of the industry and breaching the code of the newly formed Office for Media Conduct. White had told him to go home, rest up and return at seven ready for a decision as to whether he would take part in the *Newsnight* broadcast. He could have done with a nap, but he had to hang around waiting for his appointment with that ridiculous Professor whatever his name was. A load of banal questions about his personal circumstances, habits, political leanings and opinions, followed by one of those ridiculous word association tests that he thought only happened in Hollywood movies. What a waste of time!

White had given him a detailed briefing. He could have done without ninety percent of the schoolboy lecture from a man who, intellectually, simply wasn't in his class. Who was White to tell him no alcohol? Anyway, what harm could that one whiskey half an hour ago in the Green Room do? He could hold his booze and didn't need some grammar school pleb to preach to him.

The filmed introduction had finished and the feisty female anchorwoman was introducing the two guests. The Labour MP alongside Crichton was a seasoned campaigner for the abolition of the monarchy and the establishment of a republic. In her strident view, the sort of disgraceful behaviour alleged by the photos published in the French magazine and, now, on the internet, were simply further evidence that the Royals were degenerate and unfit for purpose. The sooner they were put out to graze, the better. Her adamant stance that any person born into the Royal family gave up their right to privacy annoyed Crichton to the point where he would ensure she left the interview with a flea in her ear. Stupid, ignorant bitch!

The anchorwoman swung her chair around to face him. Her eyes stared hard into his. "Mr Crichton, thank you for agreeing to join us this evening. Isn't it deplorable that the son of the King, fourth in line to the throne, completing his ecclesiastical studies to become a priest, should be photographed engaged in inappropriate sexual behaviour with other members of the clergy?"

At all costs, hold yourself in check and do not rise to the bait, White had told him. He knew that! "You will forgive me," he replied, his tone condescending, "but I consider it quite improper that you should draw conclusions from alleged photographs of a member of the Royal Family taken whilst on a private visit overseas. Your comments are inflammatory and your question is based on assumptions that you cannot substantiate."

"Have you seen the photographs?"

"No," he lied.

"Well, I have," she insisted, "and, choosing my words carefully, they certainly substantiate the assumption on which I based my question to you. I'll rephrase it. Is Prince Arthur a right and proper person to become a minister of the Anglican church if, as is indicated by these images, he is engaged in overt sexual acts with other clergymen?"

"Listen!" He was beginning to feel his hackles rise. "The entire UK public social media industry, including you at the BBC, has agreed not to reproduce, what will no doubt turn out to be digitally manipulated images, for as long as is calculated to allow lawyers in France to obtain an order on the grounds of invasion of privacy. This will oblige whoever possesses this material to cease publication and transmit it to the plaintiffs for destruction."

"You're talking about twenty four hours," she said. "Our sources tell us that the French legal process for obtaining an injunction, especially when it comes to aspects of a purely sexual nature, grind much slower than in the UK. What are you going to do if the UK media start reproducing these images?" She didn't wait for an answer. "I'll come back to the point made a few minutes ago. Isn't Prince Arthur now a liability to the standing of the Royal Family and the Anglican Church? When can we expect a direct quote from him?"

These were the questions he had been expecting. They had every confidence in the French legal system and a speedy and successful outcome. The Palace expected the British media would act responsibly and not rush to judgements which they would later regret. He was sure that the subliminal threat in the comment would hit home. As regards the Prince, Crichton had not come here tonight to discuss the Prince's private life, which was a matter solely for the Prince and his immediate family. He went on. "Contrary to the preposterous idea expounded by your crackpot guest here that anybody in the public eye should live in a sort of Big Brother house where we could all watch their antics twenty four hours a day, most decent and responsible members of society consider that privacy is a bedrock tenet of our right to live collectively."

"Are you calling me deranged!" the MP blustered.

"If the cap fits." He didn't finish the sentence. Crichton was beginning to feel very competent that he was handling this interview just the way the King would want him to deal with it.

"You pretentious prig!" the MP stormed.

"Please," the presenter implored, trying to diffuse the impending slanging match. "Can we expect a statement from the Prince? Where is he?"

Crichton deliberately avoided the glare of the woman who was sitting alongside him and moved to turn his back on her. "The Prince is away from London, totally absorbed with his religious studies. If he takes my advice, he will not deign to dignify this attack on his good character with any comment."

"Just listen to him," the MP ranted. "It's people like this stuck up, prune in the mouth, upper class hoorah Henry that we should rid our society of; him and his precious Prince!"

Crichton rounded on her. "The people we should exterminate from our society are those vermin photographers who are born in the gutter, live and thrive in the gutter by intruding into people's lives and plying their smutty trade of trying to titillate lost souls like you. The so called paparazzi should be shot at birth or hunted down like the trash they are. No civilized country needs the salacious product of these sick minds."

Thirteen - @ChasBroadhurst.kp

Broadhurst switched off the television. He had seen and heard enough. Crichton's performance had probably added another hundred thousand followers to the republican movement, but it had achieved one thing. When tomorrow's later editions hit the streets, Crichton would become the bête noir of the piece, deflecting attention away from the Prince and onto his performance on the news programme. His comments on the specific topic he had been invited to discuss had been sound, not unnecessarily evasive and had avoided any pitfalls. It was his manner that had set him apart from the watching public. They could afford to feed Crichton to the lions. He didn't matter.

There was a tap on the door. His secretary ushered in a tall, imposing figure with a shock of greasy ginger hair peeking out from under a French style beret.

"Evening, Mr Hemmings. Good of you to come at such short notice. How was the flight?"

"Let's dispense with the small talk, shall we, Mr Broadhurst?" He spoke slowly with a West Country drawl to his voice. "It's been a long day and I'd like to get home as soon as possible. What can I do for you?"

"You know why I've asked you to come here?"

"Up until a couple of hours ago, I had no idea." He seemed calm, totally in control. "All I knew prior to this was what my assistant had told me; that it was a matter of national importance I meet with you urgently. Then my wife phoned me at the airport and told me about the photos of the Prince taken in Portugal and I put two and two together."

"Before we get on to that," Broadhurst said, "can I just get some background information? You were a staff sergeant, I understand, with UKSF in the Special Reconnaissance Regiment? Presumably, you trained alongside the SAS in Hereford?"

Hemmings gave a snorted laugh. "Listen, Mr Broadhurst." He pointed to the desk. "You've doubtless got a file over there that tells you more about me than I even know myself, so why ask me to confirm facts already at your disposal?"

Broadhurst recognised that the softly, softly, get to know each other tactic was not going to work. "OK. Then tell me something that's not in the file," he responded. "How does a highly decorated and respected soldier, skilled in covert photographic surveillance, specialised in operating in highly dangerous conditions, suddenly terminate his contract and become a lay preacher in the Anglican Church?"

"Just to get your facts straight, I'm not a lay preacher, I'm a lay reader. They're two different things, but I won't bore you with that now." He sat back in his chair. "I did three tours in Iraq, twice fighting Saddam's army, if you can call it that, and, last of all, combating insurgents. Shooting at soldiers in uniform is one thing. Chasing shadows in a mutual bloodletting campaign is not war. It's savage and primeval." Hemmings leaned forward, his tone threatening. "I'm guessing you were once a serving officer, Broadhurst, but I'll warrant you've never seen the atrocities, both inflicted and sustained, that I've witnessed in my time."

Broadhurst's look was non-committal.

"After a while, those young souls fighting for their country start to lose touch with reality, the meaning of life itself. The environment is surreal. There is no viler sight on God's earth than what pain and misery one man can inflict on another."

"So you rebelled against this?" Broadhurst suggested.

The other man shook his head. "Rebel is the wrong word. I recognised that these young soldiers I was working alongside were losing faith in the concept of a benign God, discarding the morality that a religious society instils as a child becomes a man and succumbing to their fears and frailties in a myriad of ways, some violent, some sexual, some reclusive."

"The result being?"

"I made a personal pledge to help them to understand and cope with these fears and frailties by presenting God and religion, not as some esoteric concept, but as a present force in their world that could support and guide them in rebuilding their lives after the army."

"I understand," Broadhurst said, interrupting to cut short a topic on which Hemmings was seemingly prepared to wax lyrical. "Tell me about Synergy and its recent activities, would you?"

Hemmings openly admitted that Synergy had become an obsession. Following his discharge from the army, he had sought a place as a counsellor to injured soldiers suffering from burns at a specialist hospital unit in Chepstow. The local bishop had taken him under his wing and, eventually, licensed him as a lay reader attached to the South Wales diocese. His fervour apparent, progress had been swift and he found his ideals were totally in sync with the Anglican Cultural Exchange or ACE as it was known. His papers on the fears of religious intolerance between beliefs and the social and economic consequences that so often led to discrimination, segregation and, eventually, war, had brought him to the attention of a group with the acronym of SHAPE. The Synod of High Anglican Priests in England fosters the spread of Christianity throughout the Muslim world and is proactive in its condemnation of the persecution of followers in many countries. The synod's current focus was very much on areas of conflict in the Middle East.

Hemmings was invited to SHAPE gatherings around the country as a guest and it was out of these contacts that his brainchild, Synergy, came into being. "I saw it as a way of broadening the understanding of Anglican priests by encouraging them to meet and discuss with followers of other faiths in informal surroundings. We travel all over the world," he explained. "I've just returned from Van in Turkey where we propose holding a joint seminar with some Iranian and Syrian clerics. Hell of a journey to that part of the world; beautiful mind, with the lake to look out on. I'm hopeful it will bear fruit."

"These aims may be noble, but how do you reconcile these good works with sponsoring some sort of homosexual orgy in Portugal?" Broadhurst queried.

"I admit that things in Portugal got out of hand, but let me explain how we got to this stage." Hemmings took a swig from a glass of water. "Got nothing stronger, I suppose?" he asked.

"Afraid not," was the reply.

Hemmings took a deep breath and went on. Unlike the doctrine of the Anglican Church, SHAPE insists that its members do not marry. Many of its priests had homosexual leanings and Hemmings saw in many of these men the fears and frailties he had seen in the young soldiers in Iraq. If nothing was done, Hemmings believed that some would be unable to suppress their sexual urges and look for clandestine relationships or, worse still, seek and join paedophile rings. He took the view that confronting the demons and allowing these urges to be fulfilled would make these men better, healthier priests.

"So through these cultural exchanges," Broadhurst interrupted, "you actually provide R and R for a group of randy clerics? Is that it?"

"Put in those terms; yes."

"And Portugal?"

Hemmings took another swig of water. "That trip was doomed right from the start," he explained.

"How come?"

"The intention was that we hold an exchange of views with a group of Buddhist monks at their retreat. If that had been the case, then sexual activity amongst our lot would have been discreet. In the event, there was a misunderstanding. My assistant got it wrong. The Buddhists intended to be at some gathering in Nepal and simply believed that they were renting us accommodation. When we got there, we were on our own."

Broadhurst could not suppress a smile. "So you all stayed to admire the scenery?"

"I don't appreciate your sense of humour, Mr Broadhurst," Hemmings retorted. "As it was, I returned to London the same day and left them to their own devices. It seems to have got out of hand."

"Understatement of this whole sorry affair!" Broadhurst reached inside a file, pulling out two A4 size photographs which he placed in front of Hemmings. "Recognise these two men?" he asked.

"Of course *I* do, now," Hemmings replied. "The differences are subtle, but significant if you're not expecting to find Prince Arthur as one of your flock. Deacon Baxter has a definite blond tinge to his hair, it's parted differently and he wears thick rimmed glasses."

"You're not telling me you can't see it's the same man?"

"Obviously. I can only repeat the answer I just gave you."

"According to my files, Deacon Baxter already attended one of your gatherings before Portugal?"

"Yes," Hemmings replied. "We've corresponded by email for about three months. Toward the middle of that period, we had a two day seminar in Harrogate on communication skills. As far as I recall, he kept himself very much to himself. I met him, shook his hand, but I don't remember exchanging more than half a dozen words with him."

"Does anybody in your organisation know who is going on these excursions?"

"No. Absolutely not. The guest list is highly confidential. I use code names for each person. The original list is stored in an encrypted zip file. I checked before I came here. It's not been accessed since the day I put it there."

"What about the guests, as you call them? Could one of them have recognised him from Harrogate?"

"Possibly, but I doubt it. What are you driving at, exactly?"

"Someone had to have tipped off the paparazzi long before you arrived in Portugal; long enough before, for them to have selected the most advantageous vantage points to photograph. The most likely candidates are either you or one of your guests."

Hemming reacted quickly. "Well, it definitely wasn't me and it couldn't have been any of the guests?"

"How come?"

"The guests never know the final destinations, nor do they know their fellow guests' names. They are all asked to pick a pseudonym for the duration of the trip." He checked his watch. "In this case, they were given a departure airport, told to bring light wear clothing and how long the trip would last."

Broadhurst had taken the hint. "I won't keep you much longer. Let me just paint the likeliest scenario as far as I'm concerned. Here we have a highly commended soldier, a surveillance specialist, who suddenly finds God and leaves the army to survive on a miserly pension and his faith." He was watching the other man's reaction. Nothing visible. "One day our lay reader Hemmings decides that the gloss is wearing off and he needs a lot more earthly sustenance than just his pension. Recognising the Prince at Harrogate gives him the opportunity. Bingo. He fashions a sortie to Portugal. There can be no outsiders, so he comes up with a bullshit excuse for the missing Buddhists. A suitable photographer is recruited and he leaves the rest to testerone and the fantasies of a group of sex starved clerics. How does that sound?"

Hemmings stood up, smiled and extended his hand. "More than plausible, Mr Broadhurst." The handshake was firm and forceful. "Just one thing. It's not true. I'm sorry I can't help you. If it's any consolation, my distress at what has transpired may not be apparent, but it's as heartfelt as yours."

"We'll be in touch," Broadhurst said, shuffling shut the files on his table and turning off the desk light.

Hemming reacted by turning around to look Broadhurst up and down. "I'm sure we will," he said thoughtfully.

The elevator doors parted to reveal a tired looking Professor Speir leaning against the wall, a battered musician's briefcase spread-eagled between his legs. Broadhurst placed a comforting hand on the older man's shoulder. "Sorry, I've somewhat ignored you today. I do apologise. How did your interviews go?"

"Intriguing, if not conclusive," the Professor said. "I need to give one or two a little more analysis and thought."

"I understand. Do you want to set a time tomorrow so that we can discuss your findings?"

The Professor averted his eyes from the security chief. "I've been specifically requested to present my report direct to His Royal Highness tomorrow." He reacted to the look of surprise on the other man's face. "Of course, I'll be pleased to give you my interim conclusions just as soon as I'm authorised to do so."

Broadhurst began the short walk to his serviced apartment. There was something about Hemming's explanation that said he was telling the truth. There was something about the Professor's that said he had discovered something important, but he was not saying. He didn't know which one troubled him most.

Fourteen - @GerbenRosenberg

Gerben had noticed the antique grandfather clock on the way into the meeting room. It was a Chippendale with the face signed by Jacob Godschalk. These classic timepieces were a passion he had nurtured since childhood. If he could find this wretched memory card, he might invest in a more modest Hoffmeyer or something similar. The eighteenth century beauty he had stopped to admire in this instance was out of his league. One had recently changed hands for over a million dollars and it wasn't in the same pristine condition. It chimed softly on the quarter hour. Fifteen minutes and it would be one in the morning.

The eight legal long faces that stared impassively at him across the long rectangular boardroom table looked as though they were prepared to sit there all night. He had different ideas and, looking on his side of the table at the expression on the face of the dishevelled looking young lawyer that Kamal had allied him with; so did he.

They had now been at it for over an hour and the meeting was going much as the young man, Bates, had predicted. The Prince's Paris legal team had launched into a fire and brimstone attack, predicting swift legal action, injunctions, civil and criminal proceedings unless the offending photos were handed over straight away. The word *extortion* had even been bandied about, but Gerben had remained nonplussed, constantly reiterating that he was prepared to defend and counter any legal proceedings that were initiated. Then came the question of price. Gerben's six million figure was pie in the sky. They considered a figure of a few hundred thousand Euros, but Gerben remained unmoved. The price was not negotiable.

From time to time, Bates would tap his pencil lightly on the table. This pre-arranged signal was the prompt for Gerben to request a brief recession to consult with his counsel in an ante-room. He was to assume the room was bugged so that instructions could be exchanged via written notes and acknowledged by a verbal yes or no. A letter was placed in front of Gerben with the request for him to sign it. The text irrevocably authorised whoever's name was put in the space left blank to pay over any sums due to Gerben, in the event of his death, to the order of Benny Ram's lawyer. Gerben raised an eyebrow in query. The note in response said that someone wouldn't like it if his money ended up in Gerben's estate. Gerben had no intention of dying, but the note came back that you never know. He might get hit by a bus. In the end, he signed. He was in so far, there was nothing to lose.

Bates avoided the shredder and collected up all the scraps of paper which he folded carefully before returning them to his briefcase. "Let me do the talking now," he said, out loud.

The lead solicitor on the other side was an elderly man with a pitted face and wet, pouting lips. When he opened his mouth to speak, strands of saliva would stretch between his lips and then disappear as he sucked to hoover them up. At first fascinated by the man's behaviour, after an hour of watching him, Gerben had begun to find his presence nauseating.

Bates appeared not to notice. The elderly man had suggested ten years. "That's too long for my client," Bates indicated. "We accept that none of us can be sure that a copy or copies of the images have been made, although my client has taken every safeguard to ensure his material is the original and has not been reproduced. He also has assurances that no further images were taken outside of this portfolio." Untidy and badly dressed as he might be, Gerben had to acknowledge that Bates was a forceful performer.

"Portfolio. That's a rather generous term for what will doubtless turn out to be a motley collection of grainy images. When can we have sight of them, by the way? Does your client have them with him?"

Bates chose to ignore the question. "The most generous terms acceptable to my client would be a period of six years, during which time the entire six million pounds with interest accruing for his account, would be deposited with a mutually acceptable escrow lawyer proposed by us."

"Does your client have someone in mind?" the old man asked.

"Dr Martin Reinhardt in Liechtenstein." Bates paused.

"I can't see that you would have any objection to such a distinguished figure. He will also, of course, hold in trust the original source material."

"What else?"

"If, at the end of six years or upon the earlier death of my client, there has been no publication anywhere in the world of any one of the twenty nine images concerned, the funds will be transferred to the order of my client. Dr Reinhardt will be the sole arbiter as to whether these terms have been fulfilled."

"Your client might die the day after we complete."

"That's the chance you take. It's always possible, but unlikely. Mr Rosenberg is a healthy non-smoker in the prime of life. Staying alive shouldn't be a problem. He has the added incentive that at the end of six years, he will be a very rich man." He laughed. "Less my fees, of course," he joked.

"And if any one of these images does surface?"

"The entire sum, plus interest and a contribution to your fees would be returned."

"I asked about sight of the material."

"Once we have the HOTs in place. The originals are in a safe place."

"The HOTs?" Gerben queried, obviously amused by the term.

Bates smiled benignly, a gesture that said I'm on the legal high ground and know what I'm talking about. You're a pleb. "Heads of Terms," he explained.

The eight faces on the other side of the table remained silent and stony faced. Bates was in charge. "I presume you will want to take clients' instructions. If we have a deal, I'll mail a draft to your secure box. When would you anticipate completion?"

The eight stood up, almost simultaneously. "Sometime tomorrow night."

The elderly man waited until he was on his own and then sat down again. He waited for his secretary to answer the telephone. "Tell Maxwell they're on their way out, would you, and then get me the King of England."

Gerben turned, walking at pace against the traffic running eastward on the Rue du Faubourg St.Honoré, past a series of impressive shop fronts. Following the detailed instructions Bates had given as they sat in the coffee shop prior to the meeting, he would turn left into the Rue D'Elysée where the solicitor had parked his red VW Polo. Precious minutes would be gained. Confident that there would be a tail on him, the man would see Gerben enter the car and then be obliged to walk to the bottom of the road and wait whilst his driver turned east out of the embassy complex and then detoured back onto the Avenue Gabriel to join him and pick up the trail. The pursuers would not be overly concerned, because the security guard who had patted down the visitors on their arrival for the meeting had also planted a tracer pin under Gerben's lapel which would show his location within a ten kilometre radius.

It was past midnight, but the traffic on the Champs-Elysée was still heavy, stopping and starting as they made their way toward the Arc de Triomphe. "Take your jacket off now," Bates ordered, "and put on the blouson and baseball cap you'll find in the bag."

They slowed for the lights at the Camot. "Get out now! The Metro is in front of you."

As Gerben moved to open the door, somebody outside was anxious to take his place. The man pulled him out onto the road, clambering over him into the passenger seat. Car horns blasted. Gerben wheeled around to see a city bus bearing down on him. He skipped out of the road onto the central area and ran, following the signs to the Metro interchange at Charles de Gaulle Etoile. Gerben's last view of the Polo was the smoke from its wheels spinning and the new passenger struggling to put on his discarded jacket.

It looked as though the plan was working. Bates would drive to Gerben's apartment in Montreuil; the lookalike would enter the building, change clothes, put the jacket with the tracer in the closet and leave via the service exit. With any luck, the tails would waste hours before realising they had missed their man.

Gerben exited the Metro at Charles Michels, his attention set on the few people who had followed him onto the platform. There was no indication that anybody was remotely interested in him, but it didn't help his state of mind. He had decided where he would try to spend the night. Bates had been insistent. It must be untraceable and the last place that anybody would expect to find him.

As he walked toward the building where Chantelle had her apartment, he had a sense of impending doom. Every step he took was leading further and further down a one way street with no exit. Over the next twenty four hours, he would have to admit to having lost the memory card, but nobody would believe him. Both the Prince's heavies and Benny's crowd would see it as a double cross. Both would be after his blood. Worse still. When they caught up with him, and, one way or the other, they would, force would be applied to gain the information he didn't have. How far would they go before someone realised he was telling the truth and what would his fate be then?

Concentrate! He forced the bleak scenario from his mind. There was no surveillance. Chantelle's window was in darkness. He approached the entrance to the building, moving in the shadows until he was hidden behind the pillar in the outer entrance lobby. The night janitor was dozing in a chair at his desk. Gerben retrieved the mobile from his pocket and pressed the speed dial. After a long delay, Chantelle's sleep filled voice answered. "It's me," he whispered. "Do me a small favour and don't ask questions. Phone down to the janitor and tell him there's a window banging on the top floor landing. Ask him to shut it."

"Do what?" But he had already rung off.

After what seemed like an eternity, the janitor's intercom buzzed. The man woke with a start, listened and then strained to move from his chair, obviously cursing as he did so. Gerben watched him disappear up the stairs before pushing open the glass door to make his way watchfully behind the desk. The bunch of keys was hanging from the corner of a message board. He found the pass key he had seen the concierge use earlier that day and detached it from the rest, returning the bunch to the board. He made his way up to the first floor, opened the door to the broom cupboard, stepping inside until he heard the weary clump of the janitor's feet as he made his way back downstairs. The man was still cursing.

Gerben moved out into the darkness of the corridor and up the stairs. Gingerly, he made his way past Chantelle's front door, continuing to the floor above. He inserted the key in the lock and pushed the door open. Madame Lafayette's apartment was bigger than Chantelle's, about twice the size. In the darkness, he could detect the scent of perfume mixed with the musty aroma he associated with old ladies. The couch was enormous. Eventually, he found a spare blanket, fluffed up two cushions as his pillow and closed his eyes.

Sleep must have come surprisingly easily because it was bright daylight when he awoke. But it wasn't the sunshine that aroused him. It was the sound of someone banging on the front door.

Fifteen - @renemarchal

Marchal had decided to go to the office earlier than usual with a positive attitude to the handover to his successor. Last night, he had sat quietly in the lounge of his bachelor apartment mulling over a glass of a favourite wine from Alsace on a mission to rationalise the irritation – more like anger, he condescended to admit – that would suddenly overtake him without any provocation. It was not the arrival of this Colbert character, whoever he was. How could somebody he did not know provoke any kind of reaction? No, it was Arnault and his barbed comments about the seamless transition from the regressive old guard methods to the new result-based, scientific approach to criminal investigation. Marchal despised the tactic. In the final days of a long and distinguished career, his commanding officer was writing him off as a dinosaur on the verge of extinction. Arnault could play his fucking politics, he thought, but not with my reputation. For now, he would play along, but he was not going out with a whimper. No way.

The first seamless transition was to move all the bric-a-brac from his large and imposing partner's desk to the flimsy chipboard affair that Peltier had occupied. The next was to go downstairs to fetch his own double black espresso rather than send Peltier for it. The tall Moroccan from forensics met him half way up the stairs.

"I was looking for you, Capitaine," the man said. "I've reconfigured that hard drive you gave me to look at yesterday. No data was lost. I've put it in a new external case. It's on your desk. Just link the USB to your computer and you can scroll through the files. There's some very raunchy stuff on it and I've bookmarked a Tweet you might find interesting. I've also pasted shortcuts on the desktop to all the main files."

"Thank you." Listening to that polished delivery, it did make him feel like a dinosaur. Still, he reckoned, never mind. It was not his job to know all about computers. It was his job to know somebody who did.

He made his way back to the office, only to find the black box in question and a dangling lead in the hands of a woman in her mid thirties, wearing a creased black raincoat, topped by an untidy confusion of black hair. "Can I help you?" He couldn't help thinking that his remark would have been better coming from a sales assistant in Printemps.

"Sorry," she said. "This must be yours." She held the disk drive out in front of her as if it were contaminated by radiation. "You must be Capitaine Marchal. I'm honoured to meet you." She extended her hand.

Even before Marchal could react, Arnault's voice echoed from the doorway. "Glad you two have touched base." He reached out to grab the hand intended for Marchal.

"Gather around everybody." He stood at the entrance to the situations office. A few chairs scraped with a noise that suggested a begrudging acquiescence to rank. Hands in pockets, half a dozen detectives shuffled closer.

Arnault pointed at the newcomer as if she were a painting in an art gallery. "Patricia Colbert has joined us today from the Lyon Division. She will be taking the place of our dear Capitaine Marchal who retires at the end of this month."

There was a spattering of applause from the small curious, rather than welcoming, group. With his customary hubris, Arnault launched into a monologue about the need for the police to move with the times, to be at the forefront, the cutting edge of investigative technology. "That's why I'm pleased to report that Mademoiselle Colbert comes to us fresh from field training with a degree from the academy in forensic psychology."

The introduction over, Arnault strolled nonchantly away. Marchal indicated that she should sit down at his desk. "Quite a welcome," he said.

She looked around. "You must feel as though they've cut you adrift in a small boat. I really don't mind taking the other desk until you leave."

"It's not an issue for me. Anyway, the Commandant would definitely not appreciate having his suggestion countermanded."

"Well," she laughed, "I don't want to put his nose out of joint before I've even started."

Marchal felt like saying that his nose was too far up the Divisional Commissary's arse to be put out of joint, but he answered with a tame "No."

She reached for her briefcase and began shipping her belongings into the drawers. She avoided eye contact with him.

"Why did you want to become a profiler, Colbert?" he asked. "I'll call you that because we only use surnames in the office. When we're outside you can call me René."

She looked up and nodded, her big, misty dark brown eyes suggesting to him that they wanted to cry. "I've always found the way people's minds work fascinating. Translating that into predicting behavioural patterns and likely actions is a science that I've really taken to."

"You won't get much change from that dyed in the wool bunch out there. The only thing they know about forensic science is what they see on CSI Miami."

"And you?"

"I had a profiler up here on a case once. Serial killer. Six really messy homicides."

"Did it help?"

"He gave us a few pointers. Can't say it solved the crime, but it was instructive in that it made me start thinking outside of the box. In the end it came to nothing. The perpetrator walked into a gendarmerie in Toulouse, took out a gun and shot himself. That was the last I saw of Claude."

"Not Claude Betain?" She sounded amazed as he nodded. "He was my tutor, or one of them."

"Really? How is he?"

"Dead, I'm afraid."

"How? He wasn't that old."

"Classic. The husband came home early and found him in bed with the wife. No hesitation. Shot them both."

"Didn't profile the hubby too well then, did he?"

They both laughed. He recognised that the ice had been broken. Minutes later, he watched her make her way across the office in response to Arnault's summons. Trust and respect would be next. She would really have to prove herself to the hard-bitten professionals she had just walked past, who all, to a man, pretended not to have noticed her. They wouldn't give her an inch until she took it.

He was fiddling with the hard disk when Peltier rushed

in. "Immigration is pandemonium. I can't stop," spoken breathlessly.

"Yes, you can." He handed over the drive. "Fix this up for me, would you? Leave it on desktop, whatever that is."

Peltier talked as he worked. "Got some information from my sister in law on the security personnel at Kensington Palace. There's no list yet, but she's come across one of the men, a French speaker, who was with one of the Royals at the Cannes Film Festival last year. He's a French Canadian from Quebec. By all accounts a real hard nut by the name of Maxwell."

"Got a picture?"

"No, but she reckons he figures, along with another personal bodyguard, in the background of a photo that appeared in Paris Match at the time."

"Couldn't get a copy for me, could you?"

"I'm in Immigration now, remember?" He got up from the computer. "There you are, all set. Anything else?"

"Yes. The photo."

"I told you, I'm busy."

"You get a lunch break, don't you?"

Marchal decided to make two phone calls before he started working his way through the computer files. Chantelle Dubois' secretary had been expecting his call. She'd just heard the dreadful news about Sebastien. She would get straight on to Miss Dubois and ask her to contact the Capitaine's office.

The call to the Cochin was also brief. The hospital had nothing to report. Madame Lafayette's condition was stable. She was still in an induced coma, but expected to be brought out of it that afternoon if her vital signs continued to improve. Someone would contact him the moment she recovered consciousness.

There seemed to be some paranormal phenomenon about working with computers. You thought you'd been in front of the screen for thirty minutes, but, in reality, two hours had passed. So Marchal mused. With no specific plan in mind, he had ambled through file after file, program after program until he had formed a fairly comprehensive picture of Bernhard's personality. Using the office Wi-Fi facility, he had gone onto Facebook, Linked In and a handful of other social networks where the young man had been a vociferous and outspoken communicator. Whenever he came up against a user name or password problem, a brief internal telephone call and the Moroccan would emerge from the basement to help him out. The man was a genius.

Colbert had returned from the Commandant's office with an armful of files which she dropped onto the desk. Other than exchanging smiles with Marchal, she began to familiarise herself with the Division's current caseload, politely refusing his offer of a coffee. Marchal could imagine how her stomach must be churning at the newness of it all. Her field experience had been limited to providing profiling guidance to the officers in charge, not rubbing shoulders with the scum of the Paris underworld and spending countless hours when you craved to be pursuing an investigation, instead writing up reports and filling in forms. Criminal police work was made up of three components – investigation, imagination and sheer frustration. Proactive one minute; inactive the next; not every policeman was cut out for it. Maybe Arnault would cut her some slack when Marchal had left. The Commandant fancied himself as a ladies' man

The coffee was steaming hot and pressing the flimsy plastic cup, scalding to the touch, he sent a splash of liquid onto the keyboard. He quickly wiped it up with his handkerchief, now stained brown. He was angry with himself in that, unintentionally, he was doing exactly what Arnault had suggested, looking busy, but getting nowhere. He would give himself until lunchtime by concentrating on the two major file systems on the hard drive.

The animated porn movie, Jacques and Gillian had been cleverly put together. Bernhard had been a very talented artist and even Marchal, who had considered his sexual drive dormant, or, possibly extinguished, found some of the scenes in the film arousing. The animation had been created from a series of real life pornographic stills of couples in various poses. He had then cartoonized the various individuals and animated them into larger than life characters with immense sexual appetites. Marchal had to admire the technical expertise involved and the imagination that could have conceived so many varied physical poses.

The file links that he logged were to something called Twitter accounts with direct messages. Trial and error clicks with the mouse showed that these messages dealt with the contractual arrangements for the original stills used in the film.

Opening the folder entitled *Prince Arthur,* icons of two dozen photos fed across the screen, all of the Prince involved in various sexual acts with one or more other men. He recognised the five images *BV* had selected for publication which could be considered almost respectable when compared to some of the others. No wonder the UK establishment was applying pressure to stem the flow of this damaging material. Marchal clicked on the link that the Moroccan had said he would find interesting. It was a direct message on Twitter between two followers. @banderboyseb had sent the message to @papapicman6 on the morning of Bernhard's death. "Hi," it said. "Looked closely at the *#BV* prints of the Prince. Seems like original *papapicman* work. Am I right?"

Marchal scrolled back to the animation files. He had recalled the name correctly. Whoever this @papapicman6 happened to be, he was also responsible for the stills used in the animation. He wrote the name on the blank incident board on the wall behind him, followed by a large question mark.

Twitter was new to Marchal. He had never thought of using the social medium. He either had nothing to say or, if he did, it was a darn sight longer than a hundred and forty characters and links to other sites just added to his confusion. More by accident than design, he ended up on

@papapicman's home page. Whoever it was, described themselves as "pope of the paparazzi - don't look around, I might be behind you" and his location as "wherever you are." Marchal carefully copied this narrative onto the incident board. With over two hundred followers, the pope of the paparazzi was popular, although he was more selective about whom he followed, with a total of just twenty. Some of the names, bizarre as they were, appeared on both lists. @banderboyseb was one of them.

"I didn't know you were into Twitter." Colbert had looked up from her files and was watching him write with the liquid chalk pen on the board. "What's your handle?"

"My what?" he queried, prompting her to laugh. She was pretty, a genuine smile, slightly to one side, or was that the lipstick. It was her eyes. They didn't smile with her mouth.

"Your Twitter name?" she asked.

"I don't have one."

"If you did, what would it be?"

He thought for a moment. "Policemanplod," I guess," he said, finally.

Sixteen - @Bizzybuzzybee

Another cloudless sky; the temperature at its midday height; the air conditioning buzzing in the background. Even so, Benny Ram fanned himself with a large blue leque and sipped an iced mint tea which the attractive young girl had prepared for him. Dubai wasn't so bad. It had its compensations.

The particular tone on the mobile told him he had received a Tweet. He scrolled to the appropriate screen. His Twitter name, @Bizzybuzzybee displayed the message he had been expecting. "Jeremiah 4:25, Acts 21:39, Acts 28:1 Your reading for today, Sator." He thumbed through a well worn copy of the Bible. The passages listed spelled out what he wanted to know. It told him that the young man, Darek, was ready to leave Turkey. He would be travelling via Rome with a Maltese passport.

Benny nodded to himself in quiet satisfaction. Within a week, phase one would be over.

Power was a real aphrodisiac. He needed the scent of a woman on him. "Come here," he beckoned to the girl.

Seventeen - @GerbenRosenberg

Gerben looked through the spy hole at a man in blue overalls. He had a Linde identity card pinned to his breast pocket, an indication to Gerben that he could chance opening the front door. The security chain extended fifteen centimetres.

"Sure I heard somebody snoring inside; thought it was the old lady." said a chirpy voice. "I'm here to change Madame Lafayette's oxygen cylinders. It's every Tuesday."

Gerben closed the door to release the chain and then opened it fully. "Bring them in."

The man pushed his trolley into the doorway. "Concierge said Madame Lafayette had been taken into hospital and there was no one in the apartment. He looked for his pass key, but couldn't find it. He's gone off to get another one."

There were family photographs spread around the apartment. Gerben had never come across such an extensive family. More like a dynasty. "I'm her son," he said. "I've come to pick up a few of her things she'll need in hospital."

The Linde delivery man wasn't interested. He had loaded the empty cylinders back onto the trolley and was halfway out of the door. There was the sound of heavy breathing. Gerben could picture the overweight concierge, out of condition, waddling along the corridor toward the apartment. "I've got it," a hoarse voice said.

The delivery man had stopped in his tracks, not quite outside the door. "You needn't have bothered," he protested. "The lady's son is here. It's all done."

"Excuse me," Gerben said, loud enough for the concierge to hear. "Got to get done and off to the hospital." He eased the front door against the man's back, forcing him to move into the corridor. "Thank you," he added.

"Steady on," the man said. "Everybody's in a mad rush, these days."

The concierge arrived just as Gerben managed to close the door. He held his breath, waiting for a knock. A handset or telephone was making a buzzing sound. Something had fallen onto the hall carpet. "Shit!" The sound of somebody gasping for breath and then exhaling deeply. "Shit!" again. It could only be the concierge straining to pick up whatever it was.

"Hello." The concierge was clearly stressed. "I'll be right down, Monsieur Didot. It doesn't matter. I'll clear it up." There was a brief silence. Presumably, he was switching off the portable intercom. "That fucking rat he calls a dog has pissed on the hall carpet." He must be addressing his remarks to the delivery man. "Saw a cat in the street and got all excited. Pity he wasn't carrying it like he normally does." The voice started to recede into the distance. "I'll brain that cretin of a night porter. Not only does he lose the pass key, he lets her son into the building without logging his arrival. There are days when this place is more like a lunatic asylum than an apartment block."

The distraction had given Gerben some thinking time. He would need to leave without being seen, but for the time being he felt safe and could think things through.

The micro card could have only fallen out of the camera when it fell off of the old girl's lap, yet it was nowhere to be found in the corridor in front of Chantelle's apartment. That left the carer, André and the concierge. If the carer had found it, he would have given it to the concierge for safekeeping. There was a remote possibility that one of the other tenants had come across it, but he discounted that as unlikely. Most would avoid the stairs and use the elevator. He would give it a few minutes until the canine crisis had passed. In the meantime, he flicked through the correspondence in the writing desk. There was a recent letter from a loving son called Martin who lived in Strasbourg.

"This is Madame Lafayette's son, Martin. I've come over from Strasbourg to sort out a few things for mother."

"Nice to hear from you again after all this time, Sir." The concierge sounded at his grovelling best, but the enquiry proved fruitless. Five minutes explaining what a micro card looked like, only to be told that the concierge had found nothing was an entirely pointless exercise, but, at least, his last remark was worth following up. "She had one of those woolly blankets draped over her knees and touching the floor. Maybe, it got stuck to that."

A phone call to the hospital told him that the old lady was still unconscious, but if he tried again at five, it might be possible to speak directly to one of the nurses on the ward. They could not check her belongings without authorisation, so they had no idea whether or not this card thing he was asking about was in her folder.

At some point that evening, Gerben would have to come clean with Chantelle and see what she suggested. It would mean a call to Benny with consequences that did not bear thinking about. He supposed that there was an off chance that his source had been lying and did have another copy, but that hypothesis would prove his downfall either way.

He tried to justify the next move to himself. She would not mind; if she knew; just a few minutes looking around Chantelle's apartment before he left the building. It was gone ten and she would have left for *BV's* offices. While he had the pass key, he might as well make use of it. He made no pretence at stealth as he opened her front door, but stopped in his tracks as he heard her talking to somebody in the bedroom. For a moment he thought the person was with her, but she was on the phone.

"I couldn't bear it if something happened to you," she was saying. "Dad would always tell me that the end has to justify the means, so don't take unnecessary risks." After a silence, she spoke again. "Geneva, you say? Let me think about it. If I can do anything to help, I will." There was another pause as she listened. "Promise?" she implored as she started to move out of the bedroom.

Gerben backed out, silently closing the front door behind him, then knocking loudly on it.

"I've got to go," he could hear her say. "Somebody's at the door. Ring me later. Remember the date. You have to get back on time."

He could sense her checking through the spy hole and then the door opened. "What the hell are you doing here? How did you manage to get by the concierge?" There was no warmth in her voice, just concern. Or was it fear? She stood aside to let him past. "Did they see you come in?"

"Who?"

"The men in the car, stupid! They're back outside again."

"I came in by the fire escape," he lied. "Nobody saw me. You seem up tight."

"So would you be with a couple of thugs watching your every move." Tears had welled up in her eyes. "Sebastien's dead. Did you know?"

"He's what?" All his composure had evaporated in an instant. "How?" he stammered.

"I don't know the details. They're saying it's accidental, that he fell from his balcony." She had started to weep, the words choking in her throat. "I must go. I'm supposed to be meeting up with a Capitaine Marchal. I'll find out what I can. There's so much happening I've got to deal with and now this. My poor Sebastien."

He put his arms around her as she wept uncontrollably. "An accident? Impossible," he said. "They must have got to him. Unless, we're careful, it'll be us next. They were following me last night."

The tears stopped suddenly. "I wish you'd never come round, knocking on my door with your damn, stupid pictures." She thumped her fist on his chest, forcing him to release her. "Who cares whom Prince Arthur is shagging? Hope he catches Aids. It's a poor exchange for a lovely man's life. It's all my fault for giving in to your pressure. Don't you have any pride?" The display of emotion was raw. "Sebastien would be alive today. I detest you for what you do, Gerben, and the grubby little men you do business with."

That was rich, coming from her, he felt and he couldn't hold his tongue in check. "Steady on, Chantelle. We're only in this grubby business, as you call it because you and the people like you peddle this stuff to the masses in your self-righteous, pretentious scandal rags. Don't blame the dog for catching the fox. Blame the huntsman."

She held his eyes with hers. They were cold, like a fish on a slab. "I do blame myself, but that doesn't mean that you parasites don't share in it as well. I regret the day I ever let Benny talk me into joining the magazine with his 'it'll be a challenge for you, bringing the public what they want to read'." She shook her head. "It's not what they want to read, it's what we tell them they want to read. The media created the celebrity culture, not the public."

"Be that as it may, Chantelle. Unfortunately Sebastien is dead and we have to make sure we don't become accident statistics as well."

"Presumably, the moment you conclude the deal for Benny and hand over the memory card to the Prince's lawyers, we can all breathe a little easier. When's it going to happen?"

Should he confide in her about the lost card? It was on the tip of his tongue, but he drew back at the last moment. If he told her, he would be vulnerable.

"Sometime tonight," he said. "I'm waiting to hear. I guess they're using today to get the go ahead, organise the funds and try to get an injunction to stop you in your tracks."

"They're certainly doing that. They've applied for an emergency hearing, but our lawyers have objected. *BV* won't be on the news-stands until next week, so there'll be no further disclosure in France until then and the court has no jurisdiction in any other country publishing the images in the intervening period." She had finally regained her composure. "We're also arguing that the court cannot give proper consideration to a restraining order unless the public interest aspect can be considered and that's not a five minute, rubber stamp job. We should be alright, but they're throwing some big guns at us."

"You know they'll ask for all the photos if they're prepared to hand over the money. It won't just be for the unpublishable ones. Benny does appreciate that?"

"I expect so, but that's for you to agree with him." She checked her watch. "Listen I'm late for the meeting with the policeman and I want to take some time with Seb's relatives and funeral arrangements. I need to be involved." She hesitated. "By the way, what was all that nonsense about the window flapping last night and me telling the porter?"

"Oh, sorry. Nothing, really. I was thinking of coming to visit you and get into the building without being seen, but I changed my mind. Sorry. I should have said something."

She appeared to accept the explanation. "Shut the door on your way out." She gave a wry smile. "Tradesmen's exit is via the fire escape. I apologise for coming down so hard on you, but I meant every word of it."

"I know you did," he replied.

Eighteen - @ChasBroadhurst.kp

"Sit down, Lambert. Bring me up to date." Broadhurst poured a large measure of a twelve year old malt for each of them.

"Bit early for that, isn't it, Chas?"

Broadhurst shook his head. "Not today, it's not. No." He drained his glass. "Any news?"

"I just finished speaking to Maxwell. They were given the run around last night. Rosenberg knew they were tailing him and gave them the slip. They're back on surveillance at Dubois's apartment block. Lewis is covering the rear of the building. There's a fire escape which Rosenberg could be using to enter and leave the place. They presume that's where he's going at night."

"You've seen the morning papers?" He poured himself another scotch. "Crichton's outburst is headline or front page news in almost all of them. They're keeping the story warm until the twenty four hours is up. White tells me they've all bought syndicated copies of the material. He's furious, but as impotent as a neutered tomcat."

"Nobody playing ball?"

"Nobody. If I hear one more time that's it's in the public interest to know that Prince Arthur is a homosexual, I shall have to murder someone."

"And upstairs?" Lambert asked.

"Between the two of us, the King appears to be losing touch with reality. He's agreed the deal to get hold of the photos, but instead of spending his time usefully, trying to use his influence with *BV's* proprietor, Ram, he's now bewitched by that Professor Speir and all this behavioural analysis. Though God only knows where that will get us."

"Did the Professor interview you?"

"I spent a rather strange ten minutes with him, answering, what seemed to me, totally irrelevant questions."

Lambert shook his head. "By the sound of it, you were lucky. He bombarded the rest of us with enquiries about our families, attitude to the monarchy, religion, all sorts of things. He even went on about sexual habits and preferences; intimate stuff. Rounded off with those silly word association tests. You know. Think of the first thing that comes into your head when I say such and such. It must have gone on for half an hour or more."

Broadhurst ventured a smile. "With your experiences with females, I'm surprised it didn't last for much longer."

"I think you must have got me mixed up with someone else."

The internal phone rang and Broadhurst listened. "OK, Duncan," he replied. "Point taken. Leave it with me." He swung his chair around to face the window, his back to Lambert. "That was the lull before the storm." The call had changed his tone from light hearted to sombre in an instant. "*The Daily Mirror* has broken ranks. The later editions show two of the images with a shock exclusive banner. The rest will follow suit. We're in for a media feeding frenzy. They'll be after the Prince like piranha after dead flesh. Let's review security."

Lambert read from his notes. The Prince was under room guard in an Anglican retreat and training centre in Hay on Wye. He was booked in under the name of Deacon Baxter. The information was classified. His father's instructions were that he remained in his quarters where he would take all meals. There would be two half hour breaks for exercise around the grounds, one early morning, one late afternoon, but he would talk to no one and act as if on retreat.

"Cancel the breaks for the next couple of days," Broadhurst ordered. "Send an exercise bike or a treadmill up to him. I don't want him in contact with a living soul."

As far as the media was concerned, the official word would be that he was staying in one of the royal residences. A half dozen extra security personnel would be assigned to Balmoral as a decoy along with a Prince Arthur lookalike. "Let the world's press freeze their bollocks off in Aberdeenshire for the next week or two," Broadhurst said. "They can take long distance photos of him talking to the plants and chasing around the Highland terrain in a Land Rover. The fresh air will do them good!"

All the royals would "no comment" any approaches

from the press. No one would be prepared to discuss the Prince's private life under any circumstances.

Broadhurst closed the meeting. "They can all speculate and gossip until the cows come home, but we won't give them an inch. How many security men have we got undercover in Hay?"

"Two."

"Pull them off and send in two trusties to keep an eye on a foreign dignitary who's visiting. We'll give them the room number when they're in place.

"And Lambert."

"Yes."

"Tell Maxwell to find that fucking little prick who's got the memory card or whatever it is and get it back off of him before we have to pay out six million in blackmail money. If the media sniff that story, a drama becomes a crisis like we've never seen before.

Nineteen - @renemarchal

The only thing that distracted Chantelle from dwelling on Seb's death was the sight of the policeman's desk. Strange that a senior capitaine of the Judicial Police should be sitting behind a piece of furniture that looked as though it had been bought from Conforama in a sale and had been self-assembled with a few pieces left over at the end. As she shook his hand and sat down, their knees brushed together. Her apology was a spontaneous reaction which caused him to smile.

"This is my colleague, Capitaine Colbert," he said gesturing behind her to the woman of about her own age who was sitting behind a magnificent partner's desk. They exchanged pleasantries.

"Nice desk," she couldn't help herself saying. The policewoman appeared to ignore the comment and settled back into the file she was reading.

Marchal gave a brief introduction. He was dealing with two aspects which may or may not be related; the way in which Mademoiselle Dubois had come by the pictures published in *BV* yesterday and the untimely death of Monsieur Bernhard.

"I'm certain they are related," Chantelle said. "There is no way Seb could have died accidentally and he certainly would never have taken his own life. It's all to do with these wretched photos and I'd put my life on it that those two characters who have been spying on me since yesterday have got something to do with it."

He looked up in astonishment. "Can we come to that in a minute? Let me just go back to square one. How did you come by the photos of Prince Arthur in the first place?"

She omitted nothing, naming Gerben Rosenberg as the source and running through the chain of events from the time he had knocked on her door up until the point at which the magazine had reached the newsstands. Casually, she glanced at the white incident board behind him. There was a picture of a smiling Gerben and the word "@papapicman6" written in black marker. She recognised the word from somewhere, but couldn't place it.

"How did you come to know Mr Rosenberg?"

"He comes via the magazine's office from time to time. He's an agent for some low life paparazzi. Every now and again, he wants to sell an exclusive."

"Do you know which photographers he represents?"

"No idea. You never know their names. The main ones all work under the cover of nicknames or pseudonyms. With the sort of misery they peddle, I guess they must all live in the shadow of a violent reaction from many of their victims."

"For somebody whose stock in trade relies on these people, you don't seem very enamoured with the profession?"

"Are you?" she countered.

"Can't say I've ever given it much thought. Why do you think this Rosenberg came to you and not one of the majors? No offence intended. They'd probably pay a lot more."

"Gerben knows that our proprietor would make an instant decision, no hanging about waiting for the lawyers' 'on the one hand, on the other' speak."

"How much did he pay?"

Her reply was instant. "Again, no idea. They discussed it over the phone in private. I wasn't privy to the conversation."

"Didn't you and your proprietor realise the furore you would create if you published these pictures?"

She threw back her head and gave a false laugh. "So now we're getting to the real reason for this meeting, are we?" She shook her head in a theatrical display of disbelief. "You're just following up where that other policeman left off last night. Back off, Chantelle! People in high places, all that crap!"

"Sorry, what other policeman are you referring to?"

"Please don't insult my intelligence, Capitaine. You know exactly who I'm talking about." Another snorted laugh. "Arnold, or something like that. Little man, with wispy hair; cold, distant eyes like he was staring at a corpse."

A hesitant tap on the office door broke off the conversation. Marchal excused himself, walked outside, shutting the door behind him. Peltier was holding out a black and white photocopy of an enlarged photograph. "This is what you are looking for?"

Marchal gave it no more than a cursory glance. "Listen, I want. ."

Peltier interrupted. "Don't ask me to do anything else. I'm in enough trouble, already. My boss says that while I'm frigging around doing things for you, at least thirty illegal immigrants will have made it into the country."

"Tell him you're tidying up loose ends," Marchal suggested. "Anyway, you should be grateful."

"Grateful? Why?"

"Statistically speaking, of those thirty illegals, at least

two, maybe as many as eight will end up committing a crime. That keeps us in work. It'll help pay for my pension, buy you some acne cream and." He stopped as he watched Colbert rise from her desk and patted down her skirt, at the same time, mentally chiding himself for admiring her slender legs. "And keep our new Capitaine in panty hose!" he added.

"You amaze me, Capitaine." Peltier shook his head in mock disbelief. "By the way, the man in the front of the picture with the dark hair is Maxwell. The heavy set guy to his left is with him. His name's Lewis."

"I'm impressed. That's good detective work for an aspiring lieutenant."

"Not really," Peltier replied. "I took this print off of a digitally enhanced blow up. There are name tags on their lapels. Presumably it was the intention that they should appear as delegates rather than security. I'll put the details on the computer for you with Interpol access. OK?"

Marchal nodded absentmindedly. The first thing he noted as he returned to his office was that Colbert had perched herself on the edge of her desk and that her skirt had risen further up her thighs. She was deep in conversation with Chantelle.

"Sorry, I'm not interrupting anything, am I?" he asked.

If Colbert sensed his irritation, it was well disguised. "I was just reassuring Miss Dubois that we're trying to get to the truth, not influence her actions." She slid off of the desk and returned to her chair.

"Tell that to this Arnold man!" Chantelle exploded.

As both irritated and curious as he was concerning Arnault's conversation with her, right now he needed her cooperation and not her antipathy. "I'll certainly look into that," was his bland comment. He placed the photograph in front of her. "Recognise either of these two men?"

She studied the faces carefully, drawing her finger slowly around the image of Lewis. "This face seems vaguely familiar, as if I've seen him casually somewhere; in the street or on the Metro. The other one doesn't ring any bells." She looked across at Marchal. "Are these the men responsible for Seb's death?"

"Possibly, but if you see either of them again, well, you know the routine. Call me. I'll leave you my number. On no account, approach them."

"I think it's more likely they'll be approaching me rather than the other way around."

"Let's talk about Mr Bernhard's role in all this." Marchal said. "You say he copied the images you had acquired from Rosenberg from this memory card onto his computer?"

"Rosenberg had already copied the images from the card onto a USB memory stick, which Bernhard then transferred onto his laptop so that he could play around with them to provide an interesting front cover montage."

"He copied around thirty images. Is that right?"

"That's what we purchased."

"Each exposure has a number printed along the bottom, presumably a sequential listing of the order in which they were taken."

"And?"

"Some of the numbers are sequential, some aren't. There are gaps in the numbering. The last one is in the fifties. What does that suggest to you?"

She put her arms behind her head, extending her elbows outward and, at the same time, inhaling deeply. "Where are we going with this, Capitaine? Is it some kind of quiz? Because if it is, I really do need to get to work."

He ignored the objection. "It suggests to me that a lot more than thirty photos of the Prince were taken, almost twice as many. Any comment?"

"Listen. I don't know how many times I have to repeat myself. We looked at thirty. What *BV* bought was thirty and that's the be all and end all of it. What more can I say?"

"And if there were more, who would have them?"

She shrugged her shoulders. "Gerben Rosenberg, I imagine."

"There's no clause in your contract with him prohibiting the sale of such photos to your competition?"

"Obviously. We insist on a blanket, all encompassing restriction."

Marchal decided to change tack. She was getting impatient and he needed some more background information. It wouldn't be much longer, he told her. How had she come to know Benny Ram? She went to say something, but seemed to think better of it. He guessed she was about to comment on the relevance of the question.

"Somehow, he came to know of my father's plight. I'm not sure exactly how."

"His plight?"

"My parents are originally farmers from the Alsace. My father suffered a serious accident which meant he couldn't work anymore. He tried to claim compensation, but failed. I think there was a local newspaper article. Mr Ram took an interest in it, paid for lawyers to reopen the case and press the claim."

"Successfully?"

"I guess so. It paid for me to go off to boarding school in Paris, then on to university and a media sciences degree. It was all down to Mr Ram's intervention. He was always in the background. He sort of became my sponsor."

"Your good Samaritan?"

"If there is one in the Hindu religion."

"And after you got your degree?"

Chantelle checked her watch again. In a couple of sentences, she summarised how her benefactor had arranged a position for her with an influential publisher in London, where she had spent four productive years. Benny's acquisition of *BV* and her appointment as editor had been a natural progression.

"Any brothers or sisters?"

She shook her head vehemently.

"I know you want to get away," Marchal said. "Just one more question. I've seen all thirty of these photos. Some are bad enough and I can only suppose that the ones we haven't seen are even worse."

"If there are more."

"Indeed. If there are more, as you say." He was reflective. "You've chosen to publish this week what, in my opinion, are five of the least compromising. Do you intend to go on publishing the rest?"

She was on her feet. "Let me answer your question with a question, Capitaine. This man is about to be ordained as a priest in the Anglican Church. Would you want him to put his hands on the shoulders of your young son and bless him as he gave him communion? I very much doubt it."

She had left the room and Marchal had turned toward the marker board to make some notes.

"You know she was lying, don't you?" Colbert was talking to his back.

He carried on writing. *Chantelle Dubois – Father – Benny Ram.* "I'm sure you're going to tell me what and why. You seem more interested in my swansong investigation than that juicy pile of violence and death on your desk."

"Yours is active. These are all moribund." He knew she wanted him to turn around, but he kept pointing toward the board. "She's an accomplished liar," Colbert continued regardless. "I suppose it comes with the job."

"With most jobs, I should think. That's if you want to climb the career ladder."

"Most of your questions, she would reflect, hesitate slightly, before answering. Her reply would be studied."

"Go on."

"When she was lying, she had already prepared the response, knowing you would ask the question. The answer was out of her mouth almost before you had finished asking."

"So you worked out that our Miss Dubois knew how much Benny Ram had paid for the photos and that she had already seen the ones that were missing from the sequence?"

"You guessed?" She sounded mildly surprised as he

118

twisted his chair back around to face her.

"Guessed? That understates the intuition, insight and experience accumulated from talking to people just like her over the last thirty five years."

"I didn't mean to sound patronising."

"You didn't?"

"No."

"Then tell me what else you gleaned from her demeanour, actions etcetera."

"She's normally a very self-assured person, but she found some of your interrogation technique disturbing. I thought, at one point, she started to become afraid of you."

"Meaning?"

"This is just a hunch. I suspect that she saw some aspects of the relationship of an only child with her father or a male figure in her life, perhaps Mr Ram, and it disturbed her."

"Maybe she's like that with all men."

"You think she's a lesbian?"

"Quite possibly," he replied. "Though I doubt it's got anything to do with anything. Did you enjoy talking to her?"

She launched a pencil eraser in his direction that caused him to duck his head.

"You two seem to be getting on famously." Arnault was standing in the doorway. He gave her a turn the tap on and off smile. "How's the Bernhard investigation going?" he asked Marchal.

"Nowhere really, at this stage," Marchal replied. "I'm just collecting a little background information for the file. I may have to interrupt the investigation and absent myself for one or two days; some personal matters to attend to before I leave."

"Splendid. Take all the time you want." Arnault turned to his new recruit. "I'd be interested in hearing your views on the Beauclerc murders. Five years and still no conviction. Shall we say thirty minutes in my office, Patricia." He was gone as quickly as he had arrived.

"Background information; family matters. Were you deliberately misleading him?" She stared at Marchal.

"Lying, you mean?" He laughed. "You tell me. You're the expert."

Twenty - @renemarchal

The spire of the American Cathedral in Paris dominates the skyline on the Avenue George V, tucked in between the Champs-Elysee and the River Seine. It had started to drizzle and the fine spray was nestling on the lenses of Marchal's glasses as he made his way into the vestry. His appointment was with a Father Richmond, but there was no sign of a cleric, just a dozen or so members of the public, either with a genuine interest in the Cathedral or just sheltering from the rain. The notice board told him that alongside the religious schedule, the venue hosted a wide range of community based services. Tonight, there was a meeting of Alcoholics Anonymous. He could do with a stiff drink. This wasn't going to be easy.

A hand tapped him gently on the shoulder. Marchal wheeled around to find himself looking at the smiling face of a very old man who could be no more than five feet one or two in height "You're the only person in sight who looks like a policeman." His French was flawless, but it wasn't his natural tongue.

"Father Richmond?"

"At your service." He ushered his guest to a seat in a small room alongside the kiosk that sold postcards and religious artefacts to the tourists. The cleric had large floppy ears and jowled cheeks that made him look like a happy bulldog. "I assume you have not come to seek spiritual guidance, my son?"

Marchal smiled. "In a way, I have; guidance of a very delicate nature."

"How so?"

"To start with, I'm a little confused. This is an American cathedral, but it's not exclusively related to the States?"

"Of course not. We are part of the worldwide Anglican community. As you as a catholic are linked to Rome and the Vatican, we, Anglicans, are related to Canterbury, or more correctly, to Gibraltar."

"Gibraltar?" Marchal sounded incredulous.

"Amazing as it sounds, it's true. The Diocese of Gibraltar in Europe is probably the largest diocese in the Anglican community. It encompasses most of Europe, the former Soviet Union and stretches from Morocco to Iceland."

"Unbelievable. An entire church controlled from a rock at the entrance to the Mediterranean."

"In structure, yes, but not in practice. You see the Diocese of Gibraltar has seven Archdeaconries throughout the large territorial area it encompasses. Each is headed by an archdeacon and France is one of these seven. Our archdeacon is based in Nice."

"So Gibraltar is just a symbol?"

"Not really. The Anglican equivalent to your Pope is the Bishop of Europe. He is based in Canterbury, but is enthroned in the Cathedral of the Holy Trinity in Gibraltar, which is the link between all the Archdeaconries and other faiths as well."

"I'd never have imagined it."

The priest wriggled in his chair, obviously uncomfortable. "But you didn't come here, Capitaine, for a briefing on the hierarchy of the church. So what is this guidance you seek? May I suggest that It's something to do with this week's edition of *Bien à Vous*, is it not?"

"I'm afraid it is." Marchal drew several sheets of photographic paper from an envelope. "My sources tell me that Father Richmond has many contacts within the Anglican Communion."

"I rarely forget a face; more often now than in years gone by."

"The photographs in the magazine are but a small selection from a larger collection. I regret that some are sexually explicit, but all the same, I would like you to look at them."

"To what end?"

"I need the names of any of the people you recognise in these prints."

He hesitated. "I don't know. You put me in a difficult position. Will they face criminal proceedings?"

"Absolutely not. No crime has been committed in France in any of the images and I can guarantee that anything you tell me will go no further. I may request an interview with one or other of them, but their anonymity will be protected." Whatever my personal sentiments was an unspoken afterthought.

The old man looked closely at the policeman, weighing his decision, the dilemma apparent. "Let me see them," he said finally.

"I warn you, they're not pretty."

"The church has faced many crises of confidence. It will surpass this one."

Fifteen minutes later, Marchal had a list of ten names. The old man was visibly shaken, slumped in a chair, head buried in his chest. He slowly raised his eyes. "Please go now," he said.

Marchal was glad of the fresh air, even if there was still a trace of rain in the blustery wind. Father Richmond had been seriously disturbed by what he had seen. The ten names were all ordained ministers, a sprinkling of deans in their midst. The rest were either strangers he might have seen at synod meetings or trainee ministers whose names were not familiar to him. Of the ten names, only one was French, a minor dean from Lyon. The remainder were spread across Europe.

His train of thought was distracted by the vibration of his mobile. It was Colbert. "Hope you don't mind me ringing, but there's something I think you should know."

"Great to have a conduit back to base," he said.

"There's a note on your desk. Madame Lafayette has regained consciousness. The doctors will give you five minutes and no more."

He rang off. How the hell do you find a taxi after lunch on a rainy afternoon in Paris? They were about as scarce as a hen's teeth.

Twenty-one - @GerbenRosenberg

Maxwell's two way radio crackled. He resented the intrusion into a daydream of a summer's day in Quebec watching the only woman he had ever loved toss a ball across the park for their golden retriever to chase. She turned toward him and laughed. Where was the adulterous bitch now, he wondered?

"Target on fire escape." Lewis's whispered voice was hoarse. "Mid thirties, short stocky build, beer gut, physically challenged."

"Physically challenged! What the fuck does that mean?"

"He's having difficulty climbing down the stairs. Shall I take him out? There's nobody about."

"Negative. Lambert's issued an MF on this one. Anyway, he's unlikely to have the material with him. We must assume he's on his way to pick it up."

Lewis shook his head. The target had reached the first floor, gingerly moving down. Just imagine. An MF – minimum force to achieve objective. Give him five minutes in a cul-de-sac with the man and he'd have exactly what they were after. Now, they were going to pussyfoot about with all the potential for another cock-up.

"I'll come round and pick you up. We'll tail him. There's three hours until his scheduled meeting with the lawyers. Let's see where he goes."

Rosenberg had walked away from the apartment block and was waiting at the corner of an intersection, looking one way and then, the other.

Lewis entered the black Mercedes. "What's all this about? I had him, bang to rights!"

"The Palace is being cautious. There's a local police investigation into our activities." Maxwell moved the car forward as Rosenberg waved down a taxi. "Lambert says it's only a token move. People in high places have been talking. They've only got one copper on the case and he's about to retire, but we don't want to attract any attention that would move their investigation up a notch."

The taxi moved off. Maxwell kept two cars behind. He glanced around at Lewis and smiled. "Just to be sure, it's now a belt and braces job. We've been given accredited diplomatic status as attachés. I'm with trade and you're with cultural relations." He couldn't suppress a laugh. "With your technique, you should be good at that."

They stayed two or three car lengths behind the taxi as it made its way through the heavy traffic on the Left Bank toward Montparnasse. Just after the Paris Observatory, it turned right and came to a halt at the front of the Cochin Hospital.

Rosenberg made his way through the arched entrance to the information desk, spoke briefly with the attendant and then headed toward the staircase in the east wing. Lewis could only watch his target disappear up the stairs as his progress was halted by a procession of excited children in wheelchairs heading for the therapy gym. "Lost sight of him," he whispered into the two way radio.

"This is where the ambulance was taking the old lady. Look for the female wards." Maxwell was playing a hunch. "If he dropped the memory card into the old lady's purse, he'll be looking to retrieve it from wherever they keep her belongings. He's certainly not paying her a social visit."

"Got it." Lewis made his way door by door along the corridor, peering into each room as he progressed. There was no sign of Rosenberg. Visitors crowded around some of the beds, others had one or two sitting either side of the patient. A few watched on, alone and unattended. Nurses were moving from room to room along the busy corridor. A uniformed police officer passed by without giving him a second glance. Very few people did, except the guy in the third room on the right after the fire exit door. Whoever was in the bed was out of view, shielded by the nurse who was attending to her, but the visitor was holding the hand that extended from beneath the sheet between both of his. He looked up, caught and held his gaze for as long as it took Lewis to establish that Rosenberg was not in the room.

Lewis moved on. Three doors down, there was an acrylic sign – *Salle du personnel – infirmiéres*. He had no idea what it meant, his French non-existent, but he recognised Rosenberg from the back as the man rummaged through a plastic case full of large manila envelopes. There was nobody else in the room which was in partial darkness. The door was ajar and Rosenberg was far too intent on what he was doing to notice the figure standing behind him. Lewis slipped the double-sided hunting knife from his raincoat pocket into his right hand, just at the very moment Rosenberg breathed a sigh of relief and held aloft one of the envelopes.

"I'll take that, if you don't mind," Lewis said in English.

Rosenberg wheeled round, the envelope still held above his head. "What? Who the hell are you?" He went to slide past the man, stopping suddenly when he saw the knife pointed at his stomach.

Lewis could only guess what the other man had said. Speaking in French to him was pointless. He gestured at the same time as he threatened with the knife. There was a look of total disbelief on Rosenberg's face as he handed the envelope over, his eyes transfixed on the silver blade. Lewis stashed the package under his raincoat.

The sound of the door closing caused them to turn to face the stranger who smiled benignly at them. Lewis recognised him as the man who had caught his eye a few minutes earlier.

"Good afternoon, gentlemen," the newcomer said. "A pair of thespians, I do believe."

Lewis looked blank. The knife was no longer in his hand. Minimum force. The words rang in his ears.

"I'm sorry," the newcomer had changed to English. "I didn't realise you had no French. It's Mr Lewis, isn't it? British Royal security, now masquerading as a member of our police force? Your picture doesn't do your stature justice."

It was Rosenberg's turn to look confused. His eyes, distended in fear, looked from one man to the other in quick succession.

"You do understand a little English, Mr Rosenberg, or should I call you Martin, Madame Lafayette's loving son from Strasbourg, who just happens to be working in Philadelphia at this very moment?"

Rosenberg nodded.

Marchal could sense that the man was preparing to make a run for it.

"Don't think about it, Mr Lewis. You don't want to be arrested for assaulting a real policeman, do you?" He moved to block the doorway. "By the way, my name is Capitaine Marchal from the Police Judiciaire. Just to avoid any confusion that I, too, might be playacting, this is a real warrant card." Lewis was still studying his exit route and paid no attention to the document held in front of him.

"While you're here, Mr Lewis, you might be able to help me answer a few questions about the untimely death of a young man named Sebastien Bernhard. I believe you were there at the time?"

"I don't know what you're talking about, whatever you said your name is." Lewis was openly hostile.

"No comprehension, either in French or in English," Marchal taunted. "I think we French sometimes find it insulting that so few of your countrymen bother to remember to speak our language. It is compulsory in your schools, is it not?"

"We had an option," Lewis smirked. "I chose crochet. I thought it would be more useful."

Marchal stood aside, opening the door as he did so. "Then, you had better go and do some knitting in front of the guillotine while the heads roll. Just be careful that one of them isn't yours."

Lewis pushed past him, disappearing out of view at a run as he turned the corner.

"What are you doing?" Rosenberg protested loudly, moving toward the door. "You've let him get away with the old lady's property and mine too. Are you mad, Capitaine?"

"Stay where you are, Mr Rosenberg, before I arrest you! And calm down. Let's step outside. We shouldn't be in here." They found a bench seat in a deserted out patients waiting area. "If I had arrested Mr Lewis, he would have claimed diplomatic immunity and I would have spent the next few days filling in forms and justifying my actions. I don't have that luxury."

"But you've let him escape with valuable property." Rosenberg hesitated. "At least that's what it used to be." He hesitated again. "Maybe it's not even in the envelope, anyway."

Marchal reached into the inside pocket of his raincoat to pull out an identical manila envelope. "You mean this one?"

"I'm impressed."

"I had the advantage of about ten minutes over you both. Your phone call to the hospital was ill-judged. The nurse told Madame Lafayette that her son would be visiting which I learned was a lie. I guessed it was you and I suspected that you might be followed."

Gerben whistled silently through his teeth. "Remind me not to underestimate the police in future," he said.

"Mr Lewis has a bulky envelope filled with cough sweets and a selection of the opening pages from the telephone directory. Regrettably, he won't be able to understand the instructions for reporting a fault on the line."

"May I?" Gerben reached for the envelope, only to watch it returned to Marchal's coat pocket. As if part of some magic trick, the policeman held a small black memory card between his thumb and forefinger.

"I believe that this is what you came here to find?"

"Thank God, you've found it. You've saved my life." Again he lent forward to grab the card, only to find it withdrawn from his reach. His expression was confused, quizzical, and then, alarmed. "That's my property. I need it. There's a meeting in an hour." As if to justify and persuade the policeman, he followed up with, "Don't worry, it's going to be taken out of circulation."

"Probably in exchange for a great deal of money." Marchal was beginning to enjoy himself as he sensed the other man's apparent discomfort. "I'm afraid you'll have to delay your meeting. As to whose property it is, well, at this precise moment, I retrieved it from Madame Lafayette's belongings. It's also likely to form a link in my enquiries into a suspicious death. These things have to be cleared up before I can release it to its owner, whoever that happens to be."

"I can assure you, it's me." Gerben shook his head violently. "The way you're talking, this could take weeks." He swivelled in his seat to lightly grab the lapels of Marchal's raincoat. It wasn't a threatening move, more the gesture of a supplicant. "He'll kill me. You're talking to a dead man."

"Who is he?"

"It doesn't matter." He rubbed his fingers down the lapels. "Please let me have it back. You know what's on it, don't you?"

Marchal looked down at his lapels, a sign for the other man to release his grip. Gerben backed off. "Sorry," he said. "I didn't mean anything by it."

Marchal stood up, turning to face the dejected figure sitting in front of him. "I'll do you a favour, Mr Rosenberg. I need some answers to a series of questions I keep asking myself." He looked up as two ambulance men dressed in luminous yellow vests pushed an empty stretcher trolley across the waiting room floor and exit through the double swing doors. "Here's the address you'll find me at tomorrow, nine am. Tell me all you know and I'll give you the card. Lie, and I'll have an expert on hand to tell me whether you are or not, and you won't see this again. Got it?"

Gerben nodded.

"One more thing. Don't show and by nine thirty I'll have a warrant out for your arrest. Let's see. Impersonating a social security official; attempted kidnap; theft – I can probably think of a few other charges to get you put out of circulation for some time. Be there!"

The policeman had left. Gerben had an hour before he met up with Bates at Starbuck's on the Champs-Elysee. They would go on to the meeting with the Prince's law firm together. What on earth could his excuse be this time? He shook his head. This was all getting too much, out of hand. He had lost control. Benny would kill him.

Twenty two - @Bizzybuzzybee

From his apartment on the ninety eighth floor of the Princess Tower in Dubai, tonight's exceptionally bright and star filled night time sky seemed closer to Benny Ram's touch than the toy boats in the marina below. It was time for a round of phone calls and tweets to consolidate the results of today's developments and identify the topics he should deal with first in the morning. He pushed the remote control to close the venetian blinds across the panoramic window, used the same remote to lock the double office doors and a third button to release the shutter enclosing his secure phone connection. The number was untraceable and the voice distortion capability was guaranteed non-malleable encryption proof.

The elderly man had been waiting for the call, answering after the first ring. He heard a distorted voice say "Square," to which he responded "Sator".

"Everything going to plan?" the squeaky voice asked.

"All the conditions at this end are positive," Professor Speir replied. "We are waiting patiently."

"You will not have to do so for much longer. Final preparations are in course. You will doubtless be aware of the furore which has erupted since the publication."

"I do. It has enabled us to get the chess pieces into the appropriate positions. Anything else?"

"Did you get me the name I need?"

"It's Mishka Melman. He was with a two man Kidon unit travelling in a microlight north of Palmyra six years ago. They were trying to get photographs of a Syrian military installations. A sandstorm must have brought them down. One of the two was killed on impact. Melman survived for ten days. Information got back to Tel Aviv through the normal clandestine channels that Damascus believed it was a one man operation with just the single casualty."

"And Melman?"

"Presumably, the Mossad has him listed as missing, believed dead, buried under a metre of sand somewhere, but until they have positive proof . . ." Speir's sentence tailed off into silence.

"Relatives?" Benny Ram was taking notes.

"Both parents died from a viral infection when he was ten years old. He was brought up by an elder sister, his only surviving relative." Speir hesitated. "At the time, that is."

"And?"

"She was knocked down and killed in a car accident three years ago in southern Israel."

"Who took her out?"

"Who knows. Could have been a genuine accident. If not, probably the clandestine CIA identity marketing boys. Better to have a name with no family affiliations. My contact was circumspect, but Melman's watertight."

"I'll pass the information on. Be ready. I'm expecting to get the word any time now."

Before he secured the telephone, Benny spoke briefly to thank the two mullahs, Hashen and Omar on whom he heaped excessive praise. They were humbled by his comments and confident that Darek would complete his assignment with competence and commitment. He was a clever young man.

His next task was to post a number of tweets. Two were private Direct Messages, the rest general comments on various accounts where he wanted his hashtag to appear as an ardent supporter of British royalty who rejected the recent disgusting revelations as shameful.

Benny Ram had an invitation to a private party that evening, organised by a wild playboy, son of a powerful Kuwaiti arms dealer. It could be both great fun and, ultimately, profitable. But, before he readied himself, there was one more call to make.

"How are you feeling?" he asked with genuine concern. "Are you finding it harrowing?"

"Organising funerals can never be easy," Chantelle replied. "Especially when the person you're burying has been taken before his time and was a good friend and colleague."

He could sense the tears in her voice. "He was an only child?"

"Yes."

"His parents?"

"Devastated. Apart from anything else, he supported them. Where they turn to now, God only knows."

"Leave it with me," he said. "Send me the details and I'll take care of it." He made a note to organise a monthly allowance equal to their late son's salary. Collateral damage was acceptable, but somebody had to pick up the moral debt. "Any other news?" he asked.

"Plenty, Benny." She drew a breath. "Life at *BV* is never quiet. The interest in the images is overwhelming.

We'll go on selling until the next sensation hits the newsstands."

Benny was quick to reply. "Hold off any new deals for the time being, will you. Let the dust settle."

"You're joking aren't you? You can easily quadruple your money in a matter of weeks."

"Maybe, but I'd prefer it if you didn't publish any more new images in *BV* for the time being."

"Are you afraid of possible legal action? Your attorney, Kamal was on to me today. He's been served with notice of a hearing next Monday. Even if the outcome goes against us, which he doesn't seem to think it will, we'll still have time to publish another cluster of pictures before any injunction could be granted."

His voice stiffened. He wasn't going to get involved in a discussion. "Do as I ask, please. On no account, publish or sell any more of this stuff. I have my reasons. I don't get a good feeling."

"OK." There was obvious disappointment. "You pay the bills. You call the shots. What power does a poor little editor have?"

"Don't react like that," he said angrily. "It doesn't become you, Chantelle. I wouldn't insist if I didn't have a good reason."

"Don't bite my head off. What's happened? The King promised you a knighthood?"

"That's a good thought," he joked, opting to change the mood. "Sir Benny Ram – got a nice ring to it, hasn't it?"

"Yes. Suits you."

"Listen. One more thing, Chantelle." He was back to being serious again. "Stay clear of this Rosenberg fellow. There's something about him which just doesn't ring true."

"More gut reaction?"

"More than that. I've heard a few disturbing things about him. Avoid him, and whatever you do, don't do any more deals with him. He could be dangerous. Understood?"

Confused and puzzled, Chantelle replaced the receiver.

Funny, she thought to herself. Gerben always came over as a pretty harmless pussycat, not some high profile villain. "But," she muttered out loud. She closed and bolted her front door. Benny was normally right about most things. She'd give him the benefit of the doubt.

Twenty three - @GerbenRosenberg

The noise and heat in Starbucks was overwhelming. The people with seats guarded their temporary resting places selfishly as others meandered between the armchairs and tables, searching for a home for their medium decaf lattes or mocha chocolates with squirty cream. What a business, Gerben thought. Marketing at its best. Selling a product that consumers have been buying for centuries with a slant that attracted people to willingly pay over the odds and be more than happy about it. Momentarily, the concept had distracted him from bemoaning the sheer misery of his situation.

Bates was sitting at a shelf counter facing the mirrored wall, carefully protecting another stool destined for the newcomer. Through the mirror, Bates acknowledged Gerben's arrival with a cursory nod of the head. Fighting his way through a group of gesticulating young men, spread out across two sofas, their banter loud and crude, Rosenberg edged toward the vacant stool. His mumbled apology for bumping into one was ignored by the heavy set youth. At least, if the man had taken offence and flattened him, he wouldn't have had to face the solicitor.

"You feeling alright?" Bates asked. "You look like shit!"

Gerben launched into his prepared speech. "We can't go through with the meeting today. The police have got the memory card."

Bates looked nonplussed as Gerben recounted the events at the hospital.

"So what do we say to the eight just men when we meet them in what?" Gerben checked his watch. "Ten minutes time."

"Give them this." Bates took a small passport photo sized envelope from his pocket and shook an identical memory card onto the counter. "And we'll close the deal." Gerben was aghast. "And shut your mouth. You look like a goldfish."

"How did you get that? An hour or so ago, it was in a policeman's raincoat pocket."

"Don't ask questions I'm not prepared to answer. Let me just say this. You owe Mr Ram a very big favour. Don't forget that."

"I won't. You can rely on me." A sense of relief and elation coursed through his body. His mouth was dry. He could do with a coffee.

"One more thing and this is important." He leaned closer to Gerben. "You tell me you're going for an interview with this policeman tomorrow. Well, play your part."

"What do you mean?"

"You can tell him the truth about everything, but don't mention Mr Ram, other than to confirm that you did the deal with him for the first thirty photos. You kept the second set to sell back to the Prince. Understood?"

"Yes. Perfectly." Right at that moment, Gerben would have said anything Bates wanted him to say.

"When it comes to this," he pointed to the card, "you do everything necessary to protect the policeman. Don't ever let on that it's a conspiracy. When he shows you a card and says that there's nothing on it, look shell-shocked and defeated. Say you can't understand it. How could it have been switched without you knowing? There's a scratch on the card. You put it there originally and saw that it was there yesterday. And yes. It's on the one he's just handed you. Why are there no photos? Have they been erased?"

"I see where you're going."

"Good, because after the meeting this evening, we're going to go through all this one more time. The policeman will tell you that nothing has been erased, that the card is a formatted virgin. Never used. Shock, horror and you move on. Meeting over and you never see him again."

"He's taking a big risk, isn't he?"

"He's retiring in a few weeks, I understand. Police pensions are shit; austerity, cuts and all the old excuses. Who says crime doesn't pay? Come on, we'll be late."

As the Paris nightlife began to move into gear, two hours had passed since they walked the short distance from the coffee house to the lawyers' offices. The deal had been signed off and, feeling drugged with success, Gerben clenched a fist and thrust his arm into the night air.

Sat around the table had been the eight lawyers as at the previous meeting plus a short, stocky man in his sixties who was introduced as Dr Reinhardt from Liechtenstein. Unsurprisingly, there were still a few clauses of the sale contract left to negotiate. Bates began to give ground on issues relating to Palace access to the images, the compound interest rate to be applied to the deposit and some other technical stuff which went over Gerben's head. There was a heated exchange on the possible publication of contemporaneous compromising images which were not contained on the card. Again, Bates finally agreed to accept liability.

Eventually, the old man, the lead lawyer, carefully inspected the photo files on the card, one by one, making notes as he progressed, his expression, totally without emotion or any reaction. The viewing excluded his colleagues and the escrow lawyer, Dr Reinhardt who all sat patiently, in silence, until the process was complete.

There was an awkward five minute period where everyone waited without a word passing until the secretary arrived with the final version of the agreement. Signatures were appended and the memory card disappeared into Dr Reinhardt's briefcase in exchange for a copy bank deposit slip issued by the Liechtensteinische Landesbank. Bates verified the affidavit validating the deposit and carefully filed it away. There were no handshakes. Everybody filed out of the room as if they had just bade farewell to a corpse.

The ambience in the bar couldn't have been further from the mortuary like atmosphere they had just left. Bates found a table away from the main throng of young business types who were gathered together close to the door.

"Thank God that's over," Gerben prompted as he took a large swig of lager. "You seemed to be in charitable mood tonight. Made a good few concessions." His tone was almost critical.

"Trivia," Bates replied. "I don't know how you negotiate Mr Rosenberg, but the best tactic is to never totally grind your adversary into the ground. Let him win a few points. Give ground where ground doesn't matter. Now, he can go back to his client and say that he gained some significant advantages so that his fee can be justified."

"But, just supposing there were to be some other images which aren't on the card?"

"Then you've misled him as to the product you sold him in the first place. You guaranteed there are no more images. If there were to be, the contract's null and void and you could probably be sued for the breach. The concession I agreed to was meaningless in legal terms." He sipped a ten year old malt, clinking the ice cubes around in the glass. "For now, he has what he wants. To all intense and purposes, your compromising evidence is out of circulation."

"Thanks to Benny."

"Yes, thanks to Mr Ram. Now let's go over once again just how you're going to approach this meeting with the policeman tomorrow morning."

Twenty four - @ChasBroadhurst.kp

Broadhurst tapped the screen of his mobile to end the call. Sitting on the other side of the desk, Duncan White and Lambert waited for him to speak.

"The deal's done. The images were verified and handed over to this Swiss lawyer for safekeeping. The King can appoint somebody to inspect them, if he so chooses." He yawned. "In exchange for which, he's now six million poorer."

"I'll get Maxwell and Lewis to return," Lambert said.

"Leave them where they are for another twenty four hours. Let's keep tabs on Dubois and that little shit to see what they're up to. Pages from a bloody telephone directory, I tell you! We've been made to look like complete fools. What a couple of useless cretins." Broadhurst lapsed into silence.

"In the circumstances, I wouldn't say that the media coverage has been too damning." White struck a positive note. "I understand that the Prince is to make his broadcast statement the day after tomorrow. We're finishing a draft for submission in the morning."

"What's that?" Lambert asked. "His 'I'm coming out of the closet' speech?"

"Too bloody late for that." Broadhurst was sullen. "Have you seen the photos and editorial in the Evening Standard? He's out of the closet, out of the front door and half way down the fucking street with his trousers around his ankles."

"You're overreacting Chas," Lambert said. "Listen. Can we leave this until tomorrow morning, gents? I promised Soraya I'd take her out for a celebration dinner tonight. It's her birthday and I wanted to make it special for her. She's really kept my spirits up this past week."

That's not all she's kept up, I shouldn't wonder, Broadhurst thought to himself as he waved Lambert away. The man was like a love struck adolescent and, if he cared to admit it, Broadhurst was just plain jealous.

White waited to speak until Lambert had left the room. "What's wrong, Chas? You seem really down in the mouth. Taking everything together, we can't say the result has been disastrous. Bad, it may be, but fatal, no."

"It's not that, Duncan. I'm being silly really. My pride's been dented and it's got to me."

"How come?"

"It's this damn professor and his behavioural analysis. I, at the very least, expected a briefing from the boss or his equerry as to the findings."

"And?"

"Not a dicky bird, all day. They spent all morning in total privacy, far longer than I'd imagined. Then this Professor Speir left without the courtesy of the conversation he promised me yesterday."

"Maybe there was nothing to report."

Broadhurst reached for the whiskey bottle in his cabinet. White declined the glass extended to him. "Suit yourself, " Broadhurst said. "I need one."

"It doesn't seem worth getting worked up about."

"Something's up and I want to know what it is." Broadhurst poured a refill. "There were three Royal privilege entrants into the Palace this afternoon. One, perhaps, I can accept, but three?"

"Royal privilege?"

"It's the term we use for anybody who doesn't have to pass through security procedures, other than a weapons check. They've been given special dispensation by the monarch."

"Trusted individuals?" White suggested.

"Sometimes, or in this case, individuals he didn't want Palace security to know about."

"Any idea who they were?"

"Mr Smith, Mr Jones and Mr Brown. In other words, mind your own business."

"Listen Chas," White had his own agenda to pursue. "I need to catch up with the evening news. All my team have been told no comments. Let's see what the pundits make of it all. In the meantime, your problem is bound to resolve itself."

But Broadhurst was miles away. If he heard White's parting comment, he showed no reaction to it. He could sense that his authority was being eroded; that there was no longer implicit trust in his decision making ability; he was beginning to question his own actions. For the first time in his life, he felt his self-confidence start to falter. He needed to get a grip of the situation.

BOOK TWO – AREPO THE PLOUGH

Twenty Five - #DAREK

The flight from Valetta to Rome and then the wait for the transfer flight to Malaga, followed by a two hour coach trip along the coast to complete the hundred and fifty kilometres to La Linea had left the young man exhausted, fast asleep in his seat. The hiss of the hydraulic brakes as the coach came to a jolting stop woke him suddenly, a fleeting panic as he questioned his whereabouts, followed by a gradual realisation as to where he was. Darek looked down at the creases in his trousers. The mullahs Hashen and Omar had agreed that he should wear western style clothes, so called fashionable jeans, baggy, secured around his hips rather than his waist, gathered up around his canvas shoes where they were too long. The flimsy tee shirt barely reached the trousers, leaving a band of flesh visible around his midriff when he raised his arms.

Mullah Omar had seen him off from the Maltese capital that morning after a series of gruelling sessions of lessons and instructions, first from Mullah Hashen and, then, from Omar himself, all of which had sent Darek's head spinning. As he had waved goodbye that morning, his confidence was as crisp as the cut of his clothes. Now, he felt lonely, vulnerable and confused, his mind dishevelled like the state of his new trousers. His Islamic compass pointed to the direction of Mecca. He swivelled in his seat and prayed.

As night began to fall with the sun setting big and orange on the horizon, he was the last off of the coach, gathering his holdall as he followed the half a dozen or so of his fellow travellers making their way to the Spanish and British passport controls that marked the entrance to the Rock of Gibraltar. He presented an Iranian passport that was ignored by the Spanish official and carefully scanned at the British booth. The official studied the visa closely, consulting the screen in front of him on a number of occasions. "The reason for your visit?" he asked.

"I'm here to learn about Christianity," Darek answered.

"That's a first," the official remarked, amused at the reply. "Enjoy your stay, Mr Moradi."

The tall man with the frameless glasses, dressed in a lightweight suit over a dog collar walked hurriedly toward him. There was a scar on his left cheek which gave him a slightly sinister appearance, but the warm smile and outstretched arms were all embracing. "Welcome to Gibraltar, Darek. You must be exhausted." He avoided the young man's extended hand and gave him a big hug, so firm, the surprise caused Darek to drop his holdall onto the floor.

"Sorry," the cleric said, retrieving the bag. "I'm Canon Acheson. You can call me Glover. That's the ridiculous name my parents gave me." He waved his hand in the air. "My car's over here, just a small run-around. You can't travel far in Gibraltar."

He studied Darek closely from top to toe. "This is a great pleasure. Mullah Hashen is a true spiritual friend. He told me all about you. How you are his most promising student." He talked quickly, tossing his head back from time to time in some nervous gesture. "You'll be staying at my hostel. We have foreign students and trainee sacerdotes coming all the time, either to learn about or extend their knowledge of the Anglican religion." He grasped Darek's hand, rubbing his fingers as he did so. "It's so pleasing to welcome members of the Islamic faith. It's only by mutual understanding that we can live together peacefully, without fear and not breed the suspicion that leads to isolation."

Darek could only smile weakly at this outpouring.

"Brotherly love is at the root of our tree of life, don't you agree?" Acheson didn't wait for an answer. "It's only a short ride. We have what the Americans call a combo on the westside of the Rock. It's built on land reclaimed from the sea. You'll love it. Don't mind if I smoke in the car, do you? It's a terrible vice, but I can't seem to give it up." The question was a courtesy, not seriously seeking permission. His nicotine stained fingers reached into his pocket for a packet of cigarettes.

For Darek, the landscape around him was an eye-opener. He had never seen such a vast expanse of water, almost within touching distance and stretching as far as the horizon. How could his life have changed so drastically from one day to the next, from an arid desert prison that was to be the place of his execution to this strange world of water? Four large vessels, which he later learned were loaded with containers, were anchored offshore, waiting for a berth to unload. The rows of neat, box-like buildings in the foreground were shrouded in almost total darkness, just the occasional light in a window, but there was not a soul to be seen. All the activity in this world was centred round the lights twinkling from the ships that moved to the rhythm of the swell.

He stood naked by the window of his bedroom, a spare room in the Canon's quarters, temporary accommodation until a space became available in the hostel next door. His attention was devoted to the wondrous sight he looked out upon, but the pose he struck had been practiced, engineered by the mullahs to achieve the maximum impact.

It had the desired effect. The door creaked open, barely enough for the Canon to put his head round. "I just came to check that everything was alright." His gaze was transfixed by the lean, well formed young body with the small, beautifully proportioned bottom and strong muscular legs.

In a show of embarrassment, Darek reached hurriedly for a towel, but not before exposing his genitals and a penis that lay flatulent against his thigh. He secured the end of the towel. "Everything is perfect. When do we get started?" he asked pointedly.

The older man took off his glasses, furiously rubbing his eyes, avoiding the gaze directed at him. "Tomorrow," the Canon stammered, "I will take you to see our modest, but beautiful cathedral, the Holy Trinity and explain something of our faith." He exhaled deeply. "If you need anything, my room is just across the hallway." Hurriedly, the door was closed, leaving Darek to smile broadly into the mirror and drop the sensuous posture he had adopted. With the fervour of a child in an exciting new environment, he threw himself onto the bed. Everything was going just as the mullahs had forecast that it would. Maybe as soon as tomorrow he would be able to send a tweet to his contact. One word would say everything – AREPO. He wrote the word large on the pad on his bedside table and then violently defaced it with the pen he held between his clenched fist. For what he would be forced to do, Allah would forgive him. Paradise would welcome him. He collapsed onto his knees, head bent in contrition and prayed.

Twenty six - @renemarchal

Somewhere in the distance church bells sounded. Marchal was unsure whether that meant it was nine o clock or quarter to. Whatever, he was running late. It was always the same that whenever you were tired and edgy, in a hurry, the crowds of morning rush hour workers seemed to be forever in your way, a kind of collective, unspoken conspiracy against you.

The late night phone call from his daughter, Monique, had unsettled him. Her husband was seeking a separation, unable any longer to tolerate her violent mood swings, convinced that it was unsettling the children who, temporarily at least, would be better off in his care. Marchal had tried to calm her, but his reasoned approach had been no panacea for the floods of tears and threats of angry reprisals that dominated her response. He would have to go to Lille and talk to them both before they found themselves in the throes of a legal battle that would polarise their positions, leaving their marriage and the chance of reconciliation in tatters.

Whatever the contributory factors, Marchal blamed himself. After the stroke that had left her virtually paralysed, his wife, Francoise, had pleaded with them both to help her end her misery. Monique swore on the life of her children that she hadn't given her mother the pills. Marchal had said that he didn't believe her. Who else could it have been? It wasn't him. They stood side by side, a thousand miles apart, at the funeral. In the end, Francoise had escaped, but, in doing so, she had scarred the two people in the world she had most loved.

He had dealt with the tragedy in his way, avoiding the subject with his few friends, pretending to new acquaintances that he was a confirmed bachelor. To describe himself as a widower would have been to invite enquiries on a topic he never wanted to talk about. Instead, he lived a life of comparative solitude, his leisure hours filled with the passions of classical music and the stock market. On a policeman's salary, he didn't have a big portfolio, but he loved to occupy his spare time with the research that would lead him to make his modest trades.

For Monique, the death of her mother had left her unbalanced, sometimes competent, other times totally incapable of dealing with her role as wife and, then, as mother. She had made a sort of truce with her father, but she still felt deep down that he would always see her as conspiring with Francoise behind his back and that was a heavy cross to bear, even after these ten years since their tragedy had passed.

Without realising, he had arrived at 36 and was making his way to the office, only to find that Colbert was reorganising the interview room. He had only asked if she could be available to listen in on his interview with Rosenberg, not to take control of the occasion. It added to his general feeling of discomfort. Lifted to one side was the normal interview table and in its place, a video camera on a tripod, attached to a microphone that was hooked into recording equipment on a stand. Three chairs were arranged to face each and in the centre, a tiny circular coffee table, covered by three glasses and a jug of water.

"What's all this," Marchal enquired. "Reminds me of that game where the name of a famous personage is stuck on your forehead and you have to guess who it is by asking questions of the other contestants."

"Humour me," she said with a smile. "It's just a technique we use in Lyon. If we've got time when the interview's finished, we'll play the game."

"That will really impress Arnault," he retorted.

"I heard that," came a crackled voice from the loudspeaker.

Well, well, Marchal thought. I certainly hadn't expected the big guns to be listening in on such a routine enquiry.

A self-assured looking Rosenberg smiled confidently at Marchal as he was introduced to Colbert. The objective of the interview was concerned with the suspicious death of Sebastien Bernhard. "Let me ask you," Marchal began.

"Before we get started," Colbert interrupted, causing Marchal to channel his short temper into an open stare of hostility, which she appeared to ignore by purposefully leaning forward toward Gerben. "Although you are not under arrest, we shall be filming and recording this interview."

Marchal could not believe his ears. She was, as near as damn it, reading the man his rights. Should anything come to light in the future, whatever he said today could be used in a court of law. What was she playing at? The mood of the conversation they were about to begin had immediately changed. Rosenberg became edgy. He had shifted in his chair, legs and feet pointed toward the door, neck hunched into his torso, his hand playing with the knot in his tie. "I'm here to recover my memory card," he explained. "Of course, I'll help in any way I can."

By thanking him, Marchal hoped to put him at his ease, but the glance toward him was cast with doubt. "We'll come on to the subject of your memory card in a minute, Mr Rosenberg. First, tell us about the chain of events that lead up to the conclusion of your deal with *Bien á Vous* to sell them the photos of the Prince and, especially, the part played by Mr Bernhard."

Gerben swung his body back to face Marchal and crossed his legs. He began to recount a story he had told before, changing only the detail he had discussed that previous evening with Bates.

Colbert didn't allow him to finish. "Who sold you the pictures?" she drilled at him.

Again Marchal bit his lip. What in hell's name was she up to? This was his case. She was just supposed to be sitting in.

"A client."

"Which one?"

"I'm not at liberty to disclose that information."

"Why not?"

"All my contracts with clients have confidentiality clauses written into them." He had already begun to resent the line of questioning. "Anyway," he said aggressively, "what business is it of yours?"

She ignored the question. "Who is papapicman?" she asked.

"Two, three four, five or six?"

Marchal looked confused, but Colbert pressed on. "No," she said. "Just papapicman. The one who describes himself as pope of the paparazzi."

"I don't know."

"What do you mean you don't know?" she asked with contempt in her voice.

If Marchal had to stop her, call her outside, it would be a bad sign, a signal of disunity. He didn't want that. He had to take back the initiative, gain control of the interview. "Thank you, Miss Colbert," he said, catching her eye. She stared straight back at him. "It would be helpful, Mr Rosenberg, if you could tell us as much as you can. The name does appear on Mr Bernhard's computer."

"Really? That's news to me." He stopped, putting his hands, akimbo fashion, on his hips. "What is this? Good cop, bad cop like the movies?"

Marchal shook his head, a false laugh caught in his throat. "We're just trying to get at the facts. Please bear with us."

"Okay. Okay. But what about my memory card? I need it for an important meeting."

"I promise you can have it in a minute. It's of no interest to us."

"OK. The answer is I really don't know. If you ask me about two to six, I do know, but I'm simply not at liberty to tell you. As far as the original papapicman is concerned, I genuinely don't know his or her name."

"How come?"

Gerben relaxed back into his chair. "Just over two years ago, I was struggling to make a living as a free lance journalist cum media consultant for a handful of second rate athletes and soccer players, mostly contacts made through my father. He is, or was; he's retired now, what they call a recuperative physiotherapist. When a sportsman had suffered a serious injury, dad would spend months working with them to bring them back to fitness. Very often, the nature of the injury meant they could never play at the level they had aspired to in the past."

"So you got to take them on, find work for them?"

"Yes. You work closely with someone every day, a special relationship of trust develops. Dad would suggest that I help and the person concerned normally wouldn't hesitate."

"Very interesting, I'm sure," Colbert interrupted, "but can you answer the question?"

"I'm getting there," Gerben snapped back at her.

"Go on," Marchal coaxed.

The look on Gerben's face was if he had won a round at a boxing match. "To try and develop my business, I subscribed to all the social network sites, Facebook, Twitter. You name it, I was on it. One day, I got a Tweet from a papapicman telling me he was now my follower and had an important message for me if I would become his follower so that we could exchange private messages. Normally, I avoid unsolicited approaches because it's linked to publicity or some crank who wants to see how many followers he can amass."

"But you decided to go for it?"

"I don't know why. Something about it intrigued me. Anyway, the end game was that this so called pope of the paparazzi direct messaged me with a deal. He had what he described as a dozen unseen iconic conflict photographs. He wanted me to place them with the appropriate publications. I would get fifteen percent of the deal price."

"By iconic, you mean the sort of photos like the young oriental girl running unclothed down the road or the soldier, shot, and his gun spiralling into the air?" Marchal conjured a mental picture of these terrible images.

"Yes. One was of a Saudi woman who had just been put to death by decapitation for infidelity. Her head was looking at the camera, but it wasn't attached to her body."

Colbert shook her head. "I would have remembered it, had I seen it."

"It was sold to a private collector. It never saw the light of day."

"Private collector?" She sounded horrified.

"Who knows? Maybe the Saudi authorities. Maybe the State Department. It was done through lawyers."

"And the rest?"

"A catalogue of sadism and suffering; one of a young American soldier captured by the Taliban, forced to eat pages of the bible until he was choked to death. Supposedly, it was the precursor of a revenge incident at Bagram when copies of the Qur'an were burned; others of allied soldiers who had killed or maimed themselves in order to escape their private hell."

Gerben had calculated that selling on these images would be straightforward, but without reliable providence and the name of the photographer to validate them, the task was thankless. All the major publishing houses looked upon the prints with suspicion, many suggesting that they had been digitally manipulated. In the end, he was approached by a Dubai publisher who had taken them off of his hands. It was his first contact with Benny Ram, sometime before the magnate's acquisition of *BV*. He had no idea if they had ever been published, but the price was fair, if not overgenerous and papapicman was more than happy. His share of the purchase price, Gerben had transferred to a numbered account in a Curação bank.

"You were never curious as to the identity of your benefactor?" Marchal asked.

"Curious, yes, but not to the point where it became an obsession." Gerben replied. "I soon learned that individuals like papapicman hold their anonymity dear and, besides, he began to post such glowing Tweets about my skills as an agent that I began to get enquiries from other photographers, so why should I do anything to upset him?

"You keep referring to this person as a male," Colbert observed. "You know that for a fact, do you?"

"No, I don't. It just feels more comfortable. It's not papapicwoman is it?"

"You know who the other papapicmen are?" Marchal asked.

"Of course, I've met them all. I have signed contracts with them, some using their real names, some with their pseudonyms."

"How do you contact them, always via Twitter?"

"Initially, by direct message. I then moved onto WhatsApp because the messages are encrypted and with all this surveillance business." The explanation tailed off. "You know what I mean. Anyway, I agreed with papapicman that I would use his name and simply put a number from two onwards after it. So after him, my next client is hashtag papapicman2 and so on."

"All with offshore numbered bank accounts?"

"Correct." Gerben pushed his chair back slightly, crossing his legs as he did so.

"But it was the original papapicman who sent you the

memory card with the photos of Prince Arthur? How did he get it to you?"

"It was posted through my letterbox at home in a padded envelope. And, as you're about to ask, no letter, no address on the envelope, just a pre-advice on WhatsApp for me to expect it." Gerben was beginning to tire of the inquisition. "You now know as much as I do. Can I have it back now? It's important. I need to get to a meeting."

Marchal would keep him waiting. He needed just one more piece of information. He referred to a copy of the pathologist's report on Bernhard's death which was balanced precariously on his lap. There was a thermal burn, one or two days old on the back of the dead man's right hand. Could Mr Rosenberg cast any light on this injury?

"Yes. It was on Sunday," he replied. "The *BV* cover was nearly finished. Chantelle, that's Miss Dubois, brought us both a lemon tea. Some of it was about to spill onto Bernhard's computer, so he instinctively put his hand in the way. It was a nasty scald. I took him to the bathroom to apply some anti-burn cream. He was OK afterwards."

Marchal nodded. "Well, I've got some bad news for you," he said. "This SD card we found in Madame Lafayette's possessions is blank. It's never been used."

"What do you mean blank?" Gerben's voice was raised as he began to make a series of wild accusations of police interference and tampering with the evidence. He looked all the time at Marchal, his eyes never leaving the policeman's face.

"Before you go, Mr Rosenberg, there's something I want you to think about?" Marchal deliberately spoke slowly.

"Hurry up. I need to consult my lawyers."

"Before you get carried away, think about the possibility that you've been set up as a decoy, a patsy as the Americans would call it." He had Rosenberg's attention. "Let's imagine that while you were helping Bernhard in the bathroom, the memory card was switched.

Could this so called accident be collusion, planned because they knew that you would be followed, possibly assaulted and tortured to recover what, based on your description, is a truly damning piece of evidence. The people after you sound ruthless."

"Yes, so ruthless, that you let him walk out of the hospital without a by your leave." Gerben was indignant.

"Nevertheless, I mean what I say. They are as callous as the people you are in bed with. The original card is still out there somewhere and your head is the only one above the parapet. I should take care if I were you."

Gerben was on his feet, making toward the door. "I'll do that, Capitaine." He scurried out.

Marchal's initial reaction was to ignore Arnault's entry into the room, turning directly to address Colbert. "What was all that about, Patricia, the setup in here, the need to boss the interview, the quasi caution and the Miss Angry approach to the witness? And that's what he is, remember, a witness, not a suspect. So, explain yourself!"

Arnault motioned for him to sit. "Calm down, René. Miss Colbert was working under my specific instructions without any autonomy. Tell us what your conclusions are, Patricia, would you?"

She held Marchal's angry stare. "I'm just starting my second day in this job, so I think you'll agree, Capitaine, that I don't owe you any allegiance or trust based on the time we've shared together?"

"None whatsoever, but you seem more interested in my case than the pile of files on your desk. Perhaps you'd be better off getting on with your work and leaving me to my own devices."

"And what would they be?" Arnault asked.

"What's that supposed to mean?"

"Let's hear out Miss Colbert, please."

"The Commandant asked me to do a study of Mr Rosenberg's nonverbal communications, the postures and attitudes we strike in our limbic brain, based on our spontaneous reactions. That's one of the reasons, I asked for the table to be removed."

"I don't get it."

She pointed to it. "Look. It's a barrier between us. It offers him cover and protection. Take it away and I can watch the legs and feet, areas of our bodies that never lie. For millions of years, they have reacted faster than our limbic brains, helping us to manoeuvre, escape and survive. Without uttering a word, you can gain an appreciation of why the legs and feet are such good gauges of people's true sentiments and intentions."

"Even so, it seemed to involve a fair amount of you talking, as I recall."

"I wouldn't be able to comment on his stress reactions or his comfort zone unless I could establish his baseline behaviour, a sort of starting position from which he would deviate one way or the other. Our prehistoric limbic legacy works on the three "f" principals, freeze, flight and fight."

Marchal could tell that Arnault's impatience was overriding his attempt to be a tolerant and interested listener. "Can we cut out the jargon, Patricia and go straight to the conclusions."

Colbert gave a mildly patronising smile. "When I started to come on heavy, Mr Rosenberg froze, turning his knees and feet toward the door, a sure sign he did not want to be here. But flight was out of the question, so he had no option, but to stay and fight."

"To what end?"

"On all the occasions I spoke with him, his reaction was to deny me entry into his world, either by ventral denial, leg adjustments, torso shielding, leaning back. You name it, he isolated me totally."

"You mean he didn't like you?" Marchal joked. "You can hardly blame him. You weren't exactly trying to win him over."

"You're missing my point. Not liking me is one thing, but his whole approach was as if he was trying to hide something from me."

"Such as?"

"I've no idea, but he wasn't the same with you."

"Well, with all due respect, I was trying to get information from him, not suppress it."

She shook her head. "You were still a policeman, interrogating him for all that, yet his attitude to you was almost welcoming."

"Welcoming?" Arnault queried.

"Territorially, he was more expansive, at ease, drawing the Capitaine into a relationship that was symbolic of a courtship."

"As far as I can see," Marchal protested, "you're forming a number of conclusions from very flimsy evidence. I'd be careful, if I were you."

"Like I say," she replied. "I'm giving you an expert opinion, not hard evidence. The movement between you, the orienting reflexes that draw us closer, the shoe play, were all more closely related to the harmony of a new relationship, a conspiracy, for want of a better expression."

It was the turn for Marchal to shake his head. "I'm sorry, Patricia, I just see this all as so much bullshit. Are you seriously telling me that by crossing my legs in his direction, you can decide that I'm colluding with the man? Maybe, I just wanted a pee!"

Arnault held up the palm of his hand. "You know, René, these skills which Miss Colbert has acquired are tried and tested over many years in the States. Let's not pooh-pooh them out of hand. You raised an hypothesis with Rosenberg as to what had happened to the memory chip. Let me present you with another, based on a fact which you are, seemingly, as yet, unaware."

Marchal creased his brow, but said nothing.

"I have reliable information that last night, Rosenberg handed over the actual memory card, or whatever you call it, to a firm of lawyers acting for the British Royal family in exchange for a payment of six million pounds."

Colbert whistled in amazement. There was no reaction from Marchal.

"Let's assume for a moment, that the card you came

across in Madame Lafayette's belongings was, in fact, the real one. You do a deal with Rosenberg and hand him the card in exchange for a part of the consideration. A new card is then acquired, made to look like the real thing and handed in for forensic examination. Of course, there's nothing on it. Equally plausible, I'll think you'll agree."

"Are you suggesting I'm corrupt?" Marchal could hardly believe his ears. "After thirty five years in the force, you're accusing me?"

"It's not an accusation, it's a possible explanation. After all, how did Rosenberg get the real card back? He certainly didn't risk coming into the hospital to find something he already had."

"This is incredible."

"You're days away from retirement. Perhaps the sudden realisation that your pension won't stretch to meet all those expenses is coming home to you. Opportunism reared its head. It won't be the first time."

Marchal reached for his coat as he stood up. "Listen, Commandant, all I've heard in the last hour is nothing but crap. I don't think I want to hear anymore and there's work to do. So, if you'll excuse me."

"One more thing, René. I'll have to present my findings on this to the internal investigative brigade. You'll have questions to answer. I'm sorry, but it's out of my hands."

Marchal stopped in his tracks. "Why didn't you prompt her to ask Rosenberg how he came to have the real memory card when you had the opportunity?"

"I will ask him. Don't worry." Arnault gave one of his false smiles. "Plenty of time and we need to make sure we get all the facts first, don't we?"

Twenty seven - @papapicman3

The wind was beginning to blow in from the lake, the water choppy, breaking hard onto the shoreline. On a clear day, the man could look across Lake Annecy from his cabin to the outskirts of the town. Today, the cloud had descended, dark, threatening, blotting out the landscape. There was an eerie silence, broken only by the sound of his young son, giggling uncontrollably, a sure sign that his wife was tickling the little mite as she bathed him. The mobile vibrated intermittently in the pocket of his blue overalls, a message, not a call. He climbed down the stepladder he had been using to fix the curtain rail, thumbed the tactile screen and read the message. DM@ GerbenRosenberg. Strange. They had now moved over to a new, more secure message system. This had come through on the old Twitter arrangement. Anyway, at last that overpaid agent of his was coming up with something useful.

"Have you fixed it?" his wife asked.

The man known to his wife and nearest and dearest as Andy, short for Andreion, but to the rest of the world as La Foglia, told her it would take a few more minutes as he keyed into the related mail account. The hashtag was @papapicman3 and he was number three. How many more were there? So far, he had exchanged messages with colleagues up to number six. DM or Direct Message is a confidential Tweet between two Tweeters who follow each other and his told him, in summary, that the one person he was really after would be at a GPS grid reference, arriving at four that afternoon. 'Look for the red hat', said the message. A little more research pinpointed the location as a private clinic just to the north-east of Geneva. It could only mean plastic surgery. This time he had the little tart just where he wanted her.

Five years ago, she had been a starlet. Now, she was an established actress. Way back then, he had made his mistake. He had really lusted after her. His offer had been to delete the image of that drunken scene in the nightclub in exchange for a blow job. Let's have a few drinks she had said. Then, he was sitting on a chair, his trousers and pants around his ankles, his hands loosely tied behind his back. She had tossed her head back as if she was about to come on to him when the laughing started. "I've only got my reading glasses," she had said. "I'd need a magnifying glass to see that pathetic little dick." The flash of light from her mobile and his fears were realised. She had told him to piss off and called him an arsehole. If his picture of her ever came to be published, she would make sure his wife had a framed memento of her loving husband to put on her bedside table. Neither photo had ever seen the light of day.

Today, revenge would finally be his. In his mind's eye, he could just see those pouting lips. These days, she told the world through her syndicated newspaper columns just how important was the natural look. Cosmetic surgery was for the birds, she was quoted as saying. Well, it seemed that a little nip and tuck was now needed to protect that natural look. He looked up at the clock. It would take him about ninety minutes to do the sixty odd kilometres from Annecy to Thonon-les-bains, another hour say, to find the right spot.

Still time to fix the curtain rail. "I'll finish up and then I've got a job to do," he called out to his wife. The toddler was still giggling.

More out of habit than necessity, he checked that his case was by the door. The camera and the lenses were probably worth almost as much as the mortgage left to pay on the cabin. A couple of good quality images today and he would probably be able to clear it.

They called him La Foglia, the Leaf, for two reasons. One, he was famous for taking his best exclusives from positions in trees or amongst the undergrowth. He also had a sixth sense for being in the right place at the right time. *Mangiarfe la foglia* was Italian slang for "smell a rat." Today, the tip off had come from someone else. He hadn't needed to use his rodent-like intuition.

Twenty eight - #GENEVA

"She's on the move. Let's get going." He held the door open as Lewis raced back to the car. "There's a taxi waiting for her. Hurry," Maxwell urged.

Chantelle emerged from the apartment, dressed in a long fawn coat, a bright red scarf around her neck and a matching wide-brimmed hat to shield her from the unseasonably chill wind.

"She's got a slight limp," Lewis observed. "Hardly surprising with those ridiculous stiletto heels she's wearing." The taxi pulled away from the curb, signalling left at the junction. Maxwell eased the Mercedes into the traffic flow.

The taxi made its way direct to the Gare de Paris. "Get out and follow her," Maxwell ordered. "I'll park the car."

"What if she plans to get on a train? What do I do?"

"It's a pretty good assumption that if she's come to a railway station, she either plans to meet someone or get on a train. Our orders are to shadow her movements. Buy two tickets to wherever she's going."

"What about Rosenberg?"

"He's with the police. Could be hours in there with them. Let's just stick with Dubois."

Ten minutes later, Maxwell caught up with his partner waiting in the main concourse. "Where is she?" he asked.

"She went over to check the time of the express to Geneva, then doubled back to the toilets. She's still in there."

"Tickets?"

"Checked with the guard. Unreserved seats, we can pay on the train. Have you any idea how much it costs? There and back, it's almost a bloody month's salary!"

"Never been on the TGV," Maxwell muttered. "Supposed to be quite an experience. How long does it take?"

"About three and a half hours according to the guard. There she is!"

They weaved in and out of the crowd, never losing sight of the red hat. The train was busy. Plenty of people seemed to be able to afford a month's salary!

"Her limp seems to be getting worse," Lewis remarked. They found two seats in the adjoining carriage to where she sat. Through the glass door, Maxwell strained to catch sight of her.

"This should be fun," Maxwell said.

Five minutes after the sleek looking train had pulled away from the platform, Chantelle Dubois emerged from the station toilets dressed in a blue anorak and baseball cap. She checked the message on her mobile. Things were going to plan. She would go to the apartment and change, ready for the editorial staff publication meeting at *BV* that would finalise the content for next week's edition. It would occupy most of the day. Later, she intended to shop for a suitable conservative-looking black dress. Tomorrow was Sebastien's funeral. She had agreed to read the eulogy.

As the TGV slowed approaching its destination, Maxwell was like a child with a new toy. He was studying the second hand on his watch. "Can you believe it?" he asked, to no one in particular.

"Believe what?" Lewis was fed up. Just another train ride, except in this case, you went so fast, you couldn't see very much.

"We've arrived dead on time. That's incredible."

It was close to two o clock. Lewis was hungry and punctuality wasn't of any interest to his more pressing needs. "She's on the move," he said, urging his companion to change his mental gear.

"We've travelled over two hundred and fifty miles in just over two hundred minutes. Get a grip on it, British Rail. This is the real world."

"She's heading for the taxi rank. What shall we do?" Lewis was not paid to make decisions.

"We make the next cabby's day by getting in his taxi and saying "follow that cab". Come on."

The two taxis threaded their way out of the city centre towards Vernier, joining the N1 northwards toward the airport. Lewis nudged his companion, silently urging him to look at the taximeter which was clicking up as if the mechanism had gone haywire.

Seven kilometres beyond the airport, the first taxi left the motorway, heading in the direction of the Forest of Macheter, where it finally turned into a private driveway.

Maxwell told the taxi driver to stop at the entrance. "What's up there?" he asked.

"It's a clinic," the taxi driver replied. He pulled the skin at the side of his eyes toward his ears. "It's where you go if you want that younger look. But you need plenty of this." He rubbed his thumb and index finger together.

Fifteen minutes later, the taxi with the lady in the red hat reappeared down the driveway and headed back toward Geneva city centre.

They finally stopped at the entry to La Rue de La Confederation. The red hat bobbed up and down amongst the bustling crowd of shoppers until the Confederation Shopping Mall, where she entered the external elevator. Maxwell watched her alight at the second floor. The floor plan showed that there were two offices at the end of the building. His calculated guess was proved right. As he glanced through the glass door, he could see her sitting in the reception area of the Swiss headquarters of *Hello Europe*, the magazine chain.

There was a terrace café on the floor below that gave an unobstructed view of the elevator entrance. "Let's eat," Maxwell said. "I'm famished. Aren't you hungry?"

"I thought you'd never bloody ask," Lewis replied. "It's way past four."

"Waste of time, all this," Maxwell reflected. "We should be back in the UK on protection duties, not swanning around watching somebody who's not important anymore." He looked down at the menu. "Jesus!" he exclaimed. "Have you seen the prices they charge for a toasted sandwich in this city?"

Twenty nine - @papapicman3

There was exactly an hour to go before his target was due to show up at the clinic. La Foglia had timed everything to perfection. Let's hope that Rosenberg had got his facts right. He was normally reliable, but this time he really wanted his agent to be on the ball. How desperate was he to nail the bitch? Answer; beyond words.

There was a small rise overlooking the double door entrance to the clinic, which he calculated was about eighty metres away. He had selected a small copse, situated at the highest point, an ideal distance to get a really nitid image with the 70-200mm Nikkon lens he lovingly removed from the sculpted black foam inset in the metal case. It was his favourite and most reliable piece of kit. At slow shutter speeds, the image stabilization and vibration reduction gave the professional photographer a consistently reliable result. With loving care, he locked the lens into position, adjusting the focus to bring the clinic into view.

La Foglia had a lean, wiry physique, conditioned by regular gym work, his reaction time fine tuned by practice on the squash court. True, since the baby had been born, his obsession for physical fitness had given way somewhat to the new all-consuming passion of fatherhood. Little, adorable Samuel was now the only person in the world he really cared about. To honour and cherish had been the marriage vows to which he could honestly say he had always been faithful. To love until death was one commitment he could not pledge to Madeleine.

Less than ten minutes to go. Time to put on the green balaclava that would hide his unruly mop of hair and for one final check of the camera settings. Everything was ready.

She was early. A taxi pulled up in front of the main entrance to the clinic. Through the viewfinder, he could see a woman in the back seat wearing a wide brimmed red hat, which she took off and left on the seat as she got out.

161

It was the sound of a twig cracking under foot that made La Foglia swing round. The camera was still to his eye. A pair of out of focus black trousers and thick soled suede shoes filled the viewfinder. The noise against his chest was like eggs frying in fat that was too hot.

He regained consciousness with the sensation of violent pain at both ends of his body. Through the agony he was enduring, he could see that his hands were bound by plastic ties around the trunk of a tree, the side of his head smarting against the bark. Whoever it was had a black stocking over their head. The school compass was closed with a red stain on its two tips. He tried to clear his eyes. Streams of blood were running down the side of his nose. The compass dug into his forehead, but the scream of insufferable pain was stifled by the oily rag wedged in his mouth. As he desperately tried to breathe through his nose, the blood, his blood, was being sucked into his nostrils.

Two gloved hands carefully placed the compass into a plastic bag, then into a leather coat pocket. The club hammer that took its place was crude, homemade, bound with coarse string. The victim's eyes followed the hammer. Someone had taken off his trousers and underpants. A long, thin length of tree branch was resting against his anus. This time, the utter violence of the pain that racked his body was too much. La Foglia wretched as the rag was expelled from his mouth, followed by a scream of such violence that it told the horror of his ordeal. He had a fleeting image of Samuel.

"Who?" he went to say, but a gloved hand covered his mouth.

"I'm just doing what the man said. Hunting you down like the trash you are, for all the pain and suffering you've caused." The voice stopped as the gloved hand lifted the hammer. The second blow sent the length of wood further into La Foglia's anus, rupturing his spleen and perforating the lower intestine. Blood began to seep onto the ground, forming a dark red pool. The third blow severed an artery.

"Exterminate the cause of all that misery," the voice

softly concluded.

La Foglia was barely alive, able only to turn onto his side. He watched the hammer placed into another plastic bag, as the figure retreated down the gradient. "Samuel," he called, the life ebbing fast from his body. "Samuel. Come to papa."

Thirty - #DAREK

Darek's day had been filled with wonder. The visit to Cathedral Square and the Holy Trinity may have been the intended high point of Canon Acheson's guided tour, but the young man had witnessed an amazing kaleidoscope of sights, so new and different to anything he had ever seen before that they would live in his memory until his dying day.

Yet, he had never forgotten his instructions to assimilate and learn as the Canon proudly showed him the rectangular building with its Moorish revival style horseshoe arches, so white in their purity, the reliefs all around the building, delicately picked out in the colour of mustard. This was not only the seat of the Anglican faith in Gibraltar, but the symbol of a diocese which embraced a thousand churches in a hundred countries and regulated the movement of clergy, the explanation of doctrines and the liaison with members of other faiths to promote harmony, understanding and, most definitely, brotherly love.

The Canon put his hand casually around the young man's shoulder as he led him around, explaining, in detail, the physical characteristics of the building, its artefacts and the spiritual significance they held. It was a practised, articulate and comprehensive tour which the Canon had carried out a hundred times before, but never, never with somebody he was so desperate to possess.

The touches, the glances, the actions that signalled this

flight to lust did not go unnoticed on Darek, but he pretended not to give any indication that would encourage these advances. For him, the real high point of the day was, indeed, on the highest reaches of the Rock, where the two men shared a packed lunch amidst the constant attention of a pack of Gibraltar's famous apes. So brazen and confident were these animals that they would come right up to the two men to claim food, squabbling amongst themselves for the titbits that were thrown their way. Darek wondered at the labyrinth of tunnels built into the rock to fortify the tiny enclave during the Second World War, miles of passages and cavernous chambers that served as a barrack with a fully equipped hospital and a command centre to withstand bombardment from vessels attempting to enter or leave the Mediterranean Sea. It was all so different from his world.

Back at the apartment, Darek was invited to a small office to watch as the clergyman processed the day's requests from around Europe. Most were email based and Darek, his hands resting lightly on the clergyman's shoulders, watched as he dealt with the movement of personnel from one chaplaincy to another or the referrals on religious issues up the chain to the senior deans, suffragan bishop and, occasionally, to the bishop in Canterbury.

His proximity to the young man left Acheson both nervous and excited, chain smoking, using the butt of one cigarette to light another, and his heart palpitating with the anticipation of what was to come.

Darek waited in his room, expecting the tap on the door at any moment. Acheson had unexpectedly been summoned to an ecclesiastical meeting at the dean's residence, but the noises from the lounge told Darek that he had now returned.

Acheson pushed open the door and studied the boy's slender naked body as he lay, stomach down on the bed, elbows doubled, chin in hands, reading a copy of the Q'ran propped open on the pillow.

The reprimand from the dean, founded on nothing but hearsay and innuendo, had left Acheson fuming, his stomach a tight knot. He had been treated to a bout of censorial finger waving and threats of serious repercussions. His blackened, matchstick teeth grated noisily together. How many times had he been forced to politely deny the allegations made in the letter penned by the Nicaraguan student that was waved in his face by his tormentor. He had parried every accusation with the distressed front of a victim, his answers measured, always ending with a softly spoken "Sir"; whilst all the time praying for a bolt from heaven, or hell for that matter, that would strike down the pompous old hypocrite. Now, it was his turn to exercise control.

Imagine. The young Muslim was smiling at him, but there was concern in his eyes. He was afraid and so he should be. Good. Acheson was in no mood for a civilised approach to this seduction. This was his for the taking.

As he moved further into the room, the boy backed off, the expression on his face confused as if he were asking where was the benign, well intentioned tutor who had accompanied him so considerately throughout the day. This Acheson was a bitter, angry man, out of control and uncaring.

There was no foreplay. Grabbing Darek's arms, he forced the boy onto his knees, his head level with Acheson's waist. With one hand, he released the cord of his tracksuit bottoms, the other forcing the boys head toward his distended penis. The boy's initial reaction was to arch his body backwards, tense, resisting the pressure that urged him forward. There was a mumbled incantation and then he appeared to acquiesce, his eyes squeezed tight closed as he worked the penis slowly up and down in his mouth. The rest was easy. As he felt the sensation overtake him, Acheson thrust the boy onto the bed and took him with a ferocity that released all of his tensions. Penetration was hard and fierce, every thrust causing him to gasp for breath and grunt as he forced harder and harder into the young man's body, his stale nicotine breath curdling the saliva in his mouth.

For Darek, there was no pain, no presence in this room; no participation in this senseless act. He thought of the mullahs and their wisdom; he prayed to the Prophet. He had been told what to expect and to cleanse it from his mind. It was not a consensual act. He was a victim, a victim that Allah would understand, forgive and reward.

Eventually, the rape was complete. Exhausted by his exertions, Acheson lay snoring loudly, his head twisting from side to side on the pillow as if he were trying to rid himself of some burden.

For several minutes, Darek lay in the pose of his submission, shaking nervously, gagging at the stench of urine in his mouth and the sensation of the blood that was leaking from his anus, running from his buttocks onto the bed sheet. He pulled his pyjama bottoms on tightly to stem the wound, before reaching under the bed for the ampoule and pipette he had carefully hidden earlier. His hands shook as he warmed the ampoule between his palms and then measured the sixty grams of Black Leaf 40 nicotine sulphate into the pipette. Acheson's ears were full of hair and it took several minutes to feed the droplets into his inner ear. On two occasions, the canon reacted to the introduction of the liquid by moving his head on the pillow, but he remained asleep, unaware that he would never wake again. In less than five minutes, the sulphate had been attracted to the highest concentration of water in the body, his brain, where the nicotine was absorbed into his bloodstream to fatally poison him.

Darek checked for a pulse. Satisfied, he rolled the body in a sheet, letting it fall heavily to the floor, leaving enough slack at one end so that he could drag it across the hallway back to the canon's bedroom. With every ounce of energy in his muscular body, Darek lifted the dead weight onto the bed, rolling him out of the soiled sheet to lie, as if asleep, trusting that whoever tried to wake him later would disturb the body sufficiently to compromise the scene. He carefully folded the sheet from his bed, placing it at the bottom of his suitcase. Later, far away from the property, he would dispose of it.

His alarm set for seven, Darek managed to sleep fitfully on the floor until the sun began to break above the horizon over the Costa del Sol. At the computer in the clergyman's office, he logged into the system with the password he had remembered the previous day as he had looked over the canon's shoulder. An examination of the document file revealed a host of correspondence written during the last three months. By trial and error, he found what he was looking for. The letter, personally addressed to the rector of an Anglican theological college in Canterbury, sponsored the transfer from Morocco of a young ordinand to seek approval from a selection committee of the Bishops' Advisory Panel (BAP). Acheson and the suffragan bishop had sponsored the request. Darek traced the letter as an attachment to an email and noted the terminology employed in the exchanges that led to the acceptance by the college. He copied the letter onto a USB stick, together with the address book details of the Hay on Wye centre of theology and its administrator, Geoffrey Absolom, .

Darek's next task was to use the tablet he had packed in his luggage to create an email account. Linked through the canon's wireless connection, he created a Gmail account in the name of g.acheson.dioceseineurope@gmail.com. This was as close as he could get to the canon's actual mail account which was linked to the Diocese web site as g.acheson@dioceseineurope.com.

Using the correspondence he had copied from the canon's file as a template, Darek transferred the diocese letterhead onto his tablet programme and began to write. He took out the second Maltese passport he had received from Mullah Oman before leaving, to check the correct spelling of his new identity.

The letter introduced Derek Brent, an ordinant attached to St Paul's pro-cathedral in Valetta, who had displayed significant commitment to the demands of its ordained ministry and had been thoroughly screened and recommended by both the dean and chancellor of the pro-cathedral in Malta. As there was no local Diocesan Director of Ordinands (DDO), the applicant had been directed to Gibraltar for assessment. Acheson was prolific in his praise for the young man, who had also created a very good impression with the Bishop with whom he had undergone a series of appraisal sessions.

Then came the crunch section. For personal reasons, Derek Brent was recommended for immediate transfer to Hay on Wye where the canon knew that he would be treated with care and consideration. Derek had recently suffered the tragic loss of both parents in a yachting accident and needed the intimate, sympathetic understanding of a caring rector in the person of Geoffrey Absolom to see him through these difficult times and the BAP approval process. Darek was satisfied that the coded comments would be well received at the other end. In view of the urgency of the situation, Absolom was kindly asked to give immediate approval to the transfer so that the ordinand could travel direct to the UK without having the unnecessary expense of having to first return to Malta.

Satisfied with his work, Darek appended the canon's computer signature and attached the letter to an email which was marked for urgent attention and requested a read acknowledgement. To be safe, he asked Absolom to reply to the email address shown as there were problems with the official diocese web site where incoming mail was going astray.

It was past eight before he was ready to go. His luggage now included two newly laundered and folded black cassocks that he had discovered in the canon's wardrobe, a collection of clerical collars, one with a black bib and a black poly-cotton shirt, all part of the necessary uniform of an ordinant in the Anglican Church. Neither the jacket nor trousers of a black suit fitted properly, so this he would have to buy in a day or two. Dressed casually, he collected all of his belongings and made a final visual sweep of the apartment to ensure that there was no trace of his presence. The coach would take him into Spain and the hundred and fifty kilometres along the coast to Malaga, where he would wait to finalise arrangements. With any luck, it would be mid-afternoon when the cleaner arrived before the canon's body was discovered. That was time enough.

There was only one last thing to do. Once in Spain, he would break the tablet and his broadband dongle into pieces and discard them, but right now he needed to use them one last time He accessed a Twitter account and typed one word – "Arepo".

As the Rock of Gibraltar receded into the distance, he pressed the send button.

Thirty one - @Wolf_Benjamin.Israel

Senior programmer Benjamin Wolf was sitting at his desk in the Mossad headquarters at the Glilot junction just north of Tel Aviv. A Windows screensaver was scanning across the monitor in front of him, but Benjie's mind was elsewhere. He was thinking about sex, or, to be more precise, about sex with that miraculous body of a woman who was waiting for him in their Dubai apartment. She was expensive, but, God, was she worth it? Worth every penny of his ex-oficio retainer. Just the thought was giving him a hard on. Only a week to go and they would be together.

The mobile phone vibrated in his pocket against the distended penis. There was one word on the screen – "Arepo". He reached forward for the office phone to dial his home number. He could hear the sound of at least two of his infant children bawling behind his wife's tired voice. "Everything alright?" he asked, not waiting for an answer. "Listen, I've got to work late tonight, a special assignment. I'll grab a sandwich for dinner. Don't wait up for me." He replaced the receiver. This one was a special bonus job. He would be able to buy his sex machine a lovely present.

He shook his head as he sat upright and brought the computer to life. "Let the day begin," he said.

Thirty two - @ChasBroadhurst.kp

The ten o'clock press corps staff meeting at Kensington Palace was surprisingly low key, given the fact that Prince Arthur would be making his long awaited statement to the media that afternoon. It was as if the entire world of social communication was holding its breath until the young man pleaded for forgiveness and understanding, for that was the approach that was universally expected.

"They're going to be disappointed if they expect him to fall on his sword," White observed, "He'll be contrite, but arrogance comes with the genes."

Sarah Hanson looked up at him. "I didn't expect the King to wear the part of your draft where you made him appear a commoner, a one of us, we are all in it together, sort of bonding exercise. After all, he's a Royal and all that stands for. You can't expect him to mingle as one of the crowd."

"Best he doesn't" White rejoined. "There's a federalist banner waving crowd already blocking the Mall. By the time he starts, the Met are estimating a hundred thousand plus. For all our liberal attitudes to same sex relationships, there is still a groundswell of conservatism in this country that demands the monarchy be traditional, faithful to its Anglican traditions."

Sarah had spent hour upon hour talking to journalists, editors and proprietors of a hundred publications and she was physically and mentally exhausted from the effort of mounting a rearguard action at every turn.

She sounded censorious. "We're in danger of getting

into some dead end discussion about public morality. It's something the papers have spent countless column inches on over the last twenty four hours. Arthur's sexual exploits have crystallised into two themes, one the morality issue and, two, the future of the monarchy in the light of the revelations."

"You're right, Sarah," White conceded. "It's easy to be blown off course on this one."

Sarah took advantage of the admission. "What we know right now that nobody else knows is what's in the press statement. How do we use this fact to our advantage in the hours leading up to its release?"

Rashid had said nothing up to this point. "Whatever it is, we all need to be reading off the same hymn sheet." He looked pointedly at Crichton. "Not blasting away indiscriminately at every perceived enemy, real or imagined."

"OK," White said. "Let's leak to our regular sources that what they can expect is a frank and honest admission of his sexuality, deep regret that his actions at a private gathering of like minded men was allowed to get out of hand and an apology for offending the sensibilities of so many people in this country."

"That's the "I'm a sinner part". Then what?" Sarah asked.

"He then confirms that this prankish behaviour in no way detracts from his underlying moral strengths, his total commitment to the Anglican church and his one dedicated desire to become a priest and play a full and meaningful part in both our society and the role of the Royal family going forward."

"I think that is probably an accurate reflection of his views, anyway," Crichton volunteered. "Everybody is allowed one mistake."

"And you've made yours," Rashid said, following up before his colleague could interject with, "And what happens next Monday when there's another round of salacious photos in the international press?"

White nodded. "The main impact will be in the UK as far as we are concerned. The High Court hearing applying for an injunction is later today. In France, it's on Monday. Elsewhere, I'm not up to date."

Broadhurst had been present at the meeting since it started, but other than to exchange some cursory greetings, he had remained silent, preoccupied with his own thoughts. Now, he made his presence felt. "It's like the little Dutch boy trying to put his finger in the dyke to stop the water leaking through. Every time he does, a new hole appears. Our best bet is Benny Ram. He's had quite a few conversations now with the King's equerry."

"Can he do anything once his magazine has sold on the images?" Sarah asked.

"He's a very powerful man." Broadhurst explained. "He says that he was horrified that his editor in France went ahead and purchased the goods while he was out of contact on some sortie into the desert. I'd take that tongue in cheek, but, at least, we have a cast iron guarantee that, irrespective of the outcome of the Paris court hearing, there will be no more revelations in *BV*. All further sales have been halted and he is speaking to a number of influential publishers in an attempt to buy back images already released."

"So we put our entire trust in a suspected arms dealing middleman with a dubious past?" Crichton asked.

"I'm sorry he hasn't got your impeccable pedigree, Gerald," Broadhurst replied, "but he's your best hope, believe me."

"Let's leave this topic at that," White proposed. "Whatever happens next Monday, happens and is, to a large extent, out of our control. Let's deal with it, one step at a time."

"From an international standpoint," Rashid said, "it will quickly fade. As salacious as it is, it's competing with a lot more meaty stuff on the Continent. It'll figure, but not with such prominence."

"Can we turn to the mechanics of today's press

conference?" White asked. "I expected Lambert to be with us this morning, Chas?"

It was one of the topics on Broadhurst's mind. "He's been seconded for a twenty four hour assignment. There's a low level middle-eastern dignitary in London for the day. I was asked if Lambert could take his partner, Soraya, to meet the man and show him the sights. She speaks the lingo, apparently, and the equerry doesn't want to get the Palace officially involved. It's more of a personal favour than an obligation. But, I'm up to speed with the other arrangements."

Broadhurst sighed loudly, leaning forward to rest his elbows on the table. In his briefing he explained that although the original intention had been to bring the Prince to a London venue for the statement, he would now make it in the secret location in which he had been staying since the outcry began. A small camera team was already in place. Two decoy vans would arrive at Kensington Palace and Westminster Hall virtually simultaneously and make a public display of moving in cameras and sound and lighting equipment. There would be nobody else in the room when the Prince spoke, no press or media and no opportunity for questions. A five minute statement and the transmission would revert to the studio. It was then up to White's press corps to satisfy the media feeding frenzy that would follow.

Sarah laughed.

"What do you find so funny?" Broadhurst asked.

"It's sort of like the Monarch's Christmas speech, but more raunchy," she replied.

"You've got a strange sense of humour," he said, shaking his head in disbelief.

Thirty three - @renemarchal

They were lowering Bernhard's coffin into the grave. Few

had come to witness the scene. The young man's parents stood out as two confused and bereaved souls, clinging tightly to each other, looking on almost with a disbelieving air that this tragedy could really be happening. They were certainly not Parisians. Marchal guessed they had come from some small village a world away from the chaos and confusion of his city. His heart went out to them.

Marchal's decision to attend the funeral had been a spur of the moment decision, an opportunity to get away from the office, away from the accusations and cock-eyed theories that had been levied at him. Damn Arnault and his ruthless, self-serving ambitions!

There were a few friends, contemporaries of the graphics editor and a couple of faces Marchal recognised from the images originally used by Bernhard to produce his animated sex movie. Chantelle Dubois stepped forward to speak. Her black dress was well chosen, he thought, but it hardly chimed well with the large brimmed red hat and the equally bright scarf. Maybe, she was making a statement about her employee's life as well as his parting. Her words were well chosen, sincere and respectful, never patronising, a tribute to a work colleague who was obviously more than that to her, spoken in plain and simple language. Bernhard's parents listened intently, the woman breaking down in tears as the flowers and earth were tossed onto the coffin lid. Chantelle rushed over to hug the woman, sharing her grief in an outburst of remorse that moved Marchal to wipe his eyes.

As he made his way back to the car park, Chantelle caught up with him. "I didn't expect to see you here today, Capitaine. Obviously, no suspects present."

"Policemen do have hearts as well as mere mortals," he jested. "After all, we're human too. Sometimes, our motives are not what they appear."

She put her arm through his as they walked. He must have looked at her with surprise.

"You don't mind, do you?" she said.

"Of course not. I just wasn't expecting it."

"It was what you said. It reminded me of somebody."

"I see. His parents looked so vulnerable. It's difficult when it's an only child."

"I know so well," she agreed. "The tragedy is worse whenever the parents outlive the child."

Marchal was reflective. "I think it's equally tragic whenever any family member dies suddenly, before their time. You curse God for his callous act. You curse the world for just carrying on as normal as if nothing had happened. You blame yourself. They're not meant, just outpourings of all those pent up emotions that you don't have when old people reach the end of the road and pass on."

"You seem to be speaking from personal experience?"

They had reached her car. Marchal said nothing. He released her gloved hand from his arm and put it close to his lips. "Au Revoir, Madamemoiselle," he said. "I hope we can renew our acquaintance under different circumstances." He turned and walked away.

I hope we don't, she said to herself under her breath.

Marchal had reached the main road to search for a taxi when his mobile rang.

"René?" Arnault's voice was agitated. "Do you know where Gerben Rosenberg is?"

"Of course not. Why should I?" What do you think I've done, he thought to himself, met up with him to collect my fee?

"We need to trace him urgently. The Swiss police need to speak with him."

"About what?"

"I don't know the details, but apparently there's been a murder near Geneva – some society photographer. Apparently, it's a pretty brutal affair and this Rosenberg is somehow implicated."

"I'll be right back."

"If he contacts you, get hold of him." Arnault rang off abruptly.

Marchal spat in the gutter. He was being treated by

Arnault as if he was arm in arm with Rosenberg. This had to end, and soon.

Thirty four - @GerbenRosenberg

Unlike the reception Gerben had received at their previous meeting, Mahesh Kamal seemed positively pleased to see him, collecting him from the reception area of the lawyers' office. There had barely been time for Gerben to establish that the choice of newspapers and magazines available to the visitor had not changed since his previous visit.

"I understand that last evening you successfully concluded the transaction that my client had requested?"

"With the substantial assistance of Mr Bates, I have to admit," Gerben replied.

The lawyer nodded. "I understand that the deal could not have been finalised without the intervention of Mr Ram at a crucial stage that could well have exposed him to serious repercussions."

"He seemed to have the policeman in his pocket, if that's the way it was."

Again there was a nod. "In consideration for this intervention, my client would like you to perform a small service for him that he would otherwise have allocated to a member of his staff. Regrettably, no one suitable is available."

"Suitable for what?"

"It's nothing sinister, Mr Rosenberg. It requires a reasonably good working knowledge of English. I understand you are competent."

"You can't do business across Europe like I do without speaking English, however much that pisses off us French. It's a fact of life."

"Quite so. To put it simply, Mr Ram needs you to act as a guide and mentor to accompany somebody across the Channel and into England."

"Who?"

Kamal put his hands together as if he were about to pray. "There is a young priest with special access to Prince Arthur who has been engaged to follow up on the series of photographs that you sold to Mr Ram."

"Follow up, how?"

"He is to interview the Prince, take some more, shall we say, conventional photographs that will be used as an exclusive in Mr Ram's publications to show the more human side of the man."

"Well, if he's got Royal authority to see the Prince, why do you need me?"

"That's precisely the reason. This is not an officially approved visit. It will be done with the Prince's consent, but not the Royal household. The priest will not be able to enter the place where the Prince is currently staying with any recording or photographic equipment. You will have to find a way of getting that to our man once he's inside. Do you get my drift?"

Gerben nodded. I get your drift alright, he thought. So Benny was going to infiltrate some journalist, dressed up as a priest to get cosy with the Prince and get a real life interview. This was really milking the cow dry.

Kamal went on to explain that, apart from helping to get the equipment to the priest, Gerben was needed to provide an aspect of reality to the assignment. Gerben would pose as a close friend of the family, keen to feel assured that the place where his young charge would be staying was safe and secure. "You'll have to fuss around, ostensibly preoccupied that as this young priest had recently lost his parents in a tragic boating accident, as his only close ally, you're concerned that he's in good hands."

"Where is this place?"

"It's somewhere in England. I'm not privy to the information. The security will be tight because of the Prince's presence. It needs somebody who can be trusted. That's why Mr Ram has selected you."

"How do I get the equipment?"

"You'll be staying at a local hotel. The equipment will be delivered to you. It's up to you to work out with the priest how you get it to him. It shouldn't be difficult."

Gerben sat back in his chair and crossed his legs. "OK. I guess I owe Benny a favour for helping me out. Just let me know when and where and I'll pack my things and go."

"That's the problem, I'm afraid. It has to be immediate," Kamal insisted. "You need to travel right now, today, to a hotel in Calais that's booked for you. The priest will arrive tomorrow morning and your journey will begin."

"But I need to go home and pack," Gerben protested.

"That would be unwise. Your home is under surveillance by the British authorities. You may think once the deal was done, that everything was finished. That's not the case."

"No?"

"There are men on the Royal payroll who would like to interrogate you, to satisfy themselves as to the providence of the photographs they have just purchased and to ensure that no further copies exist."

"But they've done all that."

"Legally, perhaps. But there are elements that would like some, shall we say, physical reassurance."

"You're joking!"

"Far from it. Look!" Kamal's conciliatory attitude hardened. "Mr Ram has paid you a lot of money. You're a rich man. Buy a suitcase, toiletries and some new clothes and get out of circulation for a few days. Nobody, not even close family, must know of your whereabouts. By the time you come back, this whole business will have blown over and you'll be in the clear."

The conversation meandered on for another few minutes, but Gerben had been convinced. It wasn't such a bad idea after all. A few days holiday in England, doing nothing. Time to recharge the batteries.

"Just one last thing," Kamal said. "Don't try and contact me or Miss Dubois until you come back. She is also under surveillance and Mr Ram is convinced that her phone has been tapped. It's just a precaution."

The sun had appeared from between the clouds. Gerben stood in front of a large Printemps department store, taking stock of the situation. It was years since he had gone on a spending spree. There was a nice mohair suit in the window that caught his eye. He tapped the spare tyre around his midriff. Bound to have my size, he thought to himself, as he made his way through the crowds into the store. He hadn't even looked at the price.

Thirty five - @terencehemmings_gbwy

There was something vaguely off-putting about doing what he was doing right at that moment whilst, at the same time, watching on his portable TV, as Prince Arthur picked his way through the minefield of the text he had to present to the world. Terence Hemmings had a large basement under the fine detached house in Weybridge where he lived. It was his private quarters, barred to even his wife, where he could retreat to prepare his sermons, deal with the confidential business of Synergy and generally communicate and correspond with whomever he chose to without fear of interruption. When he descended the stairs and locked the door, it was only via an intercom system that he could be contacted from the living area of the property.

The two bibles, or, at least, the appearance of two bibles sat on the table in front of him. He was nearly finished.

Whoever had drafted this speech for the Prince needed shooting. The admission of his homosexuality was couched in ambiguities, a strange cocktail of confession tinged with guilt, yet strident in the right to sexual liberalism. It was designed to appeal to supporters and critics alike, yet achieved neither of these aims, leaving, in

Hemming's view, the overriding sensation that the young man was as confused about his own sexual orientation as the watching public was bound to be.

He ran his fingers over the padded, rich maroon coloured hard cover of the Revised English Bible with its white corner patterns. His attention to detail had been inspired. The spine and front cover had been carefully grafted on to a stout cardboard box with the back cover pasted to the base. Other than the initial pages of text, he had carefully shredded the rest. Into the box, he had placed a layer of carbon paper and then sealed the receiver and transmitter, placing another carbon sheet attached to a thin acrylic plaque cut to size so that it exactly covered the electronic components. Onto this flat surface he lightly spray-glued the pages of text he had reserved. Whilst it would not stand close scrutiny, to the casual observer, it looked like a common or garden hard-bound book. The carbon would, hopefully, disguise the bible's hidden content if it had to pass through an x-ray security machine.

The contrition segment of the speech was also lacking in conviction. It was as if the Prince was apologising for getting caught at it, rather than for the flagrant abuse of the stature of his birthright and his chosen vocation. He seemed to be saying, sorry for letting these damned paparazzi catch me at it. In the circumstances, it was excessive and ridiculous behaviour, but if you hadn't found me out, I'd probably be doing it again next week. Obviously, these weren't the words, simply the impression transmitted by this pseudo act of contrition. All in all, Hemmings gave the broadcast a two out of ten rating and a warrant of execution to whoever had penned the work.

The blue coloured Oxford Study Bible had received much the same treatment as the more recently published revised version, only this time, the contents had been sealed into position by a squeeze of expanded polystyrene foam. Judgement was critical. Too large an application and the foam would expand to a point where the cover would not close over it. Too little and a tell tale gap might allow the contents to loosen as the bible was handled.

Finally, he was satisfied. An hour had passed since the Prince had spoken and, on the screen, a bevy of royal commentators and hacks from Fleet Street were picking through the remains like a pack of hyenas. He picked up one of the two remotes and aimed it at the television to put it into stand-by mode. The second remote, he concealed in silver foil, padded it with carbon paper and fed the unit into a slim chocolate bar wrapper, which he carefully packed with the two bibles into a DHL printed carton, before transferring it to the motor cycle pannier he would be using when the time came.

Job done. He sat back in his recliner chair, took the mobile from his pocket and flicked through the messages until he came to the one he wanted. "Arepo", was all it said. To Hemmings, the word was a Latin hapex, used only once as the second line in the five line palindrome that was the Sator Square. Its original meaning was obscure, but in this context could be translated as 'move stealthily toward' or 'plough onward' as the poem suggested. He knew what it meant and who had sent it. Now it could be deleted.

He locked the basement door and climbed the stairs to the hallway door, which he also locked. His wife was in the lounge, her legs tucked under her body as she sat on the sofa reading a newspaper. She let the paper slide down, looking over her glasses at him and smiling. "You look concerned, darling," she said. "Something on your mind?"

"No," he lied. "I've just been watching a news story about the fighting in Iraq."

"Disturbing?" she asked.

"Yes," he said. This time, his comment was related to the subject on his mind, though nothing to do with the field of conflict he had just mentioned. "Collateral damage," he said. "I was just thinking about all the collateral damage."

"It is terrible, I know," she agreed. "All those innocent civilians."

"Yes," he repeated thoughtfully. "All those innocent civilians."

Thirty six - @renemarchal

Unexpectedly, Marchal found himself on the express to Geneva. The liaison office with the Swiss police had confirmed that the victim, Andreion Dimitrakis, was a French citizen of Cretan origin, who lived just outside Annecy. Information had been passed to the local Police Judiciaire who had contacted the man's family. In view of the circumstances, it was to be a joint investigation lead by the Swiss, who had already analysed activity on the victim's mobile phone and were keen to understand the background to an automated SMS from Twitter early yesterday morning which simply said DM@GerbenRosenberg. Arrangements were that Marchal would be met at Geneva by the investigating officer, taken to see the pathologist at the mortuary, where he would then join up with a French police officer and driven to Annecy.

They were looking at the body, partially covered by a plastic sheet and lying on a surgical table.

"It was a particularly brutal murder." The Swiss policeman was an anxious young man with thick rimmed glasses who reminded Marchal of Woody Allen. The pathologist stood aside, listening, but saying nothing. "Symbolic."

"How come?" Marchal asked.

"According to my colleague here, the victim was tasered on the chest." He lifted the sheet, indicating a slight burn mark. "Then tied to a tree until he regained consciousness." He deferred to the pathologist who deftly rolled the body onto its chest.

"A sharpened stake had been inserted into his anus," the pathologist said. "A word was scratched with a pointed instrument on his forehead. It's difficult to tell what it says because the victim must have been moving his head violently, trying to avoid the pain. It's something like 'papa', then there's an indecipherable section, and finally the number '3'."

"Maybe, it's a message," Marchal volunteered.

"A message?" the policeman queried.

"Well, I suggest, he's hardly writing it to the man he's about to kill."

"Which he did by driving the stake with a hammer or some blunt instrument into the lower intestine. No trace of the object at the scene."

Marchal asked for some detailed close-ups of the man's forehead to be wired to his office before moving outside to wait for his lift to Annecy. "What was he there for?"

The policeman shook his head. "He was a paparazzo. There's a clinic just down the slope from where he was murdered. It specialises in plastic surgery. He must have been waiting for somebody to turn up there, but, according to the administrator, nobody of any public significance was either coming or going."

"Not that they would tell you, if there was."

The Swiss looked askance at him. "I think we can be fairly confident it's a fact," he said, without any further explanation.

The ride to Annecy was slow, traffic was heavy, the French police driver talking constantly about conditions on the force, how morale needed to be improved. Marchal's head was spinning by the time they reached the lonely timber framed cabin by the lakeside.

The woman who answered the door was young, in her late twenties, clasping a baby boy to her chest. "Madame Dimitrakis," he asked, struggling to pronounce the name, at the same time as trying to reach and show her his warrant card.

She smiled at his ineptitude, her manner strangely devoid of any sign of the emotions he normally expected in such situations.

"It's Madeleine," she said, "Madeleine Savor. We were

married in a civil ceremony, but I kept my maiden name."

"Any reason?" he asked.

"Better come in," she said, standing aside and resting the toddler on the floor. The sitting room was cramped. She indicated for him to sit on a small two-seater sofa. The toddler crawled over to him, trying to raise himself by grasping at Marchal's trousers with sticky hands. His mother made no move to stop the child, leaving it to Marchal to entertain him by holding those tiny hands with two fingers and bouncing him up and down on unsteady feet.

"Andy didn't want me to," she replied. "He lived in fear that this day would come. I told Capitaine Lafarge all this."

Marchal recognised the name as the local officer who was dealing with the case. "I appreciate that it may seem unreasonable to repeat things you may have already told my colleagues, but I'm investigating the death of your husband from another angle. That's what I've come to talk to you about. You say Andy lived in fear?"

"Let's not call him Andy," she said. "Let me talk about La Foglia, because it's he who has left us. I can still feel Andy's spirit all around me."

"La Foglia?"

"The name he was known by his colleagues. Let me ask you a question, Capitaine. How would you feel if your working life was spent preying on the fallibilities of the rich, the powerful and the famous? Your job is to reduce them to the status of mere mortals, no better, no worse. How would you feel?"

Marchal pretended to be engaged with the antics of the baby, but his mind was weighing up her question. He lifted young Samuel back into her outstretched arms. "Vulnerable, I suppose, would be my answer."

"That was exactly how he felt," she said. "He was scared, scared that sometime, somewhere, one of these victims would seek revenge."

"Was that why he operated with a pseudonym?"

"La Foglia – the leaf. More people knew of him by that name than knew his real name. His speciality was to take his photos with a long distance lens whilst hidden in the undergrowth or up a tree. That's how he became to be known."

"He jealously guarded his true identity?"

"Passionately. The man I knew and love is Andy. Since we have been together, I have prepared myself for this day - the day my baby's father would not be coming home, ever again." She pretended to look out of the window towards the lake, but Marchal could see that tears were welling up in her eyes. She cradled the baby in her arms.

"I'm sorry." It was inadequate, but all he could think of to say.

"Don't be and don't give me any details of how he came to die. I can tell you've seen him, but I don't want to know."

He chose not to remind her that she would have to identify the body. "Can I ask you a few questions relevant to my investigation?"

"Go on." As if interpreting her mood, the toddler had begun to sleep in her arms, dragging hard on the soother in his mouth.

"How did La Foglia communicate with the outside world? He had a message on his mobile phone that I'm interested in tracing."

She pointed at his laptop as if it were a poisoned chalice. "Mainly, with that thing. I never took any interest in La Foglia's work. Andy would be here one minute and the next, La Foglia would tell me he had to go somewhere, to travel, maybe a day, maybe a week. I never knew. I never asked. I never wanted to ask."

He reached for the laptop, switching it on, looking closely at her as he waited for the operating system to load. "Do you mind?" he asked.

She appeared disinterested, "He used an email account and Twitter, as far as I can recall."

"And the passwords?"

"No idea. Not a clue."

He logged into the Twitter home page. "Any educated guesses?" he asked.

She looked down at the sleeping child. "When this little fellow came along, his life changed. From being a self-centred egotist, he was transformed into an adoring and giving father, a family man who wanted only to nurture us. I guess that 'Samuel' is a word that would figure large in his mind when setting or changing passwords."

It took less than five minutes. The boy's name in small letters plus his birth date opened the Twitter account @papapicman3. The original password to his email account must have been his wife's name. The current unlock was 'MadeleineetSamuel'.

Most of the activity on the Twitter account was in the form of Direct Messages. There must have been around thirty in the data box. The most recent was from @GerbenRosenberg directing him to a certain person at a grid reference which he guessed was where the body was discovered. He made a note of the time the message had been sent. There were around six other messages he needed to look at more closely, but now was not the right time. The mail account was largely general organisational matters as far as Marchal could tell, but, it too, demanded closer examination than was appropriate on this particular occasion.

"The other policeman said that some people from his forensic department would pass by to pick up the laptop and other stuff later today," she volunteered. "You can take it with you if you want."

Guessing that a small army was on its way to go through the cabin with a fine toothcomb, he declined, saying that he didn't want to get in the way of the murder investigation. His investigation was on a specific aspect.

"The look on your face suggests you've found out what you wanted to know. Is it something you can share with me?"

Marchal didn't see why not. "Do you know who

Gerben Rosenberg is?"

"Yes. La Foglia's agent. We met at a cocktail party for some magazine launch when I was pregnant."

"I want to understand if he's involved in La Foglia's movements today. Did you get on?"

"As far as I can recall, he was a portly little man whose eyes were about level with my breasts which he seemed to study for most of the time the three of us talked. It was mainly business stuff, but he was charming enough. Again, it was La Foglia's business. Nothing to do with me."

"You don't seem to approve of your husband's choice of career?"

"Approve, disapprove; it was what allowed us to live in relative comfort. My lovely Andy would have been happy with a shop in Annecy taking passport and wedding photos, pictures of babies, that sort of thing."

"And La Foglia?"

"He was a greedy parasite with an insatiable desire to wound and maim. I can't feel sorry that he's dead."

Her final words rang in Marchal's head as the driver took him back into the centre of Annecy and a meeting with his colleague who was handling the case. Madeleine had divided her partner into two different men, a sort of mild schizophrenia that had enabled her to protect her emotions from the tragedy that she had just suffered. God help her when it passed.

"Are you alright?"

"Sorry?" Marchal replied.

"I said we've arrived," the driver said impatiently.

Capitaine Lafarge met him in reception. They were contemporaries with Marchal the older, he guessed, by around two or three years. The conversation was relaxed. They were on the same wave length. Lafarge was working on the likely theory of a revenge killing, trying to piece together the identities of the celebrities whom La Foglia had photographed over the last few years. He would be grateful if Marchal could follow up this aspect through the agent, Rosenberg.

It was the least Marchal could do. He would be interviewing Rosenberg as soon as he got back to Paris.

"There's one other thing I would ask of you," Lafarge indicated. "Geneva police were in touch about half an hour ago."

"I met the investigating officer." Marchal saw a mental picture of Woody Allen rather than the man he had talked with.

"They've collected all the CCTV images from the airport and train stations for the twenty four hours preceding the murder. They've come up with a couple of characters on FIRST which were filed by somebody in your office a couple of days earlier, name of Peltier."

FIRST was an acronym for Facial Identification Recognition Software Technology, a computer programme well known to the security services throughout Europe. Peltier had explained the technique to Marchal, something about a hundred measurements across a person's face completed in a nano second, whatever that was. The measurements were then collated, filed and compared to the visual image of people in a photograph. It was like a fingerprint comparison programme, but the rest of the technical detail provided with his former assistant's ardour for all things IT, had passed over Marchal's head.

Lafarge handed him a blurred copy of the photograph of Maxwell and Lewis that he had seen in his office, plus an equally blurred copy of two men striding along a station platform. Marchal recognised the man he had seen in the hospital. "You know who these two are?" Lafarge asked.

"Yes," he replied. "They're British security personnel. I can't understand it. The plot thickens."

"Geneva have asked us to pick them up and hold them for questioning. Can I leave that one with you?"

"Might be a bit tricky to hold them for any length of time, but I'll do my best." He explained why. "Ask Geneva to send me a formal request with better copies of these two prints. The more official it is, the more difficult it will be for them to evade custody."

It was past eleven by the time Marchal arrived back in his deserted office. There were several messages on the desk, but nothing concrete. No sign of Rosenberg, who appeared to have vanished into the ether, nor of Maxwell or Lewis, who were no longer on surveillance duties. General alerts had been posted for all three. If they were still in France, it was just a question of time. The Swiss authorities had already sent through to him a request to detain the two suspects, this time with digitally enhanced photographs.

There were two press cuttings which he assumed had arrived on his desk by mistake. He glanced at them, only to recall that following his visit to the American Cathedral, where he had talked with Father Richmond, he had posted the ten names of the clergymen which the priest had given him on the media report service. Anything that was recorded which matched a name would automatically find its way onto his desk. An article about opening a flower festival in Vienna and details of a television debate on euthanasia found their way rapidly into the waste bin.

There was just one more item, a note from Patricia Colbert, scribbled on his pad. Could they meet the following morning? There was something important she had to tell him.

Thirty seven - #DAREK

Darek had fretted all day. The weather in Malaga had turned overcast and threatening, matching his mood. The hotel was cold with the humidity and the bed linen felt strangely damp to the touch. It was a climate he was unused to, making him feel uncomfortable and irritable. Above all, he was impatient for a reply from Geoffrey Absolom to confirm his visit. Forbidden to use his smartphone to access the internet, he had searched long and hard to locate an internet café in the centre of town.

Three times he had returned to check the inbox of the account he had created. He didn't want to go back to the same place again. Too many visits would attract attention. Someone would remember him. There were no new messages. The Canon's body would have been found by now and logging onto his diocese mail account spelled danger, but he had no choice. He was forced to verify that Absolom had not ignored his request and emailed the canon's real mail account. If this log on did create any inconsistency as far as the time of death was concerned, it was a risk he was prepared to take. In any event, by the time it was discovered, he would be long gone.

He went downstairs, nodded an acknowledgement to the receptionist, glancing at the clock in the entrance hall as he made his way outside. Nearly eight. He hailed a taxi, asking the driver to take him somewhere that had computers with internet access.

The commercial centre on the outskirts of town was heaving with late night shoppers and cinemagoers. A multi-complex unit offered a choice of a dozen or so films, playing until past midnight, with a forecourt of tables and chairs surrounded by a vast array of restaurants and cafés, all teaming with people waiting for their movie session to begin and friends to arrive.

Darek stood in awe, his mouth open in amazement, as he watched. Never in his life had he witnessed so many people together in one place, seemingly enjoying themselves. Sure, he had taken part in mass religious demonstrations in Zanjan, supporting the Prophet against the foreign infidels who would condemn Islam, but these were angry, violent protests with people running in all directions, groups burning images and foreign flags, mass hysteria in play. The nearest he had ever come to this experience of controlled, peaceful behaviour were the gatherings outside the cafés in the main square after Friday prayers where the men would congregate and exchange stories. Here, there were more women, faces uncovered, sporting make up, smoking, laughing aloud as they joked with one another. Darek found himself compelled to watch, yet confused and just a little scared inside at the experience. A group of four girls turned to look at him and spoke amongst themselves. One of them smiled and winked at him, surely a gesture of provocation to a member of the cloth and then the sudden realisation that, to avoid appearing conspicuous, he had discarded his priest's attire for the evening in favour of casual western clothes.

He found a large bookstore with a café attached and three vacant internet positions. Nobody took any notice of him as he threaded his way through the tables to sit in front of a screen and keyboard. The Gmail account filled the screen. Still no reply from Absolom in the UK. He typed a message as the canon, apologising for his insistence, but requesting a reply to his request concerning Derek Brent. He commented on how he was feeling unwell and had to seek medical assistance, but wanted to clear up this outstanding issue beforehand.

The reply came back as he sat pondering on his next move should nothing happen. His dear friend Geoffrey Absolom was very sorry to hear that his colleague was ill, apologising for the delay in replying. It had been a busy and unusual day at the Hay on Wye premises and there had been little time for other matters. He would not go into detail now, but would call tomorrow when he hoped his friend was feeling better. Of course, Mr Brent would be welcome with open arms. Arrangements would be made for him to have a room the day after tomorrow. There were special measures in force at the centre which could delay registration about which he could not go into details but did not anticipate a problem. His closing remarks urged the canon to attend to his physical needs as quickly as possible.

Darek replied thanking him for his concern and confirming that the timing was perfectly acceptable. Mr Brent would be chaperoned to the UK by a concerned relative who would deliver him to the premises. He would sign off now and seek his doctor's assistance. He thanked his old friend profusely.

Clapping his hands loudly in satisfaction, he turned around embarrassed, only to find the girl who had smiled at him, standing directly behind his chair. "Sorry," he stammered for no good reason.

"You, English?" she asked with obvious difficulty.

"Yes."

With another engaging smile, she turned and walked away.

Had she seen what he had written? Did the question mean that she had read the exchanges on the screen? What should he do? Could he take the chance or was more drastic action called for? Before he could make up his mind, the payphone vibrated in his pocket. There was a message from Sator. 'Arepo on hold,' it said. 'Go first to Paris. You will be contacted.'

He watched the girl disappear toward the front of the bookstore. He swore in Arabic and followed her.

Thirty eight - @Wolf_Benjamin.Israel

Benjamin Wolf waited until the shift changed, watching as the positions around him were taken by the eleven to seven watch. One of the female collators looked over at him. "Working late tonight, Benjie?" she asked with a smile.

"There's a rumour they're going to pay overtime," he joked back.

"The Mossad?," she queried. "In your dreams, Benjie!" She laughed and moved to her place.

He checked around him. Through the window, the lights of Tel Aviv twinkled in the distance. Nobody was interested in him, except the close circuit television camera that monitored activity in the room. Did anybody ever look at it?

He isolated the disk segment he would use, noting its

reference position and then building the log. There were four entries in the Kidon section, otherwise known as 'the Bayonet', a group of elite operatives which dealt with clandestine information gathering ops in hostile territory. Two were simple address changes, one was moved from active to a pending MIA file. Had he met Stein? The name rang a bell. MIA - Missing In Action. That was tough, tough on the family who would feel it in their stomachs every time the doorbell rang from hereon in.

He turned his attention to the source of his next unofficial overtime reward. The screen was filled with a personal data sheet on Mishka Melman. He was classified as MBD, missing, believed dead. With a single keystroke, he was returned to the active file. His photograph was digitally removed, to be substituted by the photograph of Gerben sent to him by one of Ram's men. Some of the physical data was also changed to better match the characteristics of the new Mishka Melman.

All Kidon operatives use assumed names, sometimes up to five aliases when they were working in the field. Wolf eliminated the third alias, substituting it with Gerben Rosenberg and linking it to a family in Paris with whom he had been embedded some two years ago. His khuliya or operating partner was shown as killed in action, leaving the cross reference to the unfortunate microlight pilot who had accompanied the real Melman on his original mission.

Satisfied, Wolf amended the system date to an earlier period, created a new log for the amended data, then saved and closed the file.

The last operation was the most important and complicated of all his clandestine tasks. The current log showed all of the various amendments that had been made to the four files. He moved the disk segment to an area where the last defrag had left a suitable space. Reformatting a single disk segment was painstaking and had to be done without alerting one of the security alarm codes built into the system. Although it was an operation Wolf had perfected and done many times, it still brought beads of sweat to his brow. Finally, with the segment cleaned and as new, he returned it to its correct position and prepared a new data log showing only three changes to the files. Melman and Rosenberg were now as one seamless person. Job done.

A week from tonight and he would be in the apartment in Dubai, his pockets filled with dollar bills, making love to the only woman he had ever met who could hold him in check until it was time to come. Not tonight though. Just the thought had made him start to come in his pants.

Thirty nine - @renemarchal

The uniformed office on duty at the reception desk cocked his head toward the elevator and gave him a knowing wink. "She's already arrived," he said conspiratorially.

Marchal avoided the response that was on the tip of his tongue. It was all that these young officers had to think about, it seemed.

As it was, Colbert was already being chaperoned by a very anxious looking Arnault, who stepped briskly in front of him as he entered the office. "What the hell's going on, now?" he shouted.

Marchal sat down purposefully, neither reacting to the question nor looking at the questioner. He read the scrawled note on the pad in front of him.

"I've had some attaché from the British Embassy on the phone already," Arnault careered on. "Apparently, you've issued instructions to stop and apprehend two embassy staff as they were ready to board their plane to London this morning. What the hell do you think you're playing at René?"

"Listen," Marchal demanded. "In the first place, the order to apprehend these two men comes from a formal request issued by the Swiss authorities under the terms of our bilateral agreement. Secondly, the diplomatic status of both men is highly questionable. There's a third and a fourth very good reason, but two should be enough to keep us going for now."

"I warn you, René. You're overstepping the mark. We're on the brink of provoking an international incident. I don't propose to get caught in the middle of some wrangle between the two governments."

Marchal was dismissive. "Take it up with the Swiss authorities. Here's a copy of the paperwork." He threw a sheaf of papers across the desk.

"I will," Arnault replied angrily, conscious that his authority was being challenged. "Don't forget to make yourself available this afternoon," he said. "The Brigade of Internal Affairs will be talking to you about your recent conduct." He gave a peremptory nod of the head as he left the room.

"You certainly aren't taking any prisoners today," Colbert said, unaware of the pun. "It seems he's really got it in for you."

"It's nothing personal, believe me."

"Doesn't come over that way."

"He's a good policeman; known him most of my working life. Right now, he's obsessed with the politics of promotion. Making Commissaire is the one objective that consumes him and he doesn't want a retiring Capitaine with a few more days left to serve putting a spanner in his works."

"Can't he see you're just trying to do your job?"

Marchal looked straight at her, his eyes inquiring, seeking hers, but she avoided his stare. The way she was looking down at the ground reminded him of a naughty schoolgirl. "You wanted to talk to me about something important?"

She looked up. "It's important to me," she said. "I want to apologise."

"For what?"

"For rushing to judgement. I promised myself I would never do it, and there I was yesterday, being bullied into making a spontaneous analysis of the non-verbals during the interview with Rosenberg."

"What's different today?"

"I've had the opportunity to re-analyse the tapes of the meeting in greater detail. I was up half the night doing it."

She was seeking sympathy? He hadn't attached that much importance to her analysis anyway. His concern was more with Arnault's willingness to associate so readily with her initial assessment. "You take your work seriously. So do I."

"I know and I do. People often denigrate my speciality as a modern day fad, but it does have merit. Our bodies don't let us hide the way we feel."

"I don't denigrate your science."

"I'm not accusing, I'm repentant. When I looked at the tapes again, I changed my mind."

The office phone rang, forcing her to hold the explanation in check. Marchal lifted the receiver and listened to the anxious voice on the other end. He held his hand over the mouthpiece while he weighed up the options. "I understand the pressure you're under, Lieutenant," he said finally, "but keep them kicking their heels at the airport detention facility for another hour; then I'll send a car to bring them back here."

He listened again. This time he answered without hesitation. "I'll send a copy of the Swiss warrant by fax. It names me as the responsible officer, so it's me that calls the shots, nobody else. Is that understood?" There was a moment's silence. "Are you still there?" A brief answer. "Then stop panicking and do your job. These are dangerous men." He replaced the receiver. "You were saying?"

"Maybe now's not the right time?"

"No. Go on. Finish what you had to say."

"I am convinced that for some reason, Rosenberg believes totally that you are in collusion with him, on his side. Something has happened that has made him feel that you are an ally and his performance yesterday, because that's what it was, acting out a scenario to protect your alliance."

"Sounds as damning as you made it sound yesterday?"

"From his side, more so. However, I'm also equally convinced that you had, have," she corrected herself, "absolutely no idea that this play acting was being carried out. Your attitude was simply bent on discovering the facts and you put no nuance on your questions or the interpretation of his answers."

"Does that help me?"

"Before you came in, I told the Commandant I had reached a set of different conclusions and these would be submitted in my written report."

A young trainee lieutenant came into the room, handed Marchal a press cutting and gave Colbert the once up and down before he left. Marchal glanced at the text and dropped it onto the table.

"What was his reaction?"

"He didn't seem minimally interested. Told me that the wheels were in motion and couldn't be stopped."

Marchal gave an understanding nod, just as the phone rang again.

Forty - @ChasBroadhurst.kp

Broadhurst put the phone down. Where the fuck was Lambert when you most needed him? Another day when his number two had been seconded by the Royal household for special duties without saying a 'by your leave' or 'do you mind' to Broadhurst. It was like there was a conspiracy going on and he wasn't part of it.

"You look worried, Chas." White accepted the waved invitation to sit down.

"If you want the truth, Duncan, this whole affair is beginning to piss me off. Everybody seems to be operating in isolation. Where's the teamwork?"

"It's because we're in trouble, Chas. Over fifty thousand protesters spent an all night vigil outside the Palace. The media circus is in full force. The Prince's statement invited more questions than it answered. They're desperate for a Q&A session or for his father to make a statement on the issue. Nobody can really decide on the best course of action. Everybody is trying all the tricks in the book to find out where he's hiding out. Should we move him?"

"Under no circumstances." Broadhurst was adamant. "The current location is ideal. Let the press do all the ferreting they want. Everyone man jack of them will be concentrating on Royal properties or the possibility that we've shipped him secretly out of the Country. Business around us must carry on as normally as possible. No clues."

"I have no idea where he is, anyway," White observed.

"Ignorance is bliss, they say. Now, if you'll excuse me, I have to catch a flight to Paris in forty five minutes."

"Paris? Business or pleasure?"

"Very funny. I've got two operatives in custody at Charles de Gaulle, awaiting interrogation by the Swiss authorities."

White looked puzzled.

"I've just come off of the phone from someone called Capitaine Marchal. I thought it was still called the Sûreté, but, apparently, it's now the Police Judiciaire. I'm none the wiser after talking to him. Apparently, the Swiss have some fugitive protocol with France and they're being held under this authority."

"The Swiss? What are they being held for?"

"He wouldn't tell me. He suggested we meet face to face to resolve the matter." He stood up and reached for a raincoat. "I must dash. As a matter of fact, the only crumb of comfort is that I'm quite looking forward to getting out of this place for a few hours."

"If you need any assistance, remember to ask for our foreign press liaison man, Ata Rashid. He's pretty well in with most contacts over Europe. I'm sure France is no exception. I'll text you his mobile number."

The flight from London City Airport to Charles de Gaulle saw him arrive just before lunch. Broadhurst passed the flight musing that it was quicker to get to Paris from his office than drive from the centre of London to the home he rarely got to live in these days in the suburbs.

There was a smell of croissants and café in the terminal building which somehow told him where he was without having to look at the signs and publicity written in French all around him. It made him feel nostalgic. Not so the detention centre on the airport perimeter. The bare walls and wire cages looked about as inviting as the Battersea Dogs Home to a street mongrel.

The man who walked towards him, hand outstretched, was of similar height, although he had a slenderer frame and was probably a good thirty pounds lighter than Broadhurst. They were of an age, but the Scot guessed the other man shaded it by two or three years and was closer to retirement age. Lucky sod! What would he give for a pension right now and a cottage far away in the Highlands.

There was a smile of genuine welcome on the man's face. "Pleased to meet you," he said with that wonderful accent French people seemed to have when speaking English. "I'm Capitaine Marchal of the Police Judiciaire in Paris. I'm pleased you could come, Sergeant-Major."

"I see you've been doing your homework, Capitaine." Broadhurst returned the smile. "But Sergeant-Major was a long time ago. Now, I'm just plain Mr Broadhurst."

"I doubt there is anything plain about you, Mr Broadhurst."

The oozy compliment surprised the Scot. French charm was not a characteristic that Broadhurst regularly came across. In the circumstances, he found it more than a little disconcerting. "We have a problem," he found himself saying.

"As you say, Mr Broadhurst, we have a mutual problem. Let me explain the circumstances, both legal and factual, which have led us to detain your two colleagues."

"Before we start, Capitaine, let me commend you on your command of English."

Marchal acknowledged the compliment with a slight movement of the head. "France is a transit country, Mr Broadhurst. People from all over Europe move from one place to another by travelling through my homeland. France is not only for the French. Our attitudes are not, how do you say, fortress Britain. As your politics so justly indicate, insularity is all very well, but it does stifle understanding and the need to freely communicate with each other." He laughed. "Besides, we learn English at school."

"As we do French," Broadhurst retorted. "We just seem to forget more than you. I'm sorry. I interrupted you. Please do go on."

Marchal briefly outlined the existence of CCTV images in Geneva which showed the arrival of the two security men just two hours before the brutal murder of a member of the paparazzi in a secluded copse north east of the city centre. The victim was of French nationality which provided grounds for a joint investigation. In view of the close involvement of these two security personnel in the attempted recovery of paparazzi photographs of a certain royal personage, the Geneva police considered that with both motive and opportunity, there were grounds to question them. Marchal added that he was also anxious to interview them concerning the death of a young graphics artist in Paris.

"You are aware, Capitaine, that these two men are able to claim diplomatic privileges?"

Marchal raised his arm to show the palm of his hand. "Please, don't let us go down that avenue. We will get nowhere and, I, for one, need to know one thing – the simple truth."

"Protocol is protocol, is it not, Capitaine?"

"Look, Mr Broadhhurst, you appreciate as well as I do that if you choose this route, it will be counterproductive for both of us. The status of these two men is highly questionable."

"Why?"

"Neither have diplomatic passports, but simple letters of accreditation from your Embassy. It is more than reasonable for us to appeal to Brussels on the grounds that your government is simply attempting to aid these men in fleeing from justice. The two crimes are very serious."

"What are you proposing, Capitaine?"

"Instead of being embroiled in some diplomatic process for weeks, let's try and get to the facts. We can both be reasonable men. The Swiss police will cooperate, I am certain."

"If I go along with this suggestion and you find that my men have no charges to answer?"

"Subject to certain assurances from you, they will be free to go." Marchal held out his hand, seeking an agreement. The other man hesitated and then shook it. "I am not looking for a fight," Marchal said.

"To be honest, right now, I'm defending on so many fronts, I don't want to open up new battle lines."

Marchal shook his head, dismissing a comment he did not understand. "Did you order your men to go to Geneva?" he asked.

"Until you told me, I had no idea they had been there. The brief was simply to keep Miss Dubois and this Rosenberg character under surveillance for another day until my second in command could decide what they should do."

Maxwell and Lewis sat dejectedly in one of the interview rooms. Their reaction, hostile as Marchal entered the room, quickly changed when they saw that he was followed by Broadhurst. There was a nodded acknowledgement, but Maxwell's attempt at a smile was met with an expressionless face from his boss, who was first to speak. "The Capitaine will ask the questions. I am an observer. You are instructed to give full and truthful answers. Is that understood?"

Both men nodded.

The story unfolded. They had simply followed Miss Dubois in her striking red hat until she had gone into the publisher's offices in Geneva. They had waited and waited, but she never reappeared and, assuming that they had lost her, they returned on the train to Paris.

Marchal left the room, to return a few minutes later. "It may interest you to know, gentlemen, that Miss Dubois confirms that she does indeed possess a red hat. In fact, I saw it on her yesterday. Apparently, it's the fashion accessory of the year!"

"There. I told you so," Maxwell interrupted.

"Unfortunately for you, Miss Dubois also confirms that she spent the best part of the day you claim she was in Geneva at a meeting in her office with her publishing staff."

The two men under question looked disbelievingly at each other. "But it can't be," Maxwell claimed. "We never let her out of our sight until her destination."

Marchal appealed for silence. "Let me suggest another, more sinister scenario, than what appears to be a pure fabrication."

The room fell silent.

"You were contacted by a man known as La Foglia who had some more compromising photos of your Prince to sell. The meeting place was a deserted stretch of hillside about twenty kilometres outside Geneva. You went there, retrieved the photos and then killed the man. To cover your tracks, you made it look like a revenge killing. That has more the ring of truth, doesn't it?"

Both men protested their innocence. Maxwell stopped, asked for his wallet, from which he retrieved a white till receipt. "What time was this man killed?" he asked.

"Around four in the afternoon," Marchal replied.

"Look," he said triumphantly. "We followed the woman in a taxi for about an hour. She went to some clinic in the country, than back to the city centre, where we sat in this café in the commercial centre waiting for her to come out of an office. We spent hours and a bloody fortune in the process. Here's the taxi receipt and the bill from the café. It's got the time on it. Four forty five. Find the taxi driver and we're in the clear. As it is, your theory doesn't add up."

Marchal examined the document, but said nothing, handing it to Broadhurst who glanced casually at it. He decided to wipe the smug look off of his operatives' faces. "It's helpful, but inconclusive," he said. "Doubtless the Capitaine will ask the Swiss authorities to check out your story."

Lewis had said nothing up until this point. "At the station in Paris, I followed the woman onto the concourse whilst Maxwell parked the car. She had a slight limp. Went into the ladies toilet. Stayed there for some time. When she came out again, I said to Maxwell, didn't I?"

Maxwell nodded.

"Said what?" Marchal asked.

"I said her limp seemed to have got worse. She could have switched with somebody else in the toilet, sending us on a wild, bloody goose chase."

"Are you suggesting Miss Dubois contrived to send you to Geneva? What would be the reason for that?"

"You tell me," Lewis replied. "I'm just telling you what I saw."

Marchal decided to change tack. "This Monday past, you pretended to be French policemen and forcibly entered the apartment of Sebastien Bernhard. Correct?"

There was no hesitation from Maxwell. "Yes."

"You were overheard shouting at each other, then, Bernhard either jumped or was pushed off of his balcony?"

"We never touched him," Maxwell insisted. "All we were trying to do was put the frighteners on him to discover where the memory chip was that had the photos on it."

"So you broke up his equipment and roughed him up a bit. Is that the position?"

"No. I said we never touched him. He panicked, tried to

203

jump off his balcony to reach the balcony across the street. It looked closer than it was. He fell."

"There are wounds on the body inconsistent with the fall. There is a severe bruise from a strike to the top of his arm which dislocated his shoulder."

"Nothing to do with us," Maxwell lied. "He must have bumped into something on the way down."

Lewis looked away to one side, a movement that neither Marchal nor Broadhurst missed.

The interview progressed to the attempt by Maxwell to contrive an entry into Dubois's apartment. Again, there was a swift admission of guilt.

"How do you propose to proceed, Capitaine?" Broadhurst asked. The two men were sitting in the back of a cab on the way back to Marchal's office. There was mutual agreement that the two security employees be left to cool their heels at the detention centre until later in the day.

"Do you have a suggestion?"

"Yes. Look, can I call you something other than Capitaine? My name's Chas."

"René." They shook hands again spontaneously, as if it was a new introduction, provoking a smile on both of their faces.

"Listen, René, as far as the two earlier incidents are concerned, I would ask you to let me impose disciplinary proceedings back in the UK. I promise they won't be minimal."

"And the Geneva business?"

"That's a totally different matter. I presume you're going to report back to the Swiss investigating officer to ask him to check out their story?"

"As soon as I can. I don't see any reason for him to come to Paris to hear the same version of events."

"And if the story checks out?"

"I'll clear it with my superior, but I'm guessing we'll accept the assurances regarding your two men and ask you to get them back to where they belong as quickly as possible. It's a distraction as far as I'm concerned."

"If it does all stack up, your Miss Dubois enters the frame. Either that or it was the most amazing coincidence and my men accidentally followed a total stranger whom they confused with Miss Dubois because of the distinctive red hat."

"Unlikely."

"Quite, but not beyond the realms of possibility."

Colbert was not in the office, affording Marchal the chance to sit behind his original desk and offer Broadhurst a spare chair. The duty officer followed them into the room, apologised for the interruption, then taking Marchal to one side to whisper something to him.

"Ask him to come in," Marchal said.

"Should I go?" Broadhurst asked.

Marchal hesitated for a moment before replying. "I'd rather you stayed, if you don't mind. You might find the conversation interesting."

A figure in a black ankle length cope with the hood down shuffled into the room. Marchal could not have imagined the transformation in Deacon Richmond's appearance from the self-assured, composed cleric who had met with him two days earlier to the dishevelled figure who confronted him now. Obviously ill at ease, beads of sweat formed on the old man's forehead to run in tiny rivulets down his unshaven face, eventually disappearing under the folds of his double chin into the dog collar, soiled by the constant rubbing of his finger in an attempt to ease the irritation against his skin. The stress was apparent in his voice. "Can we talk in private?" he asked.

"Please feel free to say whatever you have to." He introduced the two men. "Mr Broadhurst is with the Royal household in London and is acquainted with the topic we discussed."

"You recall the ten names I gave you?"

"The clergy you recognised from the photos taken with the Prince in Portugal." The explanation was for Broadhurst's benefit.

"Yes. One of the most prominent was Canon Acheson from Gibraltar."

"He died yesterday from a seizure or stroke. I know. I read the radio report transcript earlier."

"It's not as simple as that, I'm afraid. The suffragan Bishop is very concerned."

"What's wrong?"

The Deacon glanced at Broadhurst before he spoke. "The day leading up to when his body was discovered, Acheson had been entertaining a young man who had flown in from Rome the previous night."

"Something unusual in that?" Marchal asked.

"No. That was one of his functions, apparently, liaising with visiting clergy and members of other faiths."

"So?"

"This young man has disappeared. He is nowhere to be found."

"Maybe, he came across the body, got scared and took flight. Who is he? Where's he from?"

"The bishop believes he was a young Islamic theology student, but he has no other details. The police have removed the Canon's computer. "

"There's one other thing you should know." He wiped his brow with the sleeve of the cope. "The bishop is beside himself. The press are bound to get hold of it."

"Which is?"

"The police have told the bishop that there is evidence of Acheson having had," he stopped momentarily, again checking Broadhurst's reaction, "unprotected anal intercourse shortly before he died."

"With this unidentified young man?"

"Presumably. Oh Dear!" He began to sob. "This whole business, the photographs you showed me, now this. The damage to the church will be incalculable. Gibraltar is the foundation of the Diocese in Europe. The credibility of our order is on trial."

Muttering "in all my years," the old man was helped by a uniformed officer to an empty side office where he could rest and regain his composure.

"I've not been privy to all these photographs," Broadhurst said. "All I've seen so far is what's been published and one other, rather revolting print, which was sent over to encourage us to pay up. What are the others like?"

"Much the same as the published ones, maybe a little more graphic. I'll show you later. I can't help but feeling that there is something else going on that we're not aware of, but which is somehow connected."

"I know what you mean, René. I get the same feeling." He stood up, stretching to push the door closed. "I can be of some help to you, if you'd let me."

"How?"

"I have a fairly regular contact with the police in Gibraltar. A number of my Royals are in the armed services and passing through Gib is something they'll do maybe three or four times a year whilst on duty or in transit back to the UK. Doug Wiley is a good friend of mine."

"A policeman?"

"Chief of police on the Rock. In the early days, we trained at Hereford together. He was SAS as well, but chose a different path when we left the service. I can try and Skype him for a video conference."

With the help of his former assistant, Marchal opted to change the venue for the call to an empty incident room in the immigration building. He didn't feel like providing a sideshow for Colbert and Arnault unless and until a French connection emerged. Peltier asked to sit in on the call.

"Chas! Good to see you." Wiley had heavy set features and an offset nose which Broadhurst explained was a memento from his rugby playing days.

"I'm calling from Paris." He briefly explained the circumstances for his visit, introduced Marchal and identified the reason for the contact. "What info can you give me on the death of this Acheson character?"

"Can I ask what your interest is?"

"Not certain at the moment. It's linked to these disclosures surrounding the Prince. Apparently, Acheson was present in Portugal. I just want to make sure there's no connection."

Wiley explained how the body had been discovered late in the afternoon by a cleaner. The canon had been a heavy smoker, but, even so, there was an exceptionally large concentration of nicotine in the body. There was no reason to expect foul play at the moment, but he wasn't going to rule it out.

"And the sexual content?"

It had taken place in another bedroom, presumably the one used by the young man. The top sheet had been removed from the bed and hadn't been found, but the mattress was severely stained. No conclusion as to whether it was aggressive consensual sex or rape, but it looked unpleasant.

"DNA?" Broadhurst asked.

"Two people, as you'd expect."

Marchal asked for the samples to be linked to the Interpol central server file system.

"Any idea who the young man is and where he went to?" Broadhurst enquired.

"Not at the moment. We're analysing the canon's computer files, but we've hit a slight snag. The Dean thought he knew the password to the email account, but, apparently, it's not the one he thought it was or it's been changed. Our lads are working on it. Shouldn't be long. We're also looking at the CCTV cameras posted at the frontier. I'll come back to you on that one."

"Anything else of interest?"

"Not really. There's nothing in the room to suggest anybody was staying there. Clean as a whistle. Plenty of finger prints, but no antecedents. There's just one thing. It may be nothing."

"Which is?"

"There was a small writing pad on the bedside table. Somebody had written a word on the missing top sheet and then scrawled it out. The indentation on the sheet underneath suggests that two words were written originally - 'A repo'. No idea what a repo is, may be short for report, nor why it was so forcibly scribbled over."

It was Peltier who came up with a possible answer five minutes after the call had terminated, with Wiley promising to keep his old friend in touch with developments and the promise of a dinner at the best restaurant in town the next time Broadhurst was in Gibraltar.

Peltier explained his discovery to Marchal who translated into English for Broadhurst's benefit. "If you treat what was written on the pad as one word, my easily excitable young colleague here has come up with a possibility through Wikipedia of a corruption of a Latin word, 'arrepo'. It is difficult for me to explain. Why don't you look it up?"

Broadhurst waited while Peltier found the Wikipedia page in English. 'Arepo' appeared on the page dedicated to the Sator Stone, a palindrome of five words carved in stone, first used shortly after the death of Jesus and found in various locations throughout Europe. The Sator Stone, which could be read from top to bottom, bottom to top and side to side could be arranged to form the word 'paternoster' or 'our father' and was probably used as a cryptic marker to denote a Christian house at a time when persecution was rife. 'Arepo' was the second word and could be translated as 'I creep stealthily toward' or 'the plough'.

"Do you see any relevance in this theory?" Broadhurst asked.

"Other than the religious context, no, but it's something to note on my incident board, which reminds me." Marchal stopped to write in his notebook. He must find the time to examine the direct messages on La Foglia's Twitter account. "papapicman3," he muttered to himself. "Do you fancy something to eat, Chas?" It's lunchtime and there's a restaurant nearby that does an inexpensive three course worker's lunch. Fancy it?"

They were on an oversized portion of a sickly sweet, but delicious, tarte tatin when Marchal's mobile burst into life. He acknowledged the call, his voice calm as he asked for the address. "I'll join you there," he said.

"Sounds like you're going to miss coffee," Broadhurst said with a smile.

"So are you. That was the colleague who's taking over from me when I retire at the end of the month. There's a suspicious death in a hotel near the Porte de Versaille in the fifteenth arrondissement. Shouldn't take more than twenty minutes to get there."

The Hotel Chartier was a two star conversion of part of a grey painted, four storey building which stretched from one corner of the block to the next. The long rectangular neon sign flashed on and off above a single plate glass doorway, behind which was a small reception desk. The whole appearance of the hotel said second rate and deteriorating fast. Uniformed police had cordoned off an area five metres either side of the doorway.

Both men were ushered into the reception area and past the public elevator where a white coated technician was minutely examining the handrail. The climb up the creaking staircase to the third floor caused Broadhurst to stop and catch his breath. Marchal hesitated alongside him at the sound of the raised voices coming from the bedroom.

"As the senior officer, I'm telling you to do as I requested." Marchal recognised Colbert's distraught voice, at the same time beckoning urgently to his companion not to make their presence known.

"Like I said, lady, this is a local crime scene and we take our orders from Courtois." Marchal recognised the growling voice as one of the old timers out of the 3rd Division that looked after the 15th Arrondissement. "Nothing personal," the man went on, "but the new recruit to 36 with a degree in mumbo-jumbo really doesn't need to tell seasoned officers how to do their job."

"This isn't a local matter, as you call it," Colbert retorted, a mixture of anger and frustration as she spoke. "We believe this to be part of a larger investigation we are currently undertaking. This gives me the authority to assume control."

Marchal chanced a quick glance inside the bedroom as the second man began to speak. The scene was almost surreal. The naked corpse, kept in place on an upright chair by the plastic ties around his wrists and neck that was forcing his balding head upwards, appeared to be a bystander to the argument.

"Give me your technical assessment, Charles." Marchal did not know the second policeman. The guttural, clipped accent suggested an Algerian background. The voice was heavy with sarcasm. "Do you consider that as the victim's knees are pointing toward the door that he was trying to get away? He began to laugh at his own remark, obviously enjoying the opportunity to take advantage of Colbert's inexperience in the field. The detective named Charles stifled the rejoinder as he recognised one of the two men now entering the room.

"Hello," said the second man. "She's sent for her dad!"

"Fuck off!" Marchal fired at him, producing his warrant card, which he obliged the man to look at closely. "Now, go and check with the fellow guests if they saw or heard anything. Also, find out who made the booking for the room and how it was paid for. And don't come back until you've wiped that stupid, fucking grin off of your face and have learned how to act your age." The men began to edge warily past him, defiant expressions their defence against the tirade. "Any problem with that?" he asked. There was no reply as they shuffled out.

"Bloody dinosaurs, Chas! I expect you've got a few in your world?"

Broadhurst laughed. "There are some parts of the force where it's like walking into Jurassic Park!"

Marchal turned his attention to Colbert. "Before we get down to business, just remember, you can expect a lot of that, especially in Paris. Show them you're in charge and that you can do your job. Then, they'll crawl back into their shells. Whatever you do, don't let them get to you like you have today or you won't last five minutes. Understand?"

She gave him a weak smile, the watery eyes on the verge of tears..

"Now, what have we got here? Where's pathology?"

"There's a trainee downstairs, dusting for prints. The rest are on their way. It's a busy day."

"Well, I suppose we don't need too much science to work this one out." Marchal walked over to the corpse. "Looks like he was tasered, tied to the chair, gagged and then when he woke up, his genitals were crudely hacked off with a knife and shoved into his mouth. The only thing we don't know is whether he died through loss of blood or whether he suffocated."

"Why do you say, when he woke up?" she asked.

"You don't have an expression like that on your face if you're unconscious, believe me. Do we know who he is?"

"His Press Photographers Association card shows him as 'Lover Boy'. The driving licence has his real name as Norberto Rizzi, an Italian. I've already spoken to somebody at this Association. He was another member of the paparazzi who specialised in intrusive bedroom photography. Most of his work was based around whose wife is sleeping with whose husband. All sex oriented stuff."

"Presumably, the symbolism intended by the murderer. What's all that about, do you think?" Marchal was pointing at the words scrawled in blood across the wall above the headboard.

"La Vengeance est douce – Vengeance is sweet," Colbert translated. "Seems pretty obvious that we're supposed to believe it was an ex-victim of Mr Lover Boy, taking his revenge."

"Maybe a false trail, maybe not. I expect you'll get somebody to check on his list of past victims. See if someone stands out from the crowd."

Marchal pulled on a latex glove, taken from the evidence case to reach for the mobile phone that lay on the bed. "Looks like our murderer was going through Lover Boy's call log," he offered as an explanation, flicking the keys to change the app. "Shit!" he read the message out loud, an advice from Twitter earlier that day that @papapicman4 had a Direct Message from @GerbenRosenberg. "If you were in any doubt before, you won't be now. We've got a serial killer on our hands , setting up Rosenberg's paparazzi clients so that he or she can take them out one by one." He dropped the phone into the evidence bag Colbert was holding out.

"Let's broaden the alert to find Rosenberg," Colbert suggested. "I'll get on to it. He's the key to what's going on here. Until we locate him, we're fishing around in the dark."

The senior pathologist strode into the room, panting for breath as he nodded his acknowledgement to Marchal. Behind him came the two detectives sent to interview the guests. There were only two people staying on the same floor and they were both out of the hotel. The receptionist had confirmed that the room had been booked through an internet agency by a Mr Rosenberg, prepaid with his credit card. With obvious distress at having witnessed the scene, the man was able to confirm that it was the victim who had collected the key to the room. He had not seen any other visitor, although, curiously enough, an envelope with a computer printed voucher relating to the reservation had been left on the counter.

"It was the Senegalese chamber maid who found the body," the second of the two detectives explained. "She had knocked on the door and, when there was no reply, made to enter the room. The door was pushed back against her before she could open it and a man's voice told her to come back later."

"Young or old?" Colbert asked.

"She said it seemed like a younger man's deep voice,

but she couldn't be sure. On reflection, she decided it sounded as though he was trying to disguise it."

"Did she see him?"

"About two minutes later. She was coming out of a bedroom down the hall when the man pushed past her trolley. Slim build, medium height, wearing a dark raincoat, lapels pulled up to hide his face. I'll get somebody to do a photofit."

Marchal had left his colleague to pursue her investigation and was standing outside the hotel building with Broadhurst, trying to hail a taxi. The light rain was getting heavier. He had asked to keep the mobile phone found on the bed, promising to get it dusted for prints before he examined it in detail.

"Do you think Rosenberg has anything to do with these murders?" Broadhurst asked. "It seems illogical."

"It's feasible that he could have left the interview with us, caught a flight to Geneva to be there on time to murder La Foglia, but he didn't leave with the attitude of somebody who was about to commit some heinous act. And where's the motive? He sets about destroying the people who pay his wages?"

"I agree, but whoever it is has access to a great deal of his private information."

"Yes. Mind you, if he is in some way involved, he's either very stupid or very clever. We need to locate him."

Forty one- @GerbenRosenberg

Gerben was bored out of his mind. He had spent the morning roaming around the town of Calais, stopping for a late breakfast of fresh croissant and homemade strawberry jam, numerous cups of coffee, followed by aimless hours browsing in shop windows. He watched as the ships, mainly cross-channel ferries, made their way in and out of the port and now he had nothing better to do than sit in the hotel lounge waiting for his charge to arrive.

He had made two sorties into his laptop. There was nothing new in his email inbox, other than the normal spam. It wasn't his practice to consult the sent mail or deleted files, nor the one liner at the top of the homepage which told him when the account had last been accessed. Had he checked into the deletions, he would have discovered confirmation of a hotel booking he had made at the Hotel Chartier in Paris and the voucher he would require to present at reception.

His Twitter account showed a dozen or so new tweets, two of which confused him. Yesterday's message from @papapicman3, simply saying 'thanks, will follow up' provoked the reply 'follow up what?" and the 'OK' this morning from @papapicman4 was rewarded with 'if that's a question, I'm fine. Anything for me to sell?'

Another tweet from @papapicman2 advised that the assignment in Cairo was finished and he would be back in Paris in two days time.

The last Tweet that had been posted was the most worrying. It was an urgent request from a new follower, @renemarchal, to contact him urgently on a very important life or death matter. Kamal had already told him that Mr Ram did not want him to have any contact with any of the authorities, especially the police, until his chaperoning assignment was complete, but, as Marchal was on Ram's payroll, did it matter? Under no circumstances was he to use his contract mobile phone, nor to take any calls on it. When he had crossed the Channel, he was to buy a pay as you go phone and SMS the number to a French number he did not recognise. Even so, it wouldn't do any harm to make a quick call to Kamal to find out what was going on.

The lawyer was angry. They had agreed that Rosenberg would remain incommunicado, that there would be no contact between them, but Gerben only wanted confirmation. It came and in no uncertain terms. No conversations or any form of contact with any policeman, friend or foe. The young man that Gerben was to accompany had been delayed. He had now left Paris and would be arriving later that evening at the agreed location. Tomorrow morning, they would proceed as planned. Understood? And, for God's sake, follow his client's instructions and destroy the mobile phone he had and the SIM card. Getting this exclusive interview was a delicate matter and would be put at risk if he didn't do as he had been instructed.

Gerben didn't like aggressive, pushy people trying to control him, especially lawyers. Scum of the earth! He especially took exception to Kamal's rude attitude. Who was he to boss Gerben about? What was all this cloak and dagger stuff? But he had bitten his tongue. He owed Benny a big favour for both getting him out of the hole with the SD card and providing a very healthy bank balance for his future needs. In a few days time, he would have repaid the debt and be long gone, forever out of Benny's clutches. Before he could switch off the mobile, the alert told him that there were twenty missed calls, all from the same Paris number, a number he didn't recognise. He shrugged. What the hell! He threw the mobile on the floor, stamping hard on it until it was in a dozen pieces. He flushed the SIM card down the toilet. He looked up at the ceiling. Happy now, Mr Ram?" he said.

Irritated, he flicked the remote to blank the TV screen. There was nothing worth watching. He thought about trying the porn channels, but you had to pay for them and he wasn't about to start wasting money.

Forty two - @ChantelleDubois

Chantelle looked around the boardroom table at the bewildered expressions on the faces of her editorial team. She sympathised with every single one of them. Sales of the last edition of *BV* had spiked at levels which the publication had not achieved since its early days of release, an amazing achievement in an economic climate where the market for printed periodicals was steadily declining. The buzz of optimism around the office these last few days had energised everybody, even with the tragic loss of Bernhard at the back of their minds.

The show had to go on and they had the ammunition to do it, but, for some hollow excuse she had been obliged to trot out, they were letting the opportunity slip through their fingers. There wouldn't even be a follow up story to last week's revelations, let alone another set of images which they all knew she had on file. Colleagues who would always engage with her, now looked away or fiddled with a piece of clothing or studied a piece of paper in front of them. Nobody looked at her. She sensed that they all recognised who was behind the decision and that it made her look just like the proprietor's puppet. It was blatantly obvious. With the possible exception of Bernhard's assistant who was enjoying the novelty of his temporary promotion, Chantelle recognised a demoralised group of individuals who felt betrayed and frustrated at working for an impotent chief executive with no editorial control. She wanted to say sorry, but the word stuck in her throat.

As they all ambled dejectedly out of the room, Chantelle stayed in her seat and motioned for Nana to close the door and stay. For a few fleeting seconds, they held hands across the table, neither saying a word, both searching for something to say that would ease the pain.

Eventually, Chantelle spoke. "I'm seething inside, you know that, don't you?"

Her hand was gripped tighter in response.

"I did everything possible to change his mind, to compromise. I even begged, implored him to let us pick up on the story for just one more week, but he was adamant to the point that he got so angry with me, I thought he was going to shout. He's never done that before."

"What could you do?"

"I could flout his bloody wishes, publish and be

217

damned, as they say," was the angry reply.

"And lose your job?"

"I know. I'm sickened by my own selfish frailties. It's all mixed up with a lot of other emotions, gratitude for what he's been to me all these years; fear, I suppose, at the repercussions if I were to flaunt his instructions."

"It'll all blow over." Nana wanted to get up and hold her lover to her, but something told her to back off and let the dust settle. They had been through a turbulent few days in their relationship since that obnoxious little paparazzi peddler had disturbed their weekend. Now, everything was back on track, but every move had to be made with caution.

"That's a platitude and you know it." It was said with a smile that said thanks for your understanding. "Over the next few weeks, we've got to brace ourselves for resignations from some of these." She motioned at the empty chairs. Nobody worth their salt wants to work for a publication where your hands are tied behind your back."

Nana stood up unsteadily, her hand resting on the table for support.

"Is it still hurting?" Chantelle asked.

"It's getting better. Every now and again I get a twinge. Paying the price for vanity, isn't it? Last time I wear high-heeled shoes like that."

"Traipsing around Geneva didn't help, I'm sure?"

"You're damn right. Whose idea was that anyway, to get those guys off of your back?" She put a finger over her lips. "Don't tell me. Let me guess. One of Benny's little schemes, I suppose?"

Chantelle just laughed; the less said the better.

Nana blew her a kiss from where she stood. "Let me go and sort out the troops. Put some heart into these demoralised souls." She closed the door behind her, leaving Chantelle alone. Normally, there would have been a queue of employees at the door wanting to clarify details before the edition was put to bed. Today, no one wanted to speak to her.

She made sure there would be no interruptions before dialling out on the mobile. "I haven't heard from you," she said. "Is everything alright?"

"Sorry, I can't really speak at the moment. I'm a bit shaken up, but I know which one it is now. By next week, it will all be over." The man sounded hoarse and out of breath.

"You sure you're alright?"

"Positive."

"Watch your back. You're in danger."

"Don't I know it," he replied

Forty three - #DAREK

The light was fading as Darek sat on the stopping service from Paris to Calais. The train shuddered as it came to a halt, carriage doors slamming as passengers disembarked at Arras. Over half way there. Another hour before he met up with this Rosenberg man. Would he want his body, as well? It seemed that everybody in this heathen western society was totally preoccupied with sex.

The meeting in Paris with the lawyer, Kamal, had been brief. The location was close to the Sorbonne in the Jardin du Luxembourg near the Medici Fountain. There were few people about on this chilly autumn day, which was just the way the lawyer wanted it. He explained that Darek would travel to England with an older companion. His protests that he was perfectly capable of travelling alone, that it wasn't necessary, were dismissed out of hand. Kamal said that Mullah Omah had told him it would look better, more natural, if Darek was accompanied to the theology college. He could be asked awkward questions which a more experienced ally could deal with. It was just a precaution. The simple mention of the Mullah's name was enough for Darek to accept the instruction without further question.

There was just one problem that had arisen. Although

he would continue to use the identity of Derek Brent, relying on his Maltese passport, for reasons of security, his fellow traveller would need a new identity. The document Darek had been given burned a hole in his pocket. It represented the symbol of everything he had been taught to hate and despise. He wanted to get rid of it. The man he would be meeting was an Israeli.

It was just after eleven when the train pulled in at Calais-Frèthun, where the majority of the remaining passengers alighted. Several stood alongside him, waiting for the courtesy coach that would take them to the hotel. His pre-booked room was next to that of the man who looked at him with a mixture of suspicion and curiosity as he opened the door. He was dishevelled, his hair uncombed and his breath smelt stale.

"You would be?" Gerben asked.

"Derek Brent," the young man replied, holding out his hand. Gerben ignored it, shut the door and fell back onto his bed, folding his hands behind his head as it rested on the pillow.

"Listen. Let's get one thing straight right from the start. I don't know who you really are and I don't want to know. You're here to do a job, to pretend to be a padre, infiltrate into wherever the Prince is staying, no doubt take compromising pictures and get some juicy quotes for publication. Right?"

Darek nodded.

"I've been hired to deliver you, the unfortunate orphan, in the guise of a close family friend, concerned about your welfare, to make sure you get inside wherever it is. I assume you know where we're going, by the way."

"We're to go to a place called Bristol. Somebody will contact us at the address I've got."

"Very cloak and dagger, isn't it? Anyway, once I've delivered you, that's me done. I'm on my way. From then on, you're on your own, sonny boy. If you get sussed, don't expect me to be around to help."

"You're a Jew, aren't you?"

Gerben hesitated, momentarily unsure that he had heard the question correctly. "What's that got to do with anything? You said that as if I was in a zoo, locked behind bars and you'd come to look."

Darek stared back, as if he had not understood the remark. "I met Mr Kamal today. He said your real identity has been compromised."

"Do what?"

"He told me that you would react angrily when I told you, but that you had to take his word for it. Both the French and British police will arrest you on sight if you produce your own passport."

"Why? I've done nothing wrong."

"He said to tell you that it must be a case of mistaken identity. He promises that Mr Bates will sort it out for you when you get back. On no account, can the timing of our operation be changed or the opportunity will be lost. He said to use this for the time being." He took the passport from his pocket, tossing it onto the bed as if it were a hot coal. "Preferably, destroy yours or, if you can't stomach that, make sure it's hidden."

Gerben reached for the blue Israeli passport with the central menorah design, flicked through the pages, stopping only to look at his photograph and the name alongside. Mishka Melman. He shook his head. "This is not on. It's all getting out of hand. Where did this photo come from? Suddenly, I've got a Zionist passport and a strange Yiddish name. This is crazy." He reached for the hotel phone, but Darek's fleet of hand restrained him. The strength in his grip belied his stature. Gerben's hand was held firmly in check.

"Mr Kamal predicted exactly what you would do. He is a very wise man. He said you could telephone this number, but only from a public phone booth away from the hotel."

There he was again, being manipulated by outside influences, He wasn't having any of it. He thrust on his shoes, pushing the young man's hand away in a gesture of defiance. "Go to your room. We'll speak tomorrow morning downstairs. Seven o'clock." Without another word, hc ushered Darek out and shuffled down the corridor, an unkempt figure of a man sporting red braces twisted over a crumpled white silk shirt, and holding up a pair of equally creased mohair trousers.

Forty four - @renemarchal

Arnault looked anxious. "Are you sure?"

"Looks like it," Marchal replied. "This latest victim has got exactly the same message on his mobile as La Foglia in Geneva, an SMS advice from Twitter of a Direct Message from Gerben Rosenberg. If we could just get to the source of the information."

"Arrest Rosenberg, you mean?"

"First, find him. He's just disappeared. I suspect he's not directly involved in either incident."

"How come?"

"My guess is that the killer is a person with a grudge against the paparazzi who has somehow got hold of information from Rosenberg to lure them to locations where they can be restrained and then brutally murdered. For all we know, Rosenberg may be being held captive somewhere and tortured for the information."

Arnault paced the two steps that available room in the office permitted, turning, pacing and turning again. "That's all I need, a serial killer appearing on my patch at this particular time."

"At any time, surely?"

The Commandant shook his head. "My detection and conviction statistics in this department are second to none. I mean to keep it that way.

"Congratulations," spoken tongue in cheek.

"Premature! If we've got unsolved murders, with a likely serial killer on the loose, then everything that's gone before will be disregarded."

"By whom?"

"Never mind." He drummed his fingers on the desk. "Has Colbert come up with anything?"

"I left her at the murder scene working with two detectives from the fifteenth. There was a partial sighting of a man leaving the room. By morning, we should have an artist's impression to circulate."

Arnault leaned across the desk, as if about to impart a confidence. "Help her out with this one, René, would you? She's wet behind the ears, all this behavioral bullshit."

"I saw you as a fan of this latest investigative science?"

"I am, I am," Arnault protested, "But when it comes to cases like this, sometimes a dose of old fashioned policing is what's needed. Now we've got shot of those two Brits." He stopped in his tracks. "Where's their boss, by the way?"

Marchal chose to ignore the phone that had started to ring. "He's on his way back from Charles de Gaulle after seeing them off on their flight. He should be here any minute. Promised to buy me a late supper."

Arnault nodded. "Now you've got the time, give Colbert some support." A mobile burst into life. "You'd better answer that."

Marchal listened to the caller, then replied in English, explaining that Mr Broadhurst was expected at any moment. "Is there something I can help you with, Inspector Wiley? It's Detective Marchal here. I participated in your conference call. Just a moment, please." He reached for the pad that Arnault had finished writing on. The note told him to make contact first thing in the morning. In block capitals, it said 'FIND ROSENBERG!' Marchal nodded as Arnault left the room.

"Go on please, Inspector Wiley," he said, turning to a fresh page.

Broadhurst was running late. They arranged to meet in a late night eaterie on the Left Bank that Marchal had used quite frequently in another life, when love and desire had been so precious to him. The memories came flooding back.

"You look tired and very pensive," Broadhurst noted.

"A mixture of old age and past associations, I guess. I used to dine here with my late wife. We'd meet up when I was late out of work, which was often the case; enjoy a conversation catching up on the day's events over a glass of wine and a *haché*." For the first time in as long as he could remember, he had surprised himself by volunteering information that told of him as a widower rather than a bachelor.

Broadhurst made no comment. "I guess it'll be two *hachés* and a big jug of red wine," he said, looking up at the waiter who had appeared at their side.

Marchal nodded in agreement. "Your friend Wiley called me while you were returning from the airport. There's a couple of interesting developments." Out of force of habit, Marchal reached for his notebook.

"Good. I've been giving this business a lot of thought, René."

"The Spanish police found the body of a young girl today, murdered in an apartment in Malaga. She'd been strangled."

"What's the connection?"

"She'd had sexual intercourse just prior to her death. As a matter of course, the DNA from the semen was filed in the Interpol database. It matches the DNA found at the scene of Canon Acheson's home on Gibraltar."

"Changes the possible cause of Acheson's death."

"Wiley said that they're profounding the autopsy, whatever that means. The other new piece of information is that they've got into the clergyman's email account. We now have a name for the young man who was visiting him." He looked down at the notebook. "His name is Darek Moradi, a theology student of Syrian origin.."

"Syria?"

"Yes. There's an exchange of emails with Acheson from a Mullah Hashen in a place called Van in Turkey. Wiley's mailing copies of the correspondence to your inbox. This Moradi is a refugee, supposedly going to Gibraltar to learn about the Anglican Church. He got a travel visa on Acheson's recommendation."

"Curious business."

"I don't know exactly where we go from here," Marchal said.

"I do. One of the press corps guys at the Palace, in fact the one who deals with the international media, has contacts in the region. His name's Ata Rashid. He must also know people in Spain. I'll get onto it. We need to know what this Moradi is up to."

"There's one more thing which makes this whole Acheson business look more suspicious."

Broadhurst took a long swig of red wine, nodding at Marchal with satisfaction as he returned to his steak. "Nothing surprises me anymore."

"According to Wiley, there are no new mails of any relevance on Acheson's account prior to or following the estimated time of death. He had a meeting earlier that evening with the Dean on the subject of a complaint of a personal nature which had been made against him."

"Any details?"

"Apparently, the Dean wasn't forthcoming, but he hinted that it was related to some issue of alleged sexual misconduct. However, around the time Acheson's body was discovered, his diocesan email account was accessed for eighteen seconds. The IP address of the enquirer was from the Malaga area."

"I have a very unpleasant sensation about this entire business, René. Just as well, I've been summonsed back to London tomorrow for a meeting with the powers that be. I can make some enquiries from my end that might be helpful." Broadhurst leaned forwards. "Any progress with the murder investigation?"

Until they parted an hour later, the conversation ranged across the day's developments, avenues to pursue and an expression of Broadhurst's gratitude and assurances concerning the release of his two operatives. "From my

225

conversations with both men, I'm convinced that they weren't involved in the murder in Geneva. But you could have made life difficult for me, René, and I won't forget it. I owe you."

If Marchal had taken any comfort from the statement, he didn't show it. "To tell you the truth, Chas." He looked straight into the other man's eyes. "If I had my way, they'd both be in custody tonight, not because I believe they were implicated in La Foglia's killing. I, too, am with you on this one."

"Then why, for God's sake, René?"

"I am certain that they were the cause of Bernhard's death. Fear of what they might do to him caused him to panic, try to reach the balcony across the street. But, because he had already been struck by one of them, he could not maintain his grip, resulting in the fall."

"Why did you release them into my custody if you consider this to be true?"

Marchal's laugh was deliberately false. "What are the words you just used, Chas, 'the powers that be'?" I also have powers that be who wanted the matter closed. Diplomatic niceties take precedence over natural justice, especially when proof is difficult. My regret is that Bernhard has disappeared into oblivion without making his mark on the world."

"And you wanted to make it for him?"

This time, the smile was genuine. "Not really. Next week, I, too, will slip into oblivion. We all have a cross to bear. So do your men."

"I've told you I will ensure that they are subject to severe disciplinary action."

"I believe you, Chas. It's not something I feel here." He pointed to his head and then lowered his hand toward his stomach. "It's here that it really gets at me."

Marchal didn't feel like going back to an empty house, a hungry cat and another glass of a rough red wine, so he turned left, striding purposefully back in the direction of his office. The walk would take fifteen minutes. It would give him time to think. He had already posted warning Tweets on all the other four papapicman accounts, asking them to contact his mobile number urgently. It was intended to serve two purposes, not only a warning to possible victims, but a message to the killer telling him he knew what was going on. He also needed access to the latest victim's Twitter account to compare it with the comments on La Foglia's page. On the spur of the moment, he rang Colbert's number. "Sorry to disturb you."

"You're not." She sounded wide awake. "As a matter of fact, I'm sitting in the office, going over the detail of what we've come up with so far."

Maybe he would have that glass of wine anyway. "Fancy a nightcap?" He named a café close to the office.

She was already seated with the remains of a glass of wine in front of her by the time he arrived. She reached over to touch his arm. "Thanks for what you did today. I guess I've got a lot to learn."

He ordered two more glasses before sitting down alongside her, a fatherly gesture more than a romantic one that caused him to put his hand on top of hers. "You have. Give yourself time. I remember when my daughter qualified as a veterinary surgeon."

"I didn't know you had a family. They said you were single."

"My wife died. Monique is an only child."

"I'm sorry."

She began to play with his hand, her fingers gently rubbing his. Whether intended or the subconsciously provoked by some thought process, either way, he decided not to withdraw his hand at that moment, but to take a different tack. Besides, he was beginning to enjoy the sensation. "Yes. Monique must be about your age," he lied. His daughter was probably five or so years younger.

The comparison made no difference. If anything, her attention to his fingers became even more intense. "When she qualified as a vet," he went on, now somehow ashamedly unembarrassed by her attention, "She thought that was it. She had nothing more to learn, she knew it all. Then, a few months or so later, when a mare died giving birth to a foal and the farmer responded angrily, questioning her competence, she began to realise that there really is no substitute for practical experience."

"I certainly felt that today," she said. "Thank God, you were there. You will go on helping me with this one, won't you?" She reached for a handkerchief, giving Marchal the opportunity to release her grip and slide his hand under the table. Jesus! At his age! She'd given him a bloody hard on!

"I let those two bastards get to me, didn't I?" she said.

"Look," he replied, silently chastising himself for a physical reaction that was putting him off of his stride. "Of course, I'll do everything I can to support you, but, remember, I won't be around for much longer."

"I came here, buoyed by a sense of false bravado. For a couple of days it worked; then the bubble burst."

"Now you feel you're not up to the job, your self confidence has evaporated and you're scared?"

Colbert nodded. "I can tell you that those two from the fifteenth who gave me such a hard time know a lot more about what they were doing than I do."

He waved his hand in the air to attract the waiter's attention for two more glasses of wine. "They were just putting you on trial. Listen, I'm no psychologist," he said, "but there's one thing that my old boss told me thirty odd years ago that's always stuck with me. Villains are callous, calculating individuals. Whatever the reason you joined the police, the fact is that the best and most successful officers are mentally just a thin blue line away from the crooks they chase. If you begin to think like a villain, more likely than not, you'll end up in the right place at the right time to secure a conviction. If you try and behave like Hercule Poirot, you'll end up in admin."

She was smiling again, the colour back in her cheeks. She took a long draft from the glass that had been put in front of her. "Were you ever tempted to cross that thin blue line?"

"Of course, Patricia." He was beginning to feel a bit heady himself. "Most every policeman will be offered a bribe from time to time, some more than others. It's all a matter of retaining your self-respect. Once you cross the line, you'll never be any good at either job, policeman or criminal."

"What about Commandant Arnault? Is he a good policeman?"

"He was. He had a snout like a bulldog for sniffing out the bad guy. Now, he's in admin, working hard on the Peter principal."

"What's that?"

"He's focussed on promotion. In a hierarchy, so the theory goes, you rise up the ladder until you reach the level of your own incompetence."

"I don't understand."

He rose unsteadily from the table, feeling for his wallet. "Arnault's one ambition is to keep rising through the ranks. As long as he can do the job, he'll keep getting promoted. When he reaches the point where he's not up to the task he's been promoted to, he won't rise any further."

"And what about you? How does that apply?"

He resisted her attempt to pay the check. Once again he was holding her hand. "I never got on the ladder. I was ambitious for other things, but they never worked out." He stopped to remember something. "That reminds me. I'll be in the office first thing, but I've got to drive up to Lille on a personal matter later in the day. Look after the fort for me while I'm away, will you?"

She nodded her agreement, giving him a big smile. "You're a nice man, René Marchal. Thanks for tonight." He turned his head sideways to receive her kiss, but somehow her moist lips managed to brush his on their way to his cheek.

"Remind you of your dad, do I?" was his defensive reaction.

"Not at all," she replied as they made their way out onto the street. "Thankfully," she added with a shy sideways look.

"Goodnight, Patricia." He turned and walked away.

Forty five - @GerbenRosenberg

Gerben awoke with a start and a sense of dread as he struggled to remember where he was. An intermittent glow pierced the darkness as the mobile vibrated on the bedside table. Half asleep, his eyes focussed on the screen and the one word message – "NOW". He let the phone fall from his hand, closed his eyes and let his head rest back on the pillow.

The cheapie mobile with the pay-as-you-go Maltese SIM card belonged to Darek, who had insisted Gerben use it if he was determined to carry out his threat to speak to someone about this ridiculous situation.

There was the sound of a murmuring voice from the boy's bedroom as he passed down the darkened corridor and a curt nod from a curious night porter as the front door to the hotel opened and a blast of cold, humid air hit him. Stupidly, he hadn't put a coat on, causing him to shiver even as he began to jog along the deserted road. In the coastal mist, all he could make out was the glow of the street lights above him. He knew where the public phone booth was as he had used it earlier that night to try and contact Chantelle. He had left a message on her answer phone, an urgent request for Benny to alert him on the young man's mobile and, then, ten minutes later to call him on the number at the booth.

Running up and down on the spot, he tried to stave off the damp chill that was permeating his body. He was about to return to the warmth of the hotel, when a shrill tone split the air.

"I'd almost given up on you," he said, a tremor in his voice as his teeth chattered together.

"That would be a mistake." Benny's voice was relaxed.

"I was just moving my breakfast onto the terrace to enjoy the morning sun."

"Lucky you! It's bloody freezing here. For God's sake what's going on? Why have I been given a Yiddish passport? What's wrong with mine?"

"Something's come up which would otherwise oblige me to change my plans and suggest you go back to Paris to sort things out, but I'm too far along the road to get this exclusive and, in truth, another day or two is not going to make any difference to your situation."

"My situation? What are you talking about?"

Benny was cryptic, the explanation cursory. It looked like two of Gerben's photographer clients had died under suspicious circumstances. There had been a brief report on the late French TV news station, but, as yet, the police had not released details.

Gerben was numb. What he was being told was impossible. Two of his clients dead? There must be some terrible mistake. "I'd better get straight back to Paris to deal with this," was his immediate reaction.

Benny's tone changed from conciliatory to ice cold. It was a terrible, unforeseen tragedy that had presented a problem, but Gerben had to fulfil his commitment to see the assignment through. It was a small window of opportunity that could not be missed. Benny would vouch for Gerben when the time came.

"I'm sorry," Gerben insisted, "but this makes no sense. You're telling me that I should give preference to some attempt to get some salacious material from a British Royal rather than assist with a serious issue that would have professional ramifications for the rest of his life. Of course, the police will want to talk to me. I want to talk to them."

"I've already spoken to my contact in the Police Judiciaire," Benny explained. "He understands you're going to be out of circulation for a couple of days and, anyway, you can't be much help other than to confirm that you were their agent. They have many other lines of enquiry."

"Even so," Gerben started to say, but was interrupted.

"Even so," Benny repeated, "this assignment I'm asking you to help with is not just about titillating the public. I am reliably informed that we will get details of past events which will have severe ramifications for the British Royal family. This is a potentially momentous story that must be brought to light."

"But,"

"But nothing! Because of me, Gerben, you are now a rich man who need never work again for the rest of his life. I expect and demand loyalty this one time. What has happened, I know, presents you with a serious dilemma, but we must go on. The men are dead. Whoever else is involved must be brought to justice. Can you really help with that? I suggest not. Do you know what assignments these men were working on?"

"No."

"Then think about what constructive help you can be to the police over the next two days. When you get back to Paris, you'll have a clearer picture in your own mind."

Reluctantly, Gerben agreed, against his better judgement, to give his word on the Torah that he would fulfil his obligation.

He walked back to the hotel without feeling the cold, without acknowledging the porter's 'hello' and without hearing the incantations that were still coming from the boy's room. His mind was in total confusion.

OK. He would go through with it. He looked at the passport. Mishka Melman. What a silly, bloody name. Sleep wouldn't come, but, at least, he had made one decision of his own. Fuck Benny's exclusive! At the earliest opportunity, he would call his contact in the police. What was the man's name? He cast his mind back to their meeting. Marchal. That was it. As soon as he got to England, he'd speak to this Marchal.

Forty six - @kuzkazin

He awoke to the sound of constant hammering on his front door. He was alone, the place on the mattress next to his cold to the touch. A glance out of the window told him that three police cars, blue lights flashing were parked strategically blocking this suburban street in Epsom. He fumbled, half asleep, for his dressing gown, making his way downstairs, but he was too late. The front door caved in under the blow from the 16kg enforcer ram. A police inspector confronted him. "Mr Lambert?"

"Yes."

"I'm arresting you on suspicion of a breach of the Official Secrets Act. You do not have to say anything." He went on to recite the man's Miranda rights.

"What the hell's going on?"

The question was ignored. "Can you call your wife, please?"

Lambert shook his head to clear it. "I don't have a wife." Two uniformed officers pushed past him, climbing the stairs two at a time. A third clamped a pair of handcuffs on him.

"Your partner, then?" the Inspector said as if the detail was irrelevant.

"I don't think Soraya's here. I didn't hear her go out. Must have been asleep." He looked past the policeman at the short driveway up to the house. "No. Her car's missing. Before you ask, I've no idea where she's gone. I don't even know if she came in last night. I was asleep." The two policemen walked back slowly down the stairs, shaking their heads.

"Can I put some clothes on, please?"

The Inspector led him by the elbow. He nodded to one of the officers. "We'll bring some along for you. You can change at West End Central." He placed his hand over Lambert's head as he ushered him into one of the police cars. Curtains twitched in the house across the street. "Check with the neighbours," he said. "See if anybody saw

233

her leave this morning."

The car pulled away as if it were leaving the starting grid of a Formula One race.

Thirty miles away in Brighton, the business day was slowly beginning to get underway as the blue Audi came to a racing stop outside of the Hotel Metropole. Badly parked across two bays, there was still too little activity for anybody to get hot under the collar at female drivers. The woman in the dark green trouser suit hurried past the doorman, through the revolving door into the lobby. Her shapely figure, aquiline features and a rush of long raven black hair turned a few male heads, but she appeared not to notice. She found the bank of internet computers in the business services lounge next to the elevators. Her hands were shaking as she tried to log on. Finally, she accessed her Twitter account and sent a Direct Message to @papapicman. All it said was 'News?'

As she tapped her fingers anxiously on the table, the reply flickered on the screen. 'As advised, your position has been compromised.'

Tears began to roll down her cheeks onto the keyboard as she typed furiously, her anxieties put into three dramatic sentences.

There was a one line response. 'In five minutes check your mobile.' The screen darkened.

Her passage back to the car was more measured, her attention alert for any sign that told her movements were being watched. Spotting the looks of admiration was easy. What she cared about was being caught. The car would be a problem. The police would be on the lookout for it, the distinctive blue colouring no longer an eye catching advantage, but a serious impediment.

The message indicator on the mobile sounded as she stayed on the minor roads back towards London. With a huge sigh of relief she reached Gatwick Airport and the long term car park where she could leave the vehicle, inconspicuous amidst thousands of others. On the courtesy bus back to the car rental desks in the terminal, she had her first opportunity to check the message. There was a set of GPS coordinates and the time, 1pm. The model of car she hired was irrelevant. All she needed was a really good sat nav system on board.

For the first time that morning, since the first message had disturbed her sleep in the middle of the night, she felt safe. It was nearly ten am. "Calm down, Soraya," she said out loud to herself. "Time for a coffee and a clear head." The GPS coordinates indicated a location close to Swindon, some seventy miles away. She plotted a scenic route, away from the motorways. Two hours would do it easily. She had never met the man. He was just a name on a Twitter account. How would she recognise him? She wouldn't. He would know what she looked like.

They must have arrested Lambert by now. Good riddance! The pretence was over. She was well shot of the arrogant bastard. By tonight, she would be out of the Country, on her way to meet the family she hadn't seen since she was a teenager in Iraq. The foamy milk on the latte bathed her lips. She would miss Starbucks.

Forty seven - @renemarchal

Marchal chose to reach the office early for a number of reasons. Another late night call from his daughter, Monique had convinced him that he should get to Lille as quickly as possible. Her marriage seemed to be coming off of the rails at an alarming speed. Where were the rational reactions and practical decisions that needed to be taken?

He also wanted to write a short report to Arnault that would close the Bernhard investigation, but making it clear that although accidental death by misadventure was the official verdict, the truth of the situation was plainly spelled out. It was his boss who would have to shoulder the burden of diplomacy before detection, though he doubted the issue would cause Arnault to lose any sleep.

Nevertheless, having it put on the record would not be popular, but Marchal had come to the conclusion that he didn't give a shit anyway.

There was also the issue of Dubois and the red-hatted lady in Geneva. Under normal circumstances, the assignment would have been given to someone of Peltier's status to follow up, but Marchal had been cast adrift from the hierarchy at the 36, leaving him to tie up all these loose ends on his own. He made a note to speak to Dubois the following day.

Putting these chores to one side, the real reason he had opted for an early start was to avoid bumping into Patricia. Frankly, her attentions the previous evening had roused feelings in him that he had not experienced for some years. The fact that she was young enough to be his daughter put him into the dirty old man category, unvarnished animal lust or was that overstating it? Whatever, he didn't want to put his embarrassment on show, so he restricted his hastily scribbled note to some suggestions on how she could pursue the murder investigation she was handling, with a request that she try and find out how to access the photographer's Twitter account. Comparing the activity with La Foglia's could be a useful tool in relating the two homicides.

As he finished his to-do list, the last task was to check his email inbox. He had to admire Broadhurst's operational efficiency. There was already a message from Ata Rashid regarding the murdered girl in Malaga. His contact on the local Diario Sur newspaper had gained access to some CCTV stills taken at a shopping centre on the outskirts of the City. According to her friends, she would use the venue as a place to meet boys and socialise with her peer group during the weekend. The attachments to the mail were two photographs of an attractive young girl, peroxide blonde hair and a bit heavy on the make-up, but otherwise, a pleasing face with a come-on expression and a brilliant smile.

He sent a mail back to Rashid, diplomatically thanking

him for his speedy response before requesting another favour. Were there any CCTV images of the person at whom the girl was so obviously smiling? Within ten minutes, two more images were with him, one of a sideways view of a young man leaving an internet café, his face turned toward the camera as his eyes followed the girl's movements. Then, there was a grainy image of the girl with her back to the camera with the man some three strides behind her. Marchal printed out all four images, placed them in his briefcase and made his way out. The outer office was steadily filling up. The more he thought about it, the less he wanted to be found hanging around getting involved in the normal irreligious banter that passed for male bonding in this nest of vipers.

Traffic was heavy on the motorway as drivers slowed into the mist that settled in patches, and then accelerated away as the sky cleared until their visibility was again hampered. Minor accidents were commonplace, vehicle warning lights blinking on the hard shoulder, people in luminous yellow vests waiting for assistance, red triangles posted on the ground, LCD warnings blazoned across the width of the motorway. It required every ounce of Marchal's concentration to maintain some sort of reasonable average speed amongst all the confusion.

He had planned a late morning meeting with Monique and her husband at their modest terraced house near Lomme, but it was nearly two before he reached the auberge they had suggested as an alternative meeting point when he had warned of a delay.

There was a smell of smouldering apple wood and vegetable soup as he entered the dining room that made him realise he was hungry. The couple sat either side of the table, both turning to greet him in a way that gave him the sensation that they had been waiting in silence for him to arrive. His appearance registered both fear and relief on their faces. Although they were both qualified professionals, Monique, the vet, and Hubert, an engineer in a large aero components conglomerate, Marchal couldn't help thinking that they had the appearance of a couple of farm hands who wouldn't look out of place sitting atop a tractor.

Unlike the conversation, the meal was wholesome and satisfying. The topic was both predictable and timeless. A couple in their thirties, both career minded, with two young children to bring up in an environment where neither had the time nor energy to do all the tasks that were demanded of them. Monique had many of her mother's beautiful features, but none of her personality traits. She was a neurotic and highly strung young woman, headstrong, yes, but with none of the calm, reasoned responses that Marchal had so loved in her mother. Monique was convinced that her husband was having an office affair, an accusation which Hubert strenuously denied, but which Marchal sensed was probably true. Chances were that the intense pressure he felt he was under from their constant arguments had given him the time old excuse of seeking light relief in somebody else's arms. Their combative, aggressive reaction to each other's explanations and appeals to Marchal's role as mediator told its own story. They had both accepted defeat. Divorce was the only answer.

Marchal placed a question mark over Hubert's affair. If it was serious, then the relationship had probably tipped beyond the watershed. If it was, as he suspected, a casual fling, intended as a distraction rather than a substitution, then the outcome would be largely dependent upon the pressure exerted by the woman involved and Hubert's will power to achieve what he really wanted. Sacrificing family life with two young children was a step too far for most caring fathers and Marchal suspected that there was enough deep seated affection and respect between the couple to restore love to the agenda once the strain had been lifted. It was touch and go. Monique wasn't an easy person to live with and her husband had shown he had a vindictive side to his character when his temper was tested. Nevertheless, Marchal had made his decision.

Coffee was on the table and the conversation had stalled. Watches were being checked. "I suppose you remember that I'm retiring at the end of the month?" he said. They looked up at him. "I thought it might be appropriate and, after today's conversation I'm more convinced than ever, that I should get to know my grandchildren a lot better than I do at the moment." Now he had their undivided attention. "What I thought of doing was renting a little flat near to you and helping out with looking after the kids. I could pick them up, take them to school or nursery, meet them in the afternoon, look after them for a few hours and then return them to you when you were both back from work. Maybe, once or twice a week, they could stay with me overnight. How does that sound?"

They were speechless. They had expected words of commonsense, advice, a concoction of amateur psychology that would ultimately achieve nothing constructive, certainly not physical intervention into their lives.

"I don't know what to say," Monique said. "You've no experience."

"You were born at twenty one, were you? Straight out of the womb, ready to face the world?"

"I know, but that was different. You have two very demanding grandchildren," she retorted, as if it were some unique situation.

"Tell you what," Marchal said airily. "Why don't we give it a three month trial? You make a judgement as to how I'm coping, at the same time as trying to get to know each other again with a little more free time on your hands. If it works, we'll carry on. If not, we'll reassess the position." He looked straight into Hubert's eyes. "Sounds positive, yes?"

From Monique's point of view, it was a godsend. It was Hubert he had left with the dilemma. Had he talked about divorce to his mistress? Would he leave her and give it a go? Would he try and run with the hare and the hounds?

239

These were topics he would leave for another conversation at another place, when the two men were on their own, in a few days time. Right now, he had shunted his son-in-law into a corner where his only alternative was to accept the proposal.

As he walked back to his car, Marchal was feeling pretty pleased with himself. He had intended to hang around until the kids were out of school, but the phone call changed all that. Patricia sounded breathless.

"Sorry to disturb you," she said.

"You alright? You sound as if you're running."

"I am. I'm desperate to get to the loo."

"Ring me back. I'll wait."

"No, it's alright. Listen, I've just come into the office. You asked for Rosenberg's mobile to be monitored. He used it once yesterday. He's in Calais, called a lawyer here in Paris. As you're in that neck of the woods, thought you might want to check it out."

"Thanks, I will."

"While you're on the road, I'll check the hotels in the area and the credit card companies. I'll also speak to the lawyer. Keep you posted."

"Thanks."

"By the way, really enjoyed last night. We must do it again." She hesitated. "Soon."

The thought was tempting, but Lille beckoned. Maybe his offer to help his daughter was prompted by his own reservations. He would soon be out of the Paris rat race and, more important, away from the urge to reply, "Yes, we must."

Forty eight - @GerbenRosenberg

The Kent countryside flashed by the window as the Eurostar made its way to London. Gerben had said very little to his companion, dark and confusing thoughts occupying his mind. Darek had tried to start a number of conversations on various general topics, except the one that he really was curious about, but each time his initiative had been greeted with a meaningless grunt or no reaction at all.

An over polite voice on the intercom system told them the train was twenty five minutes away from London St Pancras International, prompting Gerben to break his trance to consider the rest of their travel arrangements.

Darek saw it as his opportunity. "I've been reading about Islam," he said. "Why do you think it is that we hate the Jews?"

Gerben adopted a look of contempt as he studied the face of the pretty young man, dressed as an ordinant in his black suit, clerical collar and bib. "You are supposed to be a theology student. No one with any religious training would ask such a banal question."

"Banal? I've been concentrating on Christianity, not Judaism. I'm just curious."

"I wasn't employed to wet nurse some trainee journalist making out he's some aspiring religious student, especially one who hasn't got a clue what he's talking about."

Darek was visibly taken back at the venom in the response.

"OK. Sorry. I didn't mean to be offensive. I've got other things on my mind. Listen. Take Iran for example. The Iranians don't hate Jews. There are more Jews living peacefully in Iran than in any other Muslim country. I've read up to twenty five thousand. There are synagogues, Jewish newspapers, celebration of Yom Kippur. There has even been a Jewish representative in the Iranian Parliament."

"I didn't know."

Gerben shook his head. "There has been close ties between Islam and Judaism for many centuries. Read the Qur'an and you'll see. The prophet Muhammad had a Jewish wife. At one time, the qibla was Jerusalem and not Mecca, the direction towards which Muslims now pray."

241

"Then why must a Muslim pray for your destruction?" Darek looked confused.

"You're confusing Judaism as synonymous with Zionism. What Iran objects to is not Jews, but the existence of the State of Israel. Jerusalem is a holy city to Muslims. It's where Muhammad is said to have ascended to heaven. Iran resents the creation of a country just after the war in its revered Palestine where Zionist Jews could claim sovereignty. That's what it wants to destroy."

"You don't seem passionate about Zionism?"

"Truth to tell, I'm not particularly religious, but I love and respect my mother and father. They expect me to worship, so I do it for them. My father has some reservations about Zionism, as do many orthodox Jews."

"Iran rejects the Holocaust."

Gerben reacted angrily. "It's hard line, doctrinal nonsense from a militant regime that offends every sensibility. These fanatics reject it because the death of six million Jews is seen by Iran as the moral motive which obliged the countries that won the last world war to enforce partition to establish the State of Israel where it is. Had they stuck Israel in a part of Europe, Iran probably wouldn't care a damn. Now, can we change the subject and work out exactly where we're going when we get to London?"

Darek fell silent, looking absent-mindedly out of the window, but Gerben could sense that the conversation had disturbed him.

A taxi took them from St Pancras across to Paddington, the rail terminal serving the west of England. A delay of thirty minutes before the Bristol train departed gave Gerben the opportunity to scan the two French newspapers on sale for any reference to the murder of Rizzi. There was none.

Darek sat on a bench on the station concourse, an open copy of the Bible in his hands. It was difficult to tell if he was reading the text or simply using it as a prop to avoid talking while his mind was in another place. Throughout his life, he had been taught to listen and learn. The mullahs, those wise religious men, knew the truth and there was only one truth. The Qur'an and the Hadith, the sayings of Muhammad, encapsulated everything that he needed to know about the path that had been chosen for him in the world. He had never been encouraged to think for himself, nor to consider questioning the doctrine that Jews were treacherous and hypocritical and could never be the friend of a Muslim. Yet the Qur'an also speaks of the Jews in a more derisive than hostile tone. They were not seen as a threat to Islam. For some reason, this Rosenberg man displayed an attitude of tolerance that had prompted Darek to start asking questions, the answers to which had begun to make him feel uncomfortable.

The train had pulled into the platform and Gerben was beckoning him to get on. Maybe this man had no religion other than money, a product of a wicked capitalist society that would lead the world to destruction unless Islam was triumphant. That was the answer. It wasn't that he was tolerant, wanting Jews and Muslims to live side by side. He was decadent, selfish and uncaring. To him, religion was irrelevant. He was just like all the western infidels that the mullahs had told him about. Closing the bible as if he had reached some definitive decision, Darek boarded the train.

"What exactly is the plan?" Gerben asked. "I don't like being kept in the dark."

"My instructions are that we get off of the train at Bristol Parkway. It's outside of the city with a large car park where we will meet the person who will give us all the information we need. I know no more."

"How are we supposed to recognise this person?"

"We are not. He will make himself known to us."

243

Forty nine - @ChasBroadhurst.kp

The security guard handed Broadhurst the message as he arrived at Kensington Palace. He was to go directly to Lambert's office where he would be met. His eyebrows creased as he tried to imagine what had been going on to provoke this curt, written instruction.

Lambert's office was in turmoil. Two men were removing files from the cabinets, reviewing the contents, then placing them in various stacks on the floor. All the desk drawers had been removed, the contents emptied into black plastic bags. Professor Speir looked up from the document he had been reading to greet Broadhurst, who was looking around him in disbelief.

"Good trip?" the professor asked jovially.

"Up until now. What the hell's going on?"

"Sit down, would you." This wasn't the hunched-up, dishevelled old man who had been present at the meeting last Monday, quietly observing, an irritating distraction to the security chief's routine. The man appeared to have shed ten years, with a confident, upright posture, a person sure of himself and his surroundings.

"Where's Lambert?" Broadhurst needed to get his bearings.

"All in good time." Speir gave him a curt, unfriendly smile. "I regret that you have been involved in somewhat of a subterfuge, but it was both intentional and authorised by a higher authority. We are simply acting under instructions."

"We? Who is we?"

Speir leaned forward across the desk, as if imparting a confidence. "Apart from my role as a behavioural psychologist, I happen to be a director of the ISS Corp. You've heard of us, no doubt?"

"International Surveillance Services? I was under the impression that I was the head of security in this place. Why wasn't I told of your involvement?" The rug had just been officially pulled out from under Broadhurst's feet.

"That's not a question for me to answer, but I suggest that you were considered as equally under suspicion in the same way as all those present at your Monday morning briefings." Speir moved his chair around at an angle to face the window.

"Am I being accused of divulging classified information? If so, somebody had better start thinking of finding a replacement for me."

"Calm down!" was the imperious instruction. "You are as aware as I that there has been leakage of the private movements of a number of Royals over the past four months. Until this Prince Arthur affair, the leaks were minor, alerting the paparazzi to holiday destinations, clandestine romantic liaisons, nightclub binges, that sort of thing.

"Yes. I had asked Lambert to complete a discreet investigation. He suspected a particular person in the press corps."

"Quite. Based on my initial assessment, Sarah Hansom was on my list for further consideration. Unfortunately for your investigation, so was your man Lambert."

Broadhurst gave a cynical laugh. It was beginning to get under his skin that all the time Speir was talking to him, he was looking out of the window at, what appeared to be, nothing in particular. There was a suggestion of contempt in the action.

"Lambert? You must be joking. He's one of the old school; sound as a bell and with an unblemished record. No chance."

"Unfortunately, sometimes you get so close to people, you can't see the obvious that's staring you in the face."

"You know, Speir, you're beginning to piss me off!"

The Professor swung his chair back around, concentrating his attention on Broadhurst's face. "Good," he said. "Maybe now, you can put your resentments and hard-done-by reactions to one side and we can have a constructive conversation."

"I don't have a problem."

"Let's keep it like that. We put a high level team on the job. Everybody's phone was tapped, mobile records reviewed, all that sort of thing."

Broadhurst was about to speak.

"Before you ask, yes, your phones as well. As far as my two pre race favourites were concerned, we had surveillance vans with voice monitoring, intrusion cameras, all the gear, posted outside Hanson's and Lambert's homes."

"Go on."

"You may be interested to learn that Sarah Hansom and boyfriend have, what's laughingly called, a social drug habit. Cocaine. It uses up quite a bit of their disposable income, but it's not out of control. Anyway, she's sound, even if she should ditch the wanker she's living with."

In a million years, Broadhurst could never have imagined that word leaving someone like Speir's lips. It sounded as incongruous as asking for caviar in a fish and chip shop.

He nodded as if the disclosure was something he had suspected, although he had had no idea.

"Contrary to your unwavering confidence, I'm afraid Lambert's our man. He's in a relationship with a woman called Soraya."

"Yes. It's quite recent. About four months, I think. He's on the rebound, but appears quite besotted." Alarm bells had started to ring in his head.

Speir opened a file, flicking through the papers until he found what he was after. "Her family name is Amari. She has a Turkish passport, although we believe that she's Iranian by birth. She lived in France for many years."

"Lambert told me she was Algerian."

"Easy to believe.

"Are you saying she's getting information from Lambert to pass on to the paparazzi?"

Speir nodded. "It's pillow talk. Heavy sex and then the infamous cigarette while she cleverly pumps him for details of Royal activity. She's good at it."

246

"And you're sure?" The mobile was vibrating in Broadhurst's pocket. It was a French number. He pressed the automatic message key to say that he was occupied and would call back.

Speir found the gesture amusing. "You can answer if you like. We're not bugging it anymore."

"No. It's not important. Must be the French policeman I got friendly with over this Maxwell and Lewis business."

"To answer your question, we seconded Lambert for a few days to deal with some bogus security issues. We fed him some false information about two of the Princes, harmless tittle-tattle, the sort of dead flesh the paparazzi feed on. It was duly passed on."

"How?"

"She has a Twitter feed to two contacts with the handles of papapicman and Bizzybuzzybee. We have no idea who they are, but there's a stream of DMs from her account to them. We need to question her, but she's fled the coup. Lambert was arrested this morning, but she'd already left."

"No surveillance?"

"We'd lifted the team by the time the police got involved. It sometimes causes friction if we're hanging around when the law turns up. Awkward questions get asked. There must have been a thirty minute window. Somebody tipped her off we were on to her."

"Who?"

"Don't know yet. The police are questioning Lambert as we speak."

Broadhurst stroked his chin. "If you consider there's been a leak, do we need to move Prince Arthur to another location?"

"I don't see why. In the first place, the damage has already been done as far as he's concerned. No sign of any press attention at the location where he is. It's fresh meat the paparazzi are after. In the second place, a change of venue was one of the false leads we fed Lambert which his woman passed on. So, as we speak, there are probably a few anxious photographers freezing their balls off in some godforsaken field outside a monastery in Northumberland."

Broadhurst nodded. It wasn't assent. He was being told. Nobody was soliciting his opinion. "You might find it worthwhile if you let me speak to Lambert. We have a close relationship. If he is the guilty party, he may well confide in me."

Speir rose from his chair. "I think that's a good idea. I'll set it up. By the way, I didn't ask. How did you find France?"

"Interesting. There are links to these papapicman accounts all over the place. You've heard about the two paparazzi murders in France and Switzerland?"

"I've been keeping tabs on the limited press comment. It seems an amazing coincidence. Crichton rants on TV about exterminating paparazzi and the next day, it appears, somebody's on the case."

"You see a connection?"

"No reason to, but it's as though somebody was waiting for the word and God, in the person of Crichton, spoke." Speir laughed at his own joke.

There was the clatter of files falling on the floor behind Broadhurst. He turned to see an embarrassed young man retrieving the mess he had made. "Will Lambert not be returning to his post at some stage?" Broadhurst asked.

"No. I doubt it." Speir flicked an imaginary speck of dirt off of his waistcoat. "In fact, I'll be occupying this office from now on. His Royal Highness has asked me to stay on with a watching brief for the foreseeable future. I expect he'll be talking to you personally about the arrangements."

Broadhurst felt a cold sensation around the collar of his shirt. His position was about to be compromised. What did they call it, a sideways movement into controlled obscurity? He had lost the trust of his employer. He needed time to think.

"I've got to make a call." He moved to leave. "We'll

248

carry on with this conversation when I've had time to catch up with events in my absence."

"Good idea," Speir said, standing to offer his hand, which Broadhurst took, perhaps a little too firmly than he intended. "I'll arrange for you to see Lambert."

Broadhurst slammed shut his office door. White had left an urgent message that he wanted to speak with him. Nothing else. Normally, when he left the office for a couple of days, there were a pile of security reports and issues to resolve on his return. Today, there was an empty desk, the picture of his sister and nieces taking centre stage. His position was under threat. He decided to phone upstairs for an appointment just as his mobile sounded. The French number again. Marchal must be anxious about something.

The call was straight to the point. Marchal had been in Calais. Rosenberg had been traced to a hotel near the Eurostar terminal. Two rooms had been booked in his name and paid for in cash. The second room had been occupied by a young man who fitted the description of both the theology student in Gibraltar and the man wanted for questioning by the Spanish police in Malaga. Photos of the man provided by Rashid had been mailed to his inbox. He was waiting for any CCTV images of the men at the Eurostar terminal, but it was his opinion that both men had probably travelled to the UK. He was waiting to interview the night porter at the hotel, but, in the meantime, he suggested that Broadhurst set the wheels in motion to see if the two men had turned up in London. His closing words offered a sense of relief that the security chief was not totally isolated. "I may decide to make that visit to see you in the UK sooner than you expected, Chas. I'd like to get to the bottom of what's going on and nobody over here seems to give a damn what I spend my time doing as long as it's not presenting more problems to solve."

"I understand entirely how you feel, René. I get a feeling we're in the same boat."

His secretary arrived with coffee as the call finished.

Contacts in the British Transport police and the UK Border Agency would establish the appropriate alerts at St Pancras. As soon as he received the photos from René, he flicked these across to the two authorities. Now, it was just a question of waiting.

Upon reflection, he would leave the appointment with the powers that be for a day or so until he had time to think things through and, anyway, the note in Speir's handwritten scrawl that had just appeared advised that he could interview Lambert straight away.

He decided to walk to Savile Row. At a brisk pace, it would take up most of the thirty minutes, giving him time to get his head around a whole new train of events.

There was plenty of activity at West End Central. A demonstration of overseas students protesting about something he knew not what, had been marching from Marble Arch to Hyde Park Corner when some agitators in the crowd had broken ranks and were threatening to breach the police ranks. Uniformed officers in riot gear moved hurriedly around the corridors, voices raised as orders were given and responded to.

Lambert sat crossed legged in an interview room, a crushed can of Coke alongside a half eaten sandwich on the table in front of him. He was alone. Hair unkempt, his suit jacket creased above a pair of unmatched trousers. For all the world to see, he looked like a vagrant brought in off the street.

"Don't know whether I should be pleased to see you or not, Chas. I was expecting my cousin."

"Your cousin?" Broadhurst questioned.

"She's a criminal lawyer. On her way up from Wiltshire. Thought you must have contacted her. She phoned an hour ago to say she was leaving home to deal with everything and not to worry. That's a joke." He shook his head in disbelief.

"Speir told me the police picked you up this morning. Contravention of the Official Secrets Act That's big trouble. God, your taste in women, Lambert! You sure know how to pick them."

Lambert rolled his eyes, as though he was picturing another scene in his head. "I think it was a case of Soraya picking me, not the other way round. God, she was a woman and a half. I'll miss her."

"Who told her that the police were on their way?"

"Who do you think?" Lambert uncrossed his legs, pushing his chair in closer to the table. "I guessed they were on to me two days ago. They take you for a fool, priming you with all sorts of crap, imagining you're naive enough to fail to see what they're up to."

There was a knowing nod from Broadhurst. "You told her to leave?"

"I realised I'd been indiscreet, answering her prying questions in the mistaken belief that we were in love, a bond so strong, it didn't matter what she knew."

"She was using you to pass on info to the paparazzi?"

Lambert nodded with a grin on his face that said I've been had over. "I fed her the bogus stuff they'd given me in the hope that it wasn't passed on, but it was. She confessed that one of her Algerian relatives is a press photographer having a rough time. She was helping him out."

"Bad news I'm afraid. She's probably Iranian or Iraqi with a Turkish passport and has been living in France. More lies."

"Nothing surprises me," Lambert acknowledged with a shrug of the shoulders. "Anyway, I waited until the surveillance vehicle drove off, guessing there would probably be ten or fifteen minutes before the police showed. I packed her on her way."

"Where to?"

"Didn't ask. Best not to know in these circumstances. God, I still fancy her like mad."

Broadhurst stood up to leave. "Hope it was worth it. You know something Lambert. I hope your lawyer's got her wits about her, otherwise you're going to spend a long time banged up with nothing but memories."

"I guess so," was the matter of fact comment. "Do you ever read my personnel file record, Chas?"

"Can't say as I do."

"If you did, you'd know my Christian name was David. In all these years, you've only ever called me Lambert."

"Force of habit from the services, I guess."

"Well, from now on, I'd prefer it if you called me David. After all, things are never likely to be the same again."

"I guess they're not Lam.." He stopped himself in time. "Goodbye, David. Best of luck."

BOOK THREE – TENET THE HOLDER OF MAGICAL VOW

Fifty - @papapicman

The tyres of the blue Audi crunched on the gravel path leading up to the farm house. Beyond was a two storey, thatched cottage with chintzy curtains at the windows. The GPS coordinates not only matched those she had been given, but she knew exactly where she was.

This beautiful setting in the Wiltshire countryside featured on a series of photographs David had showed her when she had asked about his family. Lambert was very proud of his cousin. She was the one member of his small family that had done really well for herself. An eminent criminal lawyer, show jumping fanatic; his spinster cousin had chosen horses over men. She used to say that horses had all the tantrums that men displayed, but you didn't have to sit through their boring dinner conversations and, unlike a man, you could prompt a horse into action with a good dig in the ribs.

Soraya walked over to the stalls and looked inside. Three were occupied; their residents chewing away lazily gave her a disinterested stare before returning to the task of rotating their jaws so that their teeth could crush the tough fibres. For the first time that morning, she began to feel relaxed.

Beyond the stables was a copse of tall eucalyptus trees with their trunks of shredded bark reaching up to a mass of bare branches. A flock of black crows flew back and forth between the trees, their eerie calls splitting the silence, combining strangely with the pungent scent that fed from the trees into her nostrils.

"Hello." The barn door had opened and the man stood, beckoning her to join him. He was tall, slim, wrapped in a black overcoat, a long grey scarf threaded oddly in looping hoops several times around his neck, a black-rimmed hat shadowing his face. He had a handsome, angular face. Soraya felt she could get to fancy him, even if he was a little older than the men on whom she normally bestowed her sexual favours.

She walked over, reaching for his outstretched hand. "So you're the famous papapicman," she said. "I always wondered what you looked like. I used to fantasise about it." She gave him a warm smile.

"Come inside," he indicated. "It's damn cold out there."

"You must have thin blood. What are you like in the winter?"

He ignored the comment. "Listen, we don't have much time." There was urgency in his voice. "You have to get out of the country." He pulled a package of documents from his inside pocket.

"Not so fast," she was anxious. "What about my family? I've completed my part of the deal. The lawyer in Paris gave his word that my parents and sisters would be smuggled out of Iraq to Van in Turkey. The militia have them under house arrest. My father's silly politics!"

"As we speak, they're on their way. When you get to France, you can check the details with the man you spoke to."

"Kamal?"

"Give him a call. He has the confirmation."

The barn was half full of bales of hay. She coughed as particles of chafe caught in the back of her throat.

"It's a diplomatic passport," he went on. "Shouldn't give you any problems."

He went to hand her the package, but it slipped from his hand, falling onto the ground. She bent down to retrieve it. The grey scarf was around her neck before she could react. The wire he had fed inside it tightened as his knee pressed into her back, providing leverage as he continued to pull with both hands. Caught off guard, she had little time to react. Instinctively, her left hand reached to release the grip around her neck. She thrust her right behind her to try to grasp at his leg, knock him off balance. He felt her nails dig into his trouser leg, tearing at the skin below before he had time to take a step back out of her reach.

He tensed, ready to react to her next move, but there was none. Her head slumped forwards, body relaxed, as she slid slowly to the ground. There was still a pulse. Lack of oxygen had caused her to lose consciousness. If he continued to exert pressure, her brain would be starved, but he released his grip. That was not the plan.

Carefully removing his shoes and hers, then forcing tight latex gloves over his fingers, he fed the wire out of the scarf so that the material could be tied firmly around her neck, making sure that her hyoid bone was covered. Taking the loose end of the scarf, he knotted it firmly to one of two hooks on the end of a chain that was dangling over the rail of the upper gallery corridor which gave access to a view over the lower floor where he now stood.

The portable generator fired into life, the noise penetrating the eerie silence caused the woman to stir. He checked outside the barn. There was no sign of life, other than the restless movements of the horses. Closing the door, he returned to the generator, engaging the winch that it powered. The chain slithered upward, taking up the slack, pulling at the scarf until it met the resistance of the weight of her body. It began to lift her, stretching the material of the scarf, throttling her as she became suspended in mid air, her head slumped forwards, arms hanging limply at her side.

It wasn't the winch that concerned him. That was guaranteed to pull a two ton four by four out of a ditch. The scarf had been selected because the synthetic material was strong and resistant. He had already tried it out elsewhere on a fifty kilo sack of cement without a problem, but now the material seemed to be under such strain, it had extended in size and was little more than the thickness of a cord.

Time was of the essence. If the material eventually gave, well that was to be expected. They would find her body on the floor of the barn. Pulling a rope from his large rucksack, he began to climb the stairs in stockinged feet, treading only on the side edge of each step so as not to disturb the dust and chafe that had collected over the weeks or months since someone had trodden on them.

The scarf was swaying with the weight of her body. He leaned over the gallery rail, threading the rope under her arms, across her body, retrieving the loose end so that he could pull the two tightly together, knot them and tie them to the second hook. Painstakingly, he retraced his steps, restarting the generator momentarily so that her body climbed another few inches. Now the strain of her weight was being taken by the rope and not the scarf which had slackened.

He took her shoes, placing a hand inside each one and began to climb the stairs once more. This time, he progressed slowly, imprinting the sole of each shoe in the dust in the middle of each step. He repeated the process on the gallery floor. There was now enough slack in the scarf to allow him to undo the knot around the hook and re-attach it to the gallery handrail. He pulled on it to test the strength and satisfied, carefully dropped her shoes over the side so that it would appear that they had fallen from her feet.

One more visit to the generator was necessary in order to give him enough slack to untie the rope he had placed under her arms. Before releasing the rope, he grasped one of her hands, lifting her slightly so that the scarf could take up the strain of her weight without the jolt that might finally tear the material.

He collected the rope and the cloth that had stopped the chain from excessively marking the handrail before tossing it down onto a convenient bale of hay. In five minutes, he had stowed all the signs of his presence in the boot of a black Mercedes which he had parked out of sight.

He was almost out of the barn when the realisation flickered through his mind, causing him to retrace his steps. It wasn't to look up at the lifeless body which swayed gently above him like a carcass in an abattoir, but to search for the envelope filled with the sheets of blank paper that had passed as her getaway documents. He put them in his pocket and pulled the barn door tight shut behind him.

His route would take him across country through Bath, a spa town he loved with its crescents of elegant stoned terraced houses. He stopped at a coffee house near one of the Roman spas. It was rather appropriate, he thought. Taking his mobile phone, he typed one word, 'TENET', found the number and pushed 'send'. If everything went to plan, her death would not have been in vain. Collateral damage they called it. All being well, her family would soon be free.

Fifty one - @renemarchal

Marchal had been in two minds. It seemed somehow irresponsible to just get on a train and head off for England without advising someone or asking permission. A policeman's instinct told him that the responsible thing to do would be turn round, head for Paris and follow up this Geneva business with Chantelle Dubois. There had to be a connection. Was the photographer waiting for the woman in the red hat that Maxwell had talked about? If she wasn't Dubois, who was she? What the hell! It could hold fire for another twenty four hours. Arnault would be glad to see the back of him and, by the time he had returned, Patricia might well have established the link between the two murders.

Feeling lightheaded even before the alcohol, he decided on a large gin and tonic in the buffet car. A phone call to Broadhurst had provided a bed for the night at the security man's grace and favour apartment in an annex to Kensington Palace and the promise of a dinner at some swanky restaurant where the bill would give you indigestion unless you could link it to some expense account or another. However important it was to find Rosenberg as soon as possible, right at that moment, the thought of some selfish pleasures tinged with guilt dimmed his professional objectives.

Broadhurst greeted him as an old friend. Somehow, security and carpet slippers didn't seem to go together, but Broadhurst managed to combine domestic relaxation and an air of readiness for any emergency with consummate ease. He poured his guest a stiff gin and tonic as they settled into the two armchairs. Marchal was beginning to feel unusually relaxed.

"Does the name, Mishka Melman, mean anything to you, René?" Broadhurst asked, couching a glass of whiskey between both hands. Marchal shook his head. "It's not really a lead, but some feedback from Border Control about two guys who matched the description of Rosenberg and our mystery young man arriving at St Pancras today."

"What's the Melman connection?"

"Maybe nothing. The older man had an Israeli passport with this name. Border Control stopped him because the screen recorded that the last entry from Melman was some years ago with a diplomatic passport. The officer asked the man about it and was given the reply that he had retired from the diplomatic service years and this was simply a sightseeing visit to introduce a friend of the family to London."

"And the young man's passport?"

"He's not too sure, because it was an EU entry. He had a vague recollection that it could have been Maltese. Probably just coincidence."

"And your Royal scandal?" Marchal laughed. "Had it been in France, it would have been a day's titillation and then 'sans fait rien'. Here it's a crisis. I think we French have a much different moral approach to what goes on above and below the waistline."

Broadhurst saw the humour in the remark. "Things have quietened down a great deal. International problems have overtaken the headlines. Benny Ram has committed not to publish or sell any more photos of the Prince, who is nicely tucked away out of public view until the storm clouds blow over." He thought about mentioning the problem with Lambert, but decided against it. "Let's freshen up and go out to dinner."

The call came through as they were studying the dessert menus. Broadhurst listened carefully. "Does Lambert know?" he asked and waited for the reply. "Don't tell him tonight. Leave it until I can see him in the morning." There was another pause. "Ask for a copy of both the police and pathologist's report, would you. Make sure they're on my desk first thing in the morning, please."

"Problems?" Marchal enquired.

Broadhurst decided to give his guest a sanitized version of the position with Lambert. "On the face of it, it seems that this Soraya went looking for his solicitor cousin, discovered that the lawyer who was, in fact, visiting Lambert, wasn't at home and hung herself in the barn. It looks like suicide, but I'll have a more complete picture in the morning."

"You are concerned about Lambert's state of mind?"

"In a word, yes. He's been duped by the woman he loved, sent her away while he stayed to face the music, only to discover that she didn't run, but took her own life instead. It's enough to destabilise anybody, especially somebody who already feels a sense of despair."

Fifty two - @GerbenRosenberg

Carriage doors thumped shut as the stream of daily commuters arrived at Bristol Parkway, heading briskly for the exit and home in the fading light of day. There was really no place else to go. The station was situated in a semi rural location, well outside and to the north of the city centre, its attraction, a large free car park in the direction of which the two men made their way.

Within five minutes, a parade of cars had made their

way past them, leaving them standing alone in silence, unsure of what they were now to expect. A lone car engine fired into life and a large black Mercedes saloon with tinted windows pulled from its parking position into the exit lane, cruising slowly toward them. The driver was wearing a black hat with a large brim that obscured his face and an overcoat with the collar turned up. A blue scarf was wrapped around his neck. He stopped alongside and indicated with his hand for them to get into the back.

He spoke without turning around. "I have some instructions for you from Mr Kamal," he said.

"And you would be?" Gerben asked.

"You'll find out soon enough. Tonight my identity is not relevant. Now, listen."

He spelled out an itinerary which would take them by car to Hay on Wye where rooms had been booked in the names of Brent and Melman at the Red Dragon Hotel in the town centre. Tomorrow morning, they would drive to the St John's Trinity Theological College at a set of coordinates which Darek noted in biro on his wrist. As Mr Brent was aware, the administrator, Geoffrey Absolom, would be expecting the new arrival. Melman would explain that he was a close family friend who had taken the young man under his wing after the tragic death of his parents. He would ask for a brief inspection tour of the premises, specifically acquainting himself with the layout of the grounds and then, satisfied that his charge was in good hands, he would return to the hotel where further contact would be made.

"Why all this cloak and dagger business?" Gerben asked. "I need to get back to France as soon as possible."

"I know," the man replied. "The day after tomorrow, you'll be gone." He began to chew noisily on a stick of chewing gum. "This is a one off opportunity to get close to the Prince for an in depth analysis of the man. If anybody were to suspect or doubt Brent's credentials, the project would fail. Military style precision and secrecy is essential. We're not going to take any chances,

Understood, Mr Rosenberg?" There was menace in the question.

Gerben made no reply.

"Now, Mr Brent. Your role is this. Once you've settled in to your quarters, you discover the location of the east wing. The Prince has private quarters there where he stays for most of the day, taking his meals in private. At around eleven in the morning and then, just before dusk at around six, he strolls around the grounds, often down to the lake. He talks freely to the other students who are not aware of his identity. Are you with me, so far?"

The young man was listening intently. The driver went on to explain that there was a lawn facing the east wing with a park bench. As soon as possible after his arrival, Brent would ask for some private moments with his bible and make his way to the bench where he would sit for an hour or so. "The weather forecast is good, but it will be cold, so wrap up warm." He was banking on the Prince looking out of the window and seeing the new arrival. "If he's true to form, he'll try and introduce himself under a false name when he goes for his late afternoon stroll. Make sure you're in the grounds ready to receive his attention. You've already been told how to react."

"I have. That part is fully understood."

"If all goes well, you'll get an invite to his quarters that evening. Don't ask too many questions. Keep the conversation theological, but let slip about your parents." He went on to expound on how the meeting should progress, taking such care over the detail that Gerben began to feel the boredom and sense of frustration build up inside him. The man seemed obsessed with the task at hand.

"One last thing," the driver concluded. "There are two security men in charge of the Prince's safety. Don't do anything which would make them suspicious. They'll probably do a background check on you through Absolom, but it should all stack up okay. On day one, they'll pat you down, run a metal detector over you, that sort of thing.

Make sure you're not carrying anything suspicious." He pushed the automatic transmission into drive, cruising back around the car park until he stopped in front of a green Astra. "This is your car, Melman. For God's sake drive carefully, remembering to stick to the left hand side of the road." He passed over a set of keys. "Try to avoid the police, at all costs. If you're stopped for any reason, asked to show a driving licence, tell them you've left it in the hotel or some such story." Gerben detected a sense of nervousness in the man's voice. He was obviously a control freak, who now had to depend on other people's initiatives. He must find it unnerving. Tomorrow, they would meet on an equal footing. He would look forward to that. He made a move to open the door.

"Brent!" the man exclaimed. "Whatever you do, don't sleep with him or let him fuck you on day one. Keep him on tenterhooks. That way you'll get more information out of him. He's the Prince, but you take charge. Don't let him boss you about. He likes to be made to feel subservient in the bedroom."

As Brent made to get out of the Mercedes, the man began to speak in measured tone in a language that Gerben did not even recognise, yet understand. Darek's body, half in, half out the car became rigid, transfixed by the words that were being said to him. He made a one word reply.

"What was all that about?" Gerben asked as he sat behind the wheel of the Astra, his brow creased, trying to get his bearings in a right hand drive vehicle he had never experienced in his life.

"He was wishing me good luck in Arabic," Darek replied, unconcerned at the look of disbelief on his companion's face.

"I get it," Gerben replied, now more intent on the workings of the vehicle than his companion. "Now, I understand the connection with Benny."

Gerben drove twice around the car park to get a feel for this unusual environment before chancing an exit onto the main road. He was relying on a sat nav that would direct him the seventy five miles across the Severn Bridge into Wales and from Newport, turning north toward the Usk Valley in the direction of Hereford.

Darek passed the journey in silence, appearing to try to make out the landscape through the darkness wherever he could from the headlights of the car and those of the oncoming vehicles. It was so, so different to the world he knew with these vast areas of rich, agricultural land, rolling hills; so much activity on the road.

As Gerben turned into the hotel car park, the challenge had become a conquest. He was feeling really pleased with himself. Apart from one near miss when it had seemed more natural to circle a roundabout in the wrong direction, a mistake he swiftly corrected, he had negotiated the journey in two hours, feeling ever increasingly confident as they neared their destination.

The hotel was an old coaching inn, warm and friendly with a log fire burning fiercely in the bar, where Gerben set himself in a winged armchair with a pint of local brew as a reward for his achievement. Darek had disappeared up to his room with the promise that he would be down for dinner in less than half an hour. Restaurant service finished at ten and Gerben was in no mood to hurry through what appeared to be a very interesting menu.

Draining the last remnants of a bottle of an expensive French burgundy, Gerben pushed back his chair and contemplated coffee with a Remy Martin to round off the meal.

"You like your food, don't you?" Darek's tone was censorial. By contrast, he had watched Gerben work through three courses as he sat with a tuna salad and a glass of mineral water in front of him.

"One of life's great pleasures," came the reply, "especially when someone else is paying the bill." He raised his empty glass in a toast. "Thanks Benny," he joked.

"Is Mr Ram a good man?"

"He is when he's dishing out money!" The

accumulation of alcohol mixed with the stress release when the drive was complete had left Gerben feeling very lightheaded. "Why do you ask?"

"I just wondered what his motives are?"

"Money, plain and simple. Benny doesn't shake your hand unless there's something in it for him."

"I can't believe it's just money."

"Look, Brent, or whatever your real name is, I don't understand exactly why he would choose someone like you to do his dirty work for him. As far as I can tell, he's picked an inexperienced, naive pretty boy who I guess, from all the murmurings I heard last night from your bedroom, is a devout Muslim. How come you are expected to play the part of a homosexual trainee Anglican priest. That just doesn't make sense."

Darek looked at him, but offered no answer..

"You're hoping to get into bed with a Royal with the sole purpose of getting a few more compromising photos and a recording of a Prince talking dirty, just to publish in his smutty little magazine. Doesn't ring true to me." He called over the waiter to place the order. "Anymore water for you?" he laughingly asked. "Best not. You'll be pissing all night." The waiter left with a smile on his face.

"Why do you belittle me in front of others? You seem to despise everything and everybody."

"Not so. I don't particularly like you, but I don't have to. It's just a job for a couple of days. Tomorrow, I'm on my way back to Paris and I can leave you to it."

"So why insult me?"

Gerben took a mouthful of brandy which he swilled around before swallowing. "I'll tell you, if you like. You can sell your body for a few bucks. That's just being a whore. But I know what you and Benny are really up to."

The young man had his fists clenched under the table. "You do? What's that?"

Gerben closed his eyes. "Someone, somewhere is paying Benny to create enough stink to bring down the British monarchy." He held his thumb and forefinger close apart. "The British are this far away from ditching the monarchy in favour of a republic and you and your patron are trying to help tip it over the edge."

"Is that so wrong?" He unclenched his fists.

"I don't care a damn. But what I don't like is being kept in the dark about the real motive for this little venture. Why couldn't he tell me in the first place what he was up to, instead of all this James Bond business?"

"Maybe he doesn't trust you? Maybe, he thinks you'll compromise his plans."

"Why should I? My motives are just like his. I'm in it for the money, that's all. Nothing else counts."

Darek nodded his head. "I can see that," he said.

Gerben staggered unsteadily to his feet. "I'm going to have a nightcap in the bar. I suggest you go and get your beauty sleep. Best to put the Qur'an aside tonight and brush up on the bible, Moses, Jesus and turning the other cheek." He laughed as he turned his back, ignoring the young man's outstretched hand and retraced his steps to the bar.

Darek climbed the creaking stairs to the bedroom area. He was cursing under his breath. "Death to you, Rosenberg and to all the infidels like you who try to threaten Islam." This was the fatwah of the Imam and he, Darek, would fulfil his chosen task.

Fifty three - @renemarchal

Patricia Colbert was coming to terms with a reality check that the honeymoon at 36 was well and truly over. She had to face the facts that her first three days had been an unmitigated disaster and that the promise of a new dawn to police detection techniques that her arrival had heralded was now dismissed, at best, as flawed and, amongst the brigade, as a sick joke. When furtive sideways glances took the place of open, honest smiles, she did not need a degree in behavioural sciences to know that she had been marginalised.

Arnault was impatient, anxious, not only for progress, but for a suspect and an arrest in the Rizzi murder; something positive he could announce at his daily press conference that would break the cycle of his 'following up a number of positive leads' speak. His mood was further darkened by the seeming lack of progress in linking the Paris murder to the killing in Geneva where the Swiss investigation had also stalled.

Colbert was now the butt of his shamefaced anger, harangued because of her inability to trace the perpetrator. The unspoken criticism in his barbed comments implied that she was a lightweight compared to her predecessor who would, in his opinion, already have solved the case. Gone was the caring veneer of a senior officer. Now, all she could see was the desperate self interest of the ruthless career policeman that Rene had described.

He had caused her to lose her temper just once. If he was so convinced of Marchal's ability to bring the killer to justice, why didn't he put him back in charge of the case. How the hell would she know where Marchal was? It had been Arnault who had suggested that Marchal back off the investigation, take a few days to deal with personal issues. No she didn't know where he was, but she'd damn well soon find out. Now, if the Commandant didn't mind, she'd like to get on with her job. Yes, she knew she was on a short fuse, but his constant reminders and snidey innuendos weren't helping. He had slammed her office door behind him with a venom that had brought the entire outer office to a standstill.

Marchal heard the mobile ring just at the critical moment in the preparation of the eggs Benedictine he had promised Broadhurst for their breakfast. His culinary skills were limited and a soft *oeuf poché* was essential if the dish was to succeed. It was touch and go whether he suggested a call back in a few minutes, but the tone of her voice and the vice of professionalism obliged him to turn the gas

267

down. Broadhurst, clad in a dressing gown that could have only been a birthday present from an elderly relative who didn't like him, stood by, waiting with a percolator of boiling coffee in his hand. Marchal was wearing his host's best white towelling robe, the sleeve wet where he had unintentionally dipped it in the pan of boiling water. Broadhurst smiled to himself. Talk about Jack Lemonn and Walter Matthau. They looked like the odd couple now.

Marchal moved from the stove, taking a seat at the kitchen table. "I understand," he said several times as he listened to her. "I'm in London with a friend," he said finally. "I'll be back tomorrow at the latest. It's important that I try to locate Rosenberg. He holds the key that will unlock this business." He waited while she spoke again, before replying in a tone which Broadhurst interpreted as more like a father than a colleague. "First of all, forget Arnault. He changes colour like a chameleon. Put him out of your mind. There are two things you can do which will help us. Make some background checks on Chantelle Dubois. Go to her office and interview her. There's something about this Geneva business, the woman in the red hat on the train, a visit to a clinic where the first paparazzi was killed. It doesn't make sense. Also, find out everything you can with Interpol on this Benny Ram character. He must be on file. Lastly, no, not lastly," he corrected himself. "Second to last, this is a long shot. See if there's anything on file about an Israeli named," he put his hand over the phone and asked Broadhurst for the information. "That's right," he continued, "Melman, full name Mishka Melman. It's probably nothing, but a background check, if only to eliminate him, would be useful."

He waited again, while she copied all the information down. "Yes, I did say second to last. Lastly, take a Xanax or something and calm down. You've been put under so much stress that you're not thinking straight. Sometimes, investigations stall when there are no obvious links, but more than often, they come to life again when you're least expecting it. Read through your background checks on the two victims again. See if there are any links between the subjects of their past exposés. Remember what I told you? You're in control. Take the lead. When I'm back, I'll give you all the support I can. You know that."

Broadhurst poured him a second coffee as he listened to a translation of the gist of Marchal's telephone conversation. "By the way, the eggs were very good," he said. "My compliments to the chef."

Marchal smiled. "A little on the overdone side if I'm being critical. Cooking requires my full time concentration."

"You sounded as though you were talking to your daughter."

This time, Marchal laughed out loud. "Did I?" he asked. "If I did, listening to the way she talks to me, she'd like the relationship to be incestuous."

Before Broadhurst could retort, Marchal's mobile rang again. The call lasted several minutes, time for Broadhurst to clear away the dishes and mime to his guest that he would go and get dressed.

He returned suited and booted. Marchal was on another phone call to Colbert. "Sorry about all this," Marchal apologised. "I'll be ready in five minutes. Interesting developments."

"How come?"

"You remember I told you there are six papapicman Twitter accounts, the original one and then the five Rosenberg added as he accumulated his clients. Three and four are the murder victims. I'd left a Tweet on five and six to contact me, put them on their guard. The call I took was from an Italian woman based in Turin, claims to be number five and to be in contact with number six whom she was also speaking for."

"You told her to ignore requests for a meeting until she'd checked with you?"

"She was already on her guard. I told her to contact Patricia to arrange a meeting as soon as possible. The link could be the breakthrough we need."

"So you're still missing number two?"

"Exactly. Worrying, isn't it? For all we know, he could be lying dead in some hotel room. Everywhere you turn in this business leads right back to Rosenberg."

"If he's still in the UK, we'll trace him, believe me." Broadhurst checked his watch. "While you're getting dressed, I'm going to speak with Lambert. I just hope he hasn't heard about Soraya from another source. If you arrive at the office before me, they'll hold you in reception until I get back. I won't be long. Those reports I asked for are already on my desk."

As it transpired, the taxi journey to West End Central was a waste of time. Although his secretary had primed the police in both the Wiltshire constabulary and London that Broadhurst would tackle the disclosure of Soraya's death to Lambert, neither had remembered to say anything to Lambert's lawyer cousin. Distraught at discovering the scene of police activity at her country home, she had not calculated the emotional cost of disclosing the tragedy by phone to Lambert. By the time Broadhurst had reached Savile Row, it was already too late. During the night, Lambert had tried to slit his wrists with the jagged edge of a china saucer he had broken. By the time he was discovered, there had been severe blood loss. A transfusion at Charing Cross Hospital had barely saved his life and he was now in a coma under police guard in a private ward.

As he made his way back to the office, Broadhurst cursed himself for the simple lack of foresight that could have prevented what the doctor advised as a touch and go situation with the possibility of permanent brain damage.

Duncan White was waiting for him as he reached his office. White's concerns were twofold. The increasing involvement of Professor Speir in security issues around the Royal family was confusing him. Had Broadhurst's position been compromised?

"Honest answer is, I don't know," Broadhurst said. "I

haven't had the opportunity to go upstairs yet to clarify the position, but, yes, you are right, there does appear to be a parallel security presence in play."

"Let me know what's going on? Before you ask, there's nothing in the press yet concerning Lambert's arrest, nor is there to be any press release. Speir has had it OSA classified."

"The Official Secrets' Act. What are they so worried about?"

"No idea, but the classification is extended to Soraya's apparent suicide as well. There's a complete press blackout."

"How did you hear?" Broadhurst asked as he scribbled a note requesting an appointment with the King which he passed to his secretary.

"Speir briefed me this morning." White raised his eyebrows. "Looks like a power play for your job, Chas."

Broadhurst shook his head. "There's more to it than that. They've got every right to get upset about the leak surrounding the Prince's escapade, even to question the integrity of the security setup, but I've got some niggling feeling that there's another dimension to all this which we don't know about."

White stood up to leave. "Keep me in the loop Chas. By the way, I hope Rashid was useful."

"My French colleague told me he was an absolute star. You've got a good man there."

"I hope so. Right now, we spend as much time looking behind us as we do looking forward. You don't know who to trust."

Their final exchange was a brief conversation about the diminishing public appetite for more news about Prince Arthur, a story which was now confined to comment and analysis rather than a sensationalist headline approach.

Broadhurst flicked through the brief police and pathology reports, highlighting with a marker pen the odd passage that interested him. He asked for Marchal to join him. He was beginning to see the Frenchman as his one true, uncompromised ally in this whole affair, albeit that their objectives were not exactly the same. Right now, he wasn't quite clear what his were or, for that matter, what they should be.

"If he survives, what's in store for him?" Marchal asked, after hearing about Lambert's attempted suicide.

"A custodial sentence in an open prison if he's okay. Otherwise, some mental institution if he's not. In many ways, he'd be better off dead. He's a good, proud man, a professional policeman, like you. This business will destroy him."

"Any news on Rosenberg?"

"Nothing. I've read the reports on Soraya's death. There are one or two inconsistencies which could lead away from suicide, but they're tenuous."

"How tenuous?"

Broadhurst flicked through the pages. The death was consistent with suicide in that there was one set of footprints to indicate that she appeared to have climbed the staircase in the barn up to the galley, tied the scarf around the rail and her neck and jumped to her death. "The police report makes reference to the facts that the scarf was expertly knotted around both her neck and the balustrade."

"It's possible she belonged, how do you say in English, *Federation du Scoutisme?*" Marchal made a gesture as if he was adjusting a toggle at his throat.

"Guides, we call them. Girl guides. It's possible, but the investigating officer goes on to make the observation that had she simply climbed onto the wooden balustrade and launched herself off, it would have been amazing that neither the scarf, even though it was made of a strong polyester weave, nor the handrail gave way to the momentum of her fall."

"The suggestion being what?"

"Either that she carefully lowered herself off of the gallery banister or that somebody got her body up there somehow?"

"Anything to support that theory?"

"The crime scene pathologist found traces of oil on the barn floor amongst the straw. It's the sort of oil you mix with petrol in a two stroke machine. Lambert's cousin who owns the property swears blind that no equipment is kept or used in the barn. It's solely for food for the horses."

"Is the idea that she was somehow craned up there?"

"Who knows? A study of the balustrade handrail shows a small area that was highly friction polished. Could be, but considered in the round, unlikely to convince a coroner to grant an open verdict, let alone unlawful killing."

"Anything else?"

Broadhurst thumbed the pages before closing the files. "Some more circumstantial stuff. There are three sets of tyre prints in the yard. Two cars can be identified as Soraya's and the owner's. The third has, unfortunately, been spoiled by a couple of police cars that were called to the scene, but there is an unidentified third car to add to the puzzle. Also, there is no trace of her mobile phone. They're checking her call register with the network operator."

"Footprints?"

"The yard was reasonably muddy, but no strange prints. If there was somebody else on the scene, they walked around in bare feet!"

"All in all, it gets you no further forward."

"You're right, but there's one last hope. They're doing a full autopsy this morning. Something may come up. I've asked to be kept informed."

"Do you have anything on my Mr Rosenberg?"

Broadhurst smiled. "You read my mind, I was just about to organise another coffee for us and make some calls. Let's see where we're up to."

Fifty four - @GerbenRosenberg

Gerben looked at the full glass of beer on the bar in front

of him. He couldn't make up his mind whether he liked this English real ale or not. There was no froth and little gas. He took a mouthful, savouring the flavour, as he sat back on the stool.

It had been a good morning, in that it had been absolutely uneventful. Brent had appeared dressed for breakfast, to all intents and purposes, as if he was a member of the Anglican clergy. His smart black suit was complemented with a clerical collar and black bib, two bibles nestled under his arm. To Gerben, he looked the part of a pretty boy Anglican ordinant, an appraisal which appeared to be endorsed by Absolom's spontaneous, approving reaction.

The college administrator welcomed him literally, with open arms. Absolom was a very tall man with some sort of spinal defect that had produced round shoulders and a stooped look that turned his head downward, burying his pointed chin into his chest. He clasped the young man to him. Welcome, Derek Brent. How tragic the circumstances of his arrival. Gerben imagined he was talking about the boy's fictional parents, but it turned out to be some canon or other who had died of a seizure in Gibraltar. Brent expressed genuine surprise and sadness, going a little over the top in Gerben's opinion, by offering a prayer to God for his soul.

Absolom was equally enthusiastic in his greeting to Gerben, thankful that this young man had such a caring friend in Mr Melman and apologising for the rigorous security check at the entrance to the college. Unfortunately, such procedures had become a part of modern life. Gerben made the appropriate comment, aware, in the back of his mind, that this degree of thoroughness could only mean that Benny's inside information was spot on. Somewhere, within a few metres of the route of their guided tour around the college, there was another young man who was fourth in line to the throne of England.

The college was a conversion of a former stately home,

set in immaculate large grounds, beautifully appointed with views over the Welsh hills and maintained with such care and precision that it looked as if the grass had been trimmed with scissors. There were plenty of inmates roaming around the place, mostly men of all ages with the odd sprinkling of sober looking women, most of whom who also found Derek Brent worth a second glance. Ruefully, Gerben recognised, it was more than they gave him.

Away from the college building, down toward the lake, Brent was most enthusiastic about the spot. This was the most beautiful setting. He turned to Gerben, staring intently at him. Here, he would spend his free time in contemplation, feeling close to the works of God. Gerben got the picture.

Absolom's offer of lunch was politely declined. Mishka Melman would stay one more night in the town, check that everything was alright with young Brent at the college, before making his way back home to Malta. He would use the available time doing some sightseeing.

Gerben took another swig of beer. This was about all the sightseeing he wanted to do. A stroll around town, a bite of lunch in that nice looking pub in the high street. Perhaps, he would buy a mobile phone to make a few essential calls. Events in France were weighing heavy on his mind. He needed to take action.

The pretty receptionist tapped him on the shoulder. A man had left a message whilst Mr Melman was out that morning. The note was succinct. A set of sat nav coordinates and a time. Two o' clock. That gave him forty five minutes. Lunch would have to wait for another time. He ordered a sandwich at the bar, exchanging the half finished glass of beer for a bottle of mineral water. The warning above the bar that talked of drinking and driving was a message he heeded. The last thing he wanted was a run in with the UK police.

"You have reached your destination," said the friendly female voice on the sat nav. "Thank you," he replied. The location was familiar. He parked just off the road amongst a stretch of oak trees and undergrowth that lead to the fence that bordered the college grounds by the lake he had so recently visited. The sound of another vehicle coming to a stop made him turn around. The driver of the black Mercedes wound down the window, beckoning Gerben to join him in the passenger seat. There was nobody else in the car. In fact, there was no sign of any other life whatsoever. The road was empty of traffic noise, the only sound, that of the birds chirping in the trees around him.

He closed the car door, turning to face a large, well built man in good condition, whom Gerben recognised from the car park in Bristol. He guessed late forties, early fifties. The man had taken off his hat to reveal a shock of curly, ginger hair that gave him a mischievous little boy look. It was accompanied by a warm grin and an outstretched hand. "Thanks for coming, Mr Rosenberg, or should I call you Mr Melman? My name is Terence Hemmings and I'm pleased to formally meet you." He had a deep, booming voice that suggested he was addressing a crowd.

Gerben felt the tight grip on his hand. "You're Benny's contact in the UK, I take it?"

"Something like that. Now, I'll be quick. I know you're keen to get back to France to sort out some problems, so let's get this sordid little business done and finished with." He reached onto the seat behind him, retrieving a battered old music briefcase which he carefully undid.

"This is like a military operation," Gerben volunteered, keen to lighten the atmosphere.

"It has to be. You witnessed the security in force at the college to safeguard the Prince? There's no way you could get past them with a tape recorder and camera. It must be done clandestinely."

"I understand."

"Tomorrow afternoon at four precisely, you come to this spot. Brent will be waiting for you. You hand him these two bibles. The dark red one has the recorder inside, the blue one, the camera. In turn, he will give you the two bibles he has carried from the college."

"Why me? Why can't you do that?"

Hemmings looked askance at him. "Obvious, man. If anybody comes upon you both, it will sound plausible that you are saying goodbye to your charge. If he's found talking to a stranger, it will alert security and we're done for."

"Of course. I get the picture."

"Good. Now this is the most important aspect. You wait here in your car with this mobile. If he's in trouble and needs to make a fast getaway, he will text you the number nine, nine, nine – nine hundred and ninety nine. Understand."

"Yes."

Gerben nodded.

"In this case, you drive to the main gate, wait for him and drive off in a hurry before security get hold of you both. Now," he looked at Gerben intently, as if willing him to concentrate. "If, as we anticipate, he gets past security with the bibles you have given him, you will obviously not receive the emergency signal. In this case, you wait in the car, in this very spot until midnight at the latest."

"Midnight! You mean I'm stuck here for eight hours, just waiting?"

"Absolutely," Hemmings impressed on him. "Your presence here is absolutely vital if Brent runs into trouble."

"You don't sound very positive."

Hemmings patted him on the shoulder. "These are contingency arrangements. In truth, I'm very optimistic everything will work out fine. So much so, I suggest you bring a good read, sandwiches and plenty to drink. I'm expecting it to go on until around ten o'clock at least."

"And then what?"

"As soon as he's about to be tucked up nicely in bed with the Prince, you'll get a confirmation text, one, one, one – one hundred and eleven. That will tell you everything is going to plan. Now, this is especially important. As soon as he sends you the one, one, one signal, you reply with eight, four, two – eight hundred and forty two. That will tell him that you know everything is okay and I'll contact you to establish all is in order."

"Eight, four, two," Gerben repeated.

"It's easy to remember. Eight divided by four equals two. Got it?"

"Then what?"

"You get the hell out of here. Set the sat nav to Heathrow and catch a plane back to France. Remember the long term parking reference, so when I call you can let me know. Leave the parking ticket in the glove compartment."

"And if he doesn't contact me by midnight, how does Brent get out?"

"That's not your problem. I'll see to that. Everything clear?"

Gerben made to get out of the car, briefcase in hand, but Hemming's grasp restrained him. "One more thing. You have twenty four hours to kill before you finish your part in this business. You may feel tempted to re-establish contacts in France, your family, friends, find out what sort of shit is going down. A word of warning. Don't even think about it. If the British police are alerted, they'll pick you up, return you to France under lock and key."

"I was tempted to buy a mobile, pay as you go version and make a couple of calls."

"Whatever you do, promise me you won't. It's just another day and you're free to do exactly what you choose. Travel back to France using the Melman passport, then destroy it. Surely, you can understand that you'll be much better off, if you turn up of your own free will to sort things out, rather than be sent back as some sort of fugitive from justice."

Gerben nodded. "I take your point. You can rely on me."

"Good. Go and visit some bookshops. Hay on Wye is famous for them. Remember, Benny's relying on you. This is the biggest coup in his journalistic career."

Hemmings watched as Gerben ambled casually back to his car. "Poor fucker," he said out loud. "Forgive me for blaspheming, Lord."

Fifty five - #DAREK

Darek must have shaken a hundred hands and smiled a thousand smiles as Absolom introduced him to every person they bumped into on their stroll around the college. Most of the inmates were males, ranging in age from early twenties, with the majority in their forties and fifties and a handful of aged clerics.

Declining the invitation to lunch in the refectory on the grounds of a mild headache, Darek retired to his appointed room in the main building where one of the staff delivered a tray with salad, dessert and a bottle of mineral water. He was far too charged with adrenalin to eat. The task in front of him consumed his attention.

He needed to pray, first locking the door, bowing low, hands on knees then prostrating himself on the floor as he quietly chanted the third rakat of the midday dhur, submitting himself to God's will, calling on the Prophet to guide him to his destiny. As if freed from the practical concerns of his mission, the act of seeking solace in the readings from the Qur'an gave him an inner peace and strength that sharpened his resolve to follow the path that would lead him to his prescribed destiny.

Calm and at peace, Darek picked at the tray of food, then packed the water together with his two bibles in a small carrying case which he tucked under his arm as he made his way downstairs and into the grounds. His objective was the bench on the lawn in front of the east wing. Most of the students were still lunching in the refectory, so the passage to his designated spot was untroubled by the need to acknowledge fellow students or engage in polite introductory conversation.

Relieved, he arrived at the spot, pointedly taking his time to arrange the contents of his case on the bench to dissuade others from joining him. His bible choice was the New Testament and the books of John and Mark which were his favourites. John told of what this Christian Jesus said whilst Mark concentrated on what the man did. The language was plain, simple to understand and he soon became engrossed.

It was a movement of the curtains at the window of a room on the first floor which distracted him. Darek had the distinct feeling that he was being watched, the hairs on the back of his neck beginning to stick up with the anticipation that he was now the object of someone's attention. He opted for some mildly effeminate gestures, tossing his long hair back over his head, playing with his eyebrows and smoothing the underside of his neck with the palm of his hand. After a while, he returned to his reading before, finally, repacking his case to return to his room. The whole charade had lasted just over ninety minutes, lunch was long since passed and the grounds had filled with students moving from one lecture room to another.

Absolom was totally understanding. It must feel very strange to be suddenly cast into such a different environment. Of course, he must take the rest of the day to rest, familiarise himself with his surroundings. Tomorrow morning, Derek Brent would be introduced to his tutors, his study programme finalised so that his course could begin in earnest. Today, he could engage with the other students. Lectures finished at six with supper at seven thirty. Do try and make it, Absolom urged. Almost all of the ordinants, clerics and staff would be there. It was a good opportunity to get to know people.

Darek, openly enthusiastic about the invitation, was far more interested in just who would not be present at the evening meal. Just after five, he made his way back to the lawn in front of the east wing, deliberately stopping an elderly cleric on the path in front of the window he had noted earlier to engage the man in some light hearted banter as he sought directions to exactly where he wanted to be.

Signs of dusk were in the still air as he stood, looking out over the rippling waters of the lake. Swans moved gracefully in and out of the rushes, ducks landed clumsily on the water, splashing with their wings as they came to a halt. Birds flew in flocks, making strange patterns in the sky, seemingly anxious as they heralded the ending of the day.

"Peaceful here, isn't it?" said the voice behind him.

Darek wheeled around to find himself confronted with a man of similar height and build, but thick set with a receding hairline that was flattened with gel toward the back of his head. He would be a good five or six years older than Darek. He smiled, showing an immaculate set of teeth which he brushed lightly with his tongue.

"You must be new here. I haven't seen you before." He held out a hand, clammy to Darek's touch, the grip of fingers only. "I'm Deacon Baxter. Pleased to meet you."

Darek introduced himself, setting off around the perimeter of the lake as if to terminate the introduction. The other man kept pace. Their conversation was general, topics which were intended to break the ice. Darek increased his stride, but the other man kept alongside. He put one hand on Darek's shoulder. "Look," he said, "it's getting a little chilly out here. Why don't you come back to my lodgings for a cup of tea before supper? I've got a place in the east wing."

Darek made as if to decline, but Baxter was insistent.

They walked briskly back up the incline toward the main building before veering off right to the east wing. The area was beginning to come alive with students finishing their formal tuition programmes, but Baxter steered a course which kept them away from inquisitive eyes or unnecessary attention. Darek made no comment, although the tactic warranted an enquiry.

Entrance to the east wing was through a double glass doorway. The lift was out of order, so they climbed the stairs turning right at the first floor to be confronted by another set of double doors, this time made of steel and firmly locked. Baxter tapped at the door, provoking someone to open a glass plated peep hole. The door was slowly opened, allowing them just enough room to step inside.

"I have a guest for tea," Baxter rattled off in regal tone. "Let us through, please."

The man to whom the remarks were addressed towered over them. Although not unusually tall, his body was the physical specimen of a heavyweight boxer, muscular with powerful arms, giant hands, which he used to frisk Darek before allowing him to pass.

"Is this behaviour really necessary, Lewis?" Baxter asked. "He's a clergyman, for God sake."

"Rules are rules, sir," came the reply. "Can I see the bibles, please?" He flicked through the pages of the two volumes which Darek handed to him. He nodded his assent.

The area was nothing like the quarters in which Darek was housed. This was an apartment with a large lounge, a kitchen which he spotted through an open door and a corridor which, presumably, led to the bedroom or rooms; he couldn't tell.

A log fire was burning in the grate, giving off a pleasing heat. There was no television.

"Sorry about all the fuss," Baxter said with a toothy grin. "Bit off the beaten track here. Lots of break-ins and robberies. Plenty of security needed." It was the tamest excuse Darek could have imagined, but he just smiled in response.

"I'll get us some tea. Do sit down," Baxter said, indicating the two-seater sofa, before he disappeared into the kitchen, closing the door behind him.

Somebody else had been waiting in the kitchen. Their voices were raised in that 'talking angrily, but trying not to let anybody else hear' tone. Darek could only make out a word here and there, but 'not authorised', 'compromising', 'stranger' and 'difficult position' told Darek that someone was unhappy with his presence in the apartment. There was silence for a few minutes, during which the kitchen door drifted ajar.

"Look at it this way, Maxwell," Darek heard the man, Baxter, say, this time in measured tone. "I'm cooped up in this place with you and the incredible hulk out there, twenty four hours a day. I understand why and I accept that, but I need the company, the stimulus of other people. Now be a good chap and just keep stum. Let me have a bit of fun, for the sake of my sanity."

The two men emerged from the kitchen, Baxter holding a tray with a silver teapot and two cups. The other man studied Darek closely without acknowledging his presence as he strode past in the direction of his colleague in the entrance hall. There was the sound of the two men laughing briefly.

"They nanny me, that's the problem," Baxter complained, without explaining the context. "Anyway, let's have tea." He sat down on the sofa next to Darek. "I've put the lemon in the teapot. Hope you like it that way."

As he poured the tea, he moved closer to nestle up alongside Darek, who made no move to distance himself. "Now," he said, in a commanding voice, "tell me what brings you to this enclave of godliness."

It was well rehearsed. Darek had recounted the story several times on the instructions of Mullah Omah to ensure that he could render it with both plausibility and emotion. His attachment to the Anglican church in Malta, the development of his religious training, various references and quotes from the bible."

"Yes. I know all that stuff," Baxter interrupted impatiently. "Tell me about your personal life, your friends, family, physical interests, relationships." He turned toward Darek, their legs touching, his elbow on Darek's shoulder so that his hand dangled, allowing him to play with the lapel on the young man's jacket. Darek's reaction was a sideways, self-conscious smile.

Darek told of the loneliness of his upbringing, the love of his parents who had died so tragically, his lifelong friendships with male friends from the village. There was no mention of any female interest.

"Did you come to England with anybody?" Baxter asked.

Darek talked of his close family friend, Mishka Melman, who cared greatly for him.

"Is this Melman what you might call a special friend," Baxter asked. "Do you have a close, intimate relationship?"

"Very much so," Darek replied.

They talked on for another ten minutes before the supper bell rang out around the grounds. Baxter raised himself, by placing a firm hand on Darek's thigh, lifting himself and leaning over to kiss the younger man on the forehead in what could have been construed as a religious gesture. "Why don't you come around tomorrow evening at this time. We'll have supper here. I'll get Maxwell to knock us up a vegetarian chilli. He fancies himself as a chef, so we'll try him out. How about it?"

"Sounds great to me, but won't it upset your companions?"

"You let me worry about them. You just turn up." Baxter gave him a brief hug, then holding him at distance with both arms as he gave him a wink of the eye. "We'll have some fun tomorrow."

Darek strode jauntily back to the main building. He would have to meet up with Absolom in the refectory, otherwise it would start to look odd.

The administrator patted the chair next to him, indicating for Darek to sit. "Are you feeling better? I saw you strolling around the grounds." He placed his hand on Darek's knee. "You mustn't overdo it on your first day."

Darek gave a weak smile, all the time thinking, what was it with all these clerics? Were they all like this? "I sat and read a little Luke and then some Psalms. It's better than an aspirin for curing a headache."

Absolom laughed, squeezing Darek's knee before retrieving his knife to start the meal. "I'm sure you'll get on very well here," he observed.

"I think I will, "Darek replied.

Following evening prayers, Darek managed to excuse himself from Absolom's attentions, seeking the solitude and the opportunity for the chance to silently practice his evening dhur. It was just after ten before he climbed into his bed, fumbling inside his rucksack for the mobile phone that had been with him since Malta. There was still twenty Euros of credits remaining. He tapped out the message, smiling to himself as he read it back.

Tenet. Opera tomorrow this hour. He tapped out the number and pressed send.

Fifty six - @ChasBroadhurst.kp

The apron really didn't suit or fit Broadhurst, but it was just as well he had it on. The boiling bolognaise sauce spat at him as he stirred it, causing him to retreat from the stove.

"You under attack?" Marchal enquired.

Broadhurst turned the heat down. "In more ways than you could imagine , René. Have you managed to open the wine?"

"I've nearly drunk half the bottle, waiting for this culinary masterpiece to appear."

"Wait no longer. I guarantee you'll have never tasted a spaghetti bolognaise like this in your life before."

"That's what I'm afraid of, Chas."

Broadhurst gave him an imaginary swipe around the head with a long French baguette, which he then preceded to slice.

As Marchal was planning to return to Paris early the following day, Broadhurst had suggested they dine at his apartment that evening, his menu selection based on some very limited kitchen skills. There had been no new information on the whereabouts of Rosenberg, as opposed to Colbert's enquiries in France that had generated lines of enquiry which he needed to follow up. Broadhurst would contact him if and when the authorities had managed to locate Rosenberg. As Broadhurst observed, there was every possibility that the fugitive could have already returned to Paris.

"I spent the best part of the day doing the tourist route," Marchal said, as they finally sat down to an oversize portion of pasta and a fresh bottle of red wine. "Now, I'm sitting in the heart of London, being truly cosmopolitan, eating Italian with an Australian Cabernet and, as a sop to your guest, a crusty French style baguette."

Broadhurst smiled. "You don't know how much I've appreciated your company over the last couple of days, René." He held his glass up in a toast to his companion. "I feel that there's a chill wind blowing around me at the moment, uncertainties and loose ends, neither which can I happily tolerate."

"How did you get on, "upstairs", as you put it?"

"Inconclusive, unfortunately." He wiped bolognaise sauce from his chin with a paper serviette. "The meeting was brief and the answers to my questions, cagey, as if something was being held back. I think I'm suspected of being more in the know about Lambert's behaviour than is the case. I think my position is tenuous."

"I'm sorry you feel that way. How is your colleague?"

"Touch and go, I'm told. The coma appears to be more profound than anticipated, but he's a tough character. If anybody can see it through, he can."

The rain began to beat heavily on the French windows. "Looks like we're in for a mother of a storm," Broadhurst observed, rising from his chair to draw the curtains. "What time's your flight?"

"I haven't booked anything yet. I'll give Patricia a call after dinner to assess how to get back. I'm not a great flyer. My preference would be Eurostar. I'd like to return your hospitality by inviting you to stay with me when you next get the opportunity."

Broadhurst looked up at the ceiling. "Can't tell you when that will be, René. Like I say, loose ends to tie."

"You're referring to the death of Lambert's girlfriend?"

"Amongst other things. The autopsy report highlights some further inconsistencies with a simple suicide." He creased his brow as he tried to recall the wording. "There was evidence of hematoma under both armpits; something called petechiae or bloodspots. The suggestion is that she was gripped tight under both arms in the hours leading up to her death."

"Possibly a hug from Lambert?" Marchal asked.

"He's strong, but do you grip somebody under the arms as an affectionate gesture?"

Marchal shrugged.

"No. It supports the theory of her being dragged in some way. There were also signs of her having been subjected to female genital mutilation when she was younger. This may suggest a clue to her family background or punishment by some strict Islamic fundamentalist in her teenage years. Taking into account the crudity of the act, sex must have been painful for her, so using your body to illicit information, as she did with Lambert, may indicate that whoever was controlling her exerted enormous psychological pressure."

"Did they find the mobile?"

"No. Again, the only activity on the phone was an SMS from an unidentified pay as you go number during the morning."

"Can you retrieve the content of the message?"

"It's difficult to say. All messages are stored on the telecom operator's SMS server for a minimum of a couple of days, but to access them, the police have to have a very good reason. Whether this instance justifies further investigation, I just don't know."

His landline telephone interrupted the conversation,

giving Marchal the opportunity to show willing by clearing away the dishes into the kitchen. All he heard as he set on his quest to find the dishwasher tablets was Broadhurst's welcoming voice saying "Hello, Trevor. Didn't expect to be hearing the voice of my trusted sergeant-major at this time of night."

The interlude gave Marchal the opportunity to consider his own position. Apart from cementing a friendship with a valued ally, this trip to London had done nothing to move Patricia's investigation forward. Where the hell was Rosenberg and why was he in the UK with an unknown, suspected murderer of a young woman in Malaga? What were they up to?

It was an hour later in France, nearly midnight, but Colbert assured him that he hadn't woken her. She was doing some background work on her early morning interview tomorrow. She sounded excited, anxious that a breakthrough might be imminent. For some stupid reason, it made Marchal feel sad, as though something was missing from his own life. There wasn't anything he could remember in recent months that had got his adrenalin pumping.

"So tell me about it," he urged.

"Your papapicman5 and 6 are a couple who work together. They live on a farm in Provence. She's Katarine Legrand; he's Tomas Osman. We've got a nine o clock meeting at 36 tomorrow, or is it today?"

"What do you know about them?" he asked.

"Well," he could sense her interrupting the flow of conversation to take a drink. "Their paparazzi activities are just a small string to their bow. From time to time, they get involved in sting operations. She sets up the target and he takes the pics."

Marchal could hear that Broadhurst had finished his conversation and was moving toward the kitchen. "So what's their big bowstring?" he asked.

"Pornography. They make blue films for the adult market."

The comment jolted Marchal's memory. There was a reference to papapicman on Bernhard's hard drive. They must be the couple who had provided him with the real life stills on which to base his animation. He asked Colbert to verify the information.

"Apparently, this Tomas Osman is a real photography nerd. He's into the technical aspects. He's asked to see the rest of the photographs of Prince Arthur. He's got some information for me about them, so he says."

"Let him see them, but don't let the pictures out of your sight," he urged.

"What do you take me for, a novice?" she chided him.

"Just my policeman's natural caution," he replied.

"By the way, I've managed to dig up a lead on Chantelle Dubois' family background. I've got an address for her parents in a town near Rheims." She stopped, Marchal guessed, for another drink. "The information was hard to find, mind you. Funny enough, it was this Katarine Legrand who put me on to the trail. Anyway, when are you back? We miss you."

He laughed. "Tomorrow. Who's the 'we'? You and Arnault?"

"OK. Well, just me. The Commandant has only mentioned your name on the few occasions we've exchanged words to remind me that you would have already solved the case."

"That sounds true to form. Expect me in the afternoon and we'll tackle the Dubois issue together."

"Look forward to it," she said.

Broadhurst was absentmindedly cleaning the kitchen surfaces. "You look preoccupied," Marchal said.

"The more I learn, the more questions that need answers, rather than produce answers to the questions."

"What's happened?"

Broadhurst held the cognac bottle up to which Marchal nodded his agreement. He poured two stiff measures. "Trevor was a colleague in the army. We served together. He's with the uniformed police now. This week, he's night duty sergeant at West End Central."

"You seem to have contacts in most places."

"Comes with the job. Anyway, last night, about forty minutes before Lambert was discovered with his wrists slashed, he had a visitor. One of Speir's men asked to be let into his cell to continue the interrogation. Trevor checked with Special Branch. He was told that the visit was authorised and, one more thing."

"You intrigue me."

"He was instructed not to record the visit in the police log. Officially, no one ever came to see Lambert last night."

Fifty seven - @Bizzybuzzybee

The newly developed Limassol marina in Cyprus had been Benny Ram's strategic choice as a home berth for his fifty three metre Baglietto super yacht. The craft could comfortably accommodate twelve guests in five staterooms, plus a spectacular full beam master suite and private office. With a top speed of seventeen knots, the twin screw, five thousand horse power Caterpillar engines could cruise around the globe at fifteen knots while the guests could enjoy a large sundeck, Jacuzzi and gym facilities.

Ram employed a crew of nine men and three women, captained by a thick set Croatian from Split who, as dawn broke, was completing a detailed maintenance check in preparation to sail. His decision to tackle the top deck first was a conscious one. Once the day was underway, tourists who had come to see the construction work at the marina would congregate around the berth, trying to imagine who could be the owner of this majestic vessel and just how much it was worth. Few guessed right. Benny Ram had seen little change out of thirty two million dollars, but, so what. It was his folly and, anyway, it was only money.

290

Benny Ram was still in Dubai City, but all that was about to change. There was no need to erase the message from the mobile. Before tomorrow was over, the expensive little handset would be at the bottom of the Mediterranean and its message that "tenet" was in play and "opera" would be fulfilled within 24 hours never to be seen again.

Benny alerted his captain. The yacht would be sailing late tomorrow night. The destination would be advised in due course. No. He would be travelling alone.

His final contact was to charter a plane for the following night to take him to Limassol. It would be between two and three in the morning, Dubai time. He would give thirty minutes notice of his arrival. The exact timing was out of his control. Now, it was up to others to complete their allotted tasks.

Fifty eight - @ChasBroadhurst.kp

The ring of the telephone woke Broadhurst. Nearly nine o' clock. They had both overslept. His mouth was furry from too much alcohol. "René!" he shouted through the doorway. "Time to get up. It's late. Your fault for insisting on that second brandy." He made it to the phone by the fifth ring.

"You accuse me," said the voice from the second bedroom door. "You almost forced it down my throat and I thought you Scots just drunk whiskey!" He laughed, but Broadhurst's mood had changed as he listened to the voice on the end of the phone.

"I see," was all he said. "Thank you." He replaced the receiver purposefully into the cradle.

Without asking, Marchal could tell what had happened from the look on the other man's face. "Bad news?" he said, unnecessarily.

Broadhurst puffed his cheeks out with a loud sigh. "Lambert died earlier this morning. They had him on a life support machine, but he had, what we call, a stroke. It's a seizure, a thrombosis." He stopped to reflect for a minute. "His last words to me were to question why I always called him by his surname and not his given name of David. I guess that it was important that I remember him as a good friend and not just as a loyal ally."

"I'm sorry," was all Marchal could say.

"Professor Speir has got a lot to answer for in more ways than one." He checked his tie in the mirror. "I'll choose my moment."

The process of getting washed and dressed, preparing and eating breakfast was carried out in almost total silence. Broadhurst moved around the kitchen like an automaton, totally lost in his thoughts. Marchal remained in the lounge, making arrangements for his return journey to Paris. Colbert could cope. He would take the train after all. It would see him in the office by around four that afternoon. Time to make his goodbyes. It was getting on for eleven o'clock. He would have to hurry.

This time, it was Broadhurst's mobile ringing that interrupted their conversation.

"Hello, Doug," he said. For five minutes he listened intently to the Gibraltar police chief's narrative. "Just confirm one more time who this Absolom is?" He made a brief note. "Good on you, Doug. You don't know how much help you've been."

He pocketed the mobile and turned to face Marchal. "I know where your Mr Rosenberg was this time yesterday. Let's hope he's still there. Come on. I'll talk as we drive."

Doug Wiley had just come from the funeral service held for Acheson on the Rock. As a courtesy, he had attended, accompanying the mourners to the crematorium. The Bishop had thanked him for coming and for the discretion he had shown locally regarding the circumstances surrounding the death of his canon. One good piece of news. The administrator of the theological college in the UK had phoned earlier that morning to offer his condolences. He also confirmed the safe arrival of young Derek Brent, accompanied by his family friend, Mr Melman. The Bishop had simply acknowledged the comment, assuming it was a routine matter that Acheson had been dealing with prior to his death.

"Do you understand the significance?" Marchal asked as they made their way along the crowded A40.

"Totally," Broadhurst replied. "The guy who phoned is a Geoffrey Absolom. He's in charge of the theological college at Hay on Wye where Prince Arthur was staying before we moved him on."

"You think this Melman is Rosenberg?"

"Almost certainly. It also puts a new complexion on the death of Soraya. She must have been feeding information on Prince Arthur's whereabouts to Rosenberg. Obviously, with David under suspicion, she didn't find out that Speir had given the instruction to relocate the Prince."

"Are you suggesting that Rosenberg killed Soraya?"

"Why not? She was no use to him any longer, just an embarrassment, perhaps even a threat. The place she was found is only a couple of hours away from where we're heading. He could have easily made a detour. Remember, his travelling companion is a suspected murderer."

"It's hard to imagine Rosenberg as a killer."

"They come in all shapes and sizes. You know that." Broadhurst moved into the overtaking lane to pass a stream of heavy goods vehicles. The BMW's acceleration was impressive. "Rosenberg must be after another sting, believing he can compromise the Prince with more revealing sexual material, recorded conversations, that sort of thing."

"Do you think there's more in it than straightforward publicity?" Marchal was uncomfortable with the conversation. It all seemed to be moving too fast for his liking. Assumptions were being made and assumptions were dangerous. "You need to be careful in jumping to conclusions," he cautioned.

"Can't you see, René? It's all falling into place." Broadhurst's mind was working overtime. "The real objective is to try and bring down the monarchy. It's under threat for a host of reasons, financial, social and moral. Whoever Rosenberg is working for, his job is to help tip the Royals over the edge of the republican precipice."

"Are you suggesting that Rosenberg could really be the original papapicman, that he is the person responsible for the death of the two paparazzi?"

"It's possible. Maybe, the victims knew too much about what Rosenberg was up to. He had to kill them."

Marchal's expression was quizzical. "But he was never in the right place at the right time. How come?"

Broadhurst chortled. "Don't be so naive, René." He patted the wallet in his back pocket. "I've got enough money in there to contract some out of his mind drug addict to commit half a dozen murders. You don't have to be there." He swerved to avoid an oncoming car.

"You're not going to resolve anything if you keep driving like that, Chas. As it is, it's like a nightmare just being a passenger in a car that's driving on the wrong side of the road!"

"Sorry. I'm just anxious to get there. Absolom's secretary gave me a total shut out. He's on some tutorial awayday at Winchester Cathedral and, even if he wasn't, there is no way he would discuss any matters concerning inmates of the college over the telephone. I told her who I was, but she laughed at me. She said I couldn't imagine the persona adopted by inquisitive journalists who were trying to get information."

"You can't blame them for that line of defence."

"I know." He checked the signpost. They were in the Forest of Dean. Not too far to go now. "I just want to get my hands on these two buggers before any damage is done."

Fifty nine - @PatriciaColbert.36

Patricia Colbert looked through the one way window at the couple sitting in the interview room. The kindest way that she could describe their appearance was bohemian. She could imagine them sitting on the pavement outside the entrance to the Metro, covered by a blanket, the obligatory docile mongrel dog at their side, an old woolly hat pushed out in front of them to collect the odd coin from a passer-by. The only paradox was the expensive looking camera case on the table in front of the man and the gold charm bracelets on the woman's wrist which partially obscured the tattoo design which ran up her arm and disappeared into the sleeve of an old chintzy blouse. Both were small in stature, she, about a metre fifty, he, another ten centimetres taller, maybe. She had long, matted auburn rinsed hair. He was bald. They both had a one stud earring in their right lobes.

Talking to them soon demonstrated that appearances are, more often than not, deceptive. They were a cultured, intelligent couple who were obviously very much in love.

Colbert ran through the formalities of identification, residence and background before she got onto the reason for the interview. She explained that Gerben Rosenberg had six clients who had been allocated the papapicman hashtag. They were five and six. Three and four were dead and two was missing.

"No, he's not," Tomas said. His English was spoken with an eastern European accent. "He's on his way back from Cairo. He was delayed. He should be arriving late tomorrow."

"Can you give me details?" Colbert asked.

He was cagey. It could wait until the meeting was finished.

"Do you know who the original papapicman is?"

"No idea." He retreated into a shell of suspicious silence.

Katarine found the idea inconceivable that the two

victims of a vicious killer had been lured to the locations where they met their fate at Rosenberg's hand. He had been their agent for about eighteen months and had secured a couple of good deals for them with the redtop tabloids. In one case, they had secretly filmed interviews of a meeting with an indiscreet top flight football club manager where she had posed as the wife of a Russian oil magnate and, in the second, she had assumed the identity of a member of the Iranian secret police trying to buy secrets from a disaffected nuclear scientist from Hungary.

"We have very little dealings with him," she explained. "He comes over as your archetypal hard-headed Jewish businessman. There was nothing in Rosenberg's demeanour that suggested violence. Anyway, why would he want to kill the sources of his income? It doesn't make sense."

The couple's main area of activity was making and distributing blue movies which, in no way, involved Rosenberg. They had been in the business for ten years, achieving a reputation as market leaders in new angles of presenting a well worked and tried and tested theme. Katarine looked around at her partner with pride. "Tomas is a genius in the genre. His storylines, cast selection, direction and, above all, his photographic skills are second to none."

For the first time, Osman gave a wry smile. "We don't touch anything really hard or illegal. We like to keep it light hearted, fun for the viewer. What the kind of people who buy our work want, is explicit sexual reality, the ability to put themselves in the place of the man or woman who is performing. The cast have to be convincing actors."

His enthusiasm roused an interest in Colbert to see an example of his movies, but she kept the urge to herself.

In answer to her question, yes, of course, they remembered Bernhard very well. He was a talented graphic designer. The idea of an animated porn film based on the images they had supplied him was intriguing. They'd like to buy the work from his family. Did that sound cruel and heartless? They were very sorry he was dead.

Embarrassed, Osman changed the subject. "You said on the phone that we could see the rest of the images taken of Prince Arthur?"

Colbert tapped the mouse alongside the computer screen, bringing it to life. "Is this general professional interest or is there an ulterior motive?" she asked.

"I just need to confirm something," he said. He looked closely as she scrolled through the images one by one on the screen.

"Well," she said at the end. "Anything to tell me?"

"The suggestion is that these stills were taken by paparazzi with long distance equipment. Yes?" He took a photo from his pocket. "This was taken, hand held, at a range of a hundred metres. See any difference?"

Colbert studied the image, then shook her head. "You tell me."

"In my photo, you can see two things. The outline of the person in focus is very slightly blurred. That's because opportunism normally means you have to be holding the camera at the right moment. You can't mount it on a tripod and hope the victim accommodates you."

"I see that."

"Second, because I've got one subject in focus, the surrounding environment, nearer or father away is blurred, out of focus. See the trees behind him?"

He pointed at the computer monitor. "Now look at all these images. Not one is blurred and everything is in focus." He scrolled quickly through the stills. "In my opinion, whoever took these photos had mounted cameras all around the building and swimming pool area. They're not security cameras. The images are much, much more nitid and carefully defined. It must have taken a couple of days work to install all this kit."

"You're suggesting it was an inside, pre-planned job? Someone had access to the building before the guests arrived?"

He nodded. "Get a second opinion, if you like, but as far as I'm concerned it's a no brainer."

"These images were sold to *BV* as having originated from papapicman." She was reading from the file of interview notes which Marchal had prepared.

"Your call," he said. "On the face of it, find out who was in the building beforehand and you've identified the link to papapicman. Why don't you ask Dubois if she's got any information."

Colbert reacted at the mention of the name. "You know Chantelle Dubois?"

Osman immediately clammed up.

"This is important, I promise," Colbert pleaded, first to a passive, non-reactive Osman, then turning her attention to Katarine. "Please," she said.

"We met her once," Katarine finally replied. "It's her partner we really know well. Nana is a very old friend of ours."

Colbert waited for the explanation.

"Look," Katarine leaned forward across the table, glancing quickly toward her partner for some sort of acknowledgement. He was stony faced. "It's an unwritten rule in our profession that you never talk about the people who work for you. It's like a priest at the confessional or a doctor with the Hippocratic oath."

Colbert allowed herself a giggle. "Pretty dramatic and disproportionate comparisons, don't you think?"

"Not to us." There was a trace of annoyance in the retort.

"I'm sorry. I meant no offence." She reverted to a serious tone. "We're trying to solve two murders, at the same time as protecting you two from the possibility of joining the victims' list, so please, give me all the help you can, however irrelevant you may feel it to be."

Osman gave an almost imperceptible nod of the head.

"Nana Breton is one of the mainstays of our cast list," Katarine whispered. "She has been with us for several years. Brilliant at what she does. There's nobody to touch her acting skills."

Colbert looked surprised. "She's a porn star?"

Osman interrupted. "Call her what you will. She's a lesbian, but when she's writhing around with some young stud's oversized member inside her, you'd think she was the horniest heterosexual woman you could wish to meet. And many men do. She's brilliant at acting the part. It's not just moans and grunts. The viewer feels like she's emotionally committed to the act. We could do with another dozen like her."

"And the connection to Dubois?"

"Nana's very versatile. For obvious reasons, her woman to woman interpretations are extra erotic. Dubois was in between relationships, betrayed and vulnerable. She got hold of one of our videos. The credits at the end of the film refer to our trade mark company OSKA."

"Let me guess," Colbert interrupted. "She looked you up, asked for an introduction to Nana?"

Katarine took up the story. Chantelle Dubois had apparently developed a fixation with the image of Nana, every day the urge to get to know her growing stronger and stronger. One day she turned up unannounced at the warehouse they used as a studio. By this time, she was the newly appointed chief executive of an influential weekly magazine, *BV*. This was a contact Katarine and Tomas were more than pleased to have.

"I could see she was nervous, embarrassed and afraid that her advances to the woman who had become an obsession would be rejected." Katarine recalled the chain of events, her eyes fixed on a point in the middle of the table. "I think that's why she brought the man with her, a sort of prop to turn to in case things went wrong."

"A man?" Colbert quizzed. "Bernhard?"

"No." She shook her head. "Dubois introduced him as her brother. He must have been a few years younger."

"A brother?" Colbert was puzzled. "My information is that she's an only child?"

Tomas interrupted. "We don't know whether he was

her brother, or not. We never saw him again."

Katarine nodded her agreement. "I must say, I thought there were some physical similarities between the two, but, maybe, I just saw them because she'd said he was her brother. You know, sort of auto suggestion."

Colbert was scribbling in her notebook. "But, in any event, she hit it off with Nana?"

"They got on from their first exchange," Katarine continued. "It was real chemistry. The rest, as they say, is history. Their relationship blossomed. Dubois hired her to work at *BV* as her personal assistant. They're still together now, as far as we know."

"So, it cost you the services of your star performer?"

Tomas laughed. "Good Lord, no! From what Nana tells us, as much as they love each other, they're both strong willed women. Our business pays well, much better than a PA to a magazine editor. Nana likes to spend, so she still does plenty of work for us."

"She must have a busy life," Colbert agreed.

"Unfortunately, she's out of commission at the moment," Katarine said. "She fell off of a stool she was using as a prop on one of the shoots just last week. Twisted her ankle badly. They'd had a disagreement about something. Nana came on set angry, carried on like a bull in a china shop. It was an accident waiting to happen."

"She's on the mend, "Tomas added. "At first, she needed a stick. Now, she's just walking with a limp."

Colbert flicked to a fresh page in her notebook. The interview was coming to an end. She needed to set up a meeting to visit Dubois' parents in Reims. She was looking forward to a day out with Marchal. They could find a nice spot for lunch together far away from Paris. "You were going to tell me about papapicman two?" She could see that Tomas was still hesitant. "I do need to brief him on the dangers of setting up unscheduled meetings. The three of you need to be totally on your guard and let me know about anything out of the usual."

Tomas lowered his head, obviously conscious that he

was about to betray a confidence. "He's known as the Banker. His real name is Bernie Fox. He's an American who spends most of his time moving between London, Paris and Frankfurt. All his work is either political or financial and business based."

"How do you come to know him?"

"I told you about the two stings we were involved in. It was Bernie who set them up for us. We shared the fee. It was based on mutual need."

"Do you have a number for him?"

Tomas shook his head. "We speak via Twitter. I'll send him a DM to contact you urgently.

"Tell me," Colbert was curious. "Why do all you papapicmen use Twitter? Why not mobiles or emails?"

"We use all the mediums, but Twitter's great. Everybody recognises it as an open book, exchanging comments, posting info and visuals for everyone to see. It's social communication. The fact that you can move around in Twitter posting private messages to one another is a new phenomenon to the authorities who like to hack into mails and mobile communications."

"You mean Twitter is perhaps overlooked because its main purpose is a public forum for exchanging information?"

"Exactly. We've moved onto more than one platform now. We don't use DMs when we want extra security. All the same, nothing is foolproof and you've got to be careful. The paparazzi are universally hated, especially by the people whose lives they've screwed up."

Sixty - *@ChasBroadhurst.kp*

There was a public car park at the end of the High Street. During their journey, Marchal had dug up the information that his companion had requested on the internet, though it had cost the remainder of his mobile's battery strength.

There were four possible hotels in and around the centre of Hay on Wye. Broadhurst would check them out. Marchal needed to find somewhere with an internet link to check his messages and to charge up his battery. It was now just after two thirty. In the absence of any contact, they would meet back at the car in an hour. Broadhurst disappeared at a gallop.

Marchal tracked his way through the afternoon shoppers and tourists until he found a bookshop in a street just off of the main road that boasted not only a café, but internet access and free Wi-Fi. As helpful as the young assistant was, she could not help him with his mobile. His charger had a two pin continental plug. The UK uses a three pin system. He would have to either buy a plug adaptor, like the one in Broadhurst's apartment, or a new phone charger. There were plenty of shops back in the High Street.

He wasn't going to walk back now. His decision was to run through his messages first, let Patricia know he would be delayed and buy a car charger on his return. That way, no time would be wasted. He would charge the battery up en route to wherever they were going next.

There was a musty smell from the shelves and shelves of old books that surrounded him. The café was full of people with empty cups in front of them, engrossed in the books they were reading, seemingly unaware of the world around them. Marchal hovered. The three computer stations were all occupied by students intent on copying information from the monitors into large notebooks. He could see why the printer wasn't in use. A pound per page! That was extortionate.

Eventually, a young man with a red nose and a hacking cough left the end station, shuffled to the pay desk. The sales assistant motioned for Marchal to take his place, a warm seat, perhaps, but the remainder of a feint aroma of cough sweets and an overriding sensation that the whole area was a nest of flu germs. As if it would make a difference, he ran his handkerchief over the keyboard and the screen of the monitor.

There was nothing special to note on his email account. Patricia's brief message of thirty minutes earlier was that her attempt to call him had gone straight to his answering service. Anyway, just to say that her meeting with papapicman 5 and 6 had thrown up some interesting facts which she would like to discuss with him as soon as he was back. She had made an appointment for them to visit Dubois's parents in Reims around noon on the next day. His reply was brief. Phone needed charging and he was on the trail of Rosenberg which had delayed his return. He would phone later.

There was also a one liner from Monique thanking him for the visit and looking forward to him following up his suggestion to move temporarily to Lille. She felt relieved and hoped for the best.

Marchal checked his watch. The sign had said a maximum of forty five minutes on the machines when people were waiting. He still had ten minutes left. On impulse, he logged into his Twitter account, following the link to the papapicman page. There were half a dozen Tweets, mainly comments from Tweeters whom this enigma had selected to follow. There was a single incomplete line of text which intrigued him. It was from someone with the hashtag kuzkazin. He copied the message word for word. It read "ur deal to bring my family to Van. Sator's promise". It made no sense. There was a polite murmuring behind him. It was time to go.

There were even more people pushing into the shop through the doorway. He could see why. It had started to drizzle with rain. He would have almost missed him had it not been for the man's voice just ahead of him. "Look where you're going," it said in English with a pronounced French accent.

Marchal leaned across to touch the man on the shoulder. "Rosenberg!" he exclaimed.

The man turned around, a look of sheer amazement on his face.

"You!" Rosenberg seemed agitated. "I didn't recognise you. You were on the computer at the end." He shook his head in amazement. "Don't tell me Benny's got you involved in this business as well?"

They moved to a corridor of the shop which was free of browsers. "Sorry?" Marchal was confused.

"Okay. I get the picture," Rosenberg said, a knowing smile on his face. "The policeman can't admit he's in the pay of the media mogul, but, don't worry, Bates told me all about it. That lawyer Kamal involved? He's Benny's paymaster, isn't he?"

The immediate reaction was for Marchal to say that he didn't have a clue what Rosenberg was talking about, but it was best left for now. He would have to be subtle in his follow up, just to find out what it all meant. He gave a weak smile.

"I never did thank you for sorting out that mess with the memory card," Rosenberg continued regardless. "You saved my bacon. I know a good Jew shouldn't say that." He laughed.

Marchal gripped his arm. "Listen, this is important. We need to go somewhere where we can talk. You're in serious trouble in France."

"I know, but I don't understand why. I have committed no crime. Whatever is happening, it has nothing to do with me. You should know that." They moved back toward the exit. The rain had stopped, but a glance at the sky suggested more was on its way. "I don't know what your involvement is, Capitaine, but I have to run an errand. Can we meet up later tonight?" He began to walk out of the shop onto the pavement, turning right away from the town centre.

"To be honest, now I've found you, I don't want to let you out of my sight."

Rosenberg turned on him. "If you're here as a babysitter, to make sure I do my job, then forget it! I gave my word to Benny and I'll keep it." He took the car key out of his pocket, moving toward a parked green Astra.

"Where are you going now?" Marchal was anxious. There was no way that he could restrain the man physically.

"Where do you think?" he replied. "Back to the College with the bibles. He indicated the package on the back seat of the car. "I've already packed my luggage and checked out of the hotel. There's a McDonalds on the roundabout just on the edge of town. Wait for me there. I can't give you an exact time, but it'll be between ten and eleven tonight."

"You'll be there? Definitely?"

"Of course. I need you to help me get this mess sorted out." He sat in the driver's seat, opening the window. "As soon as Brent gets his leg over the Prince, then I'm finished and out of here." The tyres screeched as he put the car into gear and accelerated away.

Marchal turned on his heels, making his way hurriedly back to the town centre where he quickly found a phone store to purchase a charger for his make of mobile. Shortly afterwards, he was back at Broadhurst's car, but it was another ten minutes before his companion showed up, breathless, stopping to bend double, hands on knees.

"I'm out of condition for all this field work," he said. "I found his hotel, but he's already checked out."

"I know," Marchal said, hurriedly providing a brief summary of his chance encounter.

"Let's get along to the college," Broadhurst urged. "We must find out what the hell is going on." Painstakingly, he set the sat nav to show the route, as Marchal gratefully plugged the charger into the cigarette lighter.

Broadhurst checked his watch. "It's ten to four now. How long ago did he leave?"

"Half an hour. Maybe, a bit less." The information prompted Broadhurst to speed up, but the weight of traffic on the Hereford road forced him to maintain a steady thirty miles per hour.

"Shit!" he exclaimed, thumping both hands on the steering wheel in frustration.

305

Marchal watched the signal bar on his phone move slowly up and back as, lost in thought, he tried to puzzle out Rosenberg's comments.

"You alright?" Broadhurst asked, looking over.

Marchal nodded. Absentmindedly, his fingers played with the piece of paper in his pocket. "Does this suggest anything to you?" He unfolded the paper, reading the words deliberately that he had copied from the Tweet. "It's incomplete, obviously," he said. "I don't understand why. I assume that the 'ur' is the end of a word. Let's say it's 'your' for the sake of argument."

"It somehow rings a bell in the back of my mind, but I can't think why." Broadhurst gave up on another overtaking move. "'Vans' not a word we use so much these days. It's sort of old fashioned, if you see what I mean. Anyway, it would be 'by van' and not 'to van'. It makes it sound like a place." Is the 'v' small or large?"

"What do you mean?" Marchal gripped the dashboard "Careful! You'll get us killed!"

Broadhurst swerved back into lane after a close encounter with an oncoming vehicle.

"Sorry." The incident abruptly ended the conversation as Marchal felt obliged to take the role of a back seat driver if they were to arrive in one piece at their destination. He replaced the paper in his pocket.

Four chimes from the bell tower rang out as they drew up at the entrance to the college. Two large iron gates barred their entrance. With one hand, Broadhurst banged on the horn; with the other he strained in his pocket to retrieve his identity card. An imposing figure of a man, dressed in a padded anorak appeared from the porter's lodge. Broadhurst flashed the card at him, provoking an instant transformation from a surly malaise into subservient attentiveness.

No, he replied in answer to Broadhurst's question. No green Astra had entered the premises in the recent past. In fact, it had been quiet all day. There hadn't been any need for him to attend to the gate since mid morning.

Broadhurst contemplated his next move. "You don't fancy taking the car around the roads that border the perimeter of the college grounds to see if he's parked up somewhere, do you?" He could see what the answer was from the disenchanted look on Marchal's face. "Alright, you walk up the drive and find this Absolom character," Broadhurst conceded. "Explain that you're with me and he is to summon Brent immediately to his office. I'll be back in ten minutes. If he's got any problems, speak to me on my mobile. You've got my number. Rosenberg can't be far away." He turned to the man on gate security. "If this Astra arrives, let him in, but hold him at the gate. Do not let him out of your sight. Understood?" He backed the car up and headed off down the road.

The man on security was using a walkie-talkie. He indicated for Marchal to start walking. It was a good two hundred metres up the driveway to the college building. As he made his way, his shoes making a crunching sound on the gravel, a figure was walking toward him. The man had a gait he recognised, but he couldn't quite make out who it was.

Sixty one - @GerbenRosenberg

Gerben had taken great pains to park the car amongst the trees, hidden as close to the fence as possible. On the other side was the lake he had walked to a day earlier. The distant chimes told him that he was right on time. Apart from the gentle sound of the wind in the trees, there was an eerie silence, broken only by the occasional swish of car tyres on the wet road some forty meters behind him. The rain had stopped, but the air was humid, threatening a further downpour at any time. He had unpacked the two bibles, which were wedged for protection between the buttoned jacket and jumper he was wearing.

Brent appeared over the rise, walking toward the lake,

turning every so often to ensure that no one was behind him. He raised a hand in front of him to acknowledge that he had seen his contact.

The two men shook hands formally, an automatic reaction, which Gerben found a little absurd in the circumstances. Brent was staring straight at him, but, somehow, seemed far away, as if he was transfixed on a point somewhere behind Gerben's head. "You want these?" Gerben handed the two bibles over the fence, receiving, in return, the two volumes which the young man was carrying. "Are you alright?" he asked, still confused by the distant look on Brent's face. "You look like shit!"

"I'm ready. Your work is nearly done. The time is near." The words were spoken softly.

"Not near enough for me. I've got to sit in this car for another eight hours waiting for your message. That's unless you get caught. If I get the nine, nine nine, I'll be round at the front gate, but I tell you this. If security's on to me, I'm off and you can look after yourself. Understand that?"

Brent nodded. "I'm sure it won't come to that."

"Well, get your leg over as quickly as possible. The sooner you page me with the one, one, one signal, I'll page you back and then, I'm off. Don't expect me to hang around. I've got a meeting with someone."

"You will hear from me." He turned to go, then turned back. "Rosenberg," he called.

"Yes."

"I want you to remember something."

"What's that?"

He held his hands together in front of him, his head bowed. "The angel of death does not forget you. And know o son of Adam, if you are heedless about yourself and do not prepare, no one else will prepare for you. You must meet Allah the Mighty and Majestic, so take for yourself and do not leave it to someone else. Peace be on you."

"Yes. Very good. You're coming on a treat. You're

beginning to sound like a real Christian rabbi, not some waster who's about to take snaps for money of the guy he's fucking as he records the groans and grunts of orgasm for posterity." He shook his head. "Now, go and get on with it and let me get home. Shalom Macher."

Gerben was alone again. He had bought a book on money management in the shop where he had bumped into the bent policeman. Flicking through the pages, his mistake was to switch on the engine of the car to generate some heat to warm the dampness in his feet. The noise must have alerted the oncoming driver. Gerben looked around. All he heard was the sound of brakes screeching as the vehicle travelling past him ground to a halt. All he saw was the figure of a man alongside, opening the driver's door as a blast of chill air hit him.

Sixty two - @renemarchal

"Still on diplomatic duty, Mr Maxwell?" Marchal couldn't help the sarcasm which was treated with a look of casual nonchalance. They had come together about half way between the entrance and the college building.

Maxwell had pocketed the walkie-talkie and was speed dialling on a mobile. "Shall we walk back to the porter's lodge." It was a command, no hint of a choice.

"Your boss asked me to make contact with Mr Absolom."

"Yes, I know. He's asked me to tell you to hold fire for a few minutes. Something's come up. He'll be in touch. Just take a seat."

The lodge was cramped and stifling hot. Marchal sat on the only chair which was stationed in front of a small counter that faced a sliding window. Behind him was a small cupboard, files on the shelves, a tray on the top, littered with dirty cups, sweet wrappers and a large thermos flask. He had no hesitation in declining the offer to help himself to a cup of coffee. The first security guard was chatting with Maxwell just outside the closed door, effectively imprisoning Marchal within. His mobile rang.

A draught of cold air hit him around the legs as Maxwell opened the door. "Best no phone calls, sir. Security alert and all that. Not until Mr Broadhurst contacts us."

Marchal checked the number. "It's my office in Paris. They'll get concerned if I don't answer."

Maxwell motioned him to go ahead, but stayed leaning against the open door.

"Hello, Patricia, "he said. "How's it all going?"

"Good, René. Listen, I got your message about the delay. Is everything alright?"

"I think so," was his non-committal reply. "I'll try and be back tomorrow at the latest."

She started to explain the revelation about the system used to photograph the Prince that Tomas had described and how she now knew the identity of the missing papapicman 2.

Maxwell was also answering a call. He spoke briefly before turning to Marchal with the gesture of running the side of his hand across his throat. The meaning was universal, but was unnecessary. Patricia's enthusiastic explanation of her plans with him for the following day were interrupted as the trickle charge in the mobile battery ran out leaving the screen blank and the phone dead. He laughed into the mouthpiece, feigning his conversation was still in progress. "That's right," he said in a relaxed voice.. "If I'm not back send out a search party." He pretended to end the call, conscious that, as a natural French speaker, Maxwell had understood every word of his side of the conversation.

But Maxwell was preoccupied with other matters.

Sixty three - @ChasBroadhurst.kp

The BMW had come to a shuddering halt. He had instinctively checked the rear view mirror as the sound of a car engine from within the wooded glade had reached his ears. Just as well there was no traffic about. The tyres had locked on the damp surface, putting the car into a skid which had forced it onto the wrong side of the road. Broadhurst took a deep breath and completed the three point turn which put the vehicle back in the direction from which he had been travelling. Weren't these cars supposed to have ABS or something?

He drove slowly until he found the way into the undergrowth along an uneven dirt track. The bushes scraped against the side of the car as the canopy of branches from the trees around him turned the remnants of light from a gloomy day into virtual darkness. As he moved forward, he could see the boundary fence of the college, the lake beyond and, just to the left, a green Astra, parked, almost out of view from the road. There was nobody in the vehicle.

He parked directly behind the Astra. Treading carefully, he checked the driver's door. Locked. Through the window, he could make out two bibles on the back seat, a thermos flask alongside a plastic food container and a French paperback. A small suitcase was propped up against the window. He moved around to the passenger side.

Whoever had come up behind him hadn't made a sound. The first thing he felt was the barrel of a handgun pressed into his back. "You know the drill, Broadhurst. Chin on the roof, legs spread out, hands behind your back. Don't try anything stupid."

As familiar as the voice sounded, he couldn't place it immediately, but the order was spoken in an uncompromising tone. He did as he was told, feeling the plastic tie bite into the flesh of his wrists as it was roughly tightened. A powerful arm swung him around.

He stared into the unshaven face of the man he had interviewed a week ago. "Hemmings," he said, half as a question, half as a statement.

He was pushed roughly into the thicket toward a large horse chestnut tree . The man said nothing. There was an unconscious figure, propped up against the trunk, his head and shoulders leaning to one side, a trickle of blood running from his ear down the side of his face. Broadhurst was pushed to the ground alongside him. He took in the scene around him, all the time with one eye on Hemmings, his concentration focussed on the information he remembered from their conversation. About to say something, Hemmings was distracted by the vibration of the mobile in his pocket. "I see," he said as he listened to the caller. "Give me a couple of minutes and I'll call you back."

He kept the mobile in his hand. "Listen to every word I say, Broadhurst. Don't interrupt and don't think for one moment that I would have any hesitation in doing what I say. I'm not bluffing."

"What's all this about, Hemmings?"

"Shut up and listen!" He grabbed a tuff of Broadhurst's hair, forcing his head back against the bark. "You couldn't keep your nose out of something which doesn't concern you. Now you and that French pensioner who's tagging along with you have become an embarrassment. No, not an embarrassment, rather a minor irritant, just like this greedy little prick."

Broadhurst looked at the unconscious figure next to him. "I imagine that this is Mr Rosenberg?"

Hemmings ignored the remark. "I want you to believe me that I will have no hesitation in killing you if I have to. As far as I'm concerned, you're just another piece of collateral damage. That also applies to your French buddy."

There was a painful sensation, excruciatingly painful, that hair was being torn by the roots from his head. It did nothing but steel his resolve. "If you think that whatever senseless, hare-brained scheme you're involved in is going to topple the British monarchy, you're deluding yourself, Hemmings. As for Capitaine Marchal, his only interest is all this nonsense is to question this individual." He nodded toward Rosenberg.

"Maybe, maybe not." He released the grip on Broadhurst's hair. "I'll give you a simple choice. You speak to this Marchal on the phone. You tell him you're involved in a domestic security issue and will be occupied for the next few days. His best option is to go back to France."

"And if I can't convince him?"

"You will." He frisked Broadhurst to find his mobile and trace the Frenchman's number. "If not, Marchal will meet with a very unpleasant road traffic accident which claims his life. I'm guessing you won't want his blood on your hands."

It would be senseless to further involve the Frenchman unnecessarily. The fate of the British monarchy was, probably, the last thing on his mind. Broadhurst nodded.

"It's going straight to his answering service." Hemmings ended the call. "Just a minute." He dialled another number. "Maxwell? Put the Frenchman on the phone. Tell him your boss wants to speak with him."

"Maxwell's in on this?" Broadhurst could not hide his surprise, but Hemmings took no notice. He held the phone to his captive's ear so that he could talk. "No funny business or it's curtains. I'm not joking."

Broadhurst gave a convincing excuse, confirmed that he knew of Rosenberg's whereabouts and would see that he was repatriated to Paris within the next few days. There really was no point in Marchal hanging on. "It's an internal issue. I can't go into details for obvious reasons, but I need to put out some small fires before they get out of control."

"Are you sure there's nothing I can do to help, Chas?" Marchal was concerned.

"No René. I'm absolutely certain. As I'm tied up,

someone from my staff will drive you now to the station. Go to my apartment and pick up your files and luggage. I'll ring the concierge to authorise him to let you in."

Marchal was about to reply, but Broadhurst cut him off. "The quickest way to City Airport is to use my service vehicle. The key to van is in the top drawer of my filing cabinet. Leave the key with information. I'll pick it up later. Enjoy your flight. I'll catch up with you in Paris in a day or two." He ended the call before Marchal could say anything. He looked up at Hemmings. "There. Satisfied?"

For the first time, Hemming allowed himself a smile. "Very concerned about his travel arrangements, aren't you?"

"He's my guest. What do you expect me to say. You're on your own, so fuck off or someone will kill you? Hardly appropriate, is it?"

Hemmings dialled the number again, giving Maxwell instructions to deliver the Frenchman to the main line station to London. "Better ring your concierge," he said to Broadhurst.

Rosenberg had started to stir, attempting to focus on the scene around him, establish the surroundings, and recall exactly what had happened. "Why?" was all he could manage to say.

Hemmings was conciliatory. "I heard you start the car engine. I imagined you were intending to drive away. I couldn't let that happen until the job's done."

Rosenberg had recovered his composure. He strained against the plastic ties that held his hands together. "You didn't have to hit me." He looked across at the gun which was tucked into a shoulder holster. "Untie me! I need some water." Hemmings hesitated, but did as he was asked.

Hemmings motioned to the other man. "I heard somebody approaching. I had to act quickly by ensuring that you didn't make a sound. It was my only option." He cut a length of medical plaster from the roll in his pocket, covering Broadhurst's mouth, pressing it hard against his cheeks.

"Who's he?" Rosenberg asked.

"He's working with the French police to try and find you, send you back to France."

Rosenberg rubbed his wrists. He was still very wary of Hemmings. "I still don't understand why you had to hit me. Anyway, you don't have to worry about the French policeman. Marchal's on our side. He's on Benny's payroll. I arranged to meet him later tonight."

Broadhurst caught the look of contempt in Hemming's eyes. His reply to Rosenberg was nothing more than a sop, but the man took it at face value. "Sorry. It was a bit over the top. Must have been a spontaneous reaction from my army days. I'll make sure you get an extra bonus for the bump on your head."

Apparently satisfied at the suggestion, Rosenberg turned to walk back to his car when the thought must have struck him. "Why were you here, anyway?" he asked Hemmings.

"On the off chance," he replied. "I just wanted to check everything was alright, that you had enough to eat and drink."

"Very thoughtful of you." Rosenberg walked off through the bushes, still pressing gently around the bruise on his head.

Hemmings leaned down, close to Broadhurst's car. "Try anything heroic and you're a dead man. If it was down to me, you'd have a bullet through your skull already. He checked his watch. We'll be here for a few more hours yet, so make yourself comfortable." He laughed out loud. "I regret that dinner will not be served."

Broadhurst wasn't listening. His mind was racing. 'If it was down to me?' If it wasn't down to him, who was it down to?

Sixty four - #DAREK

Darek had expected to feel both excitement and fear, but at the end of his fourth Salah of the day, his pleas to Allah for a swift entry into paradise and to be merciful had left him with a feeling of emptiness, the sensation that there were of aspects of his life that he was obliged to abandon before the opportunity to acquire the experiences had arisen. As he cast his arms in the air three times, his last rakat was to pray for forgiveness for such selfish thoughts. He took a deep breath. His fifth Salah would be just before the journey began.

Darek's day had been low key, uneventful. Sitting through three tutorials, he had grasped very little, but had tried to look as confident and knowledgeable as possible. In the one area of the teachings of Abraham, the relationship between the Old Testament and the Qur'an were so similar, that he felt brave enough to ask a question, which was answered with care and respect by the cleric tutor. He felt proud of himself as his fellow students looked around at him in admiration.

At break times, he had retreated to his room to pray and to be alone with his thoughts. He could not get Rosenberg's comments on their journey out of his mind. At first, the idea that they shared common ground was an anathema to him. How could they? The State of Israel had no right to exist. Jews were a curse on the face of the earth. Yet, the more he had listened to the, almost disrespectful, expressions of religious tolerance, the more he began to question the motives for his own beliefs, beliefs he had never questioned in the past, but simply accepted as the ultimate truths.

The bell for supper interrupted his thoughts. Under his arm, he carefully placed the two bibles he had been given, making his way across the lawn to the East Wing. The same man was on guard, but, this time, he simply waved him through the security check. "Hope you like it hot!" the man said, a large smile across his face. "And I'm not just talking about the chilli!"

Baxter was wearing a silk dressing gown, printed with dragons and licks of flame. He thrust both hands around Darek's shoulders, kissing him on the forehead and pressing him toward him. "Thought for a minute you weren't coming. So glad you decided to make it." He pushed Darek down next to him on the sofa, turning toward him, the dressing gown splitting below the belt to reveal that he had nothing on underneath. Coyly, he retied the belt of the gown to correct the position. "So, tell me." He grasped his guest's hand with both of his, forcing Darek to release the bibles onto a coffee table. Baxter looked at the two volumes. "We won't be needing those tonight. Now, as I was saying, how was your first day?"

Darek was half way through a detailed account of his day when a loud knock on the door, followed by a respectful delay, announced the arrival of Lewis who trundled across the room into the kitchen. "I'll get the Chilli ready," he said, looking straight ahead of him. Ten minutes later, the day's events recounted and opinions exchanged, Lewis emerged, pushing a hostess trolley with a selection of glass bowls nestled in the recesses. "I'll leave it by the table. You can serve yourselves."

"Good man, Lewis. You can take the rest of the night off."

Lewis shrugged his shoulders. "Fat chance of that, sir," he grumbled, as he left the room.

Baxter was exhilarated. "This is marvellous," he said. "First time in days, I've had some real company." He turned to face Darek and held his head between his two hands. He placed a gentle kiss on his mouth. Darek reacted by flicking his tongue around the retreating lips, a small reaction that provoked a deep intake of breath. "You're up for this aren't you?" Baxter exclaimed. Leaning forward, he thrust his tongue deep into Darek's mouth, his hand separately grasping, first to find his companion's genitals, next to lead Darek's hand to hold his. He was gasping for breath. "Let's forget dinner, shall we?"

Darek forced him away. Now, he was in control, just the way it had to be. Baxter retreated across the sofa, unsure of his ground, confused by the apparent rejection. Darek smiled, a benevolent, don't be impatient smile. "Let's eat first. I'm hungry. We can savour the pleasure of this meeting in more ways than one."

Baxter reacted by returning the smile. "People don't usually tell me what to do, but, in your case, I'll make a small exception." He ran his hand around Darek's cheek. "Provided you understand just who the master of ceremonies is when the time comes."

They moved across to the dining table, a veneer of normality as they picked their way through a meal fit for a Prince, emotions bubbling under the surface of an anxious and demanding host who would take his revenge on this young upstart in the bedroom.

Darek could read the signs. It was a little after nine. Within the hour he would make his journey into paradise. He checked the coffee table. The two bibles were exactly where he had left them.

Sixty five - @renemarchal

Not a single word was exchanged between the driver and Marchal as they sped along the final phase of their journey on the M4 to Bristol. Neither man was interested in idle chitchat. It was apparent that the security guard's sullen silence was no more than irritation that his daily routine had been upset by having to chauffeur his passenger on an unprogrammed three hour return journey. Marchal's silent preoccupation was the context of the telephone call with Broadhurst. Something was wrong. The few personal effects he had brought with him from France were in the boot of Broadhurst's car. Why was he being directed back to Broadhurst's apartment and the key to van? Why not 'the' van? The word preyed on his mind.

The driver dropped him off a few minutes before the London train arrived. He had managed to connect his mobile charger to the cigarette lighter in the car, but the trickle feed was barely sufficient for more than a few minutes conversation. His first thought was to call Broadhurst back, but he dismissed the idea. Broadhurst had deliberately cut short their conversation. For some reason, he didn't want Marchal to question his comments. Why? Was someone else present as Broadhurst had talked? Was he in danger? There were so many inconsistencies. Broadhurst knew he wouldn't take a plane. He also knew Marchal wouldn't think about driving on the wrong side of the road. In their earlier conversations, he had made it quite clear that a cab to St Pancras and the Eurostar would be his route back to Paris.

It was past eight before he was shown by the concierge into Broadhurst's apartment. Would he please call down on the intercom so that the alarm could be reset when he was ready to leave.

The key to van was in the top drawer of the filing cabinet? There was no key, just files full of personnel records. There were no clues that he could detect. He was about to shut the file cabinet when he noticed a yellow jotter note stuck to a mini disk. The memo recorder was on the table. The note said 'interview with Terence Hemmings returning from Van' and showed the date and time. Marchal began to listen. It was early on in the conversation. Now, it was all beginning to make sense.

He rushed across to the computer. It was in standby mode, but password protected. He couldn't even guess what it might be. The intercom had four buttons. One said 'office'. He pressed it on the off chance. A hesitant female voice answered. "What can I do for you, Sir?"

Marchal explained that he was Broadhurst's guest. "Is there somebody senior still there in Mr Broadhurst's department. I must speak with them."

"Professor Speir is still in his office."

"Can I talk to him, please?"

Thirty minutes later, the secretary had ushered him to a room in the Palace offices. Speir rose unsteadily from his chair to greet him. "Old age," he said. "Obscene the way we are obliged to tolerate the decay. Comes to us all, sooner or later, I hear you say, but I could do without the arthritis to emphasise the point." He gave his guest a warm smile.

Marchal found the long grey ponytail incongruous, but it was the piercing violet blue eyes that held his attention.

"You say you have some information about Chas?"

Marchal began to explain how he had come to be in Hay on Wye and the last words Broadhurst had spoken to him. "I believe I've come across something that suggests that Mr Broadhurst may be in danger." He produced the mini disc. "There's a comment from a Terence Hemmings that he had just returned from a place in Turkey called Van where he had arranged a multi-faith seminar. I'm sure that's the link Broadhurst was trying to make."

"Go on."

"Then I remembered that I was on Twitter today, on an account with the hashtag papapicman. This is the origin of the photographs of Prince Arthur." He looked over at the laptop on Speir's desk. "Do you mind?"

Speir cleared the pages he was working on, linked to the internet and turned the machine toward Marchal, who began his search.

"There you are," he said, finally. "It's part of a message to papapicman from someone called 'kuzkazin'. Right now, I'm betting that is the name used by this Soraya woman who is supposed to have committed suicide."

"Do you have any proof?" Speir looked troubled.

"No. It's what you call a . ."He hesitated.

"Hunch?" Speir suggested.

"Yes. Hunch. Until a week ago, I thought Twitter was exclusively something that birds did. Now, I've become an amateur expert. My guess is that this kuzkazin sent a DM, a private message, to papapicman. She must have got carried away and exceeded the hundred and forty character limit. Once that happens, the message is split into two and the excess is posted as a general tweet on the account, which anybody can read. I assume that this reference to her family and Van is some kind of arrangement she had made in exchange for passing on information from her lover."

Speir looked critical. "You seem very well informed, Capitaine. And the reference to Sator. Any ideas?"

"None at all, I'm afraid, other than the fact that I've come across words from something called the Sator Square, a Latin palindrome, used in the distant past to denote the presence of a Christian dwelling. It looks as though the words in the Square are being used as some kind of coded message."

"This is fascinating."

"I have to say that I'm making some pretty wild assumptions, based on a few facts and some conversations with Chas; that's Mr Broadhurst. I've got no other hard evidence to back up this theory, but the suggestion is that there are people about who are intent on undermining your British monarchy."

Speir nodded, leaning forward in his chair in a gesture which suggested he was about to impart some important information. "I can't thank you enough, Capitaine, for your contribution. There are elements of what you have told me which dovetail with classified information already in my possession. I must make one thing very clear to you."

"Please do."

"As a foreign national, I cannot bind you to the Official Secrets Act we have in the UK. But these issues you touch on are sovereign to the United Kingdom and have nothing to do with any other country. What are your immediate plans?"

"When I leave here, I'm going straight to St Pancras to catch the Eurostar train to Paris. I have a number of unfinished jobs to do before my retirement next week."

Speir nodded, a sign of relief rather than assent. "Then

can we part with this accord. I will immediately follow up on the information you have just given me, which you must promise to keep to yourself. As you say, it's unsubstantiated."

Marchal acknowledged the fact.

"On our side, we will do everything possible to assist with your investigations in France. You only have to lift the phone to speak to me or Broadhurst. But you must give me your solemn word that no element of your deductions or this conversation tonight will be shared with any other person. As soon as possible, I will arrange for Broadhurst to contact you to explain the outcome to these enquiries to demonstrate our trust and gratitude for your cooperation."

As Marchal had never had any intention of divulging what he had learned, he had no hesitation in providing the undertaking.

The two men shook hands. "Now, I must make some calls," Speir had told him, ushering him through the door towards his secretary. "Show the Capitaine out, please," he instructed. "The best place to pick up a taxi this time of night will be Queensway."

Marchal pulled the collar of his raincoat up around his neck. The night was chilly, rain was in the air. Every taxi that passed had an occupied light showing. He walked briskly toward Queensway, deciding as he did that the metro was probably the best and quickest route to the Eurostar station. A headline on the placard in front of a newspaper stand announced new startling revelations about the Royal Prince. He stopped to buy a copy of the late edition. The newspaper seller was hunched under a tarpaulin which kept his stand dry. "Here are, guv," he said, holding out the paper. "Bit more scandal. If you ask me, they should shoot the bloody lot of them!"

Marchal nodded. As he went to cross the road, his instinctive reaction was to look in the wrong direction to check the traffic. The Skoda had pulled out from the kerb, heading at speed straight toward him.

"Oy! Watch out guv!" the newspaper seller shouted.

Automatically, Marchal stepped back as the car crossed the line where he had just been standing. He was back on the pavement.

"Crazy bastard," shouted the man. "It looked as if he was aiming straight at you." He shook his head. "The times I have to tell you tourists to look right and not left. If I had a quid for every time I've done it, I'd be a rich man."

Marchal's attention was on the car. From his brief glimpse, there was something familiar about the driver. It took a minute while he regained his composure to associate the face. If he was not mistaken, the driver was very much like the concierge who had let him into Broadhurst's apartment. But he could be mistaken.

Sixty six - @ChasBroadhurst.kp

The only light to penetrate the darkness was the courtesy light in the green Astra. Hemmings was sitting in the front passenger seat, wrapped in an overcoat with a copy of the bible held at arm's length in front of him. To say he had been reading it for the previous two hours would have been an understatement. From Broadhurst's viewpoint, half lying across the back seat, his mouth still gagged, hands tied and now with restraints around his ankles, Hemmings had been totally absorbed in the text, flicking back and forth to cross reference various passages, mumbling to himself phrases every now and again. Studying the man had helped to distract Broadhurst from the terrible aching sensation in his shoulders and the shooting pain in his groin. He wriggled his body, but to no avail. Hemmings had not said a single word to him, other than to order him into the car. If he could just talk, understand where all this was leading.

Rosenberg sat sideways in the driver's seat, idly rummaging through a jumbo packet of potato crisps, from which he would eat every now and again. He had tried to interrupt Hemmings on three occasions with the suggestion that his presence was no longer required, but the rebuttal was curt and swift. If an emergency arose now, it was Rosenberg's responsibility to meet up with Brent. So, relax, do the job he had been paid to do and then go.

"I'm beginning to realise I need to get my eyes tested," Hemmings said. "I can't make out the text in this light." He rested the open bible on his lap.

Rosenberg nodded toward the man in the back seat. "What's going to happen to him?"

Hemmings looked up over his eyes. "Nothing. As soon as I get the pictures and the recording, I'll put him back in his car and report it to the police. They'll be enough compromising evidence with him to suggest his involvement in the scam."

Whether the explanation satisfied Rosenberg or not, he did not react, choosing instead to look down at the dashboard clock. Fifteen minutes to ten. If Brent was on schedule, he wouldn't have much longer to wait.

The ring of Hemming's mobile broke the uncomfortable silence. He glanced at the screen, accepted the call, but said nothing. He opened the car door. "Just a minute, please," he said, glancing to satisfy himself that his captive was securely bound before moving quickly in the direction of the wooded area to where he had earlier moved Broadhurst's car.

Broadhurst wasted no time, shaking his head furiously, rolling his eyes, any sign that would convince Rosenberg to release the tape across his mouth. He could see that the man was scared, his eyes furtively searching for Hemmings in the dark, but Rosenberg needed explanations, comfort, anything to convince him that he wasn't in danger. He pulled the tape, releasing it so that it hung from Broadhurst's cheek.

"You must alert the police that we're here." The words tumbled fast and furious from Broadhurst's mouth. "You think your role is to assist this Brent to infiltrate the college to get more revelations about the Prince. Of course, you're not. Something much bigger is underway, something I believe that is intended to destroy the British monarchy. You're a pawn in this, Rosenberg. Your life, and now mine, could well be in danger." The panic was rife in Rosenberg's expression. "If you can't do it, cut me loose and I'll find help."

Rosenberg had reached a decision. "I'm out of here," he said. "If you're not in on this business, then you can blame Marchal. He's Benny's man, a paid police informer who knows exactly what's going on." He opened the rear door and began to pull at Broadhurst's legs. "You're on your own." Grabbing at the body, he let it slide roughly out of the car, causing Broadhurst to gasp loudly with pain as his shoulder hit the ground. The man leaned forward to replace the tape over Broadhurst's mouth, sliding, as he did so, on the muddy ground as he lost his balance.

Cursing, he wiped the dirt from his hands, moving swiftly to the driver's door and reaching for the ignition key. The Astra engine burst into life, headlights splitting the darkness, highlighting the figure running toward the car. Rosenberg moved the gear shift forward, releasing the clutch, just as the passenger door was forced open. A hand reached toward the handbrake

Broadhurst forced himself to roll away from the vehicle. Still bound, all he could do was watch the scene unfold. As the car had jolted forward, Hemming's leg had been struck by the central door support, but his lunge forward had allowed his right hand to secure Rosenberg by the throat. For a moment, Broadhurst lost sight of the two men as they struggled in the well of the car. "What are you doing with that gun?" he heard Rosenberg exclaim. There was no reply. The sound of a single gunshot split the air like thunder, followed by total silence. The driver's door slowly opened and Rosenberg's body slid to lie on the ground, his eyes open, staring blindly at Broadhurst. It seemed as if he was about to say something, but Broadhurst knew that would be impossible. His right ear and half of his forehead was missing, nothing left but fragments of bone and blood.

"Bastard," he heard Hemmings curse as the man appeared, hobbling toward him, visibly in pain. "You'll have to help me, Broadhurst, but don't make any silly moves or you'll suffer the same fate." He bent to cut the ties around Broadhurst's arms and legs, still holding the gun at his side. As the blood rushed back into his limbs, he rubbed furiously at his joints, a pointless attempt to ease the painful sensation. The tape was still loosely stuck across his mouth.

"Lift him back into the driver's seat," Hemmings ordered.

Broadhurst looked at the gun pointed toward him.

"An old memento," Hemmings offered. It looked like an antique from the Second World War, but the remains of the man on the floor, evidence that it still worked.

"He's too heavy for me," he mouthed through the tape, as he pulled at the dead man's shoulders.

"Don't give me that bullshit, Broadhurst! You're a strong man. Just do as I say."

It was a full five minutes before he managed to lift the corpse into place, his hands matted in dark red blood that had started to congeal in the cold. Feeling had now returned to his limbs. He needed to find a chink in the other man's armour, an opportunity which would give him the advantage, but Hemmings was a seasoned pro. There would be no room for a mistake.

Rosenberg's body was slumped over the steering wheel, illuminated only by the single courtesy light above him. Hemming had wiped the old Browning clean of his prints, wrapping the dead man's hand around the stock. The weapon he now pointed in Broadhurst's direction was one he readily recognised, a UK army issue Glock 17, powerful enough to kill two people standing in line and, probably, capable of badly wounding a third.

Hemming's attention was on retrieving the remote pager from Rosenberg's pocket. There was still no light on the screen. He waved the Glock at Broadhurst. "Move over here," he commanded, indicating the wooded area from which he had emerged.

My turn is it now? was all Broadhurst could imagine.

BOOK FOUR – OPERA OPENS THE MYSTIC GATE

Sixty seven - #DAREK

Baxter rolled the remainder of his cognac around the bowl of the glass before downing it in one gulp. On the surface, he was calm, composed, the picture of a man used to the good things in life, but Darek could sense that he was fighting to control the desire that his eyes could not disguise. It was the same, abhorrent look, the tainted smell of breath tinged with anxiety that he had witnessed in Acheson before the cleric had so violently taken him.

"You don't know what you're missing, not drinking alcohol. We'll soon change that." He placed the glass on the mantelpiece. "I think it's time, don't you?" Baxter leaned across to kiss his companion full on the lips. "We have the night before us."

He linked arms with Darek, who managed to scoop up the two bibles from the coffee table with his free hand. They moved down the corridor into the master bedroom. Baxter pointed toward the bathroom. "Be a good boy and get yourself ready. You'll find everything we're going to need in there. I'll wait for you in bed. Don't be long."

Darek closed the bathroom door behind him, prompting an automatic sensor to turn on the light. He flushed the toilet, closing the inflow tap so that he could place the maroon bible with the extended version of his last message to the world in the empty cistern. Looking around, he could see exactly what Baxter had meant when he talked of everything they would need. Alongside a selection of creams, ejaculation depressants and funny heart shaped pills was a row of objects strange to him, a whip, handcuffs, a soft brush like looking object and a leather thong with knots tied in it at intervals. He shook his head in disbelief.

As he began his final Salah, he held up his hands, bowed, sinking slowly to his knees to prostrate himself. He had decided on three raka'ah. Fear gripped his heart. He begged for forgiveness for the weakness he had shown. Finally, sitting up, he turned his head to the right to perform the Taslim which would mark the end of his prayers.

Darek's hand was shaking as he reached in his pocket to retrieve the mobile phone. He tapped out the message – *Opera* and sent it. He opened the blue bible, activating the switch, then closed it. The next time he opened the cover, it would all be over. He waited for confirmation that his message had been received, then found the second number he needed. When the message had been sent, he would drop the handset into the bowl of the toilet. He tapped in the one, one, one code, holding his finger hovering over the send emblem.

"Meet me with open arms, father," he implored as his finger pressed down.

The only light in the bedroom was the table lamp next to Baxter. His back was turned to Darek. Surely, he couldn't have gone to sleep. With all the alcohol he had consumed, it was possible, but so improbable.

"I want you to wake up," Darek commanded. "You will listen to what I have to say."

Adrenalin surged through his body. "Wake up, you infidel!" he shouted. He reached for the bible, intent on opening the cover, but something was wrong. The body beneath the sheets was cold to the touch, icy cold. He grasped the man's shoulder, rolling it toward him. His face was white with fear. This man was not Baxter. Whoever he was, he was already long since dead. He pressed the closed bible to his chest. Not yet. He was confused. What was happening?

In another room some fifty metres from where Darek stood, a big man's hand closed around the remote with a single red button. Darek's last conscious thought was that the bed had begun to rise centimetres from the floor. The package of C4 explosives under the mattress had been ignited by remote control. There was a blinding flash of light followed by an explosion which thundered into the night sky, illuminating the grounds, spotlighting the section of the east wing which, as if in a slow motion sequence, was systematically reduced to a pile of smoking rubble.

Sixty eight - @ChasBroadhurst.kp

Broadhurst looked in awe as the night sky lit up. He could not believe his eyes.

"Stand over here and cover your eyes!" Hemmings pulled at his arm. He turned his gaze away from the college grounds to concentrate on the remote control. "Eight, four, two," he said to himself. "There!"

The Astra careered into the air like a feather in the wind. The explosion ripped open the petrol tank, sending a ball of incandescent flames around the clearing where they had just been standing. Smouldering metal debris came crashing to the ground, shards of glass landing just feet from where they had sought shelter.

Hemmings ripped the tape from his captive's mouth. "That's over, thank God," he said. "Now what are we going to do with you?" He waved the gun at Broadhurst. His mobile rang. "Everything go to plan, Maxwell?" he asked, then waited for the reply. "Good. Come and pick my car up, will you? We'll take your bosses'. You know where we're going."

"What in heaven's name have you done?" Broadhurst asked. "You've just assassinated a member of the Royal Family? And, now, this Frenchman? He was just an unwitting accomplice. Don't you realise that? You're mad, nothing more than a traitorous bastard!"

Hemmings turned to face his accuser with a smirk on his face. "Look, Broadhurst. My leg hurts, so you're going to drive. And if you don't do exactly what I say, I will kill you. As far as I'm concerned, you stumbled into something that was none of your business. Your death is desirable; just more collateral damage, but the order has to come from someone else."

Broadhurst took the driving seat. Hemming sat directly behind him. "Who is that someone else?" he asked.

"Forget it, will you. This isn't a James Bond movie where the villain has an ego so big, he has to confess all before Bond escapes and puts the world to rights. If I have anything to do with it, your fate will be a rotting corpse in a Welsh bog and the sooner the better!" He pressed the Glock into the nape of Broadhurst's neck. "Now, drive!"

Sixty nine - @Bizzybuzzybee

The powerful twin engines on the Baglietto hummed gently as the vessel slipped out of Limassol marina. Benny Ram looked on as the lights of the city began to recede in the distance.

Opera. Time to act. A group of SAS intelligence officers were housed in a stronghold, just outside Van in Turkey, where a communications centre had been set up clandestinely over the last six months. Copies of the suicide bomber's final message had already been distributed to the Arabic speaking flagship news station of Al Jazeera in Qatar. Within the next few minutes, copies would be with Al Aan in Dubai, Al-Baghdadia in Cairo and Abu Dhabi TV.

The dual language version which Darek had recorded in Arabic and then English were on their way to the BBC, Fox, Sky and CNN. In due course, copies would be posted on U-Tube and other social networks.

Benny felt he was in the best possible place, cruising at sea, away from the media maelstrom which was already surfacing, following a brief, announcement of an unconfirmed terrorist incident at a theological college in South Wales. Speculation was rife. The initial supposition of a gas explosion had soon given way to a more sinister explanation. It was still too early to say if there were any casualties or if there were any links to the recent disclosures surrounding the Royal Family.

He flicked off the satellite receiver. It was the middle of the night. He would benefit from a few hours sleep before catching up with developments. The following day he planned to be cruising at sea, destination Rome. If things turned sour, he could easily plot another course. All being well, from Rome he would catch a flight to Paris, travelling as a Saudi citizen with a false passport he had yet to examine. In two days time, he would be installed in the offices of his magazine, *Bien a Vous*. It was more than opportune that, at this critical moment, he took a personal interest in his investment in the world of publishing.

Benny looked around him at the lavish surroundings. The yacht was beginning to look a little tired, familiar. Perhaps it was time to look for a more luxurious vessel. After all, money was no object.

Seventy - @renemarchal

As news wires around the world were beginning to pick up and develop the breaking news of a major terrorist event in the United Kingdom, Marchal was blissfully unaware that he had been at the eye of the storm. Tired and confused by the turn of his recent experiences, he had just managed to catch the last Eurostar service of the day to Paris, falling in and out of sleep during a journey that was punctuated by unscheduled stops and delays coupled by profuse apologies over the tannoy system and which finally got him into Paris just after one in the morning. Avoiding the television, his only concession to the outside world was to flick the play switch on his telephone answering machine. The last call was from Patricia just before midnight. She had received with relief his text message that he was on his way back and would be round to pick him up at nine the next morning. She had arranged a visit to see Dubois' parents in Reims in the afternoon. There was concern in her voice. Her last words were a warning to avoid going into the office until she had the opportunity to speak with him.

The penultimate call was an hour or so earlier from Arnault. He was annoyed. Where was Marchal? There were serious questions to answer. Report to his office as soon as he returned. Contact him without fail immediately upon his return, whatever the hour. There was just one other message, an upbeat follow up from his daughter expressing, again, her gratitude for his initiative. She would keep her fingers crossed.

Marchal was both exhausted and preoccupied with the fate of Broadhurst and the turn of events that he had described to Speir in London. He had to be content that he had done everything possible to assist the British authorities with their enquiries. He would respect the old man's request to treat the topic as confidential until he had the opportunity to discuss it further with Broadhurst. With his mind at rest, sleep came easily.

He woke with a start. Light was streaming into the bedroom where he had left the curtains open. It was eight thirty. Hurriedly, he took a shower, shaved and organised a change of clothes. There was no time for a coffee. The doorbell rang promptly at nine.

"Are you alright?" He had never seen her look so troubled.

"Were you involved in all this business?" she asked.

"What business?" was his innocent reply.

"You haven't heard?" There was incredulity in the question. "Prince Arthur was assassinated last night. Some Jihadist suicide bomber infiltrated the place where he was staying. He blew them both up. The television's been showing some homemade video of the perpetrator claiming responsibility. Listen." She switched on the car radio. There was no other news. Every second of air time on every channel was dedicated to the story. Under the translation into French, he could hear a young man's voice speaking slowly in English. He was acting under the divine guidance of the true Islamic caliphate which was known as Isis to rid the world of a figurehead of a corrupt and worthless capitalist society bent on the downfall of Islam. The King's son was a homosexual, a pervert, a sinner in the eyes of Allah. He deserved to die, his soul condemned to hell and damnation for eternity.

Marchal sank back in his seat. His mind was racing. He had been there, present at the very place, the very time when all this was in motion. "Was anybody else involved?" he asked, eyes closed, half expecting some more terrible news.

"Apparently not," she replied. "The explosion was powerful, but localised. There are no other recorded victims. Everyone in the college has been accounted for, but the area where the Prince was hiding out is just a ruin."

He turned back to concentrate on the radio. A reporter was talking about a second explosion. The suggestion was that the bomber had an associate waiting close at hand with a back-up device which may have exploded accidentally. At this time, information was scarce.

"Hadn't we better go to the office, rather than go on pursuing your case at the moment?"

She shook her head. "I'm not supposed to know anything about this, but I was in the office last night, following up some information on Chantelle's partner. By the way, I'm pretty certain that she's the person who was in Geneva at the time the first paparazzi was murdered." She stopped. She could tell his thoughts were elsewhere. Tears were running down his cheeks. There was nothing she could think of to say or do, but ignore the emotion. He was such a wonderful, sensitive man, so unlike all the other bastards she had come across in the force. She longed to comfort him, but this wasn't the time or place. She started the car, moving slowly into the traffic flow away from the centre towards the ring road out of the city.

"Arnault had come looking for you, but he didn't see me. He was on the phone to someone. You're down as under investigation for corruption and criminal associations. There is also a suggestion that you're involved in some conspiracy with a security officer from the Royal household in the UK and this Rosenberg character. IGS have been alerted to take you into custody for interrogation."

"Internal Affairs want to arrest me?" He shook his head in disbelief.

"That's why I thought you might welcome a few hours to work things through before you put your head in the lion's mouth." She laughed, a futile attempt to lighten the atmosphere. "Besides, I could really do with your help. I think we may be on to something that might crack my murder case."

He didn't reply. He wasn't thinking straight anymore. A whole stream of unconnected thoughts were reeling around in his head. The more he tried to concentrate, the less he was able to. He needed to speak with Broadhurst. Thank goodness his mobile was fully charged.

Seventy one - @ChasBroadhurst.kp

The phone on the old wooden kitchen table rang. It was amongst the collection of items taken from Broadhurst's pockets. Hemmings walked over to glance at the screen. "It's your French policeman friend. Best we avoid his calls for the time being, don't you think?"

It was the first time Hemmings had spoken to him since the previous day without giving some sort of order.

The stream of instructions to turn right, straight on at the roundabout and so on during the late night drive into the heart of the Usk valley had brought them to a remote farm house close to Talybont. The area was pitch black, not a street light anywhere on the horizon, not a star alive in the sky. The silence was broken only by the occasional bleating of a sheep or the bark of a dog. On another day, Broadhurst could have really appreciated the serenity of his surroundings, but tonight his heart was heavy, his thoughts ridden with the guilt that he had failed to do his job of protecting a member of the Royal family.

They undoubtedly planned to kill him, but as his presence had not been calculated into the scenario, they must need the time to plan his demise.

He was led, handcuffed into the stone walled kitchen, a room, big enough to serve both to prepare food and to sit around an open fireplace in well worn, high backed armchairs. The centrepiece of the room was a gnarled pine kitchen table, positioned to gain maximum benefit from the warmth of an old solid fuel Aga oven range.

After an escorted visit to an outside bathroom, Broadhurst was settled into one of the armchairs, a chain locking a shackle around his ankle to the iron footstall in the grate. The handcuffs were removed and Hemmings handed him a pack of cereal and a child's plastic bowl and spoon. The milk was ice cold and farm fresh. He was hungry.

He dozed on and off in a fitful sleep. The chair was not that uncomfortable, but it wasn't a bed. He had forced himself to close his eyes. There was no point in trying to work it all out now. Wait until morning to collect his thoughts, to try and work out a plan to escape. It wouldn't be easy. He could hear Hemmings snoring in an adjacent bedroom. The man was a professional soldier, a seasoned campaigner who knew how to handle himself, to blank any emotions he might be feeling; insane enough to reconcile the heinous acts he had perpetrated with the words of the bible. He was as much a religious fanatic as the man who had been sent to kill the Prince. They were both terrorists.

Broadhurst had just finished another bowl of cereal when the mobile rang. Hemmings returned to the kitchen with a small portable television which he placed on the kitchen table in front of his captive.

"What's this, room service?"

Hemmings smiled, ignored the sarcasm and began to scroll through pages on Broadhurst's mobile. "Your

French friend is getting agitated. I'll dial, you speak. Everything is going well. You can't say anything over the phone. You'll call as soon as your assignment is over. Wish him well and I'll ring off." He hesitated. "One single word out of place and you will really regret it. I'll have a readymade excuse to do exactly what I've wanted to do since you started interfering. Capiche?"

Broadhurst nodded and followed the instructions.

"There's a good boy." Hemmings returned the mobile to his pocket. "Now you can watch how things are developing. I'll be asking questions later." He left by the back door, spoke to somebody outside, audible enough for Broadhurst to hear the instruction to shoot him if he tried to escape. Retreating footsteps on the gravel and then the sound of a diesel vehicle bursting into life. Broadhurst was alone, except for the occasional glance through the window from the man stationed outside. It was Lewis, his stare cursory, his face impassive, showing no sign that he recognised the prisoner.

Events had moved on. The suicide bomber's face had now been seen throughout the globe. There had been no word from the Jihadist leaders either associating or disassociating the regime from the terrorist act. The British Prime Minister had emerged after a COBRA meeting to announce that all armed forces in the eastern Mediterranean and the Gulf had been put on full alert. She would address Parliament later that afternoon. The heart of the nation had gone out to the unimaginable grief being borne by the Royal Family. So far, there had been no official statement from the Palace.

International vilification had been swift and unequivocal. However unlikely to succeed, a UN resolution would be immediately proposed to condemn the attack and establish a joint military force to monitor the situation. The US was particularly vociferous with a strongly worded expression of solidarity with its European allies. The Israeli prime minister had put his country on a state of alert. Growing unrest in Palestine and Lebanon could not be discounted. So far, the reaction from the major powers of Russia and China, together with Syria's Arab neighbours had been muted. Establishing the facts should be a priority. A belligerent response might suit certain western interests, but caution was urged until the Syrian government had spoken.

Broadhurst could imagine the frenzied activity that was going on behind the scenes at Kensington Palace. The press corps would be working flat out to control the situation. Had anybody queried why he was not at his desk, in charge of the security aspects? All other members of the Royal family would need special around the clock protection to ensure no other terrorist acts were planned. Official engagements would have all been cancelled. Every police force in the country would be on red alert. Surely somebody must have said, "Where's Broadhurst?" and somebody must have given a satisfactory answer. That troubled him.

"Keeping up to speed with events?" Hemmings had walked back through the door with a bag full of groceries. He sounded as though he was talking about the local flower show.

Broadhurst attempted to rise from the chair, but the chain restrained him. "Have you any idea of the consequences of this lunacy of yours. You could have triggered the start of a confrontation with the Russians."

"No bad thing if it changes the face of the Middle East," he said lightly. He took a pack of cigarettes from his baggy trouser pocket. "I haven't smoked a cigarette since I was fifteen. The army saw to that." He struck a match. "I thought I might try one now to remember just what it was like." He drew heavily on the filter. "I thought it might provoke memories of an age when you were told what the enemy looked like, the uniforms they were wearing, just who you were supposed to be killing."

Broadhurst was speechless. The man was deranged.

"I went to the local grocery shop this morning, as you can see." He stubbed out the cigarette violently on the floor, grinding it with the heel of his boot. "The man behind the counter was a smiling Pakistani lad, about Brent's age. I thought to myself what's the doctrine he's allied to? Is he a potential headstrong fanatic, capable of being brainwashed into some horrendous act?"

"You're paranoiac. The man probably works twenty hours a day to support his family and has a healthy respect for the land in which he lives." Broadhurst shook his head. "You see everybody in your colours, not for what they are."

The comment angered Hemmings. "You didn't serve in either of the Gulf wars or in Afghanistan, did you?"

"I was on special assignments during the Iraqi engagements. I quit soon afterwards to take up my current post."

"I was in the thick of everything. Give them a name, if you like, Al-Qaeda or the insurgents in Iraq, the Taliban in Afghanistan. Now, this so-called Islamic State in Syria. People talk about Pakistan as the breeding ground for these militants who spend every waking hour thinking up ways of blowing our young soldiers into smithereens. The truth is that intolerance is everywhere."

Broadhurst wriggled in his chair, the chain rattling against the stone floor. "Even if you are right, though I can't accept the simplicity of your belief, you honestly think that by assassinating innocent victims here in Britain, you can influence events in the Middle East?"

"I've seen a hundred coffins loaded onto planes in Basra, another hundred at Camp Bastion. Every one of them had "Another wasted life" written all over it." He took a knife from the sheaf on his belt, running the blade up his forearm to prove its razor sharpness by shaving off the hairs. He wiped the blade between his fingers before using it to slice a loaf of French bread into thick wedges. "Help yourself," he said, returning the knife to its sheaf. He prized open a bottle of mineral water. "Very biblical, isn't it?" he said. "The last supper."

"Whose?"

Hemmings shook his head. "That's enough. I've told you already, your fate is not in my hands. If it were, the end would justify the means." He looked thoughtful. "I'll say one more thing. Imagine you're under attack. One of your men may be wounded or dead, but there are a dozen young corpses lying around you, terrorists, we call them. Freedom fighters they like to be known as. Do you think the body count has improved your chances of winning the war against terrorism?" He stared at Broadhurst, his eyes threatening and angry. "Well, do you?"

"No."

"Of course not. Those dozen bodies have fathers, grandfathers, brothers, sons, cousins, nephews. By killing those men, you have just spawned another fifty freedom fighters to take their place, to detest the occupying forces, to loathe the sound of the words Britain or America."

"So this is your way of changing things?"

"You've heard of Newton's Third Law, I'm sure. It says that for every force there is a reaction force that is equal in size, but opposite in direction. That's how we fight our war. Unless we can change the critical mass of one of these forces by education and moderating influences, neither side will win unless and until one of the bodies stops pushing. If that happens, all those body bags arriving at Brize Norton will go on being a sheer waste of human life." He put some slices of bread on a plate, heading outside once more and firmly shutting the door behind him.

Seventy two - @renemarchal

By any standards, the house in Rheims, home of Clarence and Felice Dubois, could only be described as less than modest. The row of terraced houses were all in various stages of advanced decay, some structural, some in need of major repair and redecoration. The Dubois family owned one of the less derelict buildings, an end of terrace, small two storey building with an overgrown garden and peeling paintwork.

"Hardly the fitting backdrop for a high-flying magazine editor, would you say?" Colbert remarked, forcing the front gate open against the matted undergrowth.

During the course of their journey, Marchal had listened attentively to Colbert's summary of her meeting with Tomas and Katarine, the possible involvement of Nana in the decoy visit to Geneva and the urgency to contact papapicman2, the elusive American, Fox, otherwise known as the Banker.

"We'll try and meet up with him tonight," Marchal suggested. "Ask somebody to get details of flights from Cairo. There can't be many."

An announcer on the radio interrupted the music programme to announce the breaking news that British forces had been put on a state of alert in the Gulf. The French government had announced it would willingly provide logistical support, but, thus far, none had been requested. "This is looking ominous," Colbert commented, reminding Marchal that he still needed to speak with Broadhurst. How long he would honour his commitment to keep quiet was very dependent upon his need to communicate with his colleague.

The front door was opened by a frail looking woman in her mid sixties, who studied the warrant cards presented to her with, what Colbert assessed as a mixture of suspicion and fear. Behind her, in a wheelchair, was an unkempt looking man of similar age, his expression, openly hostile. "We keep ourselves to ourselves," he said without any provocation. "We don't have nothing to do with no police."

Marchal and Colbert were ushered into a small sitting room. Every available flat surface was occupied with pictures of Chantelle, some posed alone, others with single or groups of friends. Colbert stepped around the room, looking closely at the photographs as Marchal talked. The police were looking into Chantelle's background in connection with a threat against her life. Had she said anything to them?

The woman did all the talking, looking across occasionally at her husband for confirmation and reassurance. No. They hadn't spoken to their daughter for some weeks. She was very busy, you know. She had a very influential position. Their background? Well, they had originally come from the Alsace, farm workers and then, Clarence had the accident when the tractor overturned and he was paralysed from the waist down. Why had they decided to come to Reims? Well, it was all to do with Chantelle. Clarence had received the insurance money after the accident and they wanted to make sure their daughter had a good education. They heard that after High School; Chantelle was eleven by this time; there was an excellent university in Reims, the URCA, after which she could enrol at the famous RMS, the management school.

Marchal commented that they seemed very knowledgeable about higher education.

Felice smiled. She was beginning to relax into the conversation. Like all good parents, they wanted the best for their daughter.

Colbert had finished her sortie around the room, her every movement followed by Clarence who, she suspected, recognised her as the threatening element. "All these photos show that you're very proud of your daughter, but, do you have any photos of Chantelle as a baby? They all seem to start when she's about eleven. Also, there are none taken with you two. Is there a family album somewhere?"

The woman was thrown off guard. Marchal completed the new line of enquiry. "Also, for our records, a copy of the birth certificate would be useful. There was also talk of a brother?"

The old man stepped in. "We've said all we're gonna say. You'd better go. If Chantelle's in trouble, a copy of her birth certificate ain't gonna help none. You come from Paris, poking and prying into our lives. We ain't having none of it!"

Marchal took a figurative step back. "We haven't come here to upset you. We just need to know everything there is to know about Chantelle's background, her friends, contacts, that sort of thing. It might give us some clues."

The old man was unimpressed. "Just go, will you!"

Colbert took the mobile from her pocket. "If you're going to be uncooperative, I suggest I call the Police Municipale and we go down to the station to get the answers we need."

"You're a bitch," the old man spat at her.

Felice looked away from her husband. "I always knew you'd come knocking on our door one day." She cast a sideways glance in his direction. "It's no use, Clarence. They have to know the truth."

He thrust his wheelchair into a hundred and eighty degree turn and left the room. They could hear china clattering in the kitchen.

"Don't think badly of him," the woman pleaded. "He's a good man really."

"I'm sure he is," Marchal comforted.

"Chantelle is not our child. We adopted her when she was just eleven."

The truth was easy to tell, as if a weight had been lifted from her shoulders. The part about Alsace was true, only there had been no insurance money, no pension. They had been left destitute, evicted from their tied cottage. Then, one day, out of the blue, the lawyer from Paris had arrived with an offer. They would adopt a child, move away and pretend that the child was their own, from birth. The man was a lawyer. Everything was legal, but it must be kept a secret.

They moved to the house in Reims. Every month, they received a transfer of money. In those days, it was a great deal. Chantelle went to school and lived with them. When she was old enough, she transferred to university and

344

moved into the centre of the city. From then on, they saw very little of her. Nowadays, all they had was a card at Christmas. When she moved away, the money they received was reduced. It was barely enough to survive on. "Now you know the truth, I expect it will stop all together," she said ruefully.

No, she didn't know who her real parents were. They never asked and were never told. They couldn't have children of their own. Clarence's accident and all that.

"Did she have any brothers and sisters?" Colbert asked.

Again, she didn't know. The only thing she could say was that, at the start, the lawyer had offered them either a boy or a girl. "We had always wanted a girl." She hesitated. "That's if we could have had children."

Did she not have any clues at all as to Chantelle's background?

"All I can tell you is this," she said. "When she first came to us, she would have nightmares, bad dreams. She would call out in the night, 'Papa, don't leave me!', sometimes 'Richard'. On one occasion, she must have been living a dream because she said, 'Monsieur Armand is not at home' to someone. She had a very troubled mind, but it all settled down after a while."

They were standing at the front door, ready to leave. Marchal held the woman's hand between his. "I don't think there will ever be any need for anyone to know what you have told us today, so, hopefully, your money is safe. Tell your husband not to worry."

She bent to kiss his hand. "Thank you," she said.

"One last thing," he added. "Can you remember the name of the lawyer who got you into all of this?"

"He had a funny, foreign name. I can't remember it, but I think we still have his card." She scurried off into the house. They could hear raised voices as she talked to her husband.

"How did you know?" Marchal asked.

"The photographs were all planted for our benefit. All the surfaces were dusty, not cleaned for weeks, I suspect, except where she'd put the photos down. There, she must have wiped the surface with her hand before placing the frames. Had they been there all the time, the dust would have collected around them as well."

"I'm impressed," he said.

"Good."She smiled. "In that case, you can buy me lunch. I saw a nice auberge on the way into town."

The old woman reappeared, offering the card in her hand to Marchal. He copied down the details. He thanked her, taking the time once more to reassure her about the future.

They were pulling into the car park of the auberge before she punched him playfully in the arm. "So, who is it? Are you going to tell me?" she asked with a smile.

"Would you be surprised if I told you it was Mahesh Kamal?"

"Benny Ram's lawyer?" There was surprise and excitement in her voice.

His mobile phone rang.

"If it's Arnault, don't answer it," she cautioned. "We need to talk first."

He pressed the answer icon on the touch screen. "Chas! How wonderful to hear from you. I was beginning to get really worried about you. I'm so relieved to hear your voice. Can you tell me what's going on?"

Seventy three - @Bizzybuzzybee

The sea was calm, allowing the yacht to cruise at a steady twelve knots. They were making good time. With a good night's sailing, they would make Civitavecchia by dawn the following morning.

Benny had slept off and on for most of the day. The television reports had more or less followed the pattern that he had imagined. Now, they were getting to the phase that would interest him most. He intended to stay up most of the night, tuned into the BBC World Service and Al Jazeerah. These were the most factually reliable in his opinion.

Seedless grapes were what he had asked for. He looked up at the female crew member. She was attractive. Perhaps later. Take them away and remove the pips. Quiet! What were they saying?

The World Service reporter from Baghdad was talking about an unusually large amount of internet traffic in Syria, particularly centred around the areas controlled by the Jihadists. In the UK, the Prime Minister would be making an emergency statement to the Commons in a few hours.

The girl reappeared with the grapes which she bent down to place on the table in front of him. Benny switched off the sound on the television. He really didn't have a political bone in his body. He just loved the scheming, the challenge and the conquest; the financial reward that evidenced success.

Tomorrow, he must speak with Chantelle to let her know he would be making a visit. They would need to rework next week's edition of the magazine. That could all wait.

The girl went to rise, but Benny hand spread across the top of her head restrained her. He wrestled to loosen the belt of his gold silk robe to expose his groin. She did not resist as he forced her face down between his legs. He hoped that she was good at her job. She was being paid enough. He sighed with expectation.

Seventy four - @papapicman2

Bernie Fox saw the notice board with his name on as he reached the international arrivals hall at Charles de Gaulle airport. His flight from Milan had been full. At the last minute, he had decided to detour from Cairo before returning to Paris, to see an old flame in the Italian city who had contacted him out of the blue, but the news of the assassination and its Middle Eastern ramifications had forced him to cut short what he intended to be a passionate reunion. There were articles to be written, photos to be published. Bernie was an old timer with a life's experience of turning a story to suit the conditions. His exposé on corruption amongst the new Egyptian elite could easily be given another slant. He would not let niceties like the truth get in his way.

The message on his mobile from Tomas to contact him on arrival sounded important. He walked toward the young man holding up the board with his name. "Did Tomas send you to meet me?" he asked.

"You're Mr Fox?"

Bernie nodded.

"He instructed me to take you to see him. He needs to talk with you. I'm Adrian, one of his friends."

Bernie laughed. "Friends? Tomas doesn't have any friends. You're one of his film stars, are you?" He shook the man's hand.

"Something like that."

They walked to the car park together. The atmosphere all around them was charged with the sensation of a major international incident. "It feels like the day the twin towers were destroyed," Bernie said. "Maybe I can draw some parallels in my piece tomorrow."

"You're writing for a magazine?"

"Sure am. An exclusive for Paris Match with some really sensational photos. There'll always be bad men in high places doing bad things. It's corruption that keeps the wheels turning."

Alain took the man's suitcase, placing it in the boot of an old two door Peugeot, parked in the short-term car park.

"Is this the best Tomas could do for an old friend?" Bernie was in a good mood. A heavy payday was on the horizon. Rosenberg would want his ten per cent. He'd set the article up with the magazine. Maybe, Bernie could stick him for eight this time. They'd be talking about a sizeable sum, even so. He'd try and give him a call while they were on their way to meet Tomas.

The small diesel engine strained as they accelerated onto the Autoroute du Nord, heading south west toward Paris. Alain looked over as his passenger pulled the mobile from his pocket. "Is that one of these new generation smartphones?" he asked, holding out his hand. "Can I have a look, please?"

"It's the very latest, the real McCoy," Bernie replied proudly. "Only had it a few weeks. Hadn't you better wait until we stop?"

Alain already had the phone in his hand. "It certainly is something else," he agreed. The mobile slipped from his hand, falling into the well of the car alongside the pedals. "Jesus, I'm sorry," Alain mumbled. "I'll stop in a minute to retrieve it. We're turning off now anyway."

"Be careful, for God's sake. It cost me a fortune." Bernie was concentrating on the space between the driver's feet, but he couldn't see the phone.

They turned off the motorway at the Bobigny exit, heading east.

"Can you stop now?" Bernie asked. "I do need to make a call."

"If you hold on for just a minute, we're nearly there."

"But Tomas doesn't live in this direction," Bernie protested.

"He's shooting a film in an old warehouse, just around the corner." He turned the car through a pair of open, rusting gates, past a loading apron with grass springing through the concrete into an alleyway between two abandoned warehouses. "Here we are," he said. He bent down to retrieve the mobile, handing it to Bernie as they exited the vehicle.

For the first time, Bernie felt uneasy. "Where are all the other vehicles?" he asked.

Alain smiled. "They use the other entrance and park around the corner. It was just quicker for us to come this way. In you go." He held the door open.

The warehouse was deserted, in total darkness. Bernie half turned to remonstrate, but the metal tube hit him across the nape of the neck before he could utter a word. He fell to the ground like a sack of cement, his mobile careering across the floor. Alain walked over and crushed the phone with his heel into the ground, shattering it into pieces.

"No more calls for you, Mr Banker," he said as he looked down at the unconscious man.

Seventy five - @renemarchal

The old Peugeot had pulled out of the airport car park just as Colbert and Marchal were checking at the airline desk. No, there was no Bernard Fox on the passenger list from Cairo. Was it possible to do a search on the Egyptair reservations site to see if Mr Fox had flown that day? The counter assistant called a supervisor who studied the police credentials with meticulous attention. Apparently, satisfied, she entered a password into the system and used a search engine to look for the name. A Mr Bernie Fox with an American passport had flown the previous afternoon from Cairo to Milan. It was a one way flight with no onward destination. His reservation had a mobile contact. Colbert's call went straight to his message service

"What shall we do?" Colbert was perplexed. "Tomas was certain he was arriving in Paris today. Apparently, he's got some commitment with a magazine."

"Ring up someone at 36 and ask them to speak to the airlines with flights out of Milan today to Paris. There must be plenty of them. Get them to check the passenger lists." Marchal switched on his mobile as Colbert began her call. "I'll see if Rosenberg is able to answer his mobile. He might be able to give us a clue."

The operator announced that the call was being

diverted. Broadhurst must have had the number redirected to one of his officers. After what seemed an eternity, the phone was answered. Marchal spoke in English. "Is it possible for me to speak to Mr Rosenberg, please? This is Capitaine Marchal. I was with Mr Broadhurst yesterday."

There was a silence, apparent to Marchal that the phone was being passed from one person to another.

"René, how nice to hear your voice again." Arnault had a hint of sarcasm in his voice. "I see from our trace that you're phoning from the airport. Just arrived?"

"Recently." A non-committal reply that was intended to avoid prejudicing Colbert's position. "I was trying to trace Rosenberg."

"So I understand. Was that to cement another potential transaction or to collect from a previous deal?" The voice had changed. It was hard, almost vicious.

"I'm afraid I have no idea what you are talking about, Commandant."

"Please get here straight away, Capitaine. I have spent the day with two gentlemen from the Brigade of Internal Affairs who are anxious to ask you some questions, both about your involvement with Mr Rosenberg, who we and our British counterparts are currently unable to trace, and your recent activities in the UK, which were not, I must emphasise, sanctioned by me."

"Well, that should be straightforward," Marchal was quick to explain. "Just contact Chas Broadhurst, head of security at Kensington Palace and he'll explain everything and tell you where Rosenberg is being held."

Arnault was brusque. "Just get here, will you. The British are also unable to trace this Broadhurst man. They are convinced you can help to locate him, if he's still alive."

"Why wouldn't he still be alive?"

"You have kept abreast of the news, yes?"

"Of course."

The Commandant was obviously performing before an audience. "The explosion which killed Prince Arthur and which has sparked off a major international incident was accompanied by a second, less powerful, explosion which destroyed a car and at least one occupant. Maybe more than one. Simultaneously, both Rosenberg and Broadhurst, both of whom who were known to have been in the area, have disappeared. It would be rash to jump to conclusions, but as you were also in the vicinity, your assistance is urgently required." He hesitated. "Now, get here!"

As Colbert drove, Marchal began to issue a string of instructions to her. Gone was the cosy, intimate conversation of a leisurely lunch, his stories of the events of the last few days, her warm reaction to his presence, a closeness which she could not remember feeling for another man for so long. Now it was the harsh reality of business, the recognition that he was shortly to be stripped of his ability to act as a free agent within the Police Judiciaire. His march to retirement was likely to be a bumpy one.

Colbert dropped him off before parking her car and making her way independently to her office. There was no time to waste. With all this furore, it was easy to forget that another life was in danger. Until this Fox could be located, there was a serial killer on the loose, possibly after him. Following Marchal's guidance, she instructed uniform brigade to pick up Nana and bring her in for questioning. She also organised twenty four hour surveillance on Chantelle Dubois. Next, came the slow process of investigation. She logged into her computer and began to type.

Marchal made his way direct to Arnault's office suite. The two men approached him as he entered. Arnault sat behind his desk, looking on, saying nothing. A harassed looking individual with cigarette ash on the lapel of his suit, who spoke with the guttural accent Marchal associated with Marseille, moved toward him. He held a sheaf of papers in a hand that must have been emaciated by polio when he was young, the fingers warped and twisted.

"Capitaine Marchal," he recited formally, "you are under investigation for corruption, perverting the course of justice and possible complicity in a terrorist act in another jurisdiction. These are serious accusations, for which you will be suspended from all duties and taken into custody under caution, pending further investigation. Do you understand?"

Marchal nodded. He had already decided to say nothing, whatever the consequences, until he had the opportunity to speak to his lawyer. He went through the formalities of handing over his warrant card, advising the whereabouts of his police issue weapon and the ignominy of being cuffed to the second, younger man.

Arnault shook his head. "You're a big disappointment to me, René. I never suspected anything like this." He sounded as though he was chastising his dog.

Marchal reacted angrily. "Maybe, you should hold off oiling the guillotine until we've had the trial. Or are you too busy worrying about your knitting?"

The older man from Internal Affairs couldn't resist a smile as he led Marchal out of the door. A day spent with Arnault had seemed like a lifetime.

Seventy six - @ChasBroadhurst.kp

Broadhurst had spent a second night drowsing in and out of sleep, twisting and turning in the armchair, woken whenever his movements pulled against the chain that restrained him. His reflection in the kitchen window was beginning to show the haggard, uncared for look of an old man, the grey stubble, his eyes, hollow in wrinkled sockets. Worst of all, he was beginning to lose that mental agility for which he prided himself. He was starting to daydream.

He used the remote which Hemmings had left with him to flick between the news channels. There was no let up.

353

The coverage switched rapidly between reporters in Hay on Wye, royal correspondents outside Kensington Palace, political editors from the Houses of Parliament and, above all, a groundswell of public sympathy for the Royal family that had evaporated all talk of federalism. Overnight, it was as if it had become a dirty word. As the afternoon wore on, emotions heightened, with the nation expectantly awaiting the statement by the Prime Minister. A COBRA session was still in progress, but speculation as to the reaction to the Prince's death was at fever pitch.

Broadhurst had seen enough. He switched off the set to doze fitfully again. What was Hemmings waiting for? They would either release him or kill him. He knew Hemmings' preferred option.

The sound of a car drawing to a halt outside awoke him. It wasn't the rough diesel motor of the vehicle Hemmings used, but the hum of a high powered petrol engine. There was an exchange of greetings outside before Hemmings pushed open the kitchen door. "Someone's come to see you," he said.

Seventy seven - @Bizzybuzzybee

The yacht slipped into a mooring at the Port of Civitavecchia just after dawn. Benny's hired limousine was waiting to take him the sixty eight kilometres to Rome's Fiumicino Airport. En route, he called Chantelle. She seemed flat, not the normal self-assured, attentive response he had expected. Her mind was, obviously, elsewhere, but there was too much to do for him to concern himself with her mood swings. What the hell! He would be courteous. It was in his nature.

"I'll be with you by lunchtime today. We need a good human interest story to go with the general stuff that's going on. I think I've got just the thing for us."

"That's good," she replied with obvious disinterest.

"Is something wrong?" he asked. "You sound as though you've got a problem."

Her voice brightened, but he could tell she was play acting. "No, Benny. It's nothing really. A girl friend of mine has been taken into police custody for questioning and it's preying on my mind. I need to get a solicitor to her as quickly as possible."

"Forget her," he urged. "We've got some really big fish to fry before we publish. Ask Kamal to find someone to send along to look after your friend." He stopped for a second. "You're not in trouble, are you?"

"No. It's just that she's a very close friend and I think that the authorities may be trying to get at me through her. With these photos circulating of a Prince who's been brutally murdered, it makes it look as though *BV* was, somehow instrumental in his death."

"The storm will pass. Like I say, we have to look forward." Something crossed his mind. "There's nothing else, is there?"

She assured him that everything was fine, how she couldn't wait to see him again. Would he be staying in his penthouse apartment?

There was a reserve, a strange hesitancy in the way she posed the question. Alarm bells began to ring. Caution told him to make a second call.

He listened as a string of questions formed in his mind. "Your psychiatrist considered he was sufficiently well to consider a compassionate release? A week? And that was from when?" He was pensive. "I thought we had an understanding that I would be informed if circumstances changed." He listened again. "His father's death?" he questioned. "Who told you that his father had died?" There was a delay while questions were being asked. "I see," he said pensively when the answer was provided. "Thank you for your assistance."

He spoke in Marathi, the official language of Mumbai, to Kamal. "I want you to arrange extra security around the apartment tonight. Just for one night. I'll be leaving for the

UK tomorrow. Pay my respects and all that. You can retrieve the money from the account we set up for Rosenberg. He won't be needing it anymore."

The rest of the journey to the airport was spent in silence. The conversation with the supervisor at the secure clinic was an unexpected and disturbing development. He needed time to think.

Seventy eight - @renemarchal

Colbert had discovered that they were holding Marchal in the police barracks near Villette. She appeared shortly before going to work with a suitcase of clothes and toiletries she had purchased on route. They would give her ten minutes. She had asked for a senior police union representative to be present for his next interview. He would need to be briefed.

Marchal looked as though he had aged years over night, but his mood was bright and positive. He thanked her for her concern, straightening the clothes that had been rummaged through by the security guard. "There are some papers under the lining at the bottom," she whispered. "Read them." They talked of generalities, conscious that their conversation was being recorded. "By the way, she concluded, I've done everything you asked me to. Nana is in custody. To date, nothing, but she won't last long. I've got to go. Events are moving fast. We're still looking for our recent arrival, but I suspect he's not far away." She squeezed his arm before kissing him lightly on the cheek. "Best of luck. Be brave."

Marchal freshened up and changed clothes before casually slipping the pages she had sent into the newspaper he had been given earlier by one of the guards to follow events in the Middle East.

Colbert couldn't have got any sleep last night. The old lady in Rheims had mentioned Chantelle's dreams and the reference in her sleep to Monsieur Armand not being at home. Fifteen years ago, a member of the French aristocracy, Armand Bourbon, had been a minister in the French government. His position with the Ministry of Defence was arms procurement and sales. An investigative journalist had exposed Bourbon as having taken a bribe during negotiations to sell Exocet missiles to Syria, which were understood to be en route to Iran. He was also photographed in bed with two Egyptian whores either side of him. His claims that he had been drugged fell on deaf ears. His sensitive wife, ashamed at his behaviour, had first filed for divorce, then, suddenly, committed suicide. Despite protestations, the bank account in his name in the Cayman Islands convinced the government of his guilt and the President sought and obtained his resignation. Bourbon took his own life just ten days after his wife. There were two children, a girl, Madeleine and her younger brother, Richard. Both were taken into care by the social security services pending a decision as to their future by the rest of the Bourbon family members, none of whom were keen to assume responsibility.

Marchal did the calculations. The girl would now be about Chantelle's age. The boy, well, he was still a mystery.

Seventy nine - @papapicman2

Fox had been stripped naked before being bound hand and foot to an upright chair set in the middle of the deserted warehouse floor. Packed in the corner were ancient, rusting machines that must have once filled this factory with noise and vitality. Now, the only sounds were the birds that flew to and fro in the eaves and the scurrying of rats across the floor.

On a second chair, set alongside Fox was a case full of Monopoly notes. Alain was bending down over his captive, feeding notes one by one into his mouth. Every time that Fox resisted, Alain would pinch his nose and thrust even more notes into the gagging mouth. "Do you know who I am and why you're here?" he asked.

Fox nodded, his eyes transfixed on Alain's face.

"You do? I am surprised." Alain pulled the half masticated notes from the man's mouth, allowing them to fall to the floor. Fox gasped for air, his chest heaving with relief as the oxygen was sucked in. "Tell me then! Who am I?" Alain asked.

Fox breathed deeply. "The family resemblance is striking. You're Bourbon's son, Richard. You even post that same, sombre smile, just like he did."

Alain struck the man across the face. "Don't speak badly of my father. You were responsible for his death."

The blood began to weep from the side of Fox's mouth. He began to shiver. "Any chance you could put my coat over me. I'm freezing cold. You want to know the truth, don't you?"

Alain tossed the anorak over his body. He picked up a fresh bundle of notes from the case, flicking through them incessantly like a man obsessed. "Well, talk, Mr Banker! It's nearly dinner time again. Look! Your staple diet." He waved the notes in the air.

Fox nodded his head. "It's finally come to this, has it? I'm to be put to the sword for something I did fifteen years ago. How old were you when your father topped himself? Ten?" There may have been turmoil going on inside his head, but, outwardly, he sounded calm. "Tell me one thing before I say anything. How did you know I was on the flight from Milan to meet me?"

Alain took a knife from his pocket. He began to chop off small corners from the notes, allowing the pieces to fall, confetti like, to the floor. "I'm one of your followers on Twitter. A keen admirer. I was following your exchanges with, what was her name, Carlotta, in Milan. I joined in the Tweets. I'm your agent Rosenberg. I had to pick you up from the airport, but I hadn't remembered the flight number. A very cooperative lady, Carlotta. She'll probably come to your funeral." He laughed.

Fox let his chin slip down to hold the coat in position. "So, you want a confession. Well, it's true. I took the photos of your father with the women. And I was there when he took the case of notes from the courier. Yes. And it was me who intercepted the bank statement from the Cayman Islands. I sincerely believed, at the time, that he was as guilty as hell."

"At the time?" Alain held the knife under the man's eyelid. "What does that mean?"

Fox used all his strength to wheel the chair around. "Why don't you kill me? Why don't you get it over with?" he shouted.

Alain smiled, waving the blade of the knife across his torso, but not cutting the skin. "A quick and easy death would be too good for you, Mr Banker." He shaved a thin line of hairs from the man's leg. "After your dinner, we'll try shaving some of these nasty hairs off. Only, I'm not too good with a knife. There'll probably be a few unfortunate cuts."

"You're sick, you know that?"

"So they tell me. That dirty old man of a foster parent they sent me to in Perpignan saw to that. He said I tried to burn the house down. His old cow of a wife died of a stroke. He got me committed to a sanatorium. Now, he's paid the price. Good riddance."

"You've spent all these years, locked up; thinking about avenging your father's memory and now the time has come?"

"Yes. All you paparazzi need to be exterminated. It's my job to see that it's done, as painfully as possible."

There was a scurrying noise in the background. "They're getting hungry," Alain commented. "When I've gone, they'll scent the blood. At first, they'll be scared. One will approach, you'll wriggle and he'll back away. Slowly, more will arrive. You'll wriggle again, try to shout, anything, but they won't be so afraid. One will take a bite from the wound on your leg. Then they'll all be all over you. The whiskers will tickle your cheeks as one of them is brave enough to bite off your eyelids. When that happens, you'll be able to count the minutes that you've got left."

Fox looked up. "What if I tell you I know now that your father wasn't guilty? I learned a long time ago that he was an honourable man."

"Don't make me laugh. You make me feel sick. Trying to wriggle out from a death sentence with some insincere remonstration of regret. You, and you alone, killed my father."

Fox shook his head. "Unfortunately for you, that's only partially right. Killing me won't do away with the truth."

"Which is?"

"I was set up. It was a first class, professional job. I only came to realise a year after your father had taken his life that I had been duped. I've been trying to nail the bastard who did it for years, but he's too shrewd and clever to be caught."

Alain let the knife slip down beside him. "Go on. I like a good bedtime story."

"Your father was in charge of a deal to sell arms to Syria. No problem. At the time, a legitimate government trying to defend itself against Israeli threats. They were primarily Exocet missiles. Big money was involved. The middleman was crucial to ensure the transaction went to plan."

"I know all this. What's the punch line?"

"Your father was given clandestine evidence that the arms would end up in Iran. There was an international embargo. He backed away from the deal. He was adamant. The middleman couldn't let that happen, so he framed your father. Whispers got me involved and I played my innocent part in holding the revolver to your father's head. His successor was in the middleman's pocket. With your father gone, the deal went through."

Alain began to shake his head violently. "No. That

360

can't be true. My father would have spoken out. He wouldn't have sat in his office and killed himself."

"Maybe, he didn't."

"What do you mean?"

"How can you be so sure that your father committed suicide? There are many clever assassins available for hire."

"Can you prove this?"

Fox shook his head. "Do I have to?"

Alain dropped the knife, putting both hands over his ears, rocking his head back and forwards. Then, he punched Fox full in the face. "OK, Mr clever man. Who is this mysterious villain?"

Fox began to see a chink in the other man's armour. "Did you ever wonder who paid your foster parents to take you on, a disturbed, unbalanced child, knocked sideways by his parents' untimely deaths?"

"No."

"I'm guessing, but I'll think you'll discover that behind all this is the hand of Mr Benny Ram, famous Dubai entrepreneur and philanthropist."

"No." Alain was shouting. "He owns the magazine my sister works for."

"And she would be?"

"Chantelle Dubois."

"Well, well. So Chantelle is Madeleine, your sister. She's a few years older than you, yes?"

"He's been like a father to her. I don't believe it."

Fox shrugged. "It's the truth. Check it out. The magazine world was surprised when Chantelle was appointed BV's editor. It must have been guilt, preying on Ram's mind. Of course, they all realise now that it was a shrewd appointment. She does a good job."

Alain was fumbling in his coat pocket for a mobile. "Just a minute," he said. His hands were shaking as he dialled the number. "It's me," he said. "You must come right away." He gave her the address and directions. "Don't say no, you can't!" he shouted. "I want you to hear something, from somebody else's lips. I'll give you an hour. Be here or else!"

Fox drew a long breath. He was playing for time. Somehow, he had to keep the story alive and credible.

Eighty - @ChasBroadhurst.kp

"You know what you're doing is treason, don't you?" Broadhurst looked straight into the eyes of the man who sat at the kitchen table, facing him.

Professor Speir tapped his walking stick on the stone floor. "You've become an embarrassment to us, Mr Broadhurst. We never intended that you should stumble on this project. The dilemma is now what should be done with you." He sighed and tapped his stick again.

"Was it worth it, exchanging the life of a Prince for the prospect of toppling the monarchy?" There was anger in Broadhurst's voice. "Just look at the news and you'll see that your little plan is in danger of backfiring!"

The stick was banged quickly and repeatedly on the floor. Speir was quick to reply. "Don't talk to me about ridiculous relative values. Is the life of X worth Y? That's a stupid comparison. For an intelligent man, you have understood nothing."

"I'm sure you'll enlighten me." He looked up as Hemmings entered the kitchen. "Before your hired hands do their dirty work. Tell me, Hemmings how does an avid bible reader reconcile all this death with his religious zeal?"

Hemmings ignored the question, a smile on his lips. "Tea, anyone?" he asked, adjusting the kettle on the Aga.

Speir nodded. "The issue we face, Charles, is, if confronted with the facts, you oppose or live your days out with the reality that you are part of our conspiracy. For some…." He hesitated and looked over at Hemmings, "the risk is not worth taking. Fortunately, my opinion may have been sought, but I am grateful that your fate does not rest in my hands."

"Your brand of treachery must be controlled by some very influential figures if you're just an errand boy."

Speir laughed out loud. "Now, you are just trying to goad me, Charles. You must not underestimate me."

Hemmings placed two mugs of tea on the table and placed a cup in Broadhurst's free hand. "What about you, Hemmings?" he asked. Why do you act like the terrorists you denounce? Is anything you once told me true about your feelings for the fighting soldiers?"

Hemmings sat down next to Speir, nurturing one of the mugs between his hands. "More than you could ever imagine," he replied.

"Listen!" Speir commanded, banging his stick once more on the floor. "We're waiting for a phone call, Broadhurst, a phone call that will control your destiny."

They lapsed into silence, a silence that was suddenly broken by the sound of the ring of a landline. Hemmings retrieved the handset from an adjacent room and handed it to Speir, who listened without saying a word. After a minute, he handed the phone to Broadhurst.

"Yes, I do know who's talking," he said slowly. For a full five minutes, nobody within the kitchen uttered a single word. Broadhurst, brow creased, concentrated on what was being said to him, nodding and shaking his head from time to time as if the caller could see him. At the end he held the phone close to his chest as he digested the content of the conversation. "Yes," he said, finally. "I agree and give you my undertaking."

He handed the phone back to Speir who, again, listened without comment before nodding toward Hemmings, who spun around rapidly and, in one move, was behind Broadhurst, pressing his arms together with powerful hands. Broadhurst, moving forward, ducked his head, a defensive reaction to minimise the impact of the blow he expected to receive.

"Relax. The man has spoken. Cool it!" Hemmings

unlocked the chain that bound his captive to the chair. A sadistic smile at the tension his sudden action had provoked was followed by a dismissive grunt of laughter as he watched Broadhurst vigorously rubbing his wrist to combat the sensation of the blood flowing back into his hand.

The stick tapped on the floor. "I want you to go and freshen up," Speir said. "Take a long shower, shave, wash out of your system the uncertainty and apprehension you've been living with since you were brought here. What I've got to say to you is of paramount importance and I need you in the right frame of mind to pay full attention."

Broadhurst went to speak, but Speir held up his hand. "If it were down to us, you'd have perished in that car along with Rosenberg, but, as you now know, it wasn't. However, if one word of what I will tell you ever leaves your lips on purpose or by accident, your fate will be to join him."

Broadhurst went to speak, but the raised hand stopped him. "Everything will be made clear. Those are my instructions. In the meantime, please do as I say." He turned his attention to the television. "I'd like to catch up on events. Hopefully, the dawn of a new era is about to break."

An hour or so later and feeling decidedly more comfortable and confident, Broadhurst sat in an armchair in the lounge, a cup of tea balanced precariously on his knees. Speir sat on a dining chair, legs apart, the cane between them, steadied by both hands around the silver ball.

He leaned forward as if to heighten the air of confidentiality. "Eight months ago," he began, "Special Branch officers raided a house in Maida Vale. The informant had talked of drugs, but as it transpired, the police had come upon a group of paedophiles. Prince Arthur was one of these men. Expecting to find a haul of various substances, the raid included a police photographer who, in the event, had a high old time taking snaps of all present. Due to the sensitivity of the occurrence, I was asked to ensure that the entire incident was hushed up and the Prince airbrushed out of the scene and into a virtual world somewhere in the Highlands."

"Who do you work for, Professor Speir?"

The man looked at Broadhurst with a look that said you really don't need to ask me questions like that. "My credentials speak for themselves, but I won't leave you with a "none of your business" answer which may prompt you to try and satisfy your inquisitive nature in the future. Let's just say it's a very specialised section within the counter-intelligence service. Does that satisfy you?" He asked.

Broadhurst gave no indication, but it was apparent that Speir had nothing more to say on the subject.

"Good. Although the incident was kept under wraps, you know as well as I do that rumours began to surface on the internet alluding to the Prince's sexual preferences and his predilection for young adolescents."

Broadhurst nodded, sensitive to the other man's avoidance of any suggestion of a criminal intent. He remembered Lambert's. . . . . He corrected himself. . . . David's homophobic comment about the Prince being a "shirt lifter."

Speir hesitated, carefully choosing his words. "It then transpired that one of these young persons, learning of the true identity of Deacon Baxter, decided to seek money, if not from the Prince, then from any newspaper willing to publish his story. With the monarchy going through a serious trough in popular support, this could have fuelled the fire the federalists have been seeking to stoke up."

"So you paid?" Broadhurst queried.

Speir answered with a nod.

"But the problem wasn't going to go away?"

Another curt acknowledgement. "Psychology reports suggested we had a serious ongoing issue which, in the outside world, would have meant a long-term course of treatment in a secure facility."

"Equally damaging to the monarchy."

"Precisely. It was at this point that Benny Ram became involved."

"Benny Ram?" Broadhurst was incredulous. "He's in on this?"

Speir adjusted the cane so that he could bend his knee back and forth to exercise his leg. "Bloody old age. Body's falling to bits." He obviously found the other man's reaction amusing. "Very much so," he went on. "The whole scheme required a devious and daring mastermind. Mr Ram has spent his life making tightropes for other people to balance on." He smiled. "Some fall off."

For some years, Ram had been an unofficial advisor to the British government on Middle Eastern politics, Speir had explained. As a middle man, he had a unique insight and a slant into the cauldron of events and attitudes in that part of the world and had brokered several highly secret meetings between European officials and influential forces with whom no foreign dignitary would have officially been seen dead with. Ram was also an old and trusted friend of the British royal family.

At the time the King was wrestling with the problem of what to do about the young Prince, the PM was seeking Ram's assistance to try and find a way to overcome the British public's hostility to the idea of employing armed forces on the ground in Iraq and Syria to counter the Russian presence and fight the Jihadist forces. Any proposal for a joint operation with the Americans that smacked of the Bush/Blair alliance over Iraq in 2003 would never touch first base, but the PM was certain that this was the only course of action that would succeed.

"Ram had literally walked out of Number Ten when he was invited by the King to a private meeting at Windsor."

"I recall the occasion," Broadhurst intervened. "He was going to look at the last phase of the rebuilding work."

Speir raised his eyebrows. "The King chose to confide in Ram and three months later, he was back with a plan that would not only ultimately help to create a groundswell of public sympathy for the monarchy, provide a solution for the Prince, but also give the PM the means to achieve the government's objective and mobilise the armed forces."

Broadhurst took in a gasp of air. "This whole business is a put up job?"

"Far from it. It is a very daring and risky operation to create a terrorist attack on British soil that would succeed in assassinating the Prince. This afternoon, a second video recorded by a dedicated suicide bomber has been broadcast around the world claiming responsibility for the Jihadist movement, cursing the West and promising many more such hostilities in the future. Tomorrow, Parliament will be recalled to debate a motion to mobilise the armed forces and prepare a strategy for a ground offensive in Iraq and Syria."

"Presumably, already developed?"

"I's dotted and T's crossed. It's amazing just how quickly our chiefs of staff can react."

Hemmings had entered the room, choosing to stand behind Broadhurst, but just within his lateral vision. The sense of danger that had receded as Speir had begun to take him into his confidence, returned. Hemmings was capable of destabilising the situation.

"The Prince's tragic death was not in vein. It . . ."

Broadhurst rounded on the speaker. "The Prince is dead?" he demanded.

Speir looked him straight in the eye. "As I said, the Prince's unintended and unfortunate death was not in vein. It has both rallied public support for the monarchy and re-established the respect and warm affection with which the British hold the Royal family, but also fuelled the political will to bring an end to the Jihadist occupation of strategic territory in the Middle East." He breathed a long sigh. "In my view, sadly, a price worth paying."

Broadhurst held the man's gaze, his immediate response to challenge the assertion held in check by his failure to believe what he had just heard. He sensed that they were waiting for a reaction that gave them reason to consider him a risk to their mission. This conversation was being transmitted. It had to be. Somewhere, other ears must be listening. His life was still in the balance. His measured reply was to say how sorry he was and how his heart went out to the King and his family.

Speir gave a knowing smile. The man was now as much a conspirator as they were.

Broadhurst shook his head. "What I don't understand is Rosenberg's part in all this. Why was he involved and had to die?"

Hemmings shuffled his feet together as he moved fully into view. "A means to an end," he said.

"More unavoidable collateral damage?" Broadhurst queried.

"The man you know as Rosenberg is officially a highly decorated Israeli soldier who defected to the Jihadists when on a mission in Syria. The man's name is Melman and he is branded as a traitor."

Broadhurst turned to Speir with raised eyebrows that asked the unspoken question.

"Sources told us that as soon as allied forces were involved in land assaults in Iraq and Syria, the Israelis would see it as a green light to move against Hezbollah in Lebanon and seek territorial gains across the Golan Heights. This would create problems for the allies, so we needed to keep Tel Aviv out of the picture."

Hemmings took up the explanation. "A confidential briefing to the Israeli ambassador in London that one of their nationals was a co-conspirator in the plot to kill the Prince and a commitment to keep the information secret has ensured that Israel keeps its powder dry. Imagine the Zionist backlash if the news were to leak out?"

"Stopped in their tracks just as they were mobilising for military action in the West Bank," Speir added. "Ram identified the man you knew as Rosenberg to be . . ." He hesitated, seeking the appropriate wording. ". . . the suitable candidate," he added.

It was the one brutal aspect of the last thirty minutes that made any real sense. A myriad of questions coursed around in Broadhurst's head. Why had there been a need for more compromising pictures of the Prince when rumour on the internet was rife? Why involve Lambert's girlfriend in the plot?

Speir sensed the need to amplify the explanation. At some stage, people would start to ask questions. A public enquiry was bound to follow. There had to be hard facts to substantiate the course of events. Would social media gossip have been sufficient to encourage such a daring Jihadist plot? No. International outrage was needed to give credence to the attack. Someone had to have been feeding sensitive information about the Prince's whereabouts to the terrorists.

"You planted Soraya?" Broadhurst was incredulous.

"We had identified Lambert as the weak link in your set-up. He was easy prey to such a talented seductress. She thought she was feeding information to the Jihadis. In fact, she was talking to Hemmings."

"You had them both killed?"

"Her deal was that her family would be brought out of Syria to safety. That has happened. Lambert was supposed to have faced a rap across the knuckles and early retirement, but he started to react irrationally when he heard about her death. He was also brighter than we thought. He had begun to guess that all was not what it seemed; that Maxwell and Lewis, who are our men, were working to another agenda." Speir shrugged. "I'm sorry. We just could not take the risk. You will understand that."

Right at that moment, Broadhurst could have readily lunged forward and throttled the old man, but he held his anger in check. With Hemmings behind him, it would have been tantamount to suicide.

"There is one thing I just cannot accept." This was a game they were playing with him. No. A test. He sensed his life was still in the balance whatever assurances he had received. Once this conversation was over, there would never be another opportunity to mention it without fatal consequences. A thick, black shroud would be drawn over the entire business, never to be lifted.

"And that is?" There was brief eye contact with Hemmings before he smiled benignly. "You find my explanation wanting?"

"With such detailed and intricate planning, I find it inconceivable to believe that you would have placed the Prince in danger of actually being harmed. Yet, you say he is dead."

Speir visibly relaxed. They had been waiting for this, Broadhurst thought.

"Let me take you through the chain of events and then I must insist we draw this conversation to a close."

Ram's plan was that the principal participants in the plot would use a code system. The Sator Square, an ancient mystic palindrome, was chosen to monitor progress. Each word represented a development, a move forwards to the ultimate goal.

Everything was set to go. A homosexual gathering was arranged in Portugal, photographs were taken and a target selected who would transact the compromising pictures with Ram's magazine in France.

"As I've explained, he needed to be a Jew and open to corruption. At this point, things started to go wrong. We expected to provide Ram with a few compromising homosexual encounters between the Prince and whoever. What he got was a bloody orgy with all sorts of disgusting images. By the time we realised what had happened, all of the images were in Rosenberg's possession and we had to play along with his little extortion plan."

"And the Prince?" Broadhurst queried. "The move to Hay on Wye was intended?"

"Yes. By this time, Ram had ensured the target was established. Homosexuality is a sin under Islam, punishable by death. As such, there was both a fanatical religious motive and with the move to a relatively insecure environment, the opportunity for the assassin to complete his assignment."

"But you were putting the Prince in the path of danger."

"Never. The moment the Prince was scheduled to arrive at Hay, a stand-in, look-alike actor had been recruited to take his place. The Prince never came here, but ended up at a different hideout."

"But, you informed us that he'd been transferred from Hay to another location."

"That was to put any possible leak to the press off the scent. We kept Lambert close to us. He knew and, therefore, Soraya would know, that it was false. She was able to pass on the information that he remained at Hay."

"So, the Prince is safe and well?" Broadhurst looked relieved. "Where is he now?"

"You know the Prince to be a very sensitive and highly strung individual?"

"I would say that's a fair analysis," Broadhurst replied.

"Well, the tragedy in all this is that the Prince took the disclosure of all these images very much to heart. He was severely depressed and extremely contrite. Two days after he left London, he took his own life. For a number of reasons, I'm not allowed or prepared to go into details."

"I see," Broadhurst acknowledged sombrely.

"Save to say, that he left a long and detailed message that displayed his intense sensitivity. He realised that the first reaction to the news that he had taken his own life would be for the powers to be to abandon the project we were embarked upon. He did not want that to happen under any circumstances. He made a cogent argument which both his immediate family and we eventually accepted."

"Can I know the consequence of this argument?" Broadhurst asked.

Speir nodded. "There was obvious merit in the public arena if he was seen to have been assassinated in a terrorist plot than having taken his own life. The young suicide bomber was innocent and naive and could be easily handled by our experienced actor. At the critical moment, he left the scene and the corpse of an accident victim who also bore some resemblance to the Prince was arranged in the bedroom where we intended the bomber planned to detonate the device."

Broadhurst's mouth had dropped at the sheer brazenness of the plan. "But you were leaving a lot to chance," he protested. "Surely, the bomber could have realised he had been tricked before detonating the device?"

"The answers are we weren't and he did. He pulled back from opening the bible which would set his device off, so we had a close circuit camera in the room and a large charge of C4 explosive under the bed. The east wing of the building had been carefully evacuated. The remote detonator did its job. The two bodies were virtually vaporised, with the building left in ruins."

Broadhurst shook his head. "You guys are ruthless beyond belief."

Hemmings approached him. There was anger, hostility in his face. His fists were clenched. "You talk about the ruthless killing of a terrorist. I had a son, an only child. He wanted to serve his country, just like I did. He was in Sangin in Helmand province, on patrol, when he stepped on an IED. He was blown into the bits that we buried. The device had just been planted. They caught the bastard who killed my son. That was all he knew how to do. Now, that's what I call callous and ruthless, not something you deskbound, pampered pricks would know anything about! Serve your country! What did you do, Broadhurst? Chase a lot of whores around in Belize?" His fists unclenched and clenched again. The grief was raw.

Speir tapped his stick repeatedly, urgently on the floor. "Sit down, please! Everybody. Let's finish up."

The outburst had taken Broadhurst by surprise. Hemmings was breathing deeply, his gaze concentrated on a fixed point on the table, his attention, thousands of miles away from where they sat.

"Was it worth it? All the people you've sacrificed?"

372

There was a benign look from the old man as he struggled to regain his feet. "Let's just say they served their origins well. These risky projects all involve elements of personal danger." He looked at Hemmings and back at Broadhurst. "Remember what I said. Just make sure you don't join the list. You will go to your grave in the knowledge that you know something about which only a half a dozen people have all the facts. We may see each other at the memorial service for the Prince at St. Pauls in due course. Otherwise we will never see each other again."

Broadhurst raised his hand. "There is one thing I'd like you to do for me," he said.

Eighty one - @PatriciaColbert.36

Colbert arrived at the prestige building on the Av. Victor Hugo. The black Citroen was parked close by. "How long has she been in there?" she asked.

The driver looked around. "She's just arrived and gone up to the penthouse. She passed by her apartment on the way, stopped for five minutes, left the car and picked up a taxi. Everything go alright at the warehouse?"

She nodded. "It's all over," she said. "Go and wait by the elevator. When she comes out, arrest her."

Eighty two - @Bizzybuzzybee

Benny embraced her. "It's lovely to see you again, my child." He straightened his robe and slouched back on the settee. Through the window, Chantelle could see the traffic circulating around the Arc de Triomphe. It was a busy day, but she felt strangely alone.

"We have much to do," Benny offered her a seat. "There are so many human interest stories evolving from the assassination of the Prince. *BV* must be first to break the news."

"How long are you staying?" she asked. Her hand reached inside her handbag, clasping the stock of Rosenberg's ancient revolver that she had recovered from her apartment. There were two bullets in the chamber. She kept her hand in the bag.

"Overnight. With this tragic news, I must travel to London tomorrow to pay my respects, dates for the funeral arrangements, memorial service. It's a very sad time." He offered her a warm drink. "Now to work," he said. His hands slid back under the gold braided pillows as he moved forward on the sofa.

"I want to talk about my father," she said.

"Your father? What about him?" It was just mild curiosity.

"Do you remember the circumstances concerning the deal he was negotiating prior to his death?"

He looked bemused. "Of course, he was a close friend of mine. I did warn him."

"About what exactly?"

"Is there some purpose to this inquisition?" He gave a broad smile. "You're a journalist. You should have acquainted yourself with the facts."

"I have. It's what's behind the facts that I want to know about." She was trembling. "Did you betray him to the press?"

With slow deliberation, he shook his head. His attitude was patronising. "Who have you been talking to? Has that troubled brother of yours been up to something? I hear he has not returned to the institution."

She began to shout. "It's not him I want to hear about. It's you!"

"Very well. Do calm down, my child. Your father was not dealing through me, but through Karim, an unscrupulous dealer from Qatar. I warned your father about two things. I told him I believed the missiles the French proposed to sell were destined to end up in Iran, contrary to the embargo. He would have looked such a fool. It would have cost him his career."

"What was the second thing?"

"An American journalist was onto the story. He had the inside track with Karim. I warned Armand not to compromise himself at any stage. They were ready to publish."

"How come? He ended up in bed with two hookers alongside him."

Benny shrugged. "I assume he was drugged. Your father would never have done such a thing of his own freewill."

Perspiration dampened her forehead. She could feel her heart thumping. "My information is that it was you who set my father up. You needed to get him substituted because he refused to sell the missiles. It was you who had him killed."

"Who is telling you this rubbish?"

"Richard has Bernie Fox with him." She was about to lie, but it didn't matter. "Fox is prepared to swear an affidavit that you masterminded the entire deal. He said he has proof." She could detect a sudden change in his attitude.

"Look, Chantelle, Bernie Fox would sell his mother if there was something in it for him, so he'll lie to you through his back teeth if he thinks he's onto an earner." He looked pensive. "Tell me, where is Bernie now?"

She pulled the gun from her handbag. "Richard has him captive. It was you, wasn't it?" She started to weep. The gun was shaking in her hand. "I don't think I can take much more of this. All these years, I've been living a lie, believing your motives were prompted by kindness, when all the time they were founded on guilt."

He swivelled in his seat. A guard was just outside the door, but if he called, the state she was in, he was likely to be injured. "You don't know what you're saying. Richard is deranged. All he talks to the psychiatrists about is how he knows your father was innocent, how action should be taken. He's a dangerous man. Fuelled by Fox, he is capable of anything. Don't ruin everything you've achieved, Chantelle!"

"Don't call me Chantelle!" she shouted. "My name's Madeleine. Madeleine Bourbon. Get this Karim to confess that it was him."

"Please put the gun down," he pleaded. "You don't know what you're doing. Karim died some months ago."

She waved the gun again. "You had him killed, did you, Benny?" Tears streamed down her face.

His cell phone started to ring. He checked the screen. "Let me answer this, please." He touched the screen. "Yes, Mahesh." He listened, then, ended the call. "Richard is dead. The police arrived to arrest him. He took his own life."

She released the safety catch. "Suicide. Just like my father, is it? How did you get to him? You bastard!"

The policeman waiting at the elevator door clearly heard two gunshots, the second some twenty seconds after the first. He was already at the sixth floor by this time.

Eighty three - @ChasBroadhurst.kp

Broadhurst switched the station to Radio 4. Parliament had unanimously backed the deployment of ground troops to the active theatre, as the reporter called it. He smiled. They made it sound like some sort of fiction; a piece to be acted out. How many body bags would make up the last act of this tragedy.

Duncan White knocked politely at his office door. "I see you've packed up most of your things, Chas. Anything I can do to help?"

Broadhurst looked at the two open brown storage boxes at the centre of the room. "That's what I've got to show for the best part of two decades. That, and a dead Prince. Hardly a success story is it?"

376

"You can't hold yourself to blame, Chas. You did everything possible to save him. This Brent character was clever. He'd already killed twice to get to the Prince. Working with this Mossad guy…" He left the sentence unfinished.

"How do you know about that? It's classified."

"I know. It's on the QT. We can't say anything, but, as the old line goes, the wires have been buzzing with rumour, claims and counterclaims."

"Do you think we'll succeed with the invasion?" White asked.

"What's success?" Broadhurst posed. "Winning the war or winning the peace that follows? We are good at fighting, but there's no stomach for colonialism in the modern age and that's what is needed to stop the factions from civil war. You only have to look at Iraq and Lybia."

"I hope you are wrong," White acknowledged.

"Maybe, I am. Maybe, we have learnt the lessons and, together with the Russians and Yanks, can sort out the mess that follows."

White smiled, grasping his old friend's hand. "I'll miss you, Chas. We've had our ups and downs, but you're a good man. This Speir is a strange character. I don't know if I'll get on with him."

"I doubt he'll stay long. I think he's what you describe in sporting terms as an interim manager. Some professional will replace him."

"I hope he's as good a man as you, Chas." He stopped. "Hey, I'm talking as if you're an old man who's retiring. You're still young, far too soon to stop working. What are you going to do? Security work?"

"I haven't given it a thought. I'm going to take a break, travel a little, meet up with some old friends, that sort of thing."

"Good for you. I know this isn't the professional thing to do, but to hell with it!" He put his arms around Broadhurst's shoulders and gave him a brief hug. "It's been great knowing you, Chas. Keep in touch. If there's ever anything I can do." He left the rest of the sentence unsaid.

"I'll certainly bear that in mind," Broadhurst replied.

Eighty four - @renemarchal

She was already at the table when he arrived. Marchal hadn't had dinner in the Latin Quarter for months, or was it years? She stood as he came up to her, planting a more than friendly kiss on his lips.

"I hear you've had a busy day, Patricia," he said.

"No more so than yours, I guess."

"Mine was easy. I spent the morning with a couple of guys asking stupid questions when Arnault appears, all smiles and compliments."

"How come?"

"The Commandant was doing his normal political soft shoe shuffle. The word had come down that the British authorities wanted to thank me, 'most sincerely' were the words he used, for my cooperation in helping their security staff to track the group responsible for assassinating the Prince. They felt some sort of small honour might be appropriate."

"I can just see his face, the grovelling acknowledgement. Any apology?"

"What do you think? Internal Affairs had, as usual, rushed to judgement. Had it been his decision, etcetera, etcetera. Need I go on?"

She shook her head. The waiter took their order. In the time it took to write it down, her mood had changed. "Chantelle Dubois is dead, you know that?"

"I heard at 36. What happened?"

"Suicide, on the face of it. There are still some loose ends to tidy up. She heard that we had got to her brother, not in time, unfortunately. He slit his own throat with a knife as we tried to rush him. He had a photographer, a guy called Fox, captive. He had tortured him."

"Go on."

"She had a gun concealed in her handbag, what they call a palm size, purse revolver. Forensics tell me it's a Beretta 9mm, lethal at short range."

"Hers?"

"All above board, apparently, registered in her name, signed for, photograph, permit, brand new, only bought a month or so ago."

"So, what's the story?"

"She went to visit Benny Ram in his apartment. According to Ram, they had a serious argument. He was adamant that, as she knew of Richard's whereabouts and what he had been up to, the authorities should be informed immediately and Richard apprehended. Chantelle objected. She wanted her brother to become a fugitive from justice and for Ram to help financially."

"And he refused?" Marchal looked uncomfortable.

"Of course. Then, somebody from our side contacted Ram to tell him that her brother had killed himself. She lost control, fired at Ram and then turned the gun on herself."

"Was Ram injured?"

"A flesh wound to the arm. He'll live."

He sipped from the red wine glass in front of him. "Believe his story?"

She shrugged. "There's no other one. The security guard confirms he rushed in to find his boss clasping a bloody arm and Dubois lying dead on the floor with the Beretta in her hand. Game, set and match."

"I guess so. Any burn marks on his arm?"

She shook her head. "I thought of that. The wound might have been self-inflicted, but the shot was fired from distance. I've nowhere else to go."

"What about the photographer?"

"Fox? He's on a life support machine. The man was savagely beaten, made to eat Monopoly money."

"Monopoly money?" Marchal interrupted.

"It was all part of this Richard's bizarre revenge plan against the paparazzi. Both murders we know about and this attempt on Fox were supposed to have a theme linked to the victim's nickname. Fox was known as The Banker."

"The idea being he choke on the paper?"

"He has severe lacerations on his lower legs. The guess is that Richard wanted the infestation of rats in the warehouse to finish him off."

"What a dreadful thought. Even so, how does he end up on a life support machine?"

"He suffered a severe stroke. It's touch and go, but the word is he'll pull through."

They shared a fish and seafood casserole. As much as she tried to lighten the conversation, take it away from work as far as she could, there always seemed a prompt in the topic they touched upon to bring them back to the office. In the end, as the dessert trolley was paraded in front of them, she took the initiative. "It's only been a short few days, I know," she began, "but I'd like for us to see each other on a regular basis once you've retired, if you know what I mean." The colour rose in her cheeks.

"I'm not sure that I do," he replied hesitantly. "Are you proposing what I think you're proposing?" He was unsure of his ground.

She gave a nervous laugh. "I'm not sure what I'm proposing. Just, right now, the only thing I know is that it would be a shame if, just as the seeds of something were starting to grow, it were not allowed to develop because you're not around anymore on a day to day basis. Am I making any sense?"

"Have you thought that your sentiments for me might simply be a reflex reaction to our working relationship?"

"Does that mean you're not interested? I feel such a fool."

He could hear himself talking, but he couldn't believe the words that were coming out. "On the contrary, I would love for us to go on seeing each other. I like to feel I'm in control of my emotions at all times and the implications of your proposal have pulled that particular rug away from under my feet. Funny enough, it's not a particularly unpleasant experience, rather refreshing."

"Does that mean the answer's yes?" She rushed the question.

He put his hand out across the table to cover hers. "You know it won't be easy? People's first reaction will be to treat us as father and daughter."

"I knew you'd introduce the age thing. Can't we just act like two people, irrespective of all the conventional obstacles? Can't we just enjoy each other's company as individuals?" She drew her chair back and crossed her legs.

He smiled at the reaction. "What would your behavioural tutors say you were feeling right at this moment?

She moved back closer, interlocking her fingers with his. "They'd say I'm a headstrong girl who's infatuated and who feels, right now, like she's walked into a swamp and needs help to get pulled out so she can react normally again."

"Then, I'm your man," he volunteered. "Let's both get out of the swamp and see how it goes."

They parted outside the restaurant. It was the right thing to do, he felt. After he kissed her tenderly goodnight, he was surprised that his first reaction hadn't simply been to kiss her on the forehead. He was glad it hadn't. That would have seemed like a father responding to his daughter and he really didn't feel like that. They say life is stranger than fiction, but it was. The idea of moving into long forgotten, uncharted territory where he had no say over where their emotions would take them was rather appealing. He pulled the collar of his raincoat up around his neck, whistling a tune he recognised as he walked jauntily along the busy sidewalk to the metro. God, what was happening to him? He didn't even like Charles Aznavour.

Eighty five - @Bizzybuzzybee

Benny hadn't slept much. It wasn't conscience. The damn wound in his arm hurt like hell. It was like a dog bite, not serious, but excruciatingly painful. He had risen early, telling the guards that he would go out on his own. His flight to London was scheduled for midday, so there was no time to waste.

He decided to take the metro on the thirty minute journey to the Parc de la Villette. He wore a heavy half-length suede jacket with a sheepskin collar, turned up to hide the lower half of his face. A beret was pulled down over his forehead. His hands were in his coat pocket, the right grasping the rag he had put around the ancient revolver that Chantelle had drawn from her bag.

There hadn't been time to think beyond the immediate consequences of what she had said. The Beretta had been concealed under the cushion on the sofa. He had palmed it in a handkerchief as he rose from the seat to walk towards her. He was protesting his innocence. Almost simultaneously, he shouted out for the guard as he shot her at close range through the right ear, catching the gun she was holding as she collapsed onto the floor.

The guard listened to the instruction without question. He took the Beretta, stood over the body and fired at Benny's left arm. He was a trained marksman. The bullet grazed Benny's skin, ricocheting off into the wall. He took the handkerchief from the stock of the Beretta without saying a word, wiped it clean and then placed it between the palm and fingers of her outstretched hand. He pocketed the handkerchief and her gun, turned and left the room. He started to call the police, but knew that they would already be on their way up. Benny's men had been watching them since their car had arrived.

The policeman entered the apartment to find not only Chantelle's body, but an apparently unconscious Benny, slouched on the couch, blood seeping from a wound onto the gold upholstery.

Benny had never used the Paris metro in his life. The heat was uncomfortably clammy with an unpleasant scent that he guessed must have come from some bleach or cleaning fluid, but smelled like piss. The journey seemed to go on forever, but he was certain he wasn't being followed as he exited one train at an interim station and waited for the next.

Chantelle's untimely death presented him with a problem. Her partner, Nana and the rest of the staff could handle the next few issues of the magazine. Money would talk as far as Nana was concerned, but she'd have to be eliminated as soon as conveniently possible. He would need a new editor. The attendant on the yacht said she had a university degree. He wondered what it was in. Cock sucking, maybe? Perhaps, she could be groomed for the job. It was just a thought.

Kamal would need to be paid today. The solicitor was worth every penny of the two million dollars Benny would transfer into his offshore account. The idea of registering a small arm in Chantelle's name had been a stroke of genius. Kamal knew the history and had never trusted her. He had used the documentation she had provided for the visa application to China. Copies had been given to the forger. The rest was easy. Benny was glad he had taken the advice.

He left the train at Corentin Cariou, emerging into the hazy daylight as he headed in the direction of the park. He strolled, apparently aimlessly, through the maze of architectural, decorative follies which adorned the park, all the time checking that there was nobody on his tail. After a twenty minute walk, he arrived at the St Martin canal. Nobody was about. The old revolver disappeared beneath the muddy water, hopefully to be lost forever. He wiped his hands. It was symbolic, a gesture of closure.

The plane roared overhead. It must have just taken off from Charles de Gaulle. That reminded him. He mustn't be late. His black suit and tie would be laid out waiting for him. He had to pay his respects at the Court of St. James.

BOOK FIVE – ROTAS TURNS THE WHEEL OF FATE

The little Baptist chapel at Holmes St. Peter in the Yorkshire Dales was bursting to capacity. Close relatives knew that the coffin holding the remains of Barry Frisby was empty, save for his motor cycle keys, a David Bowie album and a symbolic casket of ash. His grieving parents were grateful that, even in death, his body had been used for special medical research, although, having given their authorisation, they did not know the details of this pioneering brain surgery procedure. Barry Frisby had died in a Sheffield hospital from injuries sustained in a tragic road accident two weeks earlier.

As much as the congregation had gathered to pay their respects to the popular young insurance broker who always had a cheerful smile on his face, they were distracted by the presence of an eminent man in a well-tailored, sombre black suit, standing to one side of the family group. The man claimed to have been helped by Barry to win a very substantial insurance claim at the start of his career. Barry's intervention had changed his fortunes and, as a gesture of his gratitude, he had approached the bereaved family to request their permission to pay the costs of the funeral. They could only stand in awe at a gesture which had provided their loved one with such a marvellous send-off.

As the congregation made their way from the crematorium, the King's representative sent a short text confirming that the matter was now closed. He shook the hand and sincerely thanked each member of Barry Frisby's close family before entering the taxi that would take him away from this godforsaken place.

* * * *

The man who answered the door was wearing a black mask and a cardboard pirate's hat. The sound of young children's' laughter vibrated somewhere in the house behind him.

"Hello, René," Broadhurst said with a smile creasing

385

his lips. "Haven't arrived at a bad time, have I?"

Marchal shouted in French over his shoulder. "Just a minute, kids." He turned back, putting both hands on his friend's shoulders. "So glad you could come, Chas. We're in the middle of what, I believe, the Americans call a game of cops and robbers; only I couldn't find the robber's black cap, so it's cops and bad pirates. That's me."

"I would never have guessed, had you not told me. I would have thought that this was your going out gear."

"What? Eccentric retired policeman wanders around Lille pretending to be the bad guy. My ex-boss would approve."

Broadhurst could see the two anxious young faces over Marchal's shoulder, looking furtively to see who had arrived to spoil their game. "I'd better come in and join the hunt for this dastardly villain."

Later, with Monique back home and the children, exhausted, ready for their beds, the two men strolled in the quiet of the evening to Marchal's local café/bar where he was politely greeted by a handful of the local patrons.

"Seems you've settled down pretty well to life outside Paris," Broadhurst observed as he sipped the head of foam off of the glass of blonde beer.

"Force of circumstances, really, Chas." He greeted a new arrival in the bar. "I don't think I've ever worked so hard in my life as in these last two months. The kids are a delight, but they're a real handful. I sleep well at night, I can tell you that."

"Thank God, you're in a position to be able to. No chance of a reconciliation, I suppose?"

"No. I don't think so. I doubt Monique would have him back anyway, Chas. The man had already had another affair before the woman he's now living with. As far as I could tell, he was working his way through the female office staff."

"I'm sorry to hear that."

"Hubert's an arsehole. His visits to the kids are even becoming less frequent. Mind you, my reception's pretty frosty."

"I can imagine. Still, look on the bright side. A close relationship with your grandchildren is a wonderful thing and your daughter is still a young, beautiful woman. She'll meet somebody else." He finished the beer, leaving a trace of white around his mouth. "That was good. I think I'll have another."

"Be careful. It's full of calories. You'll put on weight."

"As if I should worry." He patted his stomach. "Mind you, you're looking pretty fit. Plenty of exercise?"

"I go swimming with the kids a lot. I try to go for a jog most days when they've gone to school. I watch my diet."

"I can see, René. You look years younger."

Marchal patted his friend on the knee, leaning forward as he did so. "Truth is, Chas, I could do with losing twenty years. I've had a couple of dates with a woman who's just a bit older than Monique. An ex colleague. It's early days, but we get on well."

"Is it serious?"

"Hard to tell. With me in Lille and her, with a busy professional life in Paris, it's still a sort of novelty, but we get on well. The chemistry is right and we enjoy each other's company. It, also, still keeps me in touch with my former world."

"That was something I wanted to talk to you about later."

They ordered the dish of the day, a beef stew that Broadhurst raved over. He dunked the crusty bread into the gravy. "This is great," he said.

Marchal glanced at him. "Don't suppose there's much you can tell me about what was happening at Hay on Wye, is there?"

"Afraid not, René. It's all classified stuff and in the past now. I've left that world behind and I must say, in retrospect, I don't miss it one little bit."

"I'll just mention this, Chas. It's hard to imagine that Rosenberg was really some Mossad agent. Amongst the tears, his family scorned the idea as even a remote possibility. As far as they were concerned, he was a wheeler-dealer who had never visited the Middle East in his life. They were convinced it was a case of mistaken identity."

Broadhurst gently shook his head. "Whatever, it certainly brought the Israelis' intentions to an abrupt standstill. They must have had something on file. One day, they were determined to advance on all fronts; the next, they were urging a diplomatic solution. A volte face, I think you call it."

Their conversation meandered over a rough brandy to take in all the international developments that had taken place over the past several weeks. Marchal had received an invitation to the memorial service held to celebrate the life of Prince Arthur, but family commitments had forced him to decline. "Did you go, Chas?"

Broadhurst hadn't even been invited, but he gave a tactical answer. Marchal didn't pursue the subject, opting instead to ask what his friend intended to do in the future. "You're still a young man, Chas. You can't give up work at your age. You'll never survive."

"That's one of the reasons why I'm grateful you invited me to come and visit. Look, René, I presume these nursemaid duties of yours won't last forever?"

"Of course not. I want Monique to get settled again and feel comfortable as a single mother. Once that's done, we'll arrange an au pair and I'll commute between Paris and here to handle the kids on a part-time basis. But, why the question?"

Broadhurst looked mildly embarrassed. "When I left Royal security, I got a good lump sum payoff and a decent pension. I'm not short of a few bob as we say."

"Good for you."

"I've been asked on a couple of occasions since to tackle assignments on a private basis, investigations, security checks, that sort of thing." He waited for a reaction, but Marchal gave no hint that he knew what was coming. "Truth is, René, I can't tackle these jobs on my own. Most have an international angle to them, principally European and I thought you might like to work as a partner with me, a sort of joint venture to handle the workload. I could really do with your experience and contacts." He waited for a reply.

Marchal relaxed in his chair. "You're suggesting a sort of cross-channel private detective agency?" He laughed.

"I haven't thought it all through yet, but, yes, that sort of idea. "I've got the financial resources to back a small Paris office. No fixed pay, we just share the profits fifty, fifty. How does that sound?"

Marchal ordered two more brandies. "You know one thing, Chas?"

"What's that?"

"I had a gut feeling from the first time we met that, somehow, we were going to be friends for the rest of our lives." They exchanged a firm handshake.

"Tell me all about it, partner!"

* * * *

Professor Speir had taken a window seat on the train. The Norfolk countryside rushed by in swirls of a hundred shades of green and brown. It was a beautiful county, he reflected. Amongst many other things, he would miss it.

Six months ago, they had told him the cancer was in remission. Now, he only had a few more weeks to live. He felt cheated. It was a very cruel disease. It fooled you into thinking it had gone away, long enough only for it to deceive, to shatter any dreams you had dared to nurture. Still, he had had a good run and many would say that the world would be a better place without him. Upon reflection, he tended to agree.

Just crossing from one platform to another had left him out of breath. The local service from Ipswich was much slower, stops both in and outside stations more frequent, his fellow travellers, seemingly with more patience and time on their hands.

Nobody else left the train at Chandlers Halt. He stood on the truncated platform in solitude, accompanied only by the sounds of the wind coursing through the forest of sycamore trees that surrounded the unmanned station and the call of the black crows from within.

"Professor Speir?" The young man had appeared through a gateway on the opposite platform.

He wasn't sure whether the words were "hold up" or "hurry up", but either way he made his way to the edge of the platform and the three steps which led down to the wooden boards crossing the rails.

The draft of wind as the train sped past the platform nearly knocked him back off of his feet. The man looked on in horror as he tried to regain his footing. "You can't cross there," he chided. That's just for railway workers. Take the footpath down to the level crossing. I'll rush around to meet you.

Ten minutes later, seated in the front of an ageing Range Rover, Speir had regained both his breath and composure. The young man with the fresh face, whose name he learned was Lance, had also got some colour back into his cheeks. "God, that was a close one. You nearly ended up as an emblem on the front of the Kings Lynn express!" He looked over to apologise. "It was my fault really. I was running late and I stopped on the road outside the other platform just to let you know I had arrived. I should have parked and walked around to collect you."

In truth, Speir agreed with him, but he made a self-derogatory remark about senility to excuse the incident.

"George would never have forgiven me if I'd got you killed before you could meet up again. I think it's really special that his old theology tutor from university has taken the time out to come and see him. It's really very kind of you."

Lance had a nervous habit that Speir could not abide. He never stopped talking. By the time they had driven the ten miles to the house set back in the hills, Speir had learned that Lance was twenty three, been privy to a potted family history and was currently hearing all about the day care centre under construction in the local village for which George and he were currently busy fund raising.

"There's a rumour that someone important, maybe even a Royal, will come down for the official opening next year."

"That would be something, wouldn't it?" Speir commented.

Don't mind if I drop you off and shoot away, do you?" Lance said, more of a statement than a question. "I know George has got a lot of catching up to do with you, so I'll leave you in peace. We're at a car boot sale tomorrow. George has got a load of bits and pieces in the shed which should fetch a pretty penny." With that, he was gone.

I expect he has got plenty of bits and pieces, Speir thought to himself, as he watched the man come towards him. He looked older than his years. Maybe it was the balding head. They shook hands formally.

"How are you, Professor? Do come in. It seems like a long time, though it can only be a question of months. Seven, I guess."

They were sitting in the bay window of the lounge which overlooked a large lawn, bordered by shrubs and trees. Speir did not try to pick up the cup in front of him. The disease, or some associated illness, made his hands tremble. "This is the last time we shall meet," he said. "When I leave today, you will never have any contact with anybody who was part of your former life."

"I understand," George replied sombrely.

"That is, with one exception."

"One exception?" he queried.

"You understand that your father took an enormous risk when he saw the opportunity to allow you to live a normal life, away from the public gaze, the media judgements of proper conduct. He wanted for you what he could never have for himself or his other children."

"I will never underestimate his actions, nor can I ever thank him enough."

"You cannot," Speir agreed. "And if you ever mentioned the facts to another living soul, you would almost certainly end up forcing him to abdicate for the deception he allowed to be perpetrated on the British public."

"You will never have to convince me, Professor. I do understand the gravity of the situation and why, on earth, would I choose to prejudice my own happiness? I have never been so at peace with my world, as I am now."

"Good. Then these are the arrangements." The old man took a sheet of paper from his pocket. The following year, the King planned a tour of East Anglia. It would take in a number of local, cultural activities, including the official opening of the day care centre which he and Lance were helping to fund. The King will meet with a number of the local supporters. George Astor would have a ten minute private meeting with him before he moved on.

"How wonderful of you to arrange this, Professor."

"It wasn't my idea, George. It was all his. Make the most of it."

The conversation moved on to lighter topics, updates on relatives, births and deaths, social gossip. Lance was due to arrive to take the Professor back to the station to catch the last local service to Ipswich, where he had a hotel room booked for the night.

"I have one question to ask you," Speir announced.

"That's funny," George replied. "I have one for you, as well. You first."

"I can see how you chose the surname Astor. It's an anagram of the Sator Square. But what made you choose it?"

George smiled. "I guess the use of the Sator Palindrome as a code for the project was also the focal point in my own life, the death of a Prince and the birth of a commoner."

"Reincarnation is probably more accurate."

"Call it what you will, the Sator Square is believed to have denominated a Christian household in Roman times.

You can make a Greek cross around the central letter 'N' which gives you 'Paternoster' – Our Father, in the Lord's prayer – surrounded by the Greek letters A and O which represent the Alpha and the Omega. In the circumstances, the name Astor seemed wholly appropriate."

Speir nodded. "And your question is?"

George stood up. "I have two, in fact; both to satisfy my curiosity. Do you really believe that the security chap, Broadhurst, really bought the story you told him about my suicide?"

"I doubt it, but, at that point his life was hanging on a thread. To have questioned your death would have doubtless cost him his. He is no fool." He checked his watch. "And your second question?"

"I don't mean to sound offensive, Professor, but, in view of the precarious decision taken by my father, why does he come to trust you?"

Speir struggled to his feet. He came as close as he possibly could and looked at the young man directly in the eyes. His wholesome smile was something George had not witnessed from this serious man before. "Look. Perhaps he has something on me, a secret, which ensures my silence forever."

The Range Rover pulled away from the house. George guessed he had around an hour before Lance would return. The one thing they had allowed him to keep was an album of family photos taken from shortly after the death of Queen Victoria until the present day. It was kept in a special safe he had made in the floorboards under the cellar.

He was looking for two particular photographs. Those vivid violet blue eyes of the Professor, those prominent crow feet around the slightly squinting eyes as he smiled. They were vaguely familiar to him.

The photos were not mounted in the album, but kept in a worn foolscap manila envelope with a flap secured by a length of fine string wound around a brown washer. He guessed that somebody, at some time, had decided that the twenty or so photographs stored in the envelope were not worthy of enclosure in the main album. The two he was looking for had been kept apart in a smaller, white envelope, emblazoned with a royal crest he did not recognise. Both were yellowing around the edges. The first showed a teenage prince in aristocratic pose, standing amongst a group of people in the centre of a palatial ballroom. The future Edward VIII and Duke of Windsor stood dramatically with one leg in front of the other, a stern expression of determination on his face. The scrawled writing on the back was in a hand he recognised. It said 'Edward (travelling as The Earl of Chester) at 18 with the Marquess de Breteuil and family, Prince Arsen of Yugoslavia and friends – Château de Breuteil – June 1912'.

The second, a smaller, less professional print showed a young couple, posed, their heads turned sideways, gazing into each other's eyes, their hands clasped tightly together. The girl's beauty was in the simplicity of her appearance, the natural look of innocent happiness in her face. The future king was smiling, relaxed, a cigarette resting French style between his lips. In the background, a man was shying a ball to try and dislodge one of a row of coconuts at a fairground stall. The same hand had written on the back, 'Edward and (Marie-Leonie? Or Michelle?) – Luna Park? – Summer 1912?'

Maybe it was auto-suggestion, but the shape of her nose and the slightly pointed chin gave the game away. Gerald was not a gambling man, but he would bet that those particular features Professor Speir had inherited from his grandmother.

He closed the album. Perhaps it was better that some things were left unsaid.

Geoff Cook was born, educated and trained as an accountant in London.

He has spent the best part of his working life in Brazil and Portugal, eventually trading professional accountancy for a career in the world of ceramic tiles and, latterly, the hospitality and catering industries.

Ever since he created his first local children's newsletter and library at the age of ten, writing has always been his main interest. Geoff published his first full length novel, *Pieces for the Wicked*, as an e-book in 2010 and has since written two three act plays in the *Bloodlines* trilogy. Published under the titles of *The Painful Truth* and *The Last Chapter*, both works are set in Portugal and have a local resonance.

Now a full time author, *The Sator Square* is his first full length novel to be published in hardback and paperback.

The follow-up to *The Sator Square* will be published in the autumn of 2017 with the title of *The Last Rights*. Look out for it.

THE LAST
RIGHTS

© GEOFF
COOK

«After eighty years, the Lisbon bank will close its notorious safe deposit facility, the refuge for many hidden wartime treasures. So many boxes remain locked tight.

Who dares to come and claim the bounty? Who is watching their every move? There are victims who need closure. Wrongs need to be put right. Who can perform The Last Rights?»